John Greenleaf Adams

Memoir of Thomas Whittemore, D. D.

John Greenleaf Adams

Memoir of Thomas Whittemore, D. D.

ISBN/EAN: 9783337396787

Printed in Europe, USA, Canada, Australia, Japan

Cover: Foto ©Andreas Hilbeck / pixelio.de

More available books at **www.hansebooks.com**

MEMOIR

OF

THOMAS WHITTEMORE, D.D.

BY

JOHN G. ADAMS, D.D.

I have fought a good fight, I have finished my course, I have kept the faith.
ST. PAUL.

Next to the Bible, Christian biography is the most profitable reading.
NORMAN MACLEOD, D.D.

BOSTON:
UNIVERSALIST PUBLISHING HOUSE.
1878.

TO THE

UNIVERSALIST CHURCH OF AMERICA,

This Memoir

OF ONE OF HER ABLE AND FAITHFUL MINISTERS AND DEFENDERS
IS RESPECTFULLY AND FRATERNALLY DEDICATED.

PREFACE.

No word of apology or explanation is needed in offering to the public the memoir contained in the following pages. The subject of it was widely known for more than forty years in New England as well as in other parts of our country. He belonged to the Church Universal, and to the Universalist Church especially and emphatically. One who knew him long and intimately, and whose good judgment was unquestioned (Rev. Dr. H. Ballou), pronounced him to have been " the people's man above any other in our denominational history."

The author of this memoir can truly say that the writing of it on his part has been a labor of love. He had enjoyed a long fraternal acquaintance with Mr. Whittemore, had profited by his wise counsellings when he most needed them, and had been edified and strengthened in a sympathy of soul enjoyed as a co-worker with him in the ministry of the Gospel of Divine Grace.

In preparing this memoir for the press, it has been the intention of the writer to present the man and the minister as he was known when living, and as he is remembered by many now that he has passed on. We have aimed to condense the matter in hand. It has been more difficult to decide what to leave out than what to insert, where the materials for use were so ample.

To those acquainted with Mr. Whittemore, a perusal of these pages will, we think, bring their past realization of his person and his work vividly to remembrance. To the younger members of the Universalist fraternity we commend his busy, practical, and earnest life; and to our younger ministers that loyalty to our common cause which he so constantly manifested, and especially that devotion and zeal which made him such a kindling and magnetic life-power wherever his ministries extended. Were he now with us as in other days, they would find in him a cordial participator in all their endeavors to promote the true life of the Christian Gospel in human souls.

May the divine blessing attend the reading of this record of him.

J. G. A.

Melrose Highlands, Mass.,
Dec. 1, 1877.

CONTENTS.

CHAPTER I.

1821–1828.

AGED 21–28.

CHAPTER II.

1828–1830.

AGED 28–30.

CHAPTER III.

1830–1833.

AGED 30–33.

CHAPTER IV.

1833–1836.

AGED 33–36.

CHAPTER V.

1836–1840.

AGED 36–40.

CHAPTER VI.

1840–1843.

AGED 40–43.

CHAPTER VII.

1843–1844.

AGED 43–44.

CHAPTER VIII.

1844–1847.

AGED 44–47.

CHAPTER IX.

1847–1849.

AGED 47–49.

CHAPTER X.

1849–1851.

AGED 49–51.

CHAPTER XI.

1851–1852.

AGED 51–52.

PAGE

CHAPTER XII.

1852–1854.

AGED 52–54.

CHAPTER XIII.

1854–1857.

AGED 54–57.

CHAPTER XIV.

1857–1858.

AGED 57–58.

CHAPTER XV.

1858–1859.

AGED 58–59.

CHAPTER XVI.

1859–1860.

AGED 59–60.

CHAPTER XVII.

1860–1861.

AGED 60–61.

CHAPTER XVIII.

MEMOIR OF THOMAS WHITTEMORE.

CHAPTER I.

1821–1828.

Aged 21-28.

Autobiography — Ancestry in England — Recapitulation — Acquaintance with Rev. Hosea Ballou — First Sermon — Pastorate at Milford — At Cambridgeport — The Editor — The Preacher — Rev. Walter Balfour — Discussion with Rev. O. Scott — Visit to the West — Declines Invitation to settle there.

The subject of this Memoir has, in another volume, given us the history of the first twenty-five years of his life. It is a book of much interest, written in a plain, lively, and forcible style, full of such details as will serve to render it popular with a large class of readers for years to come.

Mr. Whittemore, in his "Autobiography," gives his family genealogy in America, beginning with Thomas Whittemore of England, who was in this country, and settled in that part of Charlestown since known as Malden, before 1645. The English genealogy of the Whittemore family is given in the "New England Historical and Genealogical Register," where the ancestor of the family in Massachusetts is seen to be descended from the Whittemores of Hitchen, County of Hereford, England. The name is written Whitamore and Whitamor in the Parish Register of the Hitchen Vicarage, from 1562 to 1636, and afterwards Whittemore.[1]

[1] N. E. Hist. & Gen. Reg., April, 1867.

The Autobiography gives an account of the life of Mr. Whittemore from his birth until a year after his settlement in Cambridgeport, in 1823. To those unacquainted with that part of his history, a brief statement of it may here be given.

He was born in Boston, Jan. 1, 1800, in that section of Charter Street that is on Copp's Hill. His parents had ten children, of whom Thomas was the fourth. They were honest toilers, — his father a baker, his mother a woman of much energy. It required their constant earnest exertions to support their growing family. Thomas was baptized in Brattle Street Church, twelve days after his birth. His parents were attendants at that Church, and were believers in the moderate Calvinism taught there.

At the age of seven, he was placed in one of the Common Schools of Charlestown, whither his father had removed two years before. In this school, he acquired all the education he ever received under a teacher, except three months at an evening school just before he was twenty-one, and a few weeks of private tuition after that time. But on this foundation he afterwards built himself up, as his subsequent history will show, into a scholar of large attainments.

At the age of fourteen his father died, leaving the care of the large family upon his mother. The boy was heedless, though not malicious, and caused the mother much anxiety. He was placed as an apprentice under two or three guardians; but circumstances were adverse to his continuance with them, until at last he was apprenticed to Mr. Abel Baker, a bootmaker of Boston, to whom he was bound by legal indenture and with whom he remained until he was twenty-one.

The parents of Mr. Whittemore were professed believers in the common orthodoxy of New England, prevalent in their early days. In the case of their son it produced what it has in many other instances, — much doubt and scepticism as to the divine authority of the Scriptures. The boy did not find the doctrines preached commendable in the light of his reason, so that he lost his reverence for them, and found his chief attraction in the music of the church service. He at length became connected with the choir of the Universalist Church in Charlestown, and there heard the Rev. Edward Turner, whose ministration drew his attention more closely than ever to the Bible, and to a consideration of the reasonableness of its teachings. But these were not such deep impressions as he afterwards received. He was subsequently employed on a salary, to play the bass-viol in the First Baptist Church in Boston. While here for two or three years, listening again to the teachings of its minister, some of his old doubts and perplexities of mind returned. Sometime in the last year of his apprenticeship, he became acquainted with Rev. Hosea Ballou, who had taken and occupied a part of the house in which Mr. Baker resided. Mr. Whittemore was anxious to make his acquaintance, which he did in a very modest way; and soon he found himself a pupil of the reverend gentleman, who, realizing his great desire for mental improvement, kindly consented to aid him in completing his acquaintance with English grammar, to which he had already given some attention. The good man invited the student to write an article for his inspection, that he might point out any defects of grammar or punctuation in it, if such there should be. The young man was surprised to see the article soon afterwards in the poet's corner of the *Universalist Magazine*, a semi-monthly sheet edited by Mr. Ballou. This was an indication that possibly other literary effusions of the new beginner might be given to the public.

A new interest was now awakened on the part of Mr. Ballou in reference to the young man. He was employed as a musician in the choir of the School Street Universalist.Church. His salary was raised by the change of places, and he was now enabled to listen to the preaching of one in whom he had the highest confidence, and under whose ministry he was led into the acceptance of the faith of the Gospel. There were new Sabbaths for him now since the new light had come in so genially and cheerily upon him. There was music in the pulpit as sweet as any which the choir could send forth, — music that uplifted him until he heard it mingling with the celestial anthem, "Glory to God in the highest; on earth peace, good will to men!" He breathed a new air; he entered upon a new life. The Bible was now to him the clearly spoken Word of the Eternal One. He had entered upon that highway of the Lord in which the feeblest may walk, and the wayfaring man, though exceedingly ignorant, be guided into all truth.

Mr. Ballou asked him one day if he had ever thought of preparing for the ministry. His answer was that he had entertained no such idea. Yet that question opened his mind to the subject. He pondered it, feared it, started back from such presumption; but still the subject grew upon him. He studied the Bible and the Christian Evidences by Paley, and listened with renewed attention to the preaching of Mr. Ballou. During the summer and autumn of 1820, he devoted every leisure hour to the study of the Scriptures.

Just three weeks before the day of his majority, he preached his first sermon in Roxbury, where the Universalists were then building a meeting-house. His text was Rom. i. 16. "I am not ashamed of the Gospel of Christ." The discourse had been written on the bootmaker's bench, and stitched together with a waxed-end. But it was a piece of strong work. It was well received. Mr. Ballou heard it, and humorously remarked that there were two good parts of it, the text and the amen! But he meant more than that, and the preacher felt that he did. He gained courage for new efforts. He was known to be poor; and, at the suggestion of Mr. Ballou to some of his society, means were generously furnished him to defray his expenses for one year. After remaining as a student in the family of Mr. Ballou for three months, he received and accepted an invitation to settle with the society in Milford, Mass. Here he formed an acquaintance with Lovice, daughter of John Corbett, Esq., whom he married in September of the same year. While in Milford, the house he occupied was burned to the ground, and his library and household effects were destroyed. His young wife was saved by leaping from a chamber window. The material loss he suffered was made up to him by the liberality of Mr. Ballou's society and some other Universalist societies in the neighborhood.

After a year's pastorate in Milford, he removed to Cambridgeport, on invitation of the Universalist society in that place to become their minister. He was installed there April 23, 1823. His pastoral relations with this society continued for nine years, when, because of the pressure of other duties, he resigned his office as pastor, but ever afterwards during his life remained a resident of the place.

It was in the early part of his ministry in Cambridgeport that he became joint editor of the *Universalist Magazine*, with Rev. H. Ballou and Rev. H. Ballou 2d. His articles usually bore the signature of " W.," but more frequently that of " Richards." He continued in this relation until the enlargement of the *Magazine* into the *Trumpet* in 1828. In the mean time, his pulpit labors were often extended beyond his own parish. He occasionally gave lectures in Malden, Medford, West Cambridge, Newton, Quincy, and other places, and preached both on the Sabbath and other days of the week in many towns in the neighborhood of Boston.

In the account of himself in the volume of which we have spoken, the subject of this memoir evidently regarded his life from his youth up as especially providential. There seemed to him to be a Divinity directing his steps. He was led onward into paths he had not dreamed of. His very induction into the ministry was attended with what to him were remarkable surprises. The conviction that he was to become a preacher gained upon him in spite of his wishes. In his own words: "I did not at first desire to preach. It gave me serious apprehensions. I was sensible that I was not prepared for the work. I had not been educated. I was a bootmaker's apprentice, of very humble parentage. My life had not been a religious one. True, I had recently been brought to believe and love the Gospel, so that I could truly say it was meat and drink to me; but I was conscious that I was not what a clergyman ought to be. My feeling was not caused by fear of persecution or the expectation of any opposition. It was the sense I had of the high calling of a minister of the Gospel and my unqualifiedness in every sense. But in this excitement the suggestion never came to my relief, 'Perhaps you will *not* be a preacher;' for it became more and more a fixed fact that such would be my vocation." [1]

In process of time this feeling changed, and he began to be reconciled with what seemed to be the divine purpose in regard to his life. He gave no thought to the question, whether it would be better for his reputation or material profit to become a Christian minister. He felt conscious of the utmost sincerity in his love of the Gospel; and in this truthfulness, united with much firmness of purpose and strong

[1] Autobiog., pp. 192, 193.

reliance in a beneficently directing Providence, he made his way onward and gave in the work of his subsequent years a full and noble proof of his ministry.

At the time of his entrance upon his ministry in Cambridgeport, the cause of Universalism was in its infancy in Massachusetts. There were not more than a dozen ministers of our faith in the State. The churches of the old " standing order," in company with many of the " new lights " that had come up during the half-century preceding 1820, all set their faces against what they considered this bold and audacious heresy. No language was deemed too strong in which to denounce it, and no means were left unused to set public opinion against it as a doctrine of doubtful and dangerous moral tendency, subversive of true piety and promotive of the rankest infidelity. This was what the lovers and defenders of our holy faith were obliged to hear on every hand, when its claims were set up and asserted. This fact, of course, put its ministers almost constantly on the defensive. They were obliged to work like the ancient builders of Jerusalem, with the trowel in one hand and the sword in the other. There are those now living who realize in their own remembrances the truth of these statements. But there are more who have since come up into life who realize but little the hardness of the strife then going on, because of the new incoming of this old and primitive Gospel of God the Father in Christ reconciling the world unto himself. To meet this bigoted and often unscrupulous opposition, great firmness, readiness, and resoluteness were needed. " Valiant-hearted men," not afraid of warfare, were called for; and they were providentially sent into the field to " vindicate the ways of God to man," and call man to love his brother and serve and imitate his Father in heaven. Among this company of our church-militant we find Mr. Whittemore at the time when he seemed to be especially needed, and under circumstances which enabled him to prove his valiant soldiership in the warfare. In bodily strength he was well fitted for his calling. He had great power of endurance, an ardent love of work, and a zeal in his life pursuits that knew no abatement or bound. A preacher adapted to the masses, he rose to a popularity that placed him among the most notable and acceptable public speakers of his time. Another has truthfully written of him: " Sound, logical, and clear, as an expository writer and preacher, he perhaps has not been excelled in the denomination. As a preacher, he was plain and simple. Without grace or beauty or melody, his mere elocution was sufficient to produce effects which melody and grace and beauty might have sighed for in vain. A picture that has been drawn of Luther's eloquence may not inaptly be applied to his. 'The homely force of Luther, who, in the language of the farm, the shop, the boat, the street, or the nursery, told the high truths that reason or religion taught, and took possession of his audience by a storm of speech, then poured upon them all the riches of his brave plebeian soul, baptizing every head anew, — a man who, with the people, seemed more mob than they.'"[1]

At the close of the volume containing his autobiography, Mr. Whittemore gives an account of his own installation at Cambridgeport; of the part taken by him at the ordination of Rev. Benjamin Whittemore at West Scituate; of his attendance at the Southern Association of Universalists in Stafford, Ct., in June, 1823; of his controversy with Rev. Charles Hudson on future punishment; of his first visit to Atkinson, to Haverhill, as also his first visit to the General Convention at Strafford, Vt., in 1824, — on which occasion

[1] Funeral Discourse by Rev. C. A. Skinner.

he preached; of his attendance at the Jubilee Meeting in Gloucester in November of this year, and his first visit to Plymouth, Mass., in December. We shall proceed from this date with our memoir.

During most of the time of his early ministry, Mr. Whittemore was a very constant contributor to the *Universalist Magazine*. In the issue of this paper, May 31, 1823, the annunciation was made of the conversion of Rev. Walter Balfour, a Baptist minister of Charlestown, Mass., to Universalism. Mr. Balfour was formerly a Presbyterian. He was well instructed in the Hebrew and Greek languages, and in sacred literature generally. He brought to America good recommendations from his Christian friends in Scotland, and was kindly received by the orthodox churches in Charlestown, where he began his life in America. He was a thoroughly honest man, and held his religious opinions in utmost sincerity of heart. His attention was first called to the question of the extent of the work of salvation, by Christ, while reading the controversy going on in 1819 between Professor Stuart of the Andover Theological Institution and Rev. Dr. Channing, of Boston. The Professor, in opposition to the Doctor, was aiming to prove the equality of Christ with the Father by stating that he was worthy of the worship of every human being, and ever will be of all souls. In proof of this he cites Phil. ii. 10, and Rev. v. 8, 14, where things in heaven, earth, and under the earth (a periphrasis for the universe), are said to bow the knee to Jesus, and ascribe blessing and honor and glory and power to him. "If this be not spiritual worship," says Professor Stuart, "and if Christ be not the object of it here, I am unable to produce a case where worship can be called spiritual and divine."

Mr. Balfour had strong confidence in the ability of Professor Stuart, and was greatly surprised when he read this passage.

He was almost alarmed. What could such a statement as this signify? The whole universe offering spiritual worship to God and Christ? Could the Professor mean this? Would he thus virtually avow the doctrine of Universalism? He determined to address him a letter stating his anxiety in reference to this subject, and asking an explanation. It was a respectful, candid, earnest letter. He pleads for more light. "Now, my dear sir, if it be true that things in heaven, in earth, and under the earth, is a common periphrasis for the universe; and if it be true that this worship is spiritual and divine, — you certainly have told us that the universe is to worship Christ with spiritual and divine worship. The worship is spiritual and divine, and the universe are the worshippers. Are we able to avoid this? The mind must be differently constituted from mine that can. Is it or can it be believed by any one that any beings in the universe who worship Christ thus shall be punished for ever?" This his first letter to the Professor appeared in the *Universalist Magazine* of Jan. 29, 1820, over the signature of "An Inquirer after Truth." He waited patiently and anxiously; but no answer came. He wrote again and again, from time to time, but still received no word in return.

Mr. Balfour's plea became more earnest, and his questions involving scripture exegesis more numerous. Why could he not have a reply to his inquiries? Was the Professor unconcerned as to what he was doing with his pen? Did he not really care what mischief this statement of his might work, yea, what unspeakable evil, with this inquirer and with others like him? Was he indisposed to notice newspaper inquiries? Bound to oppose Universalism, as the creed of the institution to which he had subscribed compelled him to be, why would he not seek to draw this inquirer away from its enticements? Such were Mr. Balfour's thoughts, and such the thoughts of others who kept their eyes upon his published letters. Inquiry after inquiry followed, up to the ninth, which appeared in the *Magazine* for June 16, 1821. For nearly a year and a half had the call been going to Andover for an explanation. The ninth letter elicits a reply from the Professor, which appears in the *Magazine*. But it was equivocal, and not at all in keeping with the open-heartedness and straightforward honesty of the inquirer. The Professor, not knowing who the inquirer was, objected to his animadversions because they were anonymous and published in newspapers. Frivolous talk when the eternal interests of souls are at stake, as they are in contact with destructive errors! Mr. Balfour replied modestly, — earnestly still, and manfully, — and concluded to apply to the Professor for guidance no longer. He took up the examination of the subject with increased interest, became thoroughly persuaded of the truth of the Gospel which certifies that God was in Christ reconciling the world unto himself, issued valuable books in illustration and defence of this faith, and devoted his remaining days to the inculcation of it. His whole life was an admirable comment on the holy truth he held. Mr. Whittemore enjoyed his acquaintance and companionship until his decease in 1852, and subsequently wrote his biography.[1]

In 1825, Mr. Whittemore was present at the Southern Association in South Wilbraham, Mass., and was one of the preachers on that occasion; and the next year, 1826, he attended the same Association at Dana, on which occasion he preached, and wrote the circular issued by that body.

In the *Magazine* of Dec. 2, 1826, there appeared the first of a written controversy between Mr. Whittemore and

---

[1] Memoir of Rev. Walter Balfour, Author of Letters to Prof. Stuart, and various other Publications. By Thomas Whittemore. Boston: J. M. Usher. 1852.

Rev. Orange Scott, at that time minister of the Methodist
Church in Charlestown, Mass.   The reverend gentleman
had sometime previous delivered a discourse against the doctrine of universal salvation, and in advocacy of the endless
punishment of mankind as a doctrine of the Bible.   By
means of others interested in the matter, Mr. Whittemore
had an interview with him, and proposed a fair discussion of
the subject on which he had lately preached.   He at first
declined ; but on being advised that this was improper, inasmuch as he considered Universalism a dangerous error, and
was therefore under obligation to endeavor to convince
those who believed it of the falsehood in which they were
trusting, he agreed to discuss the subject.   Failing to meet
his engagement for some months, he was urgently reminded
of it, and soon his first communication appeared.   One
characteristic of the discussion was, that while Mr. Scott's
articles, whatever their length, were freely placed in the
columns of the *Magazine*, and afterwards republished in
Zion's Herald, the Methodist journal of Boston, not one of
Mr. Whittemore's replies could find an insertion in the last-
named paper ; a reprehensible unfairness, to use no sharper
word, which the defenders of our faith, in controversy with its
opponents, have been called to realize in repeated instances.

One thing is especially noticeable in this discussion, and
that is the perfect coolness with which the exponent of the
Methodist theology quoted scripture in proof of a day of
general judgment and the endless punishment of the wicked,
and his general obliviousness to the full and patient examination of his positions made by Mr. Whittemore.   He did
not seem to be conscious that it was his duty to show *how*
his antagonist was a misinterpreter of the Scriptures, instead
of moving straight on himself with strings of scriptural quotations and statements of his theological opinions, as though

there was little or no dealing with them on the part of the defender of Universalism. But this course was not original with him. It was one of the expedients of theological debaters, conscious of the weakness of their positions. Mr. Whittemore appealed to his opponent. "I must remind you, Mr. Scott, that it does no good simply to quote passages of Scripture. You must show that they apply to a judgment in the future state, or you do nothing at all. This is the point at issue. I am perfectly willing that you should take the advice and receive the assistance of any or all of your ministering brethren. As I have expected it, so I shall not be disappointed. Let us have the whole strength of your argument against us."

As Mr. Whittemore suggested, it was believed by many at the time that, although Mr. Scott was the ostensible author of the communications in the *Magazine*, he was readily and largely aided by others, his clerical brethren. The discussion was continued for six months or more, and on the part of Mr. Whittemore was a close and able one. Both sides of the discussion were afterwards republished in the *Trumpet*.[1]

In June, 1827, we find Mr. Whittemore present at the Southern Association held in Springfield, Mass.; also in August of the same year in attendance at the Rockingham Association in Eaton, N.H.; on which occasion he preached twice, and prepared the Circular of the Association.

In the latter part of this year, he made his first visit to the West. He left Boston on Monday, October 8th, and went by way of New London to New York. Unfavorable weather prevented him from reaching the last-named place in season to deliver a lecture which had been appointed for him in the

---

[1] Vols. iii., iv.

Prince Street Church. He went on to Philadelphia, where he delivered two discourses on the Sabbath. From Philadelphia he passed on to Baltimore, and from thence, in three and a half days by stage, to Wheeling, Va. Unable from the low water of the Ohio River to fulfil an engagement to preach in Marietta, he journeyed through Zanesville, Lancaster, and Chilicothe, to Cincinnati. The roads were in the worst condition for travelling.

On his arrival at Cincinnati, he found that the Universalists of that place were making efforts, although under some discouragements, to erect a small church edifice. The congregations to whom he was called to preach assembled at the Supreme Court House, and at the Methodist Meeting House, where Rev. Mr. Burke officiated. The large Court room, where he preached three Sabbaths, was crowded to great inconvenience. Throngs were around the doors, and some, on one occasion, were taken in at the windows. "Go at what time I would," he writes, in a letter to the *Magazine*, "the house was crowded, and I had no reason to wait for the appointed hour. I attributed this excitement principally to the fact that our sentiments are new to many here; to the particular nature of the subjects I had been called upon to discuss; and to a report which the opponents spread, that one of the clergy intended to attack me. It is probable that some who attended were opponents, and perhaps still remain so; but the attention of many worthy persons was called up who had not before thought of the subject, and on whose minds an impression highly favorable to our sentiments was made."

He learned that the attention of the people in Cincinnati had been called to the subject of Universalism at different times for several years; that ministers residing in the West and two from the East had occasionally preached there; that in 1815 an edition of Siegvolk's "Everlasting Gospel" was published there by John Jenkinson, and subsequently an edition of a work by Dr. Joseph Young on Universal Restoration. He became acquainted with Mr. Abel M. Sargent, who issued at Cincinnati a small publication entitled the "Lamp of Liberty," and with Mr. Kidwell, who published a monthly paper at Eaton, Ohio, called the "Star in the West." He learned on every hand that the West was an inviting field for the dissemination of the doctrines of the Gospel of Universalism. He knew from the publications of the orthodox sects how anxious they were to occupy this field, and what exertions they were making to this end through the circulation of tracts and the sending forth of missionaries from some of the Eastern churches. He was convinced that in this same wide field there were yet rich harvests to be secured by faithful laborers in the name and spirit of our holy faith. During his sojourn in the West, he found occasion to circulate many Universalist books, among which were Rev. Mr. Balfour's "Inquiries," the first that had found their way out there.

Leaving Cincinnati on the 19th of November, he went to Fredericksburg, Va., to visit his eldest brother, who had been quite ill of paralysis. Here he preached by special invitation at the Town Hall, which was filled. But few present were acquainted with the doctrine of Universalism, and the preacher adapted his discourse to the circumstances from the text, Acts xvii. 19, 20: "May we hear of thee what this new doctrine whereof thou speakest is? for thou bringest certain strange things to our ears: we would know therefore what these things mean." He preached on the succeeding Tuesday evening, and on Wednesday took his departure for Philadelphia, where he had been invited to spend two Sabbaths. He here preached seven discourses to large and attentive audiences, and afterwards left for New York. On his arrival there, he preached in the church in Prince Street. He arrived home by way of Providence, on the 20th, after nearly three months' absence, during which time he had enjoyed uninterrupted health and travelled a distance of 2,500 miles. While he was away, the pulpit of the Cambridgeport Church was supplied by Rev. Joshua Flagg.

The result of the visit of Mr. Whittemore to Cincinnati was an urgent call on the part of the Universalist Society of that city for him to become their pastor. The call was duly appreciated, and the preacher was aware of the work he might be able by divine grace to accomplish should he take the new position to which he was invited. But he concluded on the whole to remain in New England; or rather Providence concluded for him.

"There's a Divinity that shapes our ends."

Here was to be the field of his hard and faithful toiling. How well and profitably that field was occupied by him the subsequent pages of this Memoir will declare.

CHAPTER II.

1828–1830.

AGED 28–30.

The *Trumpet:* its character — Visit to Rev. Dr. Emmons — Meetings — Rockingham Association — Preaches at Portsmouth, Exeter, Sterling — Meeting in New Hampshire — Dr. Lyman Beecher — Lowell meetings — Sunday Mail Question — Ancient History of Universalism — Meetings — Rev. M. Rayner — Prof. Stuart's Essay — Lectures by Messrs. Merritt and Fisk — General Convention at Winchester — Unitarian Statement — Woburn — Modern History of Universalism — At Dedham.

IN the beginning of July, 1828, the first number of the new Universalist weekly appeared, entitled the *Trumpet and Universalist Magazine,* edited by Russell Streeter and Thomas Whittemore. These gentlemen had purchased the *Magazine,* hitherto published semi-monthly in quarto form, had furnished an entirely new office, and obtained experienced workmen, that their paper might be issued in an attractive form. The proprietor of the *Magazine,* Mr. Henry Bowen, at first regarded the step as interfering with his private interests. A committee was mutually chosen, who decided that Messrs. Streeter and Whittemore should take the list of the *Magazine,* and pay its proprietors $1,250. The *Trumpet* was a sheet of royal size, published every Saturday at Boston, George W. Bazin, printer.[1]

---

[1] The name of Mr. Bazin appears on the *Trumpet* as its printer, for more than thirty years. He was a master in his business, and took a deep interest in the paper and in the cause of Universalism, and was ex-

The name of the paper, as it originally occurred to Mr. Whittemore, was attractive. The editors say that it was given for three reasons. 1. It was a short title; 2. It was one by which the paper would be easily distinguished from other religious publications, it having never been used to their knowledge as the title to any other Christian journal; and 3. It was in special conformity to their design. "We announce intelligence, we point out dangers, and excite the apprehensions of the community, and communicate a knowledge of the Gospel of God's grace. The trumpet was an instrument used in the religious observances of the Jews; and by figure the sounding of the trumpet is put for the preaching of the Gospel.

> 'Let every mortal ear attend,
> And every heart rejoice;
> The trumpet of the Gospel sounds
> With an inviting voice.' "

The editors say: " The divine command to the children of Israel was, ' In the day of your gladness and in your solemn days, ye shall blow with the trumpet.' We are reminded too that we must use great plainness of speech; ' for if the trumpet give an uncertain sound, who shall prepare himself to the battle.' Should we be called on to say that there is an increased attention to religion, that dormant societies are

tensively known in the denomination. He lived to the age of seventy-seven. Rev. Dr. Patterson said of him in his Centennial Discourse at Portsmouth, N.H., in 1874, that he had probably "put in type more arguments in vindication and illustration of our faith than any other man that ever lived."

Mr. Henry Bowen had been the printer of the *Universalist Magazine,* from its first appearance. He too was one of the steadfast friends of our church cause, and lived to an advanced age. He was deacon in the Shawmut Universalist Church in Boston, at the time of his decease, in 1874.

awakened to new zeal, or that the morally dead have heard the joyful sound of the Gospel, have come into possession of life and peace, by what means can this resurrection of the dead be better announced than by the sounding of the trumpet?" And so, in subsequent issues of the paper, the words of the old prophet appeared under its heading, in the centre of which was the flying angel, "Blow ye the trumpet in Zion, and sound an alarm in my holy mountain."[1] The editors furthermore say, "We retain the name *Universalist Magazine*, because our publication is to be what we promised it should, a *Universalist* publication. We venerate the name as that of the oldest Universalist paper now existing in the United States. And the *Trumpet and Universalist Magazine* is to be a continuation of the original paper, under an enlarged form and in a new series."

Later in life, on being reminded by a brother editor of his prosperity and wealth, he takes occasion to say: "When I began the *Trumpet*, I urged my ministering brethren in Boston and vicinity to take hold with me on equal terms; and they were afraid, with the exception of Brother Russell Streeter. These were days of peril. I mortgaged the very house that sheltered my family to secure the debts I was obliged to contract. Nobody had, up to that time, become rich by publishing Universalist books and papers; and very few, if any, have done it since. But if a man in the day when I commenced, and when the wisest of his brethren dared not take the slightest pecuniary risk with him, could get rich in publishing Universalist books and papers, it is a matter that should be spoken to his credit."[2]

The new paper was received with great favor by the Universalist public, and by many others who were sincerely

<hr>

[1] Joel ii. 1. [2] *Trumpet*, April 3, 1847.

inquiring after religious truth. It met an existing want. Subscribers came in on every hand. Contemporary papers, both religious and secular, gave it hearty greetings. Its columns were lively and full of terse and strong reasoning. Each issue was largely original; for the editors in their work had the sympathies of their fellow-ministers and of the laity of the Universalist churches warmly enlisted on their side. The tone of the paper was loyal to the cause it professed to espouse. It was wholly committed to the promulgation of Christian Universalism the truth that "God was in Christ reconciling the world unto himself;" Christian Universalism in all of its presentations, whether held by those who believed with Murray in the Trinity, with Winchester in the future punishment of the wicked, or with Ballou in the Divine Unity and the silence of the Scriptures as to the punishment of transgression beyond the present life. The Paternity of God and the Brotherhood of Man; the present blessedness of obedience and afflictiveness of sin; the rising of the race from mortality to immortality; the right of free religious inquiry, and the great need of the just exercise of this right; the exposure of religious error, fraud, and priestcraft, whether Protestant or Catholic; the commendation of the Gospel of Universalism as the Bible reveals it, in vindication of the Divine character and as the surest antidote of that infidelity engendered by false theologies under the Christian name, — these were the chief topics to which the *Trumpet* gave its constant and untiring attention.

The plainness and freedom of speech evinced in the paper were notable. It was, of course, deemed by many who adhered to the old theology as too presumptive and irreverent in questioning the claims of its defenders. It gave no respectful heed to what their *ipse dixit* might be; it would acknowledge no extra privilege of real or assumed sanctity on the part of opponents who, instead of offering argument in support of their opinions, were more ready to assume a solemn interest in the eternal welfare of the one they deemed heretical. Often was this disposition encountered on the part of this new "defender of the faith;" but just as often was the needed and firm admonition given, "not warning, not intimidation, but argument, brothers, argument! To the law and to the testimony!"

Three months after the commencement of the *Trumpet*, Mr. Streeter retired from the joint ownership, receiving as compensation for his portion of the property a sum mutually agreed upon. The sole responsibility as editor now devolved on Mr. Whittemore, and most faithfully was it sustained through subsequent years, until his surrender of his editorial work in 1860. Not only as editor but as proprietor of the paper was his work well and successfully pursued. He looked carefully and constantly after his subscription-list; appointed none for agents in whose ability and fidelity he had not strong confidence; kept his watch-care over those conscience-less ones, so afflictive to many newspaper publishers, who become subscribers without much thinking or caring whether they shall ever pay for their papers. To all such he was a vexation in the short work which he often made with them; while towards those who through misfortune were unable to be as prompt in payment as their honesty desired, he was tenderly considerate and generous.

In the summer of this year, passing through Franklin, Mass., Mr. Whittemore gratified himself with a call upon Rev. Dr. Nathaniel Emmons, — one of the most distinguished representatives of the Calvinism of the past, and still living as pastor of the parish over which he had been settled during fifty-four years. The venerable man, now eighty-five, after having been informed by his visitor as to his name, residence, occupation, doctrine, and object in calling, gave him a very cordial reception. He expressed his satisfaction in meeting with strangers who were open and free in avowing their sentiments in religion, and the disgust with which he frequently witnessed the prevarications of men of different denominations, not excepting some of his own order. He spoke with much freedom on what he considered the innovations made upon the old doctrines and methods of the Calvinistic churches of New England by such men as Dr. Lyman Beecher and others, who, he feared, were attempting to effect a change in the system they once accepted, without having the honesty to acknowledge it outright. It had been reported, he said, that he was inclined to Universalism, or was already at heart of that sentiment, but unwilling to have it known. He denied the imputation, and said he hoped the Universalists had too much sense and honesty to claim him on their side if he would be such a hypocrite as to conceal his real sentiments. Mr. Whittemore assured him that his position was well understood by Universalists, and that, differing widely in some respects as they did from him in their religious sentiments, they honored him for the sincerity with which they believed he held his own. The interview seems to have been a very agreeable one to both parties. Since that time the religious aspect of things in Franklin has been much changed. Where, in the day of Dr. Emmons's pastorate, there was none to dispute his sole oversight of the one Calvinistic church there, other sects have taken their places, and a Universalist Church and richly endowed Academy, founded by Dr. Oliver Dean of that place, now occupy the grounds once in possession of the venerable divine himself.

On Wednesday, July 23, Mr. Whittemore attended the service of Recognition of the Universalist Church in Watertown, and preached the sermon on the occasion. Rev. Messrs. Streeter of Boston, Jones of Gloucester, and Cobb of Malden, assisted in the services, which were appropriate and impressive.

On Wednesday, July 30, Rev. Sylvanus Cobb was installed as pastor of the First Church of Christ in Malden. This was the original first orthodox parish of the town; but the majority now in it had resolved that the ministry of Christian Universalism should henceforth be sustained by them and those inclined to aid them in their work. Mr. Cobb was their first choice as pastor. He had come from a successful pastorate in Waterville, Me., and proved himself in succeeding years in Massachusetts and throughout New England an able Christian preacher, writer, and advocate of the prominent reforms of the times. Mr. Whittemore offered the Prayer of Installation; Rev. S. Streeter of Boston preached the Sermon. Rev. Messrs. H. Ballou, W. Balfour, and R. Streeter took other parts in the services.

The Rockingham Association of Universalists was held this year in August at Kingston, N.H. Most of the services were in the old meeting-house on " the plains." There was a large attendance, especially on the last day. The weather was very favorable, and the meetings were of great interest to many who attended them. Mr. Whittemore preached on the evening of the first day.from Haggai ii. 6, 7, — the shaking of the heavens and the earth, and the coming of the Desire of all nations. Rev. Hosea Ballou preached to a large and deeply attentive congregation, on the afternoon of the last day. There are those now living (and the writer is one of them) who will have occasion while life lasts to remember with gratitude and thanksgiving to God the effects upon them of the meetings of that session of the Rockingham Association.

The installation of Rev. Thomas F. King as pastor of the First Universalist Church in Portsmouth, N.H., took place on Wednesday, Oct. 15, of this year. The discourse on the occasion was delivered by Rev. S. Streeter, a former pastor of the church. Mr. Whittemore gave the right hand of fellowship to the pastor, and preached in the evening. It was a day of much interest to the Portsmouth parish: Mr. King proved to be a highly acceptable and honored minister in that place. He was the father of Rev. Thomas Starr King, who was but a lad when he came with his parents from Hudson, N.Y., his birthplace, to the "old town by the sea."

On the next evening after the day of installation in Portsmouth, Mr. Whittemore preached for the first time in Exeter, N.H., in the Court House, to quite a large audience, on the Universalist faith and the profession of it. It was a forcible and scriptural discourse, and was, by special request of the hearers, afterwards published in the *Trumpet* of Jan. 17, 1829.

On Sunday, Nov. 16, Mr. Whittemore preached in Sterling, Mass. It was his first visit to that town. The pastor of the society there was a Unitarian. It had been supposed that he would consent to the admission of the Universalist into his pulpit; but he was unwilling to, and the Universalists therefore held their meeting in the town-house, a commodious building, capable of seating nearly three hundred people. The hall was closely filled. Passing on from this place through New Hampshire to Springfield, Vt., he attended according to previous appointment, a two days' meeting of the Universalists in that place. During the meetings, Mr. Whittemore preached twice, and other discourses were delivered by Rev. Messrs. J. Moore, S. C. Loveland, R. Bartlett, and W. Skinner.

The attention of the Universalist churches in and about Boston was at this time called to the expressed opposition of Rev. Dr. Lyman Beecher to their faith. He had delivered a course of lectures against it in his own church in Boston, some of which he had repeated in other churches in the neighborhood. The *Trumpet* call was made upon him to give them to the public through the press. It was understood that he had stated his intention to do this. But long waiting had caused some impatience on the part of those who most desired to greet them. Mr. Whittemore thus appeals to him: " My object in this letter, Rev. Sir, is to call on you for a fulfilment of your long-neglected promise. If there are justifiable reasons for your delinquency in this particular, the columns of this paper are at your service, that by a statement of these reasons you may satisfy a disappointed public. It is our ardent wish that you give us the sermons." These, however, were not forthcoming. The author did not seem inclined to give them publicity. But he was vigorously followed up, and in due time there appeared in the *Trumpet* a very searching review by Mr. Whittemore of one of these discourses taken down by a stenographer at Dorchester. We shall speak of it further on.

The dedication of the new Universalist Meeting-house in Lowell, took place on Nov. 27, of this year. Rev. Hosea Ballou preached the sermon on this occasion. In the afternoon of the same day, Rev. Eliphalet Case was installed as pastor of the society; the sermon was delivered by Mr. Whittemore from 2 Tim. iv. 5, " Do the work of an evangelist." Rev. T. F. King preached in the evening.

In the beginning of 1829, public attention was called to the subject of the running of the mail upon the Sabbath. Numerous memorials and petitions were sent to Congress, praying that the carrying of the mail on the Sabbath might be stopped. The plan originated in New York. It had the appearance of much propriety and fairness, and was regarded by many professing Christians of the more popular sects as a measure accordant with the religion they professed. But there were many others equally attached to Christianity, who were not inclined to favor the measure. They thought they saw in it a sectarian movement rather than one intended for the benefit of the nation. Mr. Whittemore gave much attention to this subject in the columns of his paper. He copied into it the popular report of Colonel R. M. Johnson in opposition to the Orthodox memorialists, and stated in strong terms his own objections to their course. His review of the petition signed by prominent citizens of Boston, was a close and searching one.[1] He thought that there might be quite as much to fear from the evils of a dominant religious sectarianism in the country as from the revolution of the wheels of a mail-coach on the Sabbath. The petitions for the new measure were not successful, and after a time the movements in behalf of it ceased.

There was issued from the press of Marsh, Capen, and Lyon of Boston, at the opening of this same year, a work which had for some time been promised and anxiously looked for, entitled, "The Ancient History of Universalism, from the time of the Apostles to its Condemnation in the Fifth General Council, A.D. 553 : with an Appendix, tracing the Doctrine down to the Era of the Reformation." By Hosea Ballou 2d, Pastor of the Universalist Society in Roxbury. This volume was the result of great labor and patient research on the part of its author, and opened up to the Christian public a new revelation in the field of ecclesiastical history. No man was better calculated, from his love of historical

---

[1] *Trumpet,* Vol. I., No. 29.

research, habits of accurate and close thinking, scholarly attainments, and devotion to the Universalist faith, than Mr. Ballou, to take hold of this work and make it a success in his hands. Previous to its appearing, but little was known of the advocacy of Universalism after the days of the apostles. The names of Origen and a few others were identified with it; but other historians had not made its history a specialty until this new explorer and examiner appeared and shed the broad light of day where before there was almost midnight darkness. Mr. Whittemore said of it, in a review in the *Trumpet:* "There are very few who will be able to estimate the labor which this volume has cost its author. This may in justice be considered the first attempt of the kind. In such an undertaking, the author enters a field boundless on every side, without index or guiding star, in which no footstep is seen; and here he is to seek the object of his pursuit. . . . The denomination of Universalists is laid under the most weighty obligations to Mr. Ballou for the labor he has performed."

The author of this history clearly shows that of all the early "Christian Fathers," so called, not one condemned the Universalist sentiment, although it was believed and defended among them; that orthodox bishops of greatest renown maintained it openly and zealously, without receiving censure or losing their popularity; and that it was not until about A.D. 400 that it was denounced as an error. Another fact brought to light was, that the word rendered in the Scriptures "everlasting" was familiarly and commonly used in the first three or four centuries to signify limited duration, and was applied very frequently to punishment by the Universalists of that period. Reviewers of ecclesiastical history since the appearing of this volume have been very careful in their notices of it to contradict none of the statements; and more recent explorers of the same field have not only corroborated the truth of the statements of its author, but have presented new and striking evidences of the wide prevalence and salutary Christian influence of the Universalist faith in these ancient days, especially in the third century.[1]

Mr. Whittemore was present and preached at the meeting of the Southern Association in Hartford, Ct., May 20 and 21; also, at the New Hampshire Association, in Sutton, N.H., on the 27th and 28th of the same mouth of this year. On the 4th of June, he attended the installation of Rev. L. S. Everett as pastor of the Universalist Church in Charlestown, Mass., and gave him the right hand of fellowship.

At the close of the first volume of the *Trumpet*, in June, the publishing office was removed to No. 40 (south side), Market Street, corner of Franklin Avenue. The editor states, in the last issue of this volume, "The patronage we have received thus far has exceeded any expectations we had formed at the commencement of our undertaking; a circumstance which has given vigor to all our operations, attractiveness to the paper, and satisfaction to all parties concerned."

On Wednesday, July 15, the Universalist meeting-house in Hanson, Mass., was dedicated, the sermon being preached by Mr. Whittemore. During this month, Rev. Menzies Rayner, pastor of the Universalist Society in Hartford, Ct., visited Boston and its neighborhood, and received a warm

---

[1] The statement of these facts is made with great clearness and candor in a series of articles by Dr. Edward Beecher, published in the New York *Christian Union*, Vol. VIII., No. 10. Speaking of Mr. Ballou's "Ancient History," Dr. Beecher says: "The work is one of decided ability, and is written with great candor and a careful examination of authorities. In our opinion, it would benefit Mr. Lecky and Prof. Shedd attentively to consider all the facts and authorities presented in it." These last-named gentlemen had written on the subject of Restorationism in the early churches.

welcome from his Universalist friends. He was then a recent comer from the Episcopalian into the Universalist church. He had stood well with his brethren of the former church, and made good and effective proof of his ministry in the new church relations upon which he had entered. He was then past the middle age of life; a bright, strong man, an acute thinker, a well-read theologian, and a preacher of uncommon energy. A discourse which he preached during this visit, at Cambridgeport, on "Apostolic Fidelity," heard by Mr. Whittemore, was published in the *Trumpet*, of Aug. 8, 1829.

The attention of the Universalist public was called about this time to an article in the *Spirit of the Pilgrims*, of Boston, from the pen of Professor Moses Stuart, of Andover, an essay on the Greek words αἰών and αἰώνιος, especially in their uses as expressive of the duration of future punishment. The essay had, doubtless, been called out in consequence of the increasing interest in the great question of the final destiny of the human family, and especially because of the pressure of the able inquiries of the professor from the pen of Mr. Balfour. Mr. Whittemore, in a short editorial review of the essay, expresses a hope that Mr. Balfour will take it up and lay its character before the public, — a work which that sincere and honest inquirer afterwards accomplished, to his own credit and for the good of the Christian public.

In a leading editorial of the *Trumpet* for September 12th of this year, is a review of "A Discussion on Universal Salvation, in three Lectures, and Five Answers against that Doctrine; by Rev. Timothy Merritt. To which are added, Two Discourses on the same subject, by Rev. Wilbur Fisk, A.M." These lectures, as it was stated by a New York paper at the time, were the substance of a public debate which took place in Springfield, Mass., between Rev. Messrs. Merritt and Fisk, and Rev. Lucius R. Paige, pastor of the Universalist

Society in that place.   Mr. Whittemore gave attention to the substance of these discourses, and especially to the uncandid and foolish classing of Universalists with Deists, evidently to bring the more discredit on Universalists in the eyes of other Christian believers.   "If men are Deists," said Mr. Whittemore, "who believe in Jesus Christ as the Saviour of the world, who hold to the resurrection of all the human race to a state of immortality and incorruption, then are Universalists Deists; and, we may add, then was St. Paul a Deist.   But, if these men are not Deists, then do Messrs. Merritt and Fisk stand before the world guilty of misrepresentation and slander."   Mr. Merritt had said, "If they (Universalists) deny this charge, let them meet us fairly.   Let them show, by facts and arguments, wherein we are deceived, and wherein we misrepresent them."   "Facts and arguments!" replies Mr. Whittemore; "what does Mr. M. mean by calling for facts and arguments?   There is nothing he so totally abhors.   In his controversy with Mr. Ballou, what was it besides facts and arguments that confounded him?   Universalists have been giving this man facts and arguments for ten years, and what good has it all done?   What attention did he pay to the facts and arguments offered to Rev. Orange Scott, whom he assisted in a controversy about three years since?   What attention did he give to the facts and arguments furnished by Rev. Mr. Paige, in reply to his lectures in Springfield against Universalism?   This call for facts and arguments is, in our opinion, a pretence.   If he is really disposed to deal in facts and arguments, we call on him for the proof that Universalists reject the inspiration of the Bible; that they treat experimental religion with contempt, and sneer at piety; that they pretend to a superior order of intellect; that they overlook the arguments of their opponents, and assert what has been confuted again and again; and that they employ arts of sophistry in support of their cause.   We call for proof of this, we say."

In September of this year, Mr. Whittemore was in attendance at the session of the General Convention, held at Winchester, N.H.   In the issue of the *Trumpet*, Nov. 7, he thus notices an article in the *Christian Register*, from its editor, who had stated, "Unitarians are not to be called Universalists, for they regard the doctrine of the Universal Restoration, although they believe it, of very little importance," deeming other articles of faith of far more consequence.   "It is then a certain fact that our liberal brethren, the Unitarians, feel very little interest whether all mankind are saved or not; and although some of them think that perhaps they may and probably will be, yet that this is a matter of small importance.   Well, as this is a fact, we will add our testimony to Mr. Reed's, that there is a considerable difference between Unitarians and Universalists; for we believe, with the good and great Mrs. Barbauld, that unity of character in what we adore is much more essential than unity of person. We often boast, and with reason, of the purity of our religion as opposed to the grossness of the theology of the Greeks and Romans, but we should remember that cruelty is as much worse than licentiousness as Moloch is worse than a Satyr."

On Wednesday, Dec. 23, the Universalist Meeting-house in Woburn was dedicated, and Rev. Otis A. Skinner installed as pastor of the society.   Mr. Whittemore addressed the society on this last-named occasion.

In the beginning of 1830, the "Modern History of Universalism," from the pen of Mr. Whittemore, appeared.   He had been upwards of five years in collecting materials for the work, steadily pursuing his purpose without regard to labor or expense.   It was, in fact, a continuation of the "Ancient History" by Mr. Ballou, taking up the subject where it was left by the author of that work, and bringing it down to the then present time. The volume contained a copious index, prepared with great care.

The work met with commendations from those most interested in its appearance and character. Mr. Ballou, the author of the "Ancient History," said of it: "Though somewhat acquainted with the subject beforehand, I found my previous calculations exceeded by the successful collection of materials from an unexplored field, whose extent, bounded only by the uncertain limits of modern literature, was enough to discourage research. I met with a mass of important information to me entirely new. So far as I can discover, the important facts in every part of the history appear substantiated either by unquestionable documents or by adequate and convincing proofs." Rev. T. J. Sawyer in the Ninth Annual Report of the Universalist Historical Society speaks of the work: "Great praise is due Mr. Whittemore for the manner in which he executed his task. Though less complete than the 'Ancient History,' it is still a noble monument of its author's industry and research. In this department of our history the sources of information were much more numerous and lay scattered more widely. When I consider the time when it was written, and the very little attention that had then been paid to the subject, I cannot but regard the 'Modern History' as remarkable for the variety and general accuracy of its information." And he justly adds: "Insignificant as the denomination of Universalists may now appear in the eyes of the world, it is not to be doubted that the time is coming when it will occupy in this country and throughout all Christendom a much more commanding position, and men will ask for the beginning of what they shall then see, and love to read the story of our present struggles and victories." The "Modern History" was afterwards enlarged and greatly improved by Mr. Whittemore, and one volume of it published in 1860. His death, which took place soon afterwards, interrupted his further labors, and the second volume has not yet appeared.

On Thursday, Jan. 14, the new Universalist Meeting-house in Dedham, Mass., was dedicated, and Mr. Whittemore preached the sermon on the occasion.

CHAPTER III.

1830–1833.

Aged 30–33.

Dr. E. S. Ely and Universalists — Dr. Lyman Beecher's opposition — Rev. Mr. Atkinson's ordination — Dr. Ely's Reply to Mr. Whittemore, and Answer to it — General Convention at Lebanon, N.H. — Dedication at Annisquam — Mr. Whittemore's resignation at Cambridgeport — Elected representative — Third Article of Bill of Rights — Mr. Whittemore's course and speech — Alteration effected — His interest in the town of Cambridge — Anecdote — Controversy with Universalists, how to be carried on — Rockingham Association — General Convention at Barre, Vt. — Nominated for the Senate — Notes on the Parables — McClure's Lectures on Ultra-Universalism — Singular concession of the author — Rockingham Association — Journey of a week — New edition of Murray's Life — Services in South Boston — Journey to New Hampshire — Ordination at Rumney — Meeting at Wentworth, at Concord, at Sandown.

One of the leading editors of the religious journals of the country at this time was Rev. Dr. Ezra Stiles Ely, editor of the *Philadelphian*, a Presbyterian journal. In an article of the editor, he attempts to show what Professor Stuart had, not long before, stated, that Universalists are not Christians, and ought not to be entitled to the privilege of testifying by oath in courts of justice. He, moreover, very seriously calculates that in the course of thirty years, by means of church and home and Sabbath-school training, the so-called evangelical sects of the country will be able by vote to control its interests, and thus keep out from public office all men whose opinions do not accord with their own. Mr. Whittemore copies the article entire into the *Trumpet*, reviews it fairly, and administers to the writer of it, as well as to those who would approve of its sentiments, the reproof which it so evidently deserved. It was a sturdy talk, and the Rev. Doctor must have felt its force.

The discourse against Universalism, which Dr. Lyman Beecher had been promising for some time to repeat, was, at the urgent request of the Universalists of Dorchester, delivered in one of the Congregational churches of that town, on Wednesday evening, March 17. Mr. Whittemore with others, his friends, attended and heard it. Full notes were taken, and the discourse was published in the *Trumpet*, followed by a close and thorough examination of it by Mr. Whittemore. The relative merits of the two discourses can be very soon decided by any reader disposed to examine the *Trumpets* of April, 1830. They were issued together in pamphlet at the time.

On Thursday, April 29, Rev. Joseph P. Atkinson was installed as pastor of the Universalist Society in Hingham, Mass.; sermon by Mr. Whittemore.

A long letter from Dr. E. S. Ely, in reply to Mr. Whittemore's examination of his article in the *Philadelphian*, appeared in the *Trumpet* of May 15. In the next issue, Mr. Whittemore replied to the Doctor at length, reviewing his statements respecting Calvinism, in which the Doctor had represented himself as holding a Calvinism quite different from the original theology of that name, and congratulating him on his approach towards Universalism. The Doctor had given Mr. Whittemore most earnest exhortations to embrace Orthodoxy, because of its safety. Mr. Whittemore favors his brother with an equally fervent plea in behalf of Universalism, because of its pre-eminent claims on the reason and conscience of mankind.

In September of this year, Mr. Whittemore attended the General Convention held at Lebanon, N.H. On his way he preached to a large congregation in Mason Village, and on his return, in Sutton and Bradford, N.H. The Convention was largely attended, and five discourses were preached during its session, one of them by Mr. Whittemore. He also wrote the Circular Letter. The Boston Association also held its annual session in Cambridgeport, Dec. 8. Mr. Whittemore was appointed to prepare the minutes with a Circular Letter for publication.

On Wednesday, Jan. 5, 1831, the new meeting-house in Annisquam, Mass., was dedicated. Mr. Whittemore preached the sermon. The old house had stood upon the same ground one hundred and two years. Rev. Mr. Leonard, who had been settled as a Congregationalist minister, but had embraced the Universalist faith and was sustained by his congregation, was pastor at the time. He had been settled there twenty-five years.

In March of this year, Mr. Whittemore tendered his resignation as pastor of the society in Cambridgeport. He had for some time been conscious that his many duties as editor and publisher of a weekly paper seriously interfered with the regular performance of his parochial work, thus depriving the society of one great aid to their prosperity. Notwithstanding their desire for him to prolong his services among them, he deemed it wrong to consent to sustain an office the duties of which he was conscious that he could but partially fulfil. He expressed his intention to work more freely and extensively as an evangelist, preaching in different places as his services might be desired.

In May following his resignation as pastor at Cambridgeport, he was elected a representative to the State Legislature from Cambridge. He continued to serve the town in this capacity for several years, and rendered very acceptable service to the town and State. He took a prominent part in effecting a change in the Third Article of the Bill of Rights or Constitution of Massachusetts. This article provided for the compulsory support of religion; that is, it made religion a matter of state, and provided for its support by law. Mr. Whittemore, like Jefferson and Madison and others, believed that the support of religion might be safely trusted to the piety and good sense of the public. He moved the reference of certain petitions to a select committee, of which he was made chairman, a place that he held through three successive sessions. The first year, 1831, the amendment passed the House by a vote of two-thirds, but was lost in the Senate. The next year it passed through both branches of the Legislature by a vote of two thirds in the House and a majority in the Senate, without which a change in the Constitution could not take place. The Constitution also required that it should pass both branches a second year, which was done in 1833. It was then submitted to the people and was adopted by a large majority.

As Mr. Whittemore was deeply interested in this subject, it was expected that he would address the House in advocacy of the alteration. This he did with great earnestness and effect. Expressing regret that it had fallen to him among his other numerous engagements to take the lead in this movement of reform, he proceeded to show at some length the character of the petitions received and the reasons assigned by the petitioners for the change they asked. A little space here cannot be better occupied than with a few extracts from the speech, which was somewhat extended: —

"For one, Mr. Whittemore thought it worthy of consideration, whether the civil power can, with propriety, interfere in the concerns of religion to compel people to support it. Jesus Christ never designed that his religion should be supported by the civil power. He did not apply to the civil power for support; he never had the support of the civil power, but was always opposed to it. And, furthermore, he has left no directions to his followers to seek this aid. A man's views of piety, religion, and morality, are a concern solely between his conscience and his God. He is not accountable for them to civil government unless he disturbs the public peace. Our common Master did not hold himself accountable to Jewish law in this respect.

" Men whom we should call *political religionists*, answer this argument as follows: ' That government has a right to legislate on that which tends to the public good, and that we may legislate on religion for the same reason that we may legislate concerning schools. Every man is obliged to pay taxes for the support of the public schools, not excepting him who has no children, because these schools are for the public good, and he, indirectly at least, enjoys the benefit of them. For the same reason every man should be compelled to support religion, for he enjoys the benefit of the religious state of society, though he never attends public worship.' Mr. Whittemore, in reply, said that religion and education are two entirely different things. So long as a man's religion does not disturb the public peace, the laws have nothing to do with it. But education is a fair subject of human legislation. On this all the citizens are agreed, — they are not split into innumerable sects, with a thousand conflicting interests and prejudices, — and no one's conscience suffers violence.

" ' But (said Mr. Whittemore) the argument that pure religion tends to the stability of government goes to show that we should not establish it by law. The way to keep religion pure is to leave it to the free will of the people. No religion but that which is voluntary can do good. If you force people to support it, it is only their money you can get; you do not cause them to respect religion, and therefore you do hurt, for you excite their ill will. The benefit which religion gives to the stability and good order of society is greater without the aid of law than with it; because the benefit of religion to any individual consists in its being left entirely to his conscience and his choice. Religion to do any good must operate on his heart; it must regulate his affections; it must subdue his passions; it must impress its likeness on his soul: but this a mere artificial support can never do; this a legal enactment never will effect.' Mr. Whittemore maintained, therefore, that legal support was a clog to pure and undefiled religion; a millstone hung about its neck, with the preposterous object of elevating it in public estimation. This has been precisely the effect of the legal support of religion in Massachusetts. The commonwealth has been split up into numberless and unnamable sects ; the oldest parishes in the several towns have been injured by the laws that were designed to support them; and unless they have been sustained by gifts, bequests, and funds, they have become weakened until they can with difficulty breathe the breath of life. Religion has flourished most among the dissenters from the oldest parishes; a fact undeniable in the estimation of every one acquainted with the state of religion throughout the commonwealth.

" Moreover, Mr. Speaker, you always lower the standard of religion by connecting it with human law. This all ecclesiastical history proves. Religion has always been the purest when totally disconnected from the civil power, and even when persecuted by it. This fact is stronger than a volume of speculations, conjectures, and fine-drawn inferences. What history teaches in its plainest forms, what the experience of eighteen centuries fully proves, should not be lightly passed over. In the primitive ages of Christianity, the religion of our common Master shone in its primeval lustre ; but does any one need to be told that he was not supported by human law, but opposed and persecuted and crucified by it? His followers were pursued from city to city, were scourged, stoned, and sawn asunder. But their religion was pure. Three centuries afterwards, when Constantine, the first of the Roman emperors who was converted to Christianity, linked the religion with the State, it soon became debased. Its ministers were corrupted ; they grew proud, indolent, and arrogant ; they perverted the Word of God to sustain the State that indulged and pampered them ; and it was not long before few traces of the original purity of the religion of Christ could be found. Follow religion through the dark ages, while it was the close ally of the civil power, and what do you find of that beautiful system of piety, doctrine, and morals bequeathed to the world by Jesus Christ, except the mere name and shadow of it? When the voice of Luther broke the silence of a thousand years, and he endeavored to call back the church from its wanderings and errors, by whom was he opposed? By civil rulers under the dominion of a corrupt clergy ; and, although one or two of the petty potentates of Germany espoused the cause of the Reformation, it is indisputable that the Emperor Charles V., and the civil rulers generally, at first opposed it ; and at last they were induced to aid it, principally because it gave them deliverance from the terrific power of the Roman Pontiff. The pages of ecclesiastical history are black with the accounts of the evil that has been done to religion by associating it with human law.

"It does not follow, Mr. Speaker, because a thing is beneficial to society, that therefore we must legislate about it. The shining of the sun is of vast benefit to the commonwealth, but is far above the power of human legislation ; and so is that religion above human legislation which is the ' Sun of Righteousness,' and ' the Light of the world.' The falling of the rain is of incalculable benefit to the commonwealth, but it is above the power of human constitutions and statutes ; and so is that religion which ' drops like the rain and distils like the dew, like the small rain upon the tender herb, and the showers upon the grass.' It is for the benefit of society that persons should enter into the married relation, but we make no laws to compel them to be married. What should we do if the farmers should refuse to till the earth? Society would be in a most lamentable situation ; but no one thinks it necessary to enact laws to compel them to do this. Such things are governed by laws which sway men with an irresistible force, far above the power of formal statutes. Government would very soon come to an end if every person should refuse to eat. But is it necessary to ordain that persons shall eat, and threaten them with penalties if they neglect? No, sir. The laws which God has ordained in man regulate that matter. To apply this comparison, the laws of the human mind and conscience will regulate religion with as much certainty. Religion is the aliment of the soul, the bread and water of life : the soul cannot live without it. The matter is made certain by the laws of the human constitution : it is above, far above, all legislative enactments ; they can have in the nature of things no more effect in sustaining religion than discussions concerning the motions of Saturn can control the revolutions of that planet."

After stating these general principles applicable to the case, Mr. Whittemore turned to the operation of the then existing constitutional enactment respecting religion, as it was seen in Massachusetts. This formed a very important part of his speech, and was very effective at the time of its utterance; but we have not room for it here. He concluded by saying: —

"The voice of the people, Mr. Speaker, calls loudly for the alteration of the third article of the Bill of Rights. In this country they are the supreme power. Popular opinion, in its steady course, is like the current of a river, but in its violence it is like a cataract which nothing can withstand. What are we, sir, but the straws that are borne on the surface? We are the servants of the people sent here to represent them. The power of public opinion always will be felt more or less, even in those countries where it is restrained by constitutional provisions; and where it has not legal redress it will break forth in violence. Look at the exhibition of public sentiment in England on the rejection of the reform bill by the House of Lords. It convulsed the nation. The castles of the offending peers were levelled in the dust. We have no fear of such an issue here, because the people, when aggrieved, can always avail themselves of constitutional redress. And they will. If the desired alteration does not take place now, they will speak in a voice of seven thunders, and they will be heard. We cannot resist them. There is great force and beauty in the classical apotheosis of public sentiment: *Vox populi, vox Dei.* Sir, bid the Mississippi roll back its waters to the North; say to the earth, 'Cease thy revolution;' speak to the sun in mid-heaven, command him to turn to the East: and you shall be obeyed when the force of public opinion in Massachusetts can be successfully resisted."

There was a strong minority of opposition to this alteration. Hon. Mr. Hoar, in the Senate, made a very urgent plea against it. He had said, in the Convention of 1820 for the revision of the State Constitution, that Massachusetts must retain the third article, or maintain a standing army![1]

[1] *Trumpet,* Nov. 26, 1831.

" Mr. Whittemore was deeply interested in all that concerned the prosperity of Cambridge. Subject as the town was to conflagrations, — it being principally built of wood, — Mr. Whittemore, while one of the selectmen, procured, by private subscriptions and public appropriations, some thirty reservoirs of water to be put down in a single year, which proved to be of immense service. And years afterwards, when an effort was made by the citizens of ' Old Cambridge,' so called, — it being that section in which Harvard College stands, — to obtain a division of the town, Mr. Whittemore opposed it with all his energy. He appeared as the agent of the town authorities before successive committees of the legislature; and it was principally by his instrumentality that the design was frustrated. So impressed was he with the injustice of the attempt, that he described the petitions to the committee as a proposition to incorporate the *wealth* into one town, and the *expenses* into another. Hon. Robert Rantoul, on one of these occasions, was the opposing counsel to Mr. Whittemore. Shortly after, these petitions were defeated; and, to set the matter of a division at rest, Mr. Whittemore advised an application for a city charter, which was obtained, and the town was changed to the ' City of Cambridge.' In the debates before the legislative committee on the subject of the charter, Mr. Whittemore met, as the opposing counsel, Hon. J. G. Palfrey." [1]

While Mr. Whittemore was a member of the Massachusetts Legislature, a resolution was introduced proposing to increase the daily pay of the members. Mr. Whittemore gave no countenance to the proposition, and sought to defeat it by his speeches and otherwise. It, however, prevailed. When Mr. Whittemore was afterwards asked by some friends of the

[1] Sketches of Eminent Americans, New York, 1853.

proposed measure what he did when the Legislature decided to adopt it? "Oh!" said he, "I concluded it best to *pocket the insult.*"

The *Trumpet* of April 2 contains a timely editorial on "Controversy with Universalists." It was written in view of the new interest taken by the sects in the Universalist controversy, and contains some very just and practical suggestions as to the manner in which it should be carried on. He proposes, 1st, that slander and hard names be left out of it; 2d, that affirmations as to the licentious tendency of Universalism be dispensed with, as if the doctrine is proved false the Universalists will give it up without controversy as to its tendency; 3d, to repeat arguments which have been time after time answered, without showing that these arguments are unsound, will by no means convince those for whom they are intended; 4th, to string together an assortment of Scripture texts will not satisfy Universalists that their sentiments are false; 5th, explanations of the text, and reasons for these explanations, must be given; 6th, it will avail nothing to refer to antiquity, because that may be pleaded in favor of error as well as of truth. "Universalists require of their opponents that Universalism be shown to be an unscriptural doctrine, if possible by fair and manly criticism. They cannot be frighted nor persuaded out of their opinions, except by the noble and irresistible persuasion which evidence exercises over the mind.   These hints are given that those desirous of engaging in the controversy concerning Universalism may avail themselves of them, and no longer ' labor in vain and spend their strength for nought.'"

In August of this year Mr. Whittemore attended the Rockingham Association, at Lamprey River village, N.H., preaching on his way at Kensington one Sabbath, and giving an evening lecture in South Hampton.   Large congregations were in attendance at Lamprey River, and the services were in the Methodist meeting-house, kindly granted for the occasion. Eight discourses were delivered, one of them by Mr. Whittemore. From the Association he went to Exeter, where he preached on Friday evening, in the Court-house, to a very crowded congregation. The Sunday following he preached in Atkinson.

The General Convention held its annual session this year in Barre, Vt. It was a meeting of unusual interest. Mr. Whittemore attended, and preached on the evening of the first day. Rev. Hosea Ballou delivered the last discourse, one of his most effective efforts, from Job xxxvi. 2 : "Suffer me a little, and I will show thee that I have yet to speak on God's behalf." On this occasion the house was thronged, and many who could not obtain a place within were seated in carriages outside at the opened windows.

Pending the actual election of State officers in Massachusetts this year, Mr. Whittemore's name was placed at the head of a list of persons nominated for senators in the District of Middlesex. On this he remarks in the *Trumpet:* "The editor supposes that his name was put on this ticket in consequence of the part he has taken for a year past in endeavoring to obtain an alteration of the Constitution of the Commonwealth in the third article of the Bill of Rights. It is but justice to the public that this should be said. His views on this subject are well known, and are fully expressed in another column; so that nothing further will be said on this subject in this place. We esteem it our duty to add, however, that we have but little expectation that the above ticket will be successful; for although the majority of the citizens are willing the article should be abolished, the more powerful influences of political party will control the impending elections."

Mr. Whittemore was present at the session of the Boston Association held at Lowell, Dec. 7, and preached in the evening.

Another volume from Mr. Whittemore's pen is now announced in the *Trumpet;* viz., his " Notes on the Parables of the New Testament," a work of about 290 duodecimo pages. The parables are arranged in reference to the order of time in which they were spoken ; a distinct exposition is given of each, illustrated by such helps as the best commentators and most approved travellers have furnished. As many of the parables have been used to support the doctrine of endless suffering, particular care was to be taken to show wherein orthodox expositors have agreed with Universalists in their interpretations of them. A full index is added to the work. The " Notes " are dedicated to Rev. H. Ballou, who had himself in former years issued a work on this subject.

In the *Trumpet* of June 30, the leading editorial is a notice of a new little work just then issued from the press, entitled " Lectures on Ultra-Universalism," by Rev. A. W. McClure, pastor of the Orthodox church in Malden, Mass. The object of the work, as its author affirms, is to " assail Universalism with the sharp shooting of wit." He complains of Universalists that they are " vulgar, that their coarse habits, their cultivated scurrility, their grovelling tastes, their deficient education," serve to " associate them with all that is distressingly low." As to his candor and good feeling, he remarks, that it is no part of his design to wound their (Universalists') feelings through mere wantonness and malice, or unjustifiably to pervert their favorite doctrines. " Far be it from me to pursue any such object. I am sensible that such an aim would be too inglorious, and that success would but poorly reward the labor of securing it." He considers his book as possessing " heartfelt, heaven-born piety, eternal celestial truth, genuine sincerity;" in proof of all which he proceeds to pour out upon the objects of his special attention ridicule without stint, and vituperation without measure. The professed believers in the doctrine are classed with the lowest and vilest of society, and accused of wringing and twisting Scripture so unmercifully that it can almost be heard to scream out at the hard usage it meets at their hands. He advises them all to get into glory as soon as possible by means of suicide, and wonders that they should " lag behind," and stay out of heaven as long as " rum, death, and the doctor will let them." As to their preachers, such men as Ballou, Whittemore, and Cobb, and their associates, he says, " I have no thought of vying with them in the panoply with which Satan arms them. Him they may thank for what moral power they have. He is the arch-prelate of their hierarchy, and they are the cardinals and minor clergy of the infernal See."

This is a specimen of the lectures, and Mr. Whittemore paid due attention to them. The extracts he made from them were their hardest condemnation. Poison and antidote were in the same volume. The whole thing was maliciously and ridiculously overwrought. The lectures carried their own refutation with them. Mr. Whittemore noticed the book, and animadverted upon it, not so much because of what it was in reality, as of the recommendations it received from leading ministers and reviewers of the Orthodox churches. To them, no matter how hard the abuse, or how intense the obloquy cast upon Universalists, the end justified the means. But Mr. Whittemore in all his notices of this little vituperative volume, turned its sayings in their bearing on Universalism to a profitable account.

One of the most ludicrous of Mr. McClure's statements in one of the lectures was, that Universalists had no oaths of their own ; so that when enraged they could not swear, unless they borrowed orthodox oaths! Their doctrine taught them to bless even their enemies, and how could they curse them consistently with their own faith? It has always seemed unaccountable to those who have considered this slip of the author's pen, where his thoughts could have been when he made it. But Universalists have always given him credit for truthfulness in this statement.

Nearly half a century has passed since these lectures were written. They have never injured the cause of Christian Universalism; and the author was capable of better work than he put into them. But he was in the drift of the excitement then rife against our holy faith, and seemed not to have the power of resisting a temptation to render himself conspicuous in this particular mode of warfare. There are none who envy him the laurels he gained in it. The writer of this Memoir afterwards spent years with him as a neighbor and personal friend. His heart was always better than his theology.

The Rockingham Association for this year (1832) was held in South Hampton, N.H. The meeting was well attended, and six sermons were delivered to large congregations of attentive hearers. Mr. Whittemore preached in the afternoon of the first day.

In the *Trumpet* of Oct. 27, Mr. Whittemore records the journey of a week. Leaving Boston on Friday night, Oct. 15, in a packet for Orleans, Cape Cod, he reached there at three o'clock Sunday morning; preached at Brewster that day, and on Monday evening in Orleans, in the Methodist church. He returned through Brewster to Dennis, where he preached on Tuesday at the South Village. He went to Hyannis Wednesday, to attend the annual session of the Old Colony Association. Three discourses, one by Mr. Whittemore, were preached on that day to very crowded audiences. Rev. J. M.

Spear was the pastor at Hyannis. On Thursday, Mr. Whittemore went to Plymouth, where he preached in the evening of
that day. On Friday evening, he preached in Halifax. He
was intending to rest on Saturday, but was urged to go over
to Abington and speak on Saturday evening. Universalism
had never been preached in that town. A large school-house
was filled to inconvenience with attentive hearers. He reached
West Bridgewater that night, and preached there the next day
(Sunday). "We occupied," he writes, "the Baptist Meeting-house, in the west part of the town, on the skirt of a wood,
like the house Thomas Potter built, and in which Murray
first preached on landing in America. This house had never
before been opened to Universalists. It is large, with a
gallery on three sides, and was filled above and below. I had
preached in this town several times before, but never to so
many people. We had a choir of fifty singers, who performed
some of the antique American music with great effect. . . . On
the evening of this day, I went over to Easton, and preached
in a large school-house in the south-east part of the town.
The lecture was attended by a crowd. The main house
and entry were full, and there was a throng outside. The
windows were thrown up, and all were able to hear. I
returned after lecture to West Bridgewater, and on Monday,
home."

In the *Trumpet* of March 30, 1833, a new edition of the
Life of Rev. John Murray, prepared by Mr. Whittemore, is
announced, differing materially from all that have been published. "The text will be the same in every respect as it
was in the original edition published by Mrs. Murray, as far
as it goes. But there are one or two important portions of
his biography included in his 'Works' which will be incorporated into this edition of his life. A considerable body of
notes will be added, throwing light on different parts of the

work and containing much information in regard to the early history of Universalism in America not before published. An Appendix will be added containing documents illustrative of the events in which Mr. Murray was concerned."

The dedication of the new meeting-house erected by the Universalists of South Boston, and the installation of Rev. Benjamin Whittemore as pastor of the society, took place on Wednesday, April 10. The Dedicatory Sermon was preached by Rev. Hosea Ballou, and the Installation Sermon by Mr. Whittemore; sermon in the evening by Rev. Sylvanus Cobb of Malden.

In June of this year, Mr. Whittemore was called into New Hampshire to attend the ordination of a younger brother in the ministry, John G. Adams. After preaching in Hancock, N.H., on Sunday, to "a large concourse," as he writes, he passed on to Concord Monday, where he was joined by Rev. Hosea Ballou, who preached that evening in the Unitarian Church in Concord. The house was filled, and the congregation was composed largely of the members of the State legislature then in session. A very complimentary notice of Mr. Ballou's discourse was given by one of the secular journals of the town.[1] Mr. Ballou went in company with Mr. Whittemore to Rumney. The account is thus given in the *Trumpet :* —

"On Tuesday we proceeded, in company with Brother Ballou, to Rumney, N.H., for the purpose of attending the ordination of Brother John G. Adams, which took place on the following day. The services were attended by a very large concourse of people from Rumney and the neighboring towns, so that it was judged necessary to place extra support under the galleries. The utmost silence and attention were, not-

[1] Whittemore's Life of Ballou, Vol. IIL p. 145.

withstanding, observed, and the solemnities of the ordination seemed to soften every heart and to lead every one present to pray in spirit for the divine blessing on the candidate and on the cause which he has espoused.[1] On Thursday, we went together to Wentworth, a town adjoining Rumney on the north. Here the brethren insisted that we should both preach in the afternoon. Brother W. S. Balch was present, and offered the introductory prayer. This was followed by two discourses, — the first from Brother Ballou. Brother Adams offered the concluding prayer. The congregation sustained an unremitted attention through the service, which was nearly of three hours' continuance. We had time to become acquainted with but few of the brethren here. Those we saw have been tried and found faithful. We mention with pleasure the name of Caleb Keith, Esq., a gentleman who, at the advanced age of nearly fourscore, sustains the vigor and vivacity of youth, and adorns the doctrine he professes with a corresponding life. On Friday morning, we left our friends in Rumney and returned to Concord. A lecture had been appointed for us at the Unitarian Church, which was attended by many members of the Legislature and many citizens of the place." He spent the following Sunday in Sandown, N.H., preaching to a large congregation.

---

[1] This old town's meeting-house stood on the common at Rumney Centre. In more recent time, other churches have been erected in the neighborhood, and the old one has been moved away and devoted to other uses. Within a few years, a substantial stone-post enclosure has been, by voluntary subscription, placed around the common, in the centre of which an elegant bronze fountain sends out its waters.

CHAPTER IV.

1833–1836.

Aged 33–36.

Rockingham Association, 1833 — General Convention at Strafford, Vt. — Scenery on the journey — Sippican — Opposition at Danvers — Rev. M. P. Braman — Public discussion with him — Comments upon it — Journey of a week — Ware, Brimfield, dedication at Spencer — Boston Association — Rev. Parsons Cooke, and One Hundred Arguments — Rockingham Association, 1834 — General Convention at Albany, N.Y. — Visit to northern New Hampshire — Boston Association — Discussion respecting zeal — Mr. Whittemore's views of conference, prayer, and praise meetings — Capital Punishment — Temperance — Visit to Maine, and Lectures — Brunswick, Topsham, Bowdoinham — Maine Convention — Dr. Beecher — Rockingham Association, 1835 — Jubilee Session of U.S. Convention — Boston Association — Stoughton — Dedication at West Rumney, N.H. — Meetings in New Hampshire — Discussion again on conference and prayer meetings — Mr. Whittemore's views of them.

In August, Mr. Whittemore is called again into New Hampshire to attend the Rockingham Association. In company with Rev. Abel C. Thomas of Philadelphia, he went to Haverhill, where Mr. Thomas was to preach; and, leaving him there, passed on to Kensington, where he preached on Sunday. "A large congregation," he writes, "listened to the services, among whom many of other denominations were seen. The orthodox deacon, a venerable gentleman of nearly fourscore, received me cordially to his house, and attended service, bearing witness to the truth; and his consort, bowed down with age, was prevented only by inability. She took me by the hand and wished me God-speed, and prayed the

Lord to guide me by his spirit to declare his truth to mankind. On Sunday evening, I passed over to Exeter, and preached to a full house, Brother T. K. Taylor, now located there, assisting me in the service. Brother Thomas joined me from Haverhill. On Monday, we passed on to Portsmouth; visited Brother King and some of his society. Met Brothers C. Gardner and G. Noyes. Brother Thomas preached with much power in the evening. We enjoyed a Gospel feast. After public service, we repaired to the house of a friend, and tarried until midnight, singing the praises of God. On Tuesday, we all started (Brother Gardner excepted), for the Rockingham Association at Nottingham."

This meeting of the Association was one of as much interest as any that had preceded it. Services were held in the spacious old meeting-house, and were attended by large congregations, particularly on the second day. Eight sermons were preached. The Occasional Sermon by Rev. S. Streeter of Boston was one of his happiest efforts. It appeared afterwards in the *Trumpet*, and might be read with profit at the present time. A circumstance mentioned by Mr. Whittemore, served to cast a shadow upon the meeting. "One of the esteemed friends of our cause, Colonel Joseph Cilley, was confined to his bed, in a very distressing condition, from sickness occasioned by a wound received on the frontiers in the last war, and of which he has never since been fully well. He resided near the meeting-house and was visited by as many of the brethren as he was able to see. Prayers ascended to heaven for his recovery, for the sake of his family, the town in which he resides, and the cause he has espoused."

On his return home Friday, Mr. Whittemore found that the worthy companion of Rev. L. R. Paige of Cambridgeport, had departed this life during his absence.

In September, he was present at the General Convention in Strafford, Vt., its forty-eighth yearly session. On his way to Vermont, he preached in Athol, Mass., in the Town Hall. The description of his ride to Claremont we give in his own words. "From Keene it was a delightful ride. Nothing can surpass the richness of the scenery. The first view I had of Connecticut River as I descended the Cheshire turnpike to its banks, threw into the shade all that I had ever conceived of Eden. At the head of the landscape stood the mighty Ascutney, which seemed to be presiding over a family of hills around. The river meandered through the richest meadows and fields in the highest state of cultivation. The tillage lands were gray with their ripened crops; the mowing and pasturage were dressed in their liveliest green; beautiful buildings gave variety to the scene; a clear sun crowned the entire view with glory. The whole was one of the grandest prospects I ever enjoyed. I know not what to call the feeling with which such a view inspires the heart; but it was but little lessened by the journey to Claremont village. Nature has poured down her riches in the greatest profusion through all this region. Claremont is one of the most beautiful towns in New England. It seems almost impossible that there could be more attractive farms than some that lie within and around it. At sunset I reached the house of Brother Wm. S. Balch, a distance of sixty-two miles from where I started in the morning."

The session of the Convention in Strafford, Vt., was a very harmonious one. An alteration in the character of the Convention was proposed by a committee chosen to report on the subject, in reference to which further action was deferred until the next session. Twenty-five ministers were present. Six services were holden attended by large congregations.

Mr. Whittemore preached on the last afternoon of the session.

The meeting-house erected by the Universalists of Sippican, in Rochester, Mass., was dedicated Oct. 11; sermon by Mr. Whittemore.

In the *Trumpet* of Aug. 31, 1833, there appeared an editorial article headed "Opposition at Danvers." It was called out by an attack on the denomination of Universalists by Rev. Milton P. Braman, a clergyman of that town. The editor of the *Trumpet* solicited him to give his discourse to the public, offering to publish it in his paper or in a pamphlet without expense to him; or, if more agreeable, an oral discussion is suggested by Mr. Whittemore.

Mr. Braman replied through the Boston *Recorder*. The result of the correspondence was, that the relative claims of Universalism and the dominant orthodoxy of the day should be discussed by Mr. Braman and himself, in the meeting-house occupied by the parish of which Mr. Braman was pastor in North Danvers, on Thursday, Oct. 31.

The question for discussion, as proposed by Mr. Whittemore, was, whether the doctrine of endless misery is revealed in the Holy Scriptures. It was the expressed desire of Mr. Braman that there should be two distinct propositions for discussion, — first, Will any of the human race be punished after death? and second, Is this punishment eternal? To this Mr. Whittemore objected, saying, "The subject of difference between you and me is not whether future limited punishment be true, for you do not believe that doctrine. The two opposing doctrines are endless misery and universal salvation. You hold the former, and I the latter. I propose to discuss the question, whether the former doctrine is revealed in the Word of God, and no other question." It was furthermore urged by Mr. Whittemore that Mr. Braman should pledge himself to observe in the discussion the rules of propriety and decency, without which the proposed debate would be worse than useless. How far this obligation was adhered to on the part of the latter the sequel will prove. Mr. Braman subsequently proposed to limit the discussion to an hour and a half, a suggestion at which Mr. Whittemore expressed his surprise and to which he could not agree. His final proposal was, that the discussion must continue until broken off by mutual consent. So much time was taken up in adjusting the preliminaries of the meeting, that another day was appointed for it, Wednesday, Nov. 6, at nine A.M.

The discussion took place according to this arrangement. The moderators mutually chosen were, Rev. A. W. McClure of Malden, Rev. Sebastian Streeter of Boston, and Rev. E. Taylor, the seaman's preacher, of Boston. The house in which the discussion took place was a large brick edifice with spacious galleries, strengthened by additional props for the occasion, and filled above and below in the morning, and with a large crowd in the afternoon. We present a statement of the day's work from the *Trumpet.*

"The services were introduced by a fervent and appropriate prayer by Rev. Mr. Taylor, and the rules were read by Rev. Mr. Streeter. The rules were in substance as follows: The question for discussion shall be, — *Is the doctrine of endless misery revealed in the Holy Scriptures?* The discussion shall commence at nine o'clock in the morning, and continue until twelve; to be resumed at two and continued until five; the discussion to be commenced by Mr. Braman, and the speakers to follow each other alternately. The parties shall observe the rules of fair and honorable debate.

"Mr. Braman opened with an account of the manner in which the discussion originated, and then proceeded to establish in the way most satisfactory to himself, — 1st, the doctrine of punishment in the future state; and, 2d, the end-less duration of that punishment. To prove the doctrine of future punishment he relied principally on Psalm lxxiii., and on Matt. xi. 22, ' It shall be more tolerable for Tyre and Sidon at the day of judgment than for you;' and also on John xii. 48, ' He that rejecteth me, and receiveth not my words, hath one that judgeth him: the word that I have spoken, the same shall judge him in the last day.' To prove the endless duration of the punishment, he adduced the Parable of the Rich Man and Lazarus (Luke xvi. 19–31), the passage in 2 Thess. i. 7–9, and the Parable of the Sheep and Goats (Matt. xxv. 31–46). In answer, I endeavored to show that these passages of Scripture had no just reference to the subject to which Mr. Braman had applied them; that they were not originally intended to have such a reference; and the true meaning of the passages was given, so far as time would allow, and so far as it was necessary to show that they afforded no support to the doctrine of endless misery. In addition to this, it was shown by a great variety of testimony, that the sacred writers taught explicitly the doctrine of ulti-mate universal salvation; and if this glorious doctrine is revealed in the Scriptures, the doctrine of endless misery cannot be revealed. No small share of Mr. Braman's time was occupied in endeavoring to resist the force of this tes-timony."

A full and fair report of the discussion was soon afterwards published by Mr. Whittemore in a pamphlet of one hundred pages. A much smaller one of thirty-six pages was issued by the friends of Mr. Braman, in which the most important portions of the debate are omitted. The arguments of Mr. Braman were the most fully reported in the pamphlet issued by Mr. Whittemore, which had a very extensive circulation.

The discussion on the whole was highly favorable to Universalism. It was conducted in the presence of a large number of the prominent professors and defenders of the olden Orthodoxy of New England. And in the afternoon of the debate, as Mr. Braman failed to give the arguments of Mr. Whittemore that close attention which they evidently deserved, the latter had the privilege of stating and urging with great earnestness what he believed to be the Universalism of the New Testament before many, both of the ministry and laity, who had probably never heard so much of this primitive Gospel before. He deemed it a rare occasion, and faithfully improved it.

Of course, the discussion could not pass off without eliciting some sharp criticism on the part of those who sympathized with Mr. Braman. Among these, we find a writer in the *Essex North Register* (supposed to have been Rev. Dr. L. Withington, of Newburyport), expressing his opinions in reference to the discussion, after having read a report of it. He professed to have felt much sympathy for the Universalist debater through the discussion, on account of the severe treatment he received at the hand of his vigorous opponent. It seemed "like seeing a little innocent babe mauled and beaten by a large two-fisted Irishman." The trumpeter, he thought, evidently did not appear at his best; "must have had the toothache, or have lost his sleep the night before," or have had a cold, and have been "in need of a dose of pennyroyal tea." Unlucky thrust that! for it only calls out the keen retort of Mr. Whittemore: "This seems to us very much like folly. The comparison, however, is tolerable in one particular, wherein Mr. Braman is compared to the Irishman; for we thought he gave us *bulls* enough during the discussion to entitle him to that appellation. As to the supposed trouble with the trumpeter, he regretted that the mention of it compelled him to make a statement which until then he had intended to conceal. Mr. Whittemore went to Danvers with the fullest confidence in the cause he had espoused. He had no fears to make him indisposed. But Mr. Braman was in the highest state of excitement when Mr. Whittemore arrived at his house on the morning of the discussion. We waited for him until nearly nine before he came into the room, and were then unable to account for his absence. But, in conversation with an Orthodox clergyman a few days afterwards, we learned the cause of his non-appearance. 'Mr. Braman,' he said, 'came so near fainting three times that morning, that they thought they should not be able to keep him on his feet.' Whether they gave him any pennyroyal tea we are not informed."

In justice to Mr. Braman it may be said that he had probably had but little experience in oral debates. He was an excellent scholar, a chaste and classical writer, and usually preached written sermons. He evidently risked a good reputation as a public speaker in the Danvers discussion. As Rev. Mr. Streeter, one of the Moderators at the debate, afterwards wrote of it: "It was a matter of surprise to myself and to many others that he should have risked the high reputation which public opinion had awarded him as a polemic, in a contest in which his tongue must take the place of his pen. But, all things considered, it is not a subject of regret. The results of the whole debate will, I am confident, be highly favorable to the cause which he labored to destroy."

A "Journey of a Week" is recorded in the *Trumpet* of Nov. 20. Mr. Whittemore, in company with Rev. L. R. Paige, visited Framingham, Worcester, Spencer, and Brookfield. On the succeeding Sunday, Mr. Whittemore preached in Ware Village; and, on Monday, passed over to Webster, where he preached in the parish meeting-house, both forenoon and afternoon. The minister of the parish, Rev. Mr. Fitch, was sorely displeased that the parish committee had allowed this privilege to the Universalists ; so much so, that he avowed his determination to ask his dismission as the pastor there, if the house was thus used. Being asked by some Universalists why he made this vow, his reply was, "Because you are going to hell, and are getting all you can to follow you." The persons addressed, however, were not able to see what relevancy the answer had to the subject ; for if Universalism were as bad as he supposed it, and was evidently coming into his parish, it would seem to be his bounden duty to stay there and endeavor to prevent its growth. In reference to the vow, Mr. Whittemore remarked, "It is made, and cannot be recalled ; and it remains to be seen whether the reverend gentleman will ask his dismission accordingly, or break his vow. We hope to be informed on this subject. Forty men once bound themselves by an oath that they would neither eat nor drink until they had killed Paul. They must either have starved to death, or else they all broke the oath ; for they did not kill Paul."

On Tuesday, Mr. Whittemore preached in Brimfield ; and on Wednesday morning proceeded to Spencer, to attend the dedication of the new Universalist Meeting-house in that place. The day was very pleasant, and a large congregation was in attendance. Rev. L. S. Everett preached the Dedication Sermon ; Mr. Whittemore made the Occasional Prayer, and preached in the evening.

The Boston Association held its annual session in Gloucester, Dec. 4. Mr. Whittemore preached at the evening service, and was appointed by the Association to write its Circular Letter. In it he appeals to the societies within the bounds of the Association to send their delegates to its meetings. "It is not pleasant to the clergy to be left to do all the business themselves: they always desire the presence and advice of their lay brethren; and they hope that the constitutional number of lay delegates will hereafter be sent by each society. It betokens a promising state of things when the members of our societies are attentive to the concerns of the denomination, and the clergy are not left to transact the business for themselves."

About this time Mr. Whittemore had occasion to bestow special attention on another opponent of the Universalist faith, — Rev. Parsons Cooke, then of Ware, afterwards of Lynn, Mass. Mr. Whittemore had published a tract entitled, "One Hundred Arguments for Universalism," and Mr. Cooke had issued a pamphlet in reply to it. Mr. Whittemore expressed his satisfaction at the appearance of the pamphlet, because it would call public attention to the controversy between Universalists and their opponents, and tend to give the subject importance in the minds of people who had thought but little of it before. He took up the examination of the pamphlet in the columns of the *Trumpet* from week to week, and very closely and fairly answered the statements of Mr. Cooke against the "One Hundred Arguments." The examination was afterwards issued in pamphlet form.

In August, 1834, Mr. Whittemore attended the Rockingham Association, held in East Kingston, N.H. He gives a particular account of his visit, in an editorial letter to Rev. A. C. Thomas, in the *Trumpet* of Sept. 6. He preached on the Sunday previous in Kensington, where he met for the first time William C. Hanscom, afterwards in the ministry. He then visited Portsmouth and Exeter. The meetings at East Kingston he describes as among the happiest he had ever known. Seven sermons were preached during the two days, — the last one by him. A very interesting conference concluded the meetings. It was " a painful parting " on Friday morning, as he writes.

In September, he attended the General Convention, held at Albany, N.Y.; preaching on his way in Chicopee Village, Springfield, Mass. The session of the Convention was one of much interest, and was largely attended. Mr. Whittemore gives an account of it in an editorial letter to Rev. Thomas F. King.[1] The Universalist Historical Society was formed at this session. The Convention adjourned to meet in Hartford, Ct., and to have the session noted as the fiftieth anniversary, or Jubilee, of the General Convention.

After his return from the General Convention, he visited Northern New Hampshire. On his way, he preached in New Market, and on Sunday in Epping. A lecture had been appointed for him at West Rumney; but the weather proving unpropitious, a praise and conference meeting was held at the home of Mr. Robert Morse, where he found other ministers and a circle of friends eager to greet him. From thence a number of the party went to Piermont, — twenty miles distant, — and attended the annual session of the Grafton Association. Seven ministers preached, Mr. Whittemore among them. He also went over the river to Bradford, Vt., and preached there to a large congregation in the Academy. All the meetings were well attended. Mr. Whittemore returned to West Rumney on Friday, where a conference meeting was held, at which Rev. D. D. Smith preached. Mr. Whittemore spent the next Sunday in Wentworth, where he spoke to a large congregation, notwithstanding it was a rainy day. He tarried here with Hon. Caleb Keith, an aged and steadfast friend to the cause of the Gospel. On Sunday evening, he preached in West Rumney; and, on his way home, in Haverhill, Mass.

At the annual session of the Boston Association, Nov. 4, in Acton, Mass., he preached the Occasional Sermon.

[1] *Trumpet*, Sept. 27, 1834.

In the *Trumpet* of Dec. 13, the editor takes occasion to notice a criticism made by a ministering brother whom he deeply loves, respecting undue zeal on the part of Universalists. It was Rev. I. D. Williamson, who, in the Albany Universalist Journal, commending true Christian zeal, expresses some fear that Universalists may indulge in a zeal not according to knowledge. He thinks he has seen an indication of this in accounts which have reached him of the meetings of the late session of the Rockingham Association in East Kingston. Mr. Williamson had read of "shouting praises" there, and reprobates the practice of crying "Amen!" "Glory!" Mr. Whittemore defends the East Kingston meeting, avers that it was an orderly one, and that he heard no extravagant shoutings of "Amen!" there; although there were those who made that utterance during the conference exercises. He sustains from the Old Testament the shouting for joy on the part of those who love the Lord. "Paul," said he, "recommended plainness in preaching, that the unlearned might understand and say 'Amen!'" As for himself, he has no objection whatever to these responsive words on proper occasions. He fears no danger that the zeal of Universalists will go too far, but thinks they need more of the prudent but effective kind.

As this subject may again come up for consideration in this Memoir, it may not be amiss to notice it here a little more at length. Mr. Whittemore's convictions as to the need of religious meetings, where ministers and the laity could unite in the exercises of praise, prayer, and exhortation, were very strong. He deemed such assemblings of great importance with Universalists: and, while there were those of his brethren whom he highly honored who questioned the utility of them, he was desirous of giving his testimony, by word and practice, in their favor. Not only in his weekly journal, but in his private correspondence, about this time, he expressed himself with great warmth, and even with enthusiasm (which he and others deemed justifiable), on the subject. Writing to a ministering brother in New Hampshire, not long after the meeting at East Kingston, he says: "I never shall forget that meeting. I bless God for that week; the happiest, it seems to me, that I ever enjoyed. If there ever was a heaven on earth, we had it there. I can make nobody here realize it. On my way home, I stopped at Brother ———'s, and gave him an account of the meeting, and he called it Methodism and enthusiasm! Heavens! let me always have such enthusiasm. It is no doubt the feeling that angels have around the throne of God. It is a prelibation of heaven, a foretaste of the glories of the eternal world. What raised us up to that height of enjoyment? The fact is, we went there to give up all to the influences of the Gospel. Every one felt free: there was no restraint, no holding back, except in me, for I was obliged at times to repress my feelings: I did not wish to set the example of being too highly transported. But if we were not above the people in our feelings, then, God bless them, they must have gone away happy. . . . I have had *faith* for fifteen years: it is full-grown now; it has wings, and takes me farther up than I have gone before. I want all Universalists to be truly and deeply religious. Why may not each house of ours be a house of God?"

The ordination of Rev. William C. Hanscom took place at Lamprey River (New Market, N.H.), on Feb. 8, 1835. The services were largely attended, and Mr. Whittemore preached on the occasion.

Among the reformatory questions which claimed the attention of Mr. Whittemore in these years was that of the abolition of capital punishment. In the *Trumpet* of March 1st, he notices the execution of a youth at Newburyport for arson.

After presenting the case itself, and the scenes attending the execution, he concludes by saying: "The question should be very seriously pondered by every member of the community, whether capital punishments are justifiable in any case. If they are not justifiable, then every instance of capital punishment is a murder. If the State has made a mistake in this matter, it has made a fatal mistake, one that can never be repaired. The question of policy must not come in until that of principle is first settled; viz., whether it is right for a community to take the life of a helpless man. We shall say more on this subject in future."

His interest in the temperance reform also led him to speak plainly on what he considered some of the errors of its leading advocates. In a missionary report published this year he notices the sectarian turn given by the writer to this reform. "Unitarians, Universalists, and Roman Catholics," are spoken of as having come into orthodox churches through a revival which had been preceded by a temperance reformation. Mr. Whittemore protests against this indiscreet language, and avers that he cannot in conscience work with men in a cause which ought to be free from sectarianism while they persist in such an unwise and perverse course. "If our brethren who are orthodox," says he, "can join us in truly temperance measures, and leave their sectarian dogmas out of consideration, we shall be happy to go with them; but if not, if they are determined to make temperance societies sectarian engines, we shall leave them and form temperance societies of our own. They have already injured the temperance cause in this way more than they are aware of; and we entreat them to pursue a different line of conduct."

In June of this year, Mr. Whittemore visits Maine. Preaching at Brunswick on the Sabbath through the day, and at Topsham village in the evening; and delivering a temperance lecture on Monday evening in the Orthodox church at Brunswick, to a very large audience, including the professors and students of the college, — he proceeded to Bowdoinham to attend the Maine Convention. The session was a busy one, and the public religious services were attended by a large concourse of people.

"On the last day," writes Mr. Whittemore, "every pew and avenue in the house was crowded; but there was the most devout attention. It was from beginning to end a season of holy feeling, of Christian triumph and joy." Mr. Whittemore afterwards wrote to a friend, of the Convention : "The services, so far as I can rightly speak of them, were rich in Gospel truth and feeling. G——, who never made me shed tears before, caused me to weep freely. Excellent man ! T—— and A—— preached excellent sermons. And most of the preaching in its practical appeals was to me, for I was the most guilty one there. Who is under greater obligation, and yet less thankful? 'Oh for grace our hearts to soften !' . . . The unhappy mariner whose ship is locked up amidst floating mountains of ice, and who, as far as his eye can reach, sees no avenue of escape, must feel something as I do at times when I see the coldness of many Universalists. I want to get away from this ice. We must have a new state of things. Awake, ye sleepers ! Come, Lord, with Thy quickening power upon us !" A reminiscence of this Convention is given by Rev. E. G. Brooks, D.D., who was present at the meetings, and thus describes the last one, when Mr. Whittemore preached : "The day was beautiful. The house was packed. A daughter of Father Barnes and a brother of Elhanan Winchester were present. Every thing conspired deeply to affect the preacher, and to put him into his best condition. The theme was, 'Jesus and the Resurrection,' — a familiar and favorite one with him ; and, unfolding it he warmed and rose with it, taking us upward with him, until, at an appointed place, the two representatives of the departed patriarchs stood up amidst the people. No man knew better than he how to use such material as was thus furnished; and, as he addressed the standing ones, recounting what the Fathers had done and suffered, and apostrophizing them in their ascended life, wearing the crowns they had so nobly won, the whole assembly was dissolved in tears, and he swayed us as a forest is swayed in the wind." [1]

After the Convention, he returned to Brunswick, where he had engaged to lecture on Friday evening. The Baptist Society had generously offered the use of their house for the occasion, but so intense was the opposition of their minister to the course, that he threatened to leave the town if the meeting was held according to this appointment. For the sake of peace, the Universalists chose to occupy their own house, although it was small. It was filled and running over. The temperance address on the previous Monday evening had left a very strong impression in the place. From Brunswick he went to Yarmouth and Westbrook, and gave an evening lecture in Saccarappa village. The succeeding Sabbath was spent in Portland, where Mr. Whittemore preached in the Universalist church, of which Rev. M. Rayner was pastor. On Wednesday, July 8, he preached the sermon at the dedication of the new meeting-house in West Haverhill, Mass.

In reply to a statement which had been made by one or two orthodox journals, that Mr. Whittemore was an enemy to Dr. Beecher, he makes these remarks: "When the *Trumpet* was commenced in 1828, we know that some considerable attention was paid to Dr. Beecher, particularly by one or two correspondents. We certainly had no rancorous feel-

---

[1] *Universalist Quarterly*, July, 1877.

ing towards him, as the Doctor himself will, we believe, cheerfully confess. The Doctor and the editor of the *Trumpet* in days past have had several very pleasant interviews : we have prayed together ; we have conversed on the subject of religion ; and though at the last we differed greatly in our views, yet we separated in kindness and wished each other well. We maintain the same feeling toward the Doctor still ; and we do protest most seriously against being called his enemy."

The anniversary of the Rockingham Association took place this season at Deerfield, N.H. Mr. Whittemore attended, and gave a particular account of it. He preached in Kensington the Sabbath previous, and visited Portsmouth on his way to the Association. It was a meeting to him and to many others of unusual enjoyment. He writes : "If ever pure felicity was vouchsafed to mortals on earth, we felt it there. It begun with the beginning of the services, and increased through the whole. No heart seemed to be untouched. Those who had been delivered from the fetters of the doctrine of endless wrath, and who had heretofore been led to believe that there was little or no zeal and devotion among Universalists, were surprised. They found their former prejudices to have been all wrong. They could sing their Christian songs with increased pleasure, and realize to the fullest extent the force of the hopeful words which they chanted." "At the close of the services in Deerfield," he writes, "several of the brethren proceeded about twenty miles to Lamprey River, where a lecture by Rev. A. C. Thomas had been appointed. The congregation thronged the house in every part. It was a glorious meeting." Mr. Thomas preached in Portsmouth on Friday evening, and Mr. Whittemore was with him. A very large congregation attended. Mr. Whittemore spent the subsequent Sabbath in Sandown.

The "Jubilee" session of the United States Convention was held in Hartford, Ct., this year. Mr. Whittemore was present. The business meetings were held in the hall of the House of Representatives. The principal subjects of debate were, — the expediency of establishing a theological seminary by the Universalists of the United States, and the need of seeking by all proper and laudable means to abolish the odious practice of capital punishment. Six discourses were delivered. The Occasional on the first day was by Rev. S. R. Smith of Clinton, N.Y., and was a sermon of rare ability and impressiveness. Mr. Whittemore writes: "It is almost impossible to speak of it in terms of exaggerated praise. It was profound, solemn, animated, instructive." More than eighty ministers were present. A very able report on the subject of Capital Punishment was made to the Convention and laid over for final action at its next session.

At the session of the Boston Association in Stoughton in November, Mr. Whittemore preached a sermon.

The new meeting-house in West Rumney, N.H., was dedicated on the 18th of November. A two days' meeting was held. The dedicatory services were on the first day; the sermon by Rev. John G. Adams, then residing in that place. Mr. Whittemore preached during the meeting. On Thursday evening, a meeting for social conference was held at the house of Mr. Robert Morse. Of this meeting Mr. Whittemore writes: "Our aged and venerable father Keith addressed us and warmed our hearts by his exhortations. A young gentleman recently converted from infidelity to Christianity bore testimony in a very impressive manner to the value of the truth as it is in Jesus. A lady of the Baptist Church addressed the women present on their Christian obligations and duties."

In December, we find Mr. Whittemore at meetings in New

Hampshire. He is present at the forming of the Strafford County Association, in Dover. Public religious services were held two days; five sermons were preached (including one by Mr. Whittemore), and prayer and conference meetings held. After the meetings here, most of the ministers repaired to Lamprey River, where a Christmas service was held, a newly formed church publicly recognized, and the Lord's Supper observed. Mr. Whittemore and others preached, and the meetings were full of interest. Of Mr. Whittemore's preaching on this occasion, one who was present has written: "A double portion of the spirit seemed to be upon him. We felt almost as if we were in the very presence of the apostles; and, catching the warmth of his magnetic fervor, we were all thrilled, stirred, uplifted, as it is rare for any congregation to be. I have seldom been so rapt in listening to any man, and do not remember ever to have felt myself nearer heaven than under the spell of his earnestness in that memorable hour."[1] On the next Sunday, Mr. Whittemore preached in South New Market, and in the evening at Exeter.

The public recognition of the church connected with the First Universalist Society in East Cambridge, took place on the evening of Jan. 1, 1836. Mr. Whittemore preached the sermon on the occasion. On Sunday evening, the 11th of the same month, he preached the sermon at the installation of Rev. T. F. King in Charlestown.

About this time, there appeared in one of the denominational journals certain fraternal criticisms of the "concerts of praise," or meetings of conference and prayer and praise, differing from the ordinary church services; a renewal of the

---

[1] Rev. E. G. Brooks, D.D., *Universalist Quarterly*, July, 1877.

controversy on the same subject held a year or two before. The article (by Rev. T. J. Sawyer) seems to have been called forth by what he deemed indications of an extravagant zeal on the part of certain friends and advocates of these meetings. Mr. Whittemore notices these remarks as one deeply interested in the subject. Mr. Sawyer objects to the meetings, because, according to accounts given, indescribable emotions were awakened there. Mr. Whittemore replies by asking if his brother never realized emotions which he could not describe, and refers to the "joy unspeakable and full of glory" of which Peter speaks. Then the meetings were considered objectionable, "calculated to produce religious excitement," to which Mr. Whittemore replies: "If our brother means, by religious excitement, religious warmth, zeal, earnestness, we bless God that they have such an effect. Rant we, of course, do not approve. But on the great subject of salvation by Jesus Christ, how can any one be cold? We blame no one; but, if we must take our choice, we say, Give us the feeling, even if it be sometimes a little extravagant, than coldness and indifference on a theme like this. There is no extravagance here like that of preaching on this subject without any emotion." To the truthful and strong affirmation of Mr. Sawyer, that Universalists should be really the most habitually upright of all Christians, and their hearts "constantly sending up the incense of gratitude and love to heaven," Mr. Whittemore responds a hearty Amen, and concludes his article by saying, "We dread frost more than fire. From the beginning until of late, Universalists have been in favor of pure, warm, ardent feeling, in the cause of religion. A conference meeting has been held every week by the First Universalist Society in this city (Boston) ever since the days of John Murray. Shall they now abandon it? If not, why may not other societies follow the same example? Has the meeting bred any confusion in that society? No, and never will. Let us avoid dulness and indifference, and endeavor always to speak and act on the subject of religion with sincerity, earnestness, and love." [1]

[1] *Trumpet,* March 26, 1836.

CHAPTER V.

1836–1840.

Aged 36–40.

Murray's tomb — Mass Convention at Wrentham — New musical work — Study of Harmony — Letter to a friend — Songs of Zion — Convention Sermon — Temperance — Ideas of Christ — Dedication at Malden — Rockingham Association at Epping; Dedication — U.S. Convention, New York — Dedication in Essex — Lowell and Exeter — Installation at Phillipston — Rockingham Association at Salem, N.H. — Installation at Nashua — Newton Upper Falls, grove meeting — Mass. Convention at Malden — Removal of Murray's remains to Mount Auburn — U.S. Convention at Philadelphia — Washington, Baltimore, Fredericksburg, New York — Extemporaneous speaking — Installation at Lamprey River — Ministerial education — Installation at Methuen — Prosecution of Abner Kneeland — Funeral of Rev. W. C. Hauscom — Dedication at Andover — Ministerial education again — Rockingham Association at South Hampton — U.S. Convention at Boston — Creeds — R. W. Emerson's Address at Cambridge — Chester, N.H. — Notice of Rev. E. H. Chapin — Religion and Common Schools — Worship of Christ — Nashua — Conference at Danvers — To believers scattered abroad — A theological institution — New Hampshire Convention at Nashua — Rockingham Association at Hampstead — Death of Rev. T. F. King — Dedication at Waltham; Monument to Hanscom — Fire at Cornhill — Self-sacrifice — Dedication at South Reading — Miller excitement — Plain Guide to Universalism — Debate with Rev. Parsons Cooke — Progress of Universalism — Editorial independence.

In May of this year, Mr. Whittemore with others, under the direction of one of the burial officers of Boston, went to the tomb in which the body of Rev. John Murray was deposited. The examination was proposed in furtherance of the object recommended by the United States Convention of Universalists ; viz., the removal of the remains to Mount Auburn Cemetery, and the erection of a suitable monument there. He thus records the visit : " Mr. Murray was entombed on Monday, Sept. 4, 1815, in the vault where the family of Sargents lie, of which his last wife was a member. This tomb is in the Granary Burying Ground, so called ; lying between Park Street Church and the Tremont House. The coffin in which the preacher was buried was without much difficulty distinguished from the rest. First, it is known from the records in the office of the Superintendent, that his body was placed in that tomb. Second, all the other coffins were recognized as being those of other individuals. Third, the coffin containing the remains of Murray is known by its shape, being short and broad, and in this respect different from all the rest, neither of the others being suitable for a body formed as his was. Fourth, a lady of the family present at the funeral, who knew not where Father Murray's coffin had been found by us, stated afterwards that at the funeral it was deposited on the ground, at the right hand as you enter, the precise place where the coffin we mention lay." [1]

The Massachusetts Convention met this year on June 1, at Wrentham. A large number of ministers and lay delegates were present, and the services were attended by large audiences. The Occasional Sermon was delivered by Mr. Whittemore. He preached the sermon from full manuscript ; and it was plain-spoken, timely, and effective.

A new work now engages the preacher's attention. He has always been a lover of music, and for many years has practised it vocally and instrumentally. His interest in it deepens. He enters upon the study of harmony as a science,

---

[1] *Trumpet,* May 14, 1836.

under the direction of Professor J. Webb, a distinguished organist of Boston, and one of the profoundest harmonists in New England.   He writes to a friend on the subject : —

"In addition to my customary vocations, which are numerous, I am taking lessons in harmony of Professor Webb, of the Boston Academy.   It is an herculean task, a perplexity to have the head full of common chords, perfect and imperfect, dominant sevenths, imperfect sevenths (major and minor), diminished sevenths, and dominant ninths, &c.   I am about one-third through Catel's splendid treatise on 'Harmony.'   What is it all for ?   Shall I ever publish a book ?   The Professor says it is utterly impossible to harmonize the old American tunes, generally speaking.   I can discover many errors in them now that I could not have seen six months ago. . . .

"Do you mean to study harmony?   You will, I know, study harmony in the moral sense of the word ; but I mean as a musical science.   One of the great secrets of harmony is to make use of discords so that they shall terminate agreeably in the final resolutions of them.   He who knows not the purpose for which they are used, and cannot see their beautiful terminations, rendering the harmony more diversified, and the common chords sweeter and more delighting, never can know why discords are introduced, and never can enjoy them.   Universalists understand the science of God's moral harmony.   They perceive discords in the moral world.   But these discords are not used without rule ; they are not mistakes in the great Composer.   They are designed, and are all according to the infinite Law of Wisdom.   How beautiful in their resolutions !   When, in the progression of the great Oratorio, we shall slide off these into the sweetest, purest sounds, and see the reason why every discord has been used, shall we not like the harmony the better for it ?   Shall we not sing the ' Song of Moses and the Lamb ' with a higher zest ?   Pope had this idea in mind when he said, —

> "Better for us, perhaps, it might appear,
>   Were there all *concord* and all virtue here ;
>   That never air or ocean felt the wind ;
>   That never passions discomposed the mind ;

> But ALL subsists by elemental strife,
> And passions are the elements of life.
> The general ORDER since the world began
> Is kept in nature and is kept in man.

" Again he says, — and I never realized the full force of the passage before : —

> " All nature is but art, unknown to thee ;
> All chance, direction, which thou canst not see ;
> All *discord*, HARMONY *not understood* ;
> All partial evil, universal good.

" It is so ! Praise the Lord, O my soul ; magnify his name ! Glorify Him evermore ! ''

Mr. Whittemore had in view during this course of study the publishing of a new book of church music. This work appeared before the close of this year.   It is entitled " Songs of Zion ; or, the Cambridge Collection of Sacred Music ; designed for Social Meetings of Christians and for Family Worship." It was a book of 350 pages, containing a rich variety of tunes, some from the best of the American authors ; others, European tunes then popular in this country, and a large variety of original ones which had never appeared in any work. Quite a number of the tunes were composed by the compiler, and became quite popular wherever known. One notable feature of the book was,— its hymns and anthems contain no utterance of any sentiment not in accordance with the faith of the Universalist Church.   It had a large circulation, and was used quite extensively in churches of the different Christian sects.

The Occasional Sermon, preached by Mr. Whittemore before the Massachusetts Convention, appeared in the *Trumpet* of June 25.   It is full of wise direction to the Christian life, and strong appeals to those for whom it is intended.   In an exhortation to the work of temperance, he says : " If this holy cause has been injured on the part of others by an indiscreet sectarianism, this is no reason why Universalists should hesitate to give it their warmest support. The evil to be met is a common and deadly one; and we are but carrying out the great principles which the order of Universalists have adopted to reform men, by using our utmost endeavor to suppress it." His exhortation to zeal is emphatic. He cites the Old and New Testaments to show how it is there commended by precept and example, and explains most clearly how essential it is to the growth and prosperity of the cause represented in the Universalist churches. As to the light in which Christ is to be regarded by Universalists, he says, " While our opinions differ widely from the sentiments of those who consider Jesus to be the supreme God; so, on the other hand, they differ as much from the sentiments of that class who regard him only as a reformer, — like Xenophon, Socrates, and Plato. With us, Jesus Christ is emphatically the Son of God, in a sense in which no mere man can be said so to be. He stands next to the Father in rank and dignity. ' All the angels of God worship him.' He is the Mediator between God and man, which can be said of no other being. All power in heaven and in earth was committed into his hands. The great work of redemption was entrusted to him. He shall rule in the mediatorial kingdom until every creature shall submit to his authority; and then he shall deliver up the kingdom to God even the Father, that God may be all in all."

The newly modelled church edifice in Malden was dedicated June 24: Mr. Whittemore preached the sermon. On the 21st of July, the new Universalist meeting-house in Methuen was dedicated. Mr. Whittemore preached on the occasion. This was the first of nine Universalist meeting-houses erected during the year by Universalists.

The session of the Rockingham Association was held this

year in Epping, N.H., commencing on the 31st of August. The new church in that place was dedicated, the sermon being preached by Mr. Whittemore. The other public services during the meeting of the Association were held in the town's meeting-house. " It was judged," writes Mr. Whittemore, " from an estimate made at the time, that there were 1,200 persons in the house. Epping never saw such a spectacle before. It became impossible for the visitors to obtain accommodations adequate to their needs ; and some were obliged to leave town on this account."

Mr. Whittemore was present at the session of the United States Convention this season in New York city, and preached on the occasion. There was a very large attendance of ministers, and the session was one of deep interest. In his published account of his visit to the Convention, he pays a just tribute to the work of a brother minister in New York city at a time when the cause of Universalism had been seriously injured by the defection of Mr. Kneeland and his successors. " In the midst of this state of things, Rev. Thomas J. Sawyer moved there. It was for a time a severe struggle. But by a judicious course, by a long sacrifice of private considerations, and by the exercise of the talents he so eminently possesses, he·was enabled to resuscitate the cause when others pronounced it dead. The two societies now in the city are large and flourishing."

On Wednesday, Dec. 14, Mr. Whittemore preached the sermon on the occasion of the dedication of the new meeting-house in Essex, Mass. ; and, on Feb. 11, a discourse at the installation of Rev. Zenas Thompson as pastor of the Second Universalist Society in Lowell. On the 1st of March, the new meeting-house in Marblehead was dedicated ; the sermon by Mr. Whittemore. On the 16th of June following, Rev. James Shrigley was installed as pastor of the united societies of Epping and Exeter, N.H., on which occasion Mr. Whittemore preached.

At the last of June, he made a journey by private conveyance to Phillipston, Mass., where a small but zealous company of believers in the Abrahamic faith had built a house of worship, and were now to install a pastor, — Rev. Aurin Bugbee. The installation services took place on Wednesday, June 28 ; Mr. Whittemore preached the sermon.

·The Rockingham Association held its session this year (1837) in Salem, N.H. The meetings were well attended, and of deep interest. Mr. Whittemore was present, but did not preach. Stirring conference meetings were held. On Friday, Sept. 2, he attended the installation of Rev. A. P. Cleverly, at Nashua, N.H., and preached the sermon.

On Sunday, Sept. 3, he preached at Newton Upper Falls, in a grove, near the house of Mr. Joshua Gardner. The use of every church or place of worship had been denied the friends of Universalism who had invited the preacher to officiate. An awning was extended under the trees, and temporary seats were erected, so that more than six hundred persons were accommodated. The speaker was at his best on the occasion, and delivered two discourses of some length, enforcing the doctrinal and practical claims of his faith upon attentive listeners. An account of the services appeared a week afterward in the *Dedham Patriot.*

The Massachusetts Convention was held this year (1837) at Malden, on Wednesday, June 7. It was a very full session, both of ministers and lay delegates. Two ministers were ordained, and several young men received letters of fellowship as preachers. The Convention, not being able to finish its business on Wednesday, adjourned to meet in Boston on Thursday, to attend the removal of the remains of Rev. John Murray in the afternoon of that day. The event took place according to the arrangements. Public services were observed in the First Universalist church, on Hanover Street; the remains being placed before the pulpit, where the revered preacher had so long officiated. Rev. Sebastian Streeter preached a very appropriate and eloquent discourse. A large procession followed the hearse to Mount Auburn, where Rev. Hosea Ballou delivered a very impressive address. The Convention adjourned at the grave.

The session of the United States Convention was held this year at Philadelphia. It was a very agreeable and harmonious one. Eight discourses were delivered; the Occasional by Mr. Whittemore. He continued his journey to Washington, where he was not much edified by the acrimonious debates to which he listened in Congress. On his return, he visited Baltimore, and attended the dedication of the new Universalist church, and the installation of Rev. L. S. Everett as the pastor, in that city. He next visited Richmond and Fredericksburg, Va. By urgent request, and at very short notice, he preached in the last-named place. The succeeding Sunday he passed in Philadelphia, preaching in the Lombard Street church in the morning, and in the Callowhill Street church in the evening. On his way home he spent a day or two in New York city. He reckons this journey of a thousand miles "among the pleasantest events of his life."

Quite a debate took place in the columns of the *Trumpet* about this time, on the subject of extemporaneous preaching; Mr. Whittemore advocating it strongly, and Rev. Calvin Gardner and others objecting to it as a rule, and advising the writing of sermons and preaching them with the use of the manuscript. Good points were made on either side, but the controversy ended about where it began. None of the disputants were opposed to extemporaneous preaching; but all were in favor of it where the preacher could do most justice to his own powers, and make himself most useful to his hearers. There are diversities of gifts with preachers, and each one must study his own abilities, and take the course in which he can do his pulpit-work with the greatest advantage. Some of the ablest and most effective Christian ministers have used the manuscript, and some have extemporized. The subject, although not quite so profound, is about as interminable in the hands of debaters as that of the connection of the Divine Sovereignty and the Human Will.

On the evening of Dec. 25, Rev. John Harriman, Jr., was installed as pastor of the Universalist Society at Lamprey River. Mr. Whittemore preached the sermon. In the *Trumpet* of March 24, he makes a strong plea for a more thorough preparation for the Universalist ministry than many of those who have entered it have been able to make for themselves. "We greatly need," he writes, "an institution of some kind in which young men can prepare themselves, under the help of some kind teacher, for the duties of the ministry. We are suffering in Massachusetts for the want of such a desideratum; but when we shall have it we cannot foresee. There are indispensable studies which ought to be pursued. Mankind, with few exceptions, are apt to think better of themselves than they ought to think. Young men preparing for the ministry are easily led to suppose themselves quite well qualified; and, before they have been in the ministry a year, judge themselves competent to take students in their turn. This, in truth, increases *the number* of our preachers; but does it add weight and respectability and influence to our clergy as a body? It is an error for a young man to seek a settlement too soon: it frequently is the cause of subsequent disappointment and chagrin. We want a greater number of well-instructed preachers, men of studious habits, cultivated minds, winning address, who will always seek the good of the society or societies with whom they are located, and give themselves wholly to the duties of their calling. Such are the men our cause now needs. May God send us a full supply." [1]

On Thursday, April 19, Rev. Edward N. Harris was installed as pastor of the Universalist Society in Methuen, Mass. Mr. Whittemore preached the sermon.

It was in this month that the case of Abner Kneeland, who had been indicted for blasphemy under an ancient and obsolete statute of Massachusetts, came up for consideration. As Mr. Kneeland had formerly been connected with the Universalist denomination, and had caused some trouble in it by his changeable and sceptical course, it was supposed by some that Mr. Whittemore was directly or indirectly the cause of his indictment. But he takes occasion to say : "We solemnly aver that we never had the least connection with it in any way, and that we have regretted from the beginning that the indictment was ever found. Leave his character and his opinions to be settled by the tribunal of reason and free inquiry. We agree with the editor of *Zion's Herald* in hoping that a nominal punishment merely will be decreed, and that Mr. Kneeland will be dismissed from the court to repent of the error of his ways, and to mourn for the folly which must embitter the evening of his earthly existence." Subsequently Mr. Kneeland was sentenced to sixty days' imprisonment. His offence was, his denial of a belief in the existence of an intelligent Supreme Being whom the Christians called God. Mr. Whittemore was unable to see how the imprisonment of Mr. Kneeland for this offence could be reconciled with the spirit and intent of the second article of the Bill of Rights, which declares that no " subject shall be hurt, molested, or restrained in his person, liberty, or estate for his religious professions or sentiments."

[1] *Trumpet*, March 24, 1838.

On Friday, May 25, the funeral of Rev. W. C. Hanscom took place in the Unitarian church in Waltham, Mass. Mr. Hanscom was a very devoted and promising young minister, and had but a short time before his decease been installed as pastor of the Universalist church in Waltham. He died at Cambridgeport, at the house of a faithful friend, at the early age of twenty-two years and ten months. Mr. Whittemore took a deep interest in him, especially during his last sickness, and very frequently visited him. He preached the sermon on the funeral occasion, which was published in the *Trumpet;* and truly said of the departed one: "The ministering brethren feel sensibly that one of the brightest of our young men has fallen, in whom were blended the zeal and activity of youth, and the matured judgment of ripened manhood." One who knew the departed intimately has written of him, "Our church has met with few losses in the death of its young ministers so great as the loss it suffered when his voice was hushed. Of good talents, ardent, sincere, of immense energy, he was a young man of signal promise, alive in every fibre of his being with spiritual fervor and zeal, and thoroughly consecrated to his Christian work. But the force and fire of his zeal soon consumed his physical powers, and too soon for us, as it appeared, his earthly work was ended." [1]

On Tuesday, July 3, the meeting-house erected by the Universalists in Andover, Mass., was dedicated. The sermon on the occasion was by Mr. Whittemore. In the *Trumpet* of Sept. 1, there is another appeal from the editor's pen in behalf of the education of ministers. The calls for them in the denomination impel him to this appeal for the right supply. If some ministers with small advantages for scholastic improvement have been successful in their work, this is not to

---

[1] Rev. E. G. Brooks, D.D. — *Universalist Quarterly*, July, 1877.

be regarded as the rule. Great natural qualifications cannot insure ministerial success. The best natural talents need to be aided by well-directed study. The editor regrets that there should be any opposition among his brethren the clergy to an institution for the preparation of young men for the ministry. He thinks the subject should be most seriously considered at the coming session of the General Convention.

Another session of the Rockingham Association of very deep interest, was held at South Hampton, N.H., in August of this year. Mr. Whittemore preached on the occasion, and says of the meeting: "We know that, if we describe this meeting precisely as we viewed and as we *felt* it, we shall be regarded as too enthusiastic. Nevertheless we must say that, taken altogether, it was one of the most precious meetings we ever attended. We are sure that we never before heard so much good preaching in two days. The conference and praise meetings were peculiarly interesting; all the addresses were marked by sound wisdom and deep evangelical feeling."

Boston welcomed the General Convention this year. It was very fully attended. The Occasional Sermon was preached in the School Street church, by Rev. A. C. Thomas. Rev. S. R. Smith preached the sermon on the second day at the communion service. There were eight hundred communicants present. Meetings fully attended were held in adjoining places. A meeting for devotional exercises was held at the grave of Murray at Mount Auburn.

In the *Trumpet* of Oct. 20, Mr. Whittemore in a leading editorial calls the attention of his readers to the fact that, however lightly Universalists may regard many of the man-made creeds stated and maintained in the Christian church, still they have a creed; *i.e.*, a statement of faith, the word creed coming from *credo*, which signifies, I believe. "There is no harm in having a creed. Every man who believes any thing has a creed, of necessity. The great difficulty in regard to creeds has been this, — they have been set above the Word of God, and have been the cause of religious proscription and cruelty." He then states the Universalists' Creed, in accordance with the Winchester Confession of Faith : God the just and loving Father of man ; Christ the Son of God and Saviour of all men ; the Scriptures of the Old and New Testaments as containing the Divine promise respecting man, and the most perfect rule of human conduct and life ; the ultimate redemption of all souls from error and sin and their enjoyment of life and love immortal.

In the *Trumpet* of Oct. 27, he takes occasion to notice the position taken by Mr. Ralph Waldo Emerson in his address delivered before the Senior Class at the Divinity School in Cambridge. This class consisted of six young men, four of whom in the choice of a preacher voted for Mr. Emerson, who was accordingly chosen. His discourse, as Mr. Whittemore and others regarded it, was quite redolent of Atheism and Pantheism. It seemed a denial of the existence and personality of God, and, therefore, unfitted to an occasion of advocating or encouraging a Christian ministry. The junior Professor Ware deemed it his duty to differ from Mr. Emerson, in a lecture before the Divinity School, which was afterwards published. "If this," says Mr. Whittemore, "is to be regarded as a sample of the divinity taught at Cambridge, we pray that God in mercy may deliver our land from the blighting, poisonous influence of the Cambridge Theological School." It is amusing, to say the least, to read Mr. Whittemore's notice of certain extracts from Mr. Emerson's Address. The mystical and obscure sentences of the Concord philosopher are mostly moonshine to the plain, clear, matter-of-fact intellect of Mr. Whittemore. The two could hardly have appreciated each other. Mr. Emerson did properly in leaving the Christian ministry. Evidently he had not been "called" to it. As a scholar, philosopher, and reformer, he has in subsequent years proved himself an honor to his country and to his race.

On Sunday, Oct. 21, Mr. Whittemore preached for the first time in Chester, N.H., to a large audience of persons from that and the adjacent towns. In the *Trumpet* of Oct. 27, the first extracts appear from a published sermon of Rev. E. H. Chapin, then of Richmond, Va. Speaking of the extracts, the editor remarks that "they are sufficient to show that the sermon is one of no ordinary kind."

The question involving religious instruction in our Common Schools was somewhat earnestly discussed about these days. The Suffolk County Common School Convention had been held in the vestry of the Park Street Church, Boston, where the subject was very freely debated by some of the friends of education. Certain of the speakers expressed serious fears that religious instruction was to be thrust out of our Common Schools, where the intellect would be educated at the expense of the moral faculties. Others saw difficulty in the way of teaching religion in the schools because of the differences of religious views on the part of those who sent their children to these schools. If religion was to be taught, what religion? Every parent might want a teacher of his own faith, and thus contentions might be going on in every school district. Mr. Whittemore gave quite a space in his paper to the report of this Convention, and stated his own views of the subject. He granted the importance of correct moral guidance in the Common Schools, but was strongly opposed to any course that looked to the predominance of one religious sect over another in this work. "Let us not," he says, "be too much in haste to follow the examples of European governments, in which the people are confined to professions of faith and where there is but little freedom of opinion. Their examples are opposed to the genius of our institutions."

In the *Trumpet* of Nov. 17, quite a spirited article appears from the pen of the editor on "The Worship of Christ." His opinions on this subject had been questioned by a brother minister and editor, and he proceeds to state them with great clearness. He differs from many Unitarians respecting the nature of Christ and his position in the spiritual universe. Dr. Priestley, according to a biographer, thought it most reasonable to believe that Christ's perfect moral excellence was the result of his own exertion, vigilance, and fortitude, rather than of a supernatural operation, and the biographer affirmed that it would be hard to find any considerate and consistent Unitarian who did not adopt Dr. Priestley's ideas concerning the formation of our Lord's character. Mr. Belsham, an English Unitarian of note had said: "The Unitarians disavow all those personal regards to Christ and direct addresses to him, either of prayer or praise, which properly fall under the denomination of religious worship, as unfounded in reason, unauthorized by Scripture, and derogating from the honor of the Supreme Being, — as polytheistical and idolatrous." Mr. Whittemore affirms: "I do not regard Christ as Unitarians do. I sing his praise, I make ascriptions to him in prayer, which they do not, if their own authors are to be believed. I am a Universalist. I believe in Christ as the Son of God and the universal Saviour. Unto him every knee shall bow; every tongue shall confess him Lord; the angels shall worship him; the universe — every creature that God hath made in his image shall worship God and the Lamb, and ascribe to each blessing, honor, glory, and power for evermore. I respond from the heart a full Amen."

The Universalist Meeting-house in Nashua, N.H., was dedicated Jan. 1, 1839; the Occasional Sermon was preached by

Mr. Whittemore. On the 16th, a conference of much interest, which Mr. Whittemore attended, was held in Danvers, Mass. He writes of the closing conference meeting: "It was an occasion of high spiritual joy and of great profit. We have no doubt that a large portion of the persons present were made wiser, and went home from the exercises of that occasion with holier feelings and resolutions. We are constrained once more to recommend these meetings to our brethren all over the country, and advise that our lay brethren should cultivate their abilities and take part in these services more frequently than they have done. We desire to have frequent opportunities of attending such meetings as the one at Danvers."

In an editorial entitled "To Believers Scattered Abroad," he makes an earnest and faithful appeal to all friends of Universalism, wherever they may be, to make some active exertion for the dissemination of their principles, the building up of their faith. Wherever ten believers can be found, he advises them to set up religious worship. "Ten good men are enough to make a beginning with. That number is more than there were righteous persons in Sodom. Form a society. Meet together as often as you can for conversation, for conference, for encouragement. Meet on the Sabbath; read the Scriptures, sing, pray, even if a printed form of prayer be used; select a good discourse from the great number published by our clergy, and read it for the edification of the meeting. On the next Sabbath let some other brother officiate. This practice of lay worship has been tried with very good results, and we do most sincerely recommend it to the brethren scattered abroad." Again he pleads with the laymen: "The fewness of the speakers among our laymen is not to be attributed to any lack of talents in them, but rather to the former habits of the denomination itself. It has not been sufficiently *a habit* with us for our laymen to speak. Let us break up our old habit, which was a bad one, and begin anew. It will be the duty of the laymen to encourage us in bringing about this state of things. Our brethren, by heeding these directions, we believe, would see the happiest consequences following them. Nothing would please us more than to see this course taken, in order to try the correctness of our conclusions." Sound and timely advice, and as good and applicable at this time as it was forty years ago.

In the *Trumpet* of March 16, in an article addressed to Rev. S. R. Smith, there is another appeal from the editor for a Theological Institution. He is anxious to have the movement begin. "We are behind the Presbyterians, the Baptists, the Congregationalists, the Episcopalians, Unitarians, Methodists, and others in these things. How long is this to be so?" His prophecy in another article on this subject has been verified. "We must expect to begin small, and that our institution will be weak in its infancy. But get it once into operation, give it however small 'a local habitation and a name,' it will become a focus of our best wishes, our prayers and donations. Every year will see it gaining strength."

In June of this year, Mr. Whittemore was present at the New Hampshire Convention in Nashua, N.H., and took part in the services at the ordination of Rev. A. A. Miner. He describes the session as one of much interest. Of the last conference and prayer meeting he writes: "There was a large number of speakers. We were never present at a meeting where the brethren were more ready to bear testimony. There was no painful waiting for one another. The meeting was profitable. Many members of other sects were present." In August, he attended the Rockingham Association at Hampstead, N.H. He remained but one day on account of a severe attack of cholera, which subjected him to a night of severe and incessant pain. The care of kind friends, and the skill of an able and attentive physician, enabled him to start for home, where he arrived, none the worse for the ride. The meetings of the Association were largely attended.

On Friday, Sept. 13, Rev. Thomas F. King, pastor of the church in Charlestown, departed this life, aged forty-two. He had been a preacher of the Gospel for twenty years, was self-educated, and received much of his religious instruction and inspiration by attendance on the ministry of Rev. Edward Mitchell of New York city, the place of his birth. He had been pastor at Hudson, N.Y. (where his son, Thomas Starr, was born), and in Portsmouth, N.H., before coming to Charlestown. He was an able, eloquent, and successful minister, and greatly beloved in all his pastorates. He had a lingering and painful illness, but was constantly sustained and inwardly strengthened by that holy faith which he had so long and so faithfully commended to others. The funeral was attended at the church on Monday, Sept. 16. The discourse was by Rev. Sebastian Streeter of Boston. Mr. Whittemore took part in the services, and was one of the pall-bearers.

The dedication of the new meeting-house in Waltham took place on Wednesday, Sept. 11. In the afternoon of the day, a white marble obelisk was placed over the grave of Rev. W. C. Hanscom in the cemetery in that town. The prayer on this occasion was offered by Mr. Whittemore. A very impressive address was delivered by Rev. Henry Bacon.

In October, the office of the *Trumpet*, at Nos. 38 and 40 Cornhill, was seriously injured by fire. With the exception of a few books and bundles of paper, the entire contents of the office were destroyed. The mail-books were saved. The damage exceeded the insurance on the property destroyed, and not a little delay and trouble were caused in the issuing of the paper. But the resolute publisher said: "We intend that it shall come forth phœnix-like from its ashes, and we would that we might say that it shall be the better for having passed through the fire, like gold purified in the furnace."

A good word has he on self-sacrifice in his leading editorial of Nov. 2. He alludes to Christ's teaching, to the example of the early Christians, and to the need of this spirit among Christians at the present time. He addresses those who hold the Universalist faith: "Reader, ask yourself, have you the true spirit of sacrifice? Are you willing to part with your substance for the cause of the Gospel? Have you done your duty in this respect? Have you subscribed liberally for the maintenance of the preached word? Are you willing to do your full proportion in building a meeting-house in the town in which you live? Willing to do your part in any Christian enterprise, according to the magnitude of it and according to your comparative ability? Look around you. Are there no Christians of other churches who put you to shame? Look at the Methodists. See what sums they are offering as their centenary gifts to testify their gratitude to God for his abundant mercy to their church. We are not desirous that Universalists should run into any of the injurious excesses of other sects. But where these others are right let us follow them."

The Universalist Meeting-house in South Reading was dedicated, Nov. 21 of this year. Mr. Whittemore preached on the occasion. A very large audience was in attendance, and meetings were continued through the day and evening.

About these days, the Second Adventist prophet, Rev. Mr. Miller, appeared in New England. He had fixed a new date for the end of the world, — 1843. Possibly his figures might mistake just one hundred years, but he was quite sure that the 43 of the present century was the true time. He was quite fluent in the statement of his calculations, using the imagery of some of the Old Testament prophets with strong effect with the classes of hearers disposed to accept his conclusions. The man himself was but of small account as a prophet; but he was used by other preachers to further their revival work by raising much religious excitement in reference to this second personal appearance of Christ and the general winding up of sublunary affairs. Mr. Whittemore spoke very plainly on this subject, and especially in condemnation of those who, although they had no faith whatever in Mr. Miller's theory, were ready to have it pass current with others, so that a religious revival might be promoted. He denounced this very justly as rank dishonesty. He regarded the imposture as laying the foundation for infidelity in many minds. Speaking of the admission of Mr. Miller into a Baptist Church in Cambridgeport, he says: " We agree with Dr. Sharp in a remark he is said to have made, that the Miller theory is ' all moonshine,' and are astonished that a truly respectable society should give the least countenance to such deception." But the excitement had its run. The brick tabernacle erected in Howard Street, Boston, was intended for the use of the Second Adventists until the crisis in 1843. But the gatherings there as well as elsewhere at the appointed time were followed by no realization of the event predicted, and the ground where the Boston Tabernacle stood has since been occupied by the Howard Athenæum building. During this excitement, able reviews of Mr. Miller's theory were published by ministers of the Universalist Church, — Rev. A. C. Thomas, Rev. O. A. Skinner, Rev. Thomas Whittemore, and Rev. J. M. Austin.

In February, 1840, Mr. Whittemore's new book, " The

Plain Guide to Universalism," was issued. It was a work "designed to lead inquirers to the belief of that doctrine, and believers to the practice of it." It includes a brief history of the doctrine from the earliest ages; its evidences from the Scriptures; explains controverted passages; answers the common objections to the doctrine; points out the moral tendency of the faith, and the duties of those who hold it; furnishes directions for the formation of churches and societies, a plan of church government, scriptural views of the Lord's Supper, and a form of the administration of the same. A chapter on the evidences of revealed religion includes the whole of that valuable little work, "Leslie's Short Method with the Deists." It was very favorably received by the Universalist public, and large numbers of the volume were circulated. It was not, however, very courteously received in certain orthodox quarters. A notice of it in the *Boston Recorder*, attributed to the pen of the late Dr. Storrs, of Braintree, is quite caustic. The writer says: "Every minister who has the care of souls ought to possess the book and study it; for otherwise he can know little of the length and breadth of that scheme of mischief and ruin which Satan has devised in these last days for the filling up of his kingdom." To which Mr. Whittemore replies, that "neither scorn nor bitterness will convince the author of the 'Guide' of his error, but sound arguments drawn from the Bible. This notice states that the 'Guide' should be 'in the hands of every minister who has the care of souls.' This we suppose a hint to the orthodox clergy to buy the book and read it. We have no objections: the more they read it the better. We are not afraid to have it candidly examined, and are glad that the editor of the *Recorder* recommends his clerical brethren to read it."

In the *Trumpet* of April 4, Mr. Whittemore invites Rev.

Parsons Cooke, editor of the *Puritan*, to a discussion of the question, "Is the doctrine of endless misery revealed in the Bible?" the articles of both parties to be published in the *Trumpet* and *Puritan*. Mr. Cooke gave his reasons for declining, which did not seem satisfactory to Mr. Whittemore, and for a few months the discussion was delayed; but, after repeated efforts on the part of the trumpeter to induce his neighbor to commence, Mr. Cooke, in July, entered upon the debate. Mr. Whittemore was much gratified that the arguments on both sides were to come before the readers of both papers. He deems it a rare opportunity for him to speak in defence of the Gospel. He says: "Mr. Cooke comes before the public to attack Universalism as the organ of an orthodox association. He comes out to make the greatest onslaught upon our faith, for the whole orthodox party in the county of Essex, as his brother, Mr. Braman, did in 1833. He shall be vanquished. We have but little confidence in ourself, but the truth of God cannot be overthrown. Mr. Cooke has agreed to publish both sides of the controversy in his paper. It was an unfortunate day for his doctrine when he agreed to do that."

During the discussion, Mr. Whittemore had occasion to say: "There is one fact worthy of notice. Before this controversy began, and while Mr. Cooke was carrying on his running fight with us, many of the partialist editors were in ecstasies. They could not refrain from expressing their joy that the editor of the *Trumpet* had found an opponent whom he dare not meet in fair controversy. But since the regular discussion commenced, we hear no shouts of victory from them: they have become comparatively silent. Not one of them has copied the controversy; whereas the Universalist editors have copied freely on both sides. What meaneth this, if the argument for endless punishment is well sustained?"

Mr. Cooke closed the discussion in December, much against

the desire of Mr. Whittemore, who would have continued it
through the next year if his neighbor had signified his readiness to do so.

Mr. Whittemore speaks with much gratification, in one of
his editorials, of the progress of Universalism since his
acceptance of its claims, and entrance upon its ministry.

"Where are the old-fashioned doctrines of our orthodox
fathers? Where is the doctrine of infant damnation, which
was formerly preached with so much assurance? Who
preaches the doctrines of election and reprobation as they
were preached in former times? Who dare say now, what
was so boldly and so frequently said in former times, that a
large part of the human race would be lost for ever? Who
believes now in a hell of fire and brimstone in the literal sense?
All these forms of error have passed away, and now it is conceded, even by the most rigid of our divines, that all infants
will be saved; that there is no decree which prevents the salvation of all men; that but a few of the human race will be
lost, and that by far the larger part of mankind will be finally
saved? that hell is not literal fire, but a hell of conscience;
that it is not a place, but a certain condition of the mind.
Now, mark you, reader, all these changes are toward the
doctrine of Universalism; every one of them brings society
nearer to that faith. Although there are many who start
back with horror from the name of Universalists, they are
fast approaching the sentiments of that class of Christians." [1]

In common with other editors, Mr. Whittemore was tried
at times by those who wished to have him speak their opinions
and favor their interests, whatever his own opinions as to
such courses might be. He gives all such very plainly to
understand that his independence cannot be purchased in any

[1] *Trumpet*, April 11, 1840.

such way. " We ask," he says, " for no subscribers who do not approve of our general course. We are willing to receive advice from our friends with attention and gratitude, if given in kindness ; but do not attempt to buy us, — at least until we offer ourself for sale. When people do not approve of our course, they sometimes threaten to discontinue their patronage of the *Trumpet* if we do not desist. We should be unworthy of the station we hold if we were capable of being moved by such considerations. We hope never to be insensible to the kindness of our friends ; never to be ungrateful for their steady and unfluctuating support ; we do not deny that we regret to have good patrons leave us : but when a person attempts to turn us from a course we believe to be right, either by promises of support or a threat of withdrawing it, he has a mean estimate of our honesty. Whenever the time shall come that we will sacrifice truth, honor, the good of the denomination, or a clean conscience, for the sake of gaining or retaining patronage, it will be time for the *Trumpet* to pass into other hands."

CHAPTER VI.

1840–1843.

Aged 40–43.

Unitarianism and Universalism — State Convention at New Bedford — Views on future punishment — Movement of Restorationists — Desire for union — Dedication and Church Recognition at Concord, Mass. — Statement of Rev. Dr. Lowell and comments — Dedication at Newburyport — The Banker — Theological Seminary — Temperance Reform — Rev. Theodore Parker — Gospel Harmonist — Rockingham Association — Seminary meeting at Worcester — U.S. Convention at New York — Knapp excitement — Rev. O. A. Skinner's Review of it — Temperance Lectures — Twenty years' experience — Conference at East Cambridge — U.S. Convention at Providence.— Conference at Marblehead — Rev. G. E. Channing on Unitarianism, and Mr. Whittemore's comments.

SIDE by side with the Universalist sect, there had grown up since the beginning of the present century, that of the Unitarian. It was mainly a New England movement. It did not start, like that of the Universalist, with an open avowal of certain articles of faith on which it professed to be based, although it gradually came to this avowal as its history matured. It seemed an outcome of the Arminianism that existed more or less in the churches of the orthodox or "standing order." It dwelt for a time in comparative peace with these churches, and occupied their pulpits, and shared their fellowship. But afterwards it was more outspoken. It affirmed the doctrine of the Divine Unity; it discarded the Trinity, Total Depravity, and the Decrees of election and reprobation so inseparable from Calvinism, and assumed a position such as to draw forth the opposition of the orthodox churches, and cause a cessation of pulpit exchanges and church fellowship between them. A large number of parishes originally orthodox, thus became, by vote of the majority, Unitarian parishes, still retaining the word "Congregational" in their parish titles.

Meanwhile the Unitarians were indisposed to a hearty fellowship of the Universalists. They did not generally accept the doctrine of the final salvation of all souls as a truth of the Gospel, and were not inclined to exchange pulpit services with our ministers, nor to give their support to Universalist churches in places where these churches were set up instead of their own. Indeed, it was often the case that their "liberal" Christianity inclined them to worship with the most orthodox congregations there. At the same time they were ready to complain of the orthodox because of the unwillingness of their ministers to exchange pulpit services with their own. Gradually, however, Unitarianism has more widely adopted among its articles of faith that of the ultimate reconciliation of all souls to the One Father; and many of its adherents have been asking for a score of years just past; "What is the difference between Unitarianism and Universalism? and why cannot the two sects work together in a common Christian sympathy and fellowship?"

They can in some respects; in others, they cannot so freely. The prominent theological ideas of Unitarianism, viz., the Fatherhood of God and the Brotherhood of Man, are in accordance with all the Universalism of the past or present. But Universalism has always accepted the logical conclusions growing out of these two statements of faith; while Unitarianism has often hesitated in its acceptance of them. Dr. Channing, with all the clearness and strength of his defence and maintenance of the doctrine of the Divine Paternity, failed, so far as we can learn from the record of his ministry, to see clearly and acknowledge the truth that this same Paternity will bring all the human family at last to the enjoyment and life of the one common heavenly home. Other eminent ministers of the Unitarian churches were like him in this respect. A few still seemed inclined to a belief in the unending punishment of the unregenerate; others favored the idea of the annihilation of the wicked; while a larger number were in doubt as to the disposition God would make of those who departed this life without reconciliation to him, and were disposed to regard the whole discussion of the subject as the gratifying of "an idle and useless curiosity." The Universalism that recognized in Christ that love of the Father that would surely draw all his children to him, and that deemed it essential that this truth of the Father should be clearly spoken to his children everywhere in the dispensation of the Gospel, could not be satisfied with any ministry that would dispense with it, or, holding it, would deem it wise and prudent to keep it in the background.

Then, Universalism was, practically, a democratic faith. It sought "the common people," and made its appeal to them. It cared little for social distinctions, as these were often conventionally regarded in society; for ecclesiastical precedents or establishments; for the prestige given to churches by educational institutions, or wealth, or any other like consideration, when it would make its appeals to the masses. It numbered among its friends many "plain people," and while it had the countenance and support of some of the soundest thinkers and most respected persons in society, it sought to take hold upon the popular thought and invite all classes to a consideration of its claims.[1]

Unitarianism acted in a more conservative way. It stood more upon its dignity, scholarship, and respectability. Says one of its own children : "It almost seemed like a social movement, beginning at the top and working down. Distinguished laymen, even more than distinguished ministers, gave it character. Near Boston it was fashionable. . . . It was seldom found with warm expressive feelings ; and what excited little apparent enthusiasm, even among its own followers, would fail of course to touch the general heart."[2]

Moreover, Universalism, as it made increase in numbers and means for the extension of its influences, gave special heed to the organization of its forces and the systematic advancement of its church interests ; while Unitarianism seemed to care less for its organization and growth as a sectarian force than for the work it might do as a leavening power in setting right the opinions of the churches, and of the religious world generally. It was not over-anxious to have a positive statement of doctrines around which its professed friends might rally ; and so opened a wide door for the incoming of much of the unchristian radicalism that has since caused its churches no little vexation in their attempts to draw the line of distinction between sceptical Theism or Pantheism and the teachings of the New Testament. As another has so expressively said : "The 'Address to the

---

[1] "The voice of its champions in press and pulpit, and of sturdy village propagandists, gave forth no uncertain sound. But its literary field still lay apart from that of Unitarians. It maintained its evangelical and democratic character, making an appeal to a class that would only have been offended by the high cold rationalism of the Boston set. And the Boston set, from its side, was little disposed to fraternize." — *Memoir of Dr. E. S. Gannett, by his son.*

[2] Ib.

Divinity School' (by Mr. R. W. Emerson) was the veritable proclamation of a new gospel, a gospel which indeed ' ravished the souls' of the elect, but proved too subtle and ethereal to become ' bread of life to millions.' This ambrosial food was transmuted into homelier diet by Mr. Parker, and has served to furnish the board of the later Free religionists." [1]

Pre-eminent among the Unitarian divines stood Dr. Channing, one of the brightest lights of the churches of advanced Christian thought of the present century. His greatness, however, was not like that of Ballou. Although his scholarly attainments were superior, the latter was the sturdier theologian of the two. But, as it has been truly written, "the inspiration of Channing lay in his noble ' enthusiasm of humanity.' As a scientific theologian, he cut no deep lines on our religious thought; but, as an apostle of that benignant Gospel which seeks in the welfare of man the highest glory of God, he must be reckoned a star of the first magnitude in our spiritual firmament. His true and abiding influence overruns the boundaries of sects." [2]

Such were the relative positions of the two sects soon after Mr. Whittemore entered the ministry, and through the time of his connection with the *Trumpet* as its editor. He well knew the characters of the leading ministers and writers of the Unitarian churches, and held in high esteem their mental accomplishments, as well as their Christian philanthropy and devotion. But, in his notices of them before the public, he never failed to note what he considered their shortcomings, with the same plainness which he manifested in his dealings with other sects around him. In one instance, he significantly remarks, speaking of some annual statistical reports: "A New England Unitarian endeavors to preserve a careful

---

[1] Prof. Diman, in *North Amer. Review* for Jan. 1876.   [2] Ib.

balance between Orthodoxy and Universalism, throwing weights into either scale, as the opposite is likely to predominate. Unitarianism is in a flourishing condition when the beam is exactly horizontal. There are, however, it must be confessed, some among our Unitarian neighbors who are open and independent; but these disapprove as highly as we the middle-ground policy." At a later date, in an editorial of his paper, he pays this willing tribute to them: "We might speak of the intercourse we have enjoyed with Unitarians. There are noble spirits among them, — men who would scorn a mean action; men whose tendency towards heaven has lifted them above all party warfare; whose Christianity consists in doing good; who do not so much belong to one sect as to all sects. We honor such men. It is profitable to be in their society. But all Unitarians are not of this character, neither are all Universalists. We would that the number of such might increase. If there is any thing in the effect of our labors that in the least prevents the influx of the tide of generous emotions among the different sects, God knows we do not intend it for that end. We would sooner that our right hand should be stricken off, than that it should use a pen for such a purpose." [1]

Always in readiness to co-operate with Unitarians as fellow Christians, and especially as those who claimed to be emphatically "liberal" in their Christian faith and work, he was true to his convictions of their errors in doctrine or action, and his duty to present his own faith as embracing all the excellencies of Unitarianism, and as pre-eminent in its claims upon mankind.

Mr. Whittemore was present at the session of the Massachusetts State Convention, in New Bedford, in June of this year.

[1] *Trumpet,* Oct. 16, 1847.

Reform topics were freely discussed there, the inviolability of human life and the abolition of slavery. He took part in the debate on the last-named subject, which was evidently growing in importance in the minds of the people, and especially in the churches in New England. No unanimous or decisive word respecting it was sent out to the public from this meeting of the Convention. The time had not quite come. A committee was chosen — of which Mr. Whittemore was one — to appoint a board of trustees of a Theological Seminary, to obtain a site, hold the property in trust, and erect the necessary buildings as soon as possible. Mr. Whittemore was also chosen a committee to report the condition of the denominational cause in Massachusetts at the next session of the United States Convention.

His views in reference to future punishment were in substance those of the eminent man who had been his principal theological instructor, — Rev. Hosea Ballou. A strong controversy on this subject had risen up, and Mr. Ballou had been earnestly engaged in it. He had not sought the controversy with his brethren, but it came very naturally in the order of events existing at the time of Mr. Ballou's removal to Boston. Rev. Paul Dean, minister of the First Universalist Church in that city, Rev. Edward Turner, of Charlestown, and others, believers in the doctrine of future punishment, felt called upon to affirm it; and especially in opposition to the opinions of Mr. Ballou on the subject. So strong became the feeling on the part of the believers in future punishment, that a circular was issued by them, declaring a dissolution between them and the Universalists. It appeared in the *Independent Messenger*, of Aug. 26, 1831, — a paper established to maintain their opinions and the position which they had taken in reference to them. "The intention was," says Mr. Whittemore, "to form a new sect or distinct class of Christians, bearing the name Restorationists. The design did not succeed. The organization continued for a few years only, when it died of itself, and those who composed it generally amalgamated with the Unitarians."[1]

That Mr. Whittemore was quite persistent in the advocacy of his peculiar views respecting the Divine retributions, is quite evident; some have thought him too much so altogether. But it should be remembered that there were those equally persistent on the other side; and, besides, it was honestly believed by many that one ground of opposition to Mr. Ballou by some of the leaders in the new movement was the jealousy of one of them because of the coming of this distinguished preacher to Boston. Whether this was so or not, one thing is certain; viz., that Mr. Ballou never harbored ill-will against the brethren who so strongly opposed his opinions. As Mr. Whittemore writes: "He would often speak of them with affection; and, when he referred to his intercourse with some of them in early days, it was difficult for him to refrain from tears."[2]

As to Mr. Whittemore, whatever may be said of his forwardness and persistence in defending the doctrine of no future retribution, he never manifested the least disposition to have disaffection stirred up among the brethren on account of their differences of opinion as to God's punishment of his children for their sins. As he writes in the *Trumpet* of July 25, 1840: "It has been the invariable conviction of the leading members of the Universalist denomination from the beginning, that the doctrine of the final restitution is the main point; that all who hold to that doctrine are Universalists, and ought to bear the name which Murray and Winchester

---

[1] A special account of this movement is given by Mr. Whittemore in his memoir of Ballou, vol. iii. pp. 88-90, 119; vol. ii. pp. 223, 224.

[2] Life of Ballou, vol. ii. p. 224.

bore, and which the sect has borne from the beginning. For the twenty years that we have been acquainted with the venerable Hosea Ballou, of this city, we know that the views here expressed have been his views, and we believe they have been the views of our brethren generally." In reference to those who would magnify the difference between Universalists who believe in future punishment and those who do not, he says: "Brethren, let us be moved by none of these things. Let us all go for union. Let us seek for the things that make for peace, and things wherewith one may edify another. Then will the Lord be our God, and we shall prosper still more abundantly."

On Thursday, Oct. 1, the Universalist Meeting-house in Concord, Mass., was dedicated. Rev. H. Ballou preached on the occasion. In the afternoon the services of the recognition of the church recently formed there, were observed. A discourse was delivered by Mr. Whittemore, followed by the communion service.

In an editorial of the *Trumpet* for Oct. 17, he has some pointed remarks on a statement of Dr. Lowell, the well-known Unitarian divine of Boston, made in an ordination sermon, and addressed to the candidate: "I know you will be told that you must indoctrinate your people with your own theological system, *if you unfortunately have any*, in self-defence. This language is unbecoming Christians."

"What can the good Doctor mean?" asks Mr. Whittemore. "Does he object to theology as such, or merely to a system of theology? Theology from θεός and λόγος is the doctrine of God, the science of divine things. Hooper, as quoted by Dr. Johnson, says: 'The whole drift of the Scripture of God, what is it but only to teach theology?' Theology, what is it but the science of divine things? Hence, Dr. Johnson's definition of the term is Divinity. Dr. Lowell is a Doctor of

Divinity; and this degree was a mark of honor, designed to denote a man who was pre-eminently learned in divine things. But if Dr. Lowell is *so fortunate* as to have no system of theology, then we have at least one Doctor of Divinity without any Divinity! If it be wrong to have a system of theology, is it not improper to accept a degree implying that a man is pre-eminently learned in the Christian system? What should we think of a professor of philosophy who had no philosophical system? of a professor of languages who had no system of language? What would he teach his pupils? and what would a Doctor of Divinity teach his pupils if he had no Divinity to teach them? Is the sentiment of Dr. Lowell a prevalent sentiment among the Unitarian clergy?"

Mr. Whittemore attended the services of the dedication of the new meeting-house in Newburyport, Mass., on Wednesday, Oct. 28, and preached in the evening of that day.

This year (1840) Mr. Whittemore was elected a director of the Cambridge Bank, and in a short time was made its president. "By mismanagement and misfortune this bank had been seriously injured, and Mr. Whittemore went into the direction at the most unfavorable time. The stock sold at about thirty per cent discount. He used his influence to bring the bank under the management of a board in favor of reform. The president, a worthy man, resigned his office; and Mr. Whittemore was immediately placed at the head of the institution. By the aid of the new members, a course of measures was carried out, which soon increased public confidence. Directors of unsettled pecuniary standing were induced to resign; the accommodation paper was gradually changed to that of a good business character; demand loans to directors were called in; and by these means the bank was brought up to its present high condition. No bank in Massachusetts, it may truly be said, gave greater satisfaction to the Board of Bank

Commissioners, at their examination in 1852, than the Bank of Cambridge."[1]

In January, 1841, the committee, of which Mr. Whittemore was one, appointed by the Massachusetts Convention to take action respecting a Theological Seminary, drew up certain statutes for the government of the Board of Trustees, organized the Board, and took measures for the raising of funds to the amount of $50,000. Mr. Whittemore was one of four to subscribe immediately $1,000 each.

It was during this year that the Washingtonian Temperance Reform made its strong demonstrations throughout the land. Mr. Whittemore gave it a hearty welcome. " A holy name applied to a worthy object. If our great political father can look down upon this lower world, and take knowledge of what is passing here, he will feel himself honored by the application of his name to a society formed for purposes so truly benevolent. *Washington* Temperance Societies are designed for the benefit of drunkards. None are admitted except those who need reformation ; the members bind themselves to watch over each other ; they respect the drunkard and pity him ; and they allow of no sectarian designs. We bid them God speed."

In May of this year, Rev. Theodore Parker preached his sermon which introduced him to the public as a rationalistic teacher, on " The Transient and Permanent in Christianity," at the ordination of Rev. C. C. Shackford, Unitarian minister at Lynn. Mr. Whittemore spoke in very plain terms of the sermon. He considered it as aimed at the root of all revealed religion, and deeply lamented that such sentiments should emanate from such a source. He wished to know if the theological institution at Cambridge gave countenance to such

---

[1] **Biographical Sketches of Eminent Americans.**

opinions as the discourse contained. "In some points Universalists and Unitarians agree; but we must say very explicitly, that the sentiments we have quoted from this sermon will find no countenance among us." The Unitarian editor of the *Christian Register* said of the discourse, and Mr. Whittemore indorsed his words: "If we held its sentiments, we should not claim to be called Christian, nor consent to exercise the functions of a Christian minister."

Another meeting in the interests of the proposed Theological Seminary was held in Murray Hall, Boston, June 28. A site had been offered on which to erect the building, — that where Tufts College now stands. The meeting was one of much interest. Mr. Whittemore took an active part in it, and plans were instituted for immediate operations in behalf of the object.

A new book of church music by Mr. Whittemore was now ready for the press, entitled the "Gospel Harmonist." He thought it an improvement on the "Songs of Zion" issued five years before. It was a work of much merit and had a large circulation.

In August, he attended again the Rockingham Association, held in Poplin, N.H. He preached one of the seven sermons delivered during the meetings. Friends from a large number of the towns in Rockingham county were present, the meetings were full of interest, and the entertainment given to the visitors by their friends in Poplin had in it every expression of the most cordial welcome. Mr. Whittemore's thoughts called up by the meeting are characteristic of the writer: "There is an inexpressible satisfaction in leaving the city, with its smoky walls and noisy streets, and fleeing to the hills and fields of the country. There you find quiet. The forests, fields, orchards, grazing herds and flocks, meet the eye on every side. You see the ministering brethren from the region round about, every one with a brother's heart beating in his bosom. All feel happy. Then such a gathering of friends! it keeps you half the time shaking hands. Some are in mourning; and you hear the story of the sickness and death of the beloved, how patient they were in pain, how resigned in death, how much comfort they drew from their faith in the hour of death: others speak of the living, of new connections formed, some absent friend returned, some new society or preacher in their vicinity, or, what is always regarded as of no small importance, the conversion of some friend to the truth as it is in Jesus. Perhaps the new convert is there, and desires to be introduced to you. His heart is full to tell you of his joys and to ask forgiveness for the hard things he has said; and how readily do we forgive him when ' we wot that through ignorance he did it.' The feelings that gave rise to these remarks are such as we brought home from Poplin; and we trust they will abide with us."

Another "Seminary" meeting was held in Brinley Hall, Worcester, Sept. 2. It was well attended, and a deep anxiety was manifested that the work should be forwarded. Spirited addresses were made by fifteen or more speakers,— Mr. Whittemore among them; and another meeting was proposed, to be held in Boston in October.

The United States Convention was held this year in New York. The attendance was very large, that of the ministers being nearly one hundred and fifty. The Occasional Discourse — a very able and timely one — was preached by Rev. T. J. Sawyer. Mr. Whittemore was present, and speaks highly of the session and its work. Resolutions favoring the Theological Seminary were zealously discussed and unanimously passed.

The meeting in behalf of the new institution was held agreeable to appointment, in Murray Hall, Boston, Oct. 16.

Rev. E. H. Chapin delivered a very able and acceptable address at the meeting, and was requested to repeat the same on some Sunday evening in the School Street church.

Another religious excitement came up in Boston and vicinity about this time, under the leadership of Rev. Jacob Knapp and his advisers. In his paper of Jan. 15, 1842, Mr. Whittemore takes occasion to speak plainly of the revivalist and his doings. He regards him as a bitter and reckless partisan, indulging in strains of invective against other classes of Christians, especially Universalists, towards whom he seemed to have a very hearty feeling of opposition. He had at times grossly attacked, from the pulpit, persons who differed from him in religious opinion, and had been apprehended in Rhode Island to answer in an alleged slander, uttered from the pulpit, on a widow in Providence. As a professional revivalist, however, his presence and work in Boston were sought by some of the Baptist clergymen; while the venerable Dr. Sharp, as in the case of Mr. Miller, reprobated the course of Mr. Knapp and would hold no fellowship with him. Mr. Whittemore said: "We must express the conviction that there is a retribution in store for those pastors and churches who have been instrumental in bringing Mr. Knapp to Boston." The religious press that sustained him were somewhat sharply criticised, in which course Mr. Whittemore deemed it just to take a part. Among those to whom he especially addresses himself is the editor of the Baptist *Christian Watchman.* In reply to certain strong denunciations by this editor of those who oppose and expose the course of Mr. Knapp, he says: "We advise him to sit down for a while at the feet of such men as President Wayland, Dr. Sharp, and Professor Sears, and peradventure by and by he will be a wiser man. The divisions and animosities which we predicted have already begun to appear; and many serious-minded church-members regret that Mr. Knapp ever came among us. Let the consequences fall on those who brought him here."

In March, a little volume of 144 pages from the pen of Rev. O. A. Skinner, of Boston, appeared, entitled "Letters to Revs. B. Stowe, R. H. Neale, and R. W. Cushman, on Modern Revivals." Religious excitements like the one under Mr. Knapp's ministrations, and his in particular, are reviewed with much wisdom and Christian faithfulness. The pastors named on the title-page are addressed because of their instrumentality in giving force and effectiveness to Mr. Knapp's movements.

In the spring of this season, Mr. Whittemore had frequent calls to deliver temperance lectures, — one at Jamaica Plain, in the Unitarian church, — on which occasion more than one hundred signed the pledge of total abstinence ; one at Cabotville, in the Universalist church, to a very large crowd of listeners ; one at Hingham, in the ancient church there, which was filled to overflowing ; one at Petersham, in the Universalist church ; one at Dedham, at the Town House, which was densely crowded. He is enthusiastically alive in the Washingtonian reform.

Mr. Whittemore republishes about this time an old book, entitled "The Doctrine of Endless Hell Torments Overthrown," partly original and partly selected, containing Dr. Hartley's Defence of Universalism. The book was issued more than two hundred years ago in England, and had never before appeared in America.

In the issue of his paper of May 7th, he has an article stating some of his conclusions after twenty years' experience in the ministry of Universalism. He thinks he may safely say, 1. That "we are more and more confirmed in the belief, that the distinguishing doctrine of our church, viz., the final holiness and happiness of all men, is the doctrine of the Scriptures. All our reading, all our intercourse with other sects, and the very opposition we have encountered, have tended to confirm it. Other sects themselves are fast coming to the belief. 2. The experience of these years confirms us, in general, in our views of those texts generally denominated the threatenings. 3. This same experience shows us that Universalism is consonant with a life of piety, benevolence, devotion, and prayer. This was once very seriously doubted by those of the contrary part, but they are fast changing their views in this matter. Our fathers did well in the hard pioneer work they had to do. We enter into their labors ; but our work is not precisely like theirs. What shall we do? Just what they would do if they stood in our places, — press forward. Let us bring to maturity the seed they planted. There is a moral power in Universalism which every man must feel who gives up his heart to the doctrine. Let us endeavor to bring, first ourselves, and then others, into that sweet and holy influence. Let us cultivate a living faith, and never be for a moment content with a dead one. Our faith works by love and purifies the heart. What faith can do better?"

He realizes at this time much gratification in the Union meetings for conference and prayer held in the different churches in East Cambridge. Unitarians, Methodists, and Universalists all join. Mr. Whittemore speaks of the address of Rev. Mr. Willson, the Methodist clergyman, at one of the meetings, as one of the most catholic and excellent to which he ever listened. Of the conferences he said : "We prayed together, sung together, and exhorted each other to love and good works. We wish that such meetings might be held in all our towns. How much would they diminish the evils of sectarianism. Lord, let thy kingdom come and be established in all our hearts !" Again he writes : —

"It is not religion, but sectarianism that keeps men at a distance from each other. This the Christian world is beginning to see. Sometimes we are encouraged to hope that at no very distant period there will be a great change come over the church. When that time shall come, and Christians shall all work together for Christ, what a power will the church exercise. The voice of love will be heard in all our dwellings. Her brightness will be above the brightness of the sun. Brethren, one and all, let us pray for that day. Such will be the true coming of Christ. Come, Lord Jesus!"

Of the earnestness of effort in the Temperance cause on the part of Universalists, he thus speaks : —

"It is pleasing to see by the newspapers how often Temperance lectures are given in Universalist churches. Our clergy, too, come up nobly to the work. Brother Chapin of Charlestown is winning golden opinions by his pre-eminently useful labors in this cause. Brother Spear of Weymouth and Brother Thompson of South Dedham enter heart and soul into the work. Indeed, so general is the zeal of our clergy in this great and good work, that it is almost invidious to discriminate. Let the work go on. God's blessing will rest upon it."

The United States Convention held its session this year in Providence, R.I. Rev. I. D. Williamson preached the Occasional Discourse. There was a large attendance. Mr. Whittemore took part in the excellent conference meetings, and officiated with Rev. S. Streeter at the communion table. The discourse of this occasion was by Rev. E. H. Chapin on "The Tenderness of Jesus." Mr. Whittemore said of the discourse : "It had passages of strong reasoning, of great power, and of inimitable tenderness : it convinced, it thrilled, it melted the audience." It was at this Convention that Rev. Hosea Ballou 2d preached in the Unitarian church, opened for the occasion, a most searching discourse on "Honesty in maintaining Religious Truth." His definition of Christian charity was long remembered by many who heard it:

"By charity we mean the reality, not the mere pretence. We mean that pure spirit of heaven whose eye is all light, and whose heart all tenderness, who sees things as they are, and calls them by their right names. People do wrong to screen their sheer indifference to truth under her sacred name. Whom do they take charity to be? an idiot, with great moony eyes and a stolid countenance, who knows only to babble 'good, good,' at every thing she meets! This is not charity: it is stupidity; or, worse, hypocrisy."

There was a meeting of much interest in Marblehead, in December, which Mr. Whittemore attended; the first of a series which followed. Nearly four hundred went from Salem. He writes of it: "Every eye and ear was open. The duty of self-examination was enforced, and the Gospel as exemplified in the character of Jesus was commended to all as a rule by which to guide our lives. Several who had been in the bonds of error spoke. God had opened their eyes and revealed himself, and they were now at peace. Persons not there cannot imagine the interest of the services. The next meeting is to be at Danvers, and there will be a crowd. We shall be there if possible."

He is quite interested in an article in a new Unitarian paper, *The Christian World*, edited by Mr. George E. Channing, brother of the late Dr. Channing. The article is entitled, "Condition and Wants of Unitarianism." The writer, Mr. Channing, argues that one great want of the Unitarians is greater life, zeal, activity. "Men say, 'the Unitarian doctrines seem reasonable; but the orthodox are doing more, are more in earnest, seem awake and alive. It is no answer to this to say, — Their zeal is sectarian, proselytiug, and a party spirit — they are driven on by fear of hell.' Be it so; but why do you not do more then? If you are moved by higher motives, why do you not perform greater actions? The effort of the denomination should now be to realize its own convictions more deeply, so as to be quickened by them into a profounder life. The time has come when we should adopt new measures for promoting this spirit. We should be ready to make use of every expedient to awaken the soul, — whether by social meetings, improvement in the forms of worship, lay preaching, or whatever else may be adapted to interest and edify. Our doctrines also need to be considered and modified. They were formed in order to reply to opponents. We now need to put them in forms which will enable us to apply them to our own consciences and hearts. They must be stated so as to mean *as much* and not *as little* as possible. We have been too much in the habit of saying that conversion *only* means so and so; that regeneration means *nothing more* than this, repentance is *nothing but* that, &c. Now we need to see that repentance and conversion mean a great deal, and to say so."

Mr. Whittemore takes occasion to give these suggestions of his Unitarian brother in the main a hearty indorsement, and to commend them with much earnestness to the attention of Universalists. He thinks that not a few of them may be benefited by taking heed to these words of their neighbor: "Let Universalists take these hints. Here is a testimony borne to the utility of conference meetings. Let every Universalist meeting-house hereafter built, be furnished with a good vestry. Let the laymen employ their gifts: it must be done; and, where there are no objections, let women do the same if moved thereunto. We have heard women speak with great propriety and profit in social meetings. While we see Christians of all denominations awaking to these things, let not Universalists any longer sleep. Awake, awake!"

CHAPTER VII.

1843–1844.

AGED 43–44.

Conferences at Danvers, Lynn, Charlestown, Cambridgeport, Salem, East Cambridge — Conference Hymn-book — Conference at School Street Church : at Newburyport — Discourse on Modern History of Universalism — Answer to the question, Has Universalism changed? — Conference at West Cambridge, Woburn — Massachusetts Convention at Plymouth — Dedication at Saco, Me. — Conference at South Reading — Meeting at Winchester, N.H. — Rockingham Association — Journey to the West — Visit to Niagara Falls — Buffalo — U.S. Convention at Akron, O. — Accident returning from Hingham — Conferences at Marblehead, Lynn, Danvers — Improper singing — Massachusetts Convention at Worcester — Notice of an accusation — Tour to the White Mountains.

A SPIRITED conference was held at Danvers on Feb. 1, 1843. It commenced in the midst of a driving snow-storm which continued through the day. There was a large gathering, however; in the afternoon the house was completely filled, including aisles and pulpit stairs. Mr. Whittemore, who had reached the place by a ride of fifteen miles in the face of the storm, and who arrived, as he says, " clothed in white," thus writes of the exercises : —

" There was evidently a great expectation of a good meeting. The remarks of the speakers were generally on the power of religion to purify and exalt the affections, and to give joy to the soul. And one very pleasing circumstance in regard to the meeting was, that the lay brethren were ready and willing, yea, even anxious to speak. We do unfeignedly rejoice in this increase of interest on their part. It promises great good to our churches ; it is bringing on our brighter days." Of the evening meeting he writes : "It was appointed to commence at six, — too early as many thought. We went a quarter of an hour before the time, and with much difficulty succeeded in forcing a passage through the aisle to the pulpit stairs. Two other meetings were held by other sects at the same time ; but many of their usual attendants were at our conference. We cannot give the names of the many speakers. The laymen seemed to take the lead. It was inquired by some brother if there were none out by the door whose hearts vibrated to the emotions that had been expressed. Whereupon a brother in one of the front corners of the house gave us an impressive address. It was then asked if the hearts in the other front section were not responsive. An affirmative answer was immediately given by a brother who proceeded to address the congregation. From this the suggestion arose, that the gallery was the only part of the house that was backward. A brother then arose in the gallery, and spoke with deep feeling." The next conference was appointed to be at Lynn.

Of this meeting, which was in the midst of a storm. Mr. Whittemore writes : " We found the friends in Lynn in low spirits. They knew not what to do. Should the meeting be put off or be held? For very few had arrived from neighboring towns. It was agreed that the meeting should be held at two p.m. Before that time, the friends came pouring in from Salem, Danvers, and Marblehead, as the railroad trains had been delayed by the snow. The large Lyceum Hall, engaged for the occasion, was filled. Many of the laymen engaged in the services ; and we thought that we had never heard the singing equalled on such an occasion." The evening meeting was of still greater interest, if possible. Impressive confessions were made as to the reformatory power of Universalism drawn from personal experiences. Rev. B. F. Newhall of Saugus, who had embraced the faith a year or two before, made a very acceptable address. Mr. Whittemore affirmed that it was a large, happy, and profitable meeting.

The conferences continue; one is held in Charlestown. Mr. Whittemore, who was present in the evening, says of it: "The speakers all seemed to have one object in view,—the promotion of the spiritual interests of men, the increase of divine knowledge, the quickening of zeal, the importance of purity of life and a godly conversation, and the necessity of our sympathizing with the distressed and sorrowing. The laymen took part in the exercises in all the meetings."

The next conference was in Cambridgeport. The friends there welcomed it heartily. During the morning exercises, Father Ballou spoke of the propriety and benefit of such assemblies. He referred to the customs of the Jews in ordaining gatherings and festivals,—such as the feast of the passover, of pentecost, of tabernacles,—not only to perpetuate the remembrance of great events and to worship God, but also to cultivate social feelings, to repress sectional jealousies, and to keep alive the flame of love which ought ever to burn in our hearts. Father Sebastian Streeter made a thrilling speech. The laymen took a good part in the exercises. A large number of the ministers of neighboring parishes were present. In the evening, Father Ballou gave a deeply interesting account of his conversion to Universalism. And, in reference to the experiences of his own ministry, he remarked, with much feeling, "I have seen so much of the triumphs of truth, have seen the cause blessed so much beyond my expectations, that I sometimes feel like Simeon in the temple at Jerusalem, ready to depart."

Mr. Whittemore said of the meeting: "It was the more interesting to us because it was holden in the place of our residence, and gave us the opportunity to receive at our own house some of the friends whose hospitalities we had enjoyed at other places. It also enabled the church of which we are a member to enjoy the pleasure of such a meeting, and we hope to reap a rich harvest of profit from it."

Another conference was held in Salem. Between 1,500 and 2,000 persons were in attendance at the Universalist church. The account of the meetings, day and evening, fills three columns of the *Trumpet*. Ministers and laymen were equally free and earnest in their addresses and prayers. Various churches were reported by their ministers. Vital piety, devotion in the home, and Christian consecration at all times, were repeatedly and forcibly urged.

East Cambridge was next visited. The conference there was on March 20. The Universalist chapel in the place being small, the Methodist church was at the service of the attendants at the meetings; and these were of notable interest; Methodists, Orthodox, Universalists, all holding sweet and profitable communion. Rev. Mr. Willson, pastor of the Methodist church, was especially happy. He acknowledged all men as Christians who had the Spirit of the Master. He wanted heaven while here on earth. Father Ballou and Rev. E. H. Chapin followed in warm responsive words. An Orthodox layman said, "How little my church brethren know of Universalism. If this is it, I say 'Amen' to it! Let it spread abroad!" Rev. Mr. Lambert, of the Unitarian church, made a timely and fervent address. Many laymen spoke.

A second book of "Conference Hymns" was published by Mr. Whittemore about this time. It was intended as a continuation of the first one issued by him; was of the same size, and they could be bound separately or together. Both books were quite extensively used.

The next conference of the churches was held at the School Street church, in Boston, on Tuesday, June 4. Father Ballou opened the morning meeting most appropriately. He dwelt upon the importance of Christian union. There was a large attendance, and some of the most truthful and earnest utterances of the doctrinal and practical excellencies of the Gospel of Universalism. Ministers and laymen were alike in readiness to take parts in the exercises. The report of the meetings by Mr. Whittemore is a lively one, and fills three columns of his paper.

The next day he was present at a conference in Newburyport, which is reported in the *Trumpet*. It was not so largely attended as some of the others, but was a gathering of much interest, and a very wakeful and profitable occasion. Many ministers and laymen were speakers. Mr. Whittemore said, in one of his speeches: " We read in the Bible of a certain pool at Jerusalem, which, when the water was stirred, had great medicinal qualities. It reminded him of the Gospel pool, which he hoped would be stirred mightily that day; and he hoped that even the poor old cripple who had had an infirmity thirty-eight years would this day go into the pool. Jesus now said to him, ' Arise, take up thy bed and walk.' Jacob said, when he wrestled with the angel, ' I will not let thee go except thou bless me.' We must do the same with this meeting, — determine that it shall not pass by without blessing us. He spoke of individual duty, — that each one should resolve to watch over and take care of one heart; this will make your society prosper, and you will grow in the grace of Christ." He justifies himself in giving full reports of these meetings by saying: " We do not believe there are, in any department of either sacred or secular science, any subjects of more importance than those discussed in these meetings."

In the *Trumpet* of April 2 of this year, is published a discourse of Mr. Whittemore, on " The Modern History of Universalism."   One of a series of ten discourses delivered a year previous by Universalist ministers in Boston and vicinity ; a very comprehensive and instructive presentation of the subject.   One passage in it we cannot refrain from quoting. Speaking of Universalism, he says : " When the church grew corrupt the light of this doctrine grew dim ; its holy fires almost expired ; gross darkness reigned ; and no gleam of light was seen except an occasional ray, when some daring hand stirred the smouldering embers of truth.   But, when the Reformation broke out, Universalism arose with it.   It is a planet whose orbit is near the sun.   In the fall of night, it was the evening star, that lingered for a while above the horizon to reflect the beams of the departing orb of truth ; in the Reformation, it was the morning star, harbinger of a bright and glorious day.   May we not use the language of Milton : —

> "'Fairest of stars, last in the train of night,
>   If better thou belong not to the dawn,
>   Sure pledge of day that crown'st the smiling morn
>   With thy bright circlet.'"

Another conference was held at Roxbury, April 18.   Rev. C. H. Fay, the resident pastor, opened it, and the exercises were of deep interest throughout.   Ministers and laymen were in readiness to carry them on.   Most of the addresses were strongly practical.   Mr. Whittemore says of his report of it : " We did not intend that it should be so long, and made a serious attempt to abridge it ; but what could we leave out ? It is all good.   Carefully read and meditate upon it."

An editorial in the *Trumpet* of May 6, attempts an answer to the question, " Has Universalism changed ?"   Another church journal has just been provoking this query by criticising rather pointedly the awakened religious interest apparent in the Universalist churches. This writer says, in substance: "After all their reproach of revivals, night meetings, excitements, and protracted meetings, the Universalists are going fully into the same measures. They recommend the organization of churches; make much display of immersion; use conference hymns; sing exciting tunes; advise the laity to take part in exhortation and prayer; and even the sisters hold not their peace. In this we rejoice: it is the indication of awakened religious sensibility. They are obliged to do homage to the religious spirit abroad in the land, and tacitly confess that all their past denunciations of the orthodox and their measures were false and unjust; and no severer penance would we inflict than to keep them hot at work at conference and prayer meetings; for if 'this kind goeth not out' by argument and scripture, it will flee at the approach of this orthodox machinery, and Universalism will be numbered with the things that were."

Mr. Whittemore promptly and squarely replies to these cool insinuations, by assuring the writer of them that Universalists have never reproached revivals of pure religion, but have endeavored to distinguish between these and merely animal excitement produced by false doctrines. "We have," says he, "always been in favor of any excitement which the plain preaching of the truth will produce; and as to night meetings Universalists have always been in the habit of having evening lectures ever since we knew them. It is out of place for this editor to talk of 'new measures.' His own sect has adopted them. Once it was as much opposed to night meetings as anybody else, and used to preach vehemently against the operations of Methodists and Baptists. As to churches, they have long existed among us; so have

meetings for conference and prayer. Baptism by immersion
has been practised by some of our clergy for years. As to
conference hymns, we calculate to keep up with the spirit of
the times in that matter, and do not intend that other sects
shall have better conference hymns than we. We do in
truth advise the brethren to take part in exhortation and
prayer, and are happy to add that our advice has not been
altogether without effect. Our neighbor speaks as though
conference and prayer meetings were to us a kind of penance.
What an error! They are seasons of high satisfaction. We
love them. It would be a penance to be deprived of them.
If our friend flatters himself that the present course of Universalists is to prove fatal to their doctrine, he is amazingly
deceived. We do advise him to be correct about something:
he is wrong in almost every position he has taken. Universalism will never go down. It is the doctrine of God; it is
precious to the benevolent heart; it is God's answer to the
prayers of all true Christians. It will prosper; and the conference meetings among us may well alarm those who are our
enemies, for they are giving a fresh impulse to the cause of
truth."

Another conference was held in West Cambridge (now
Arlington), on the 2d of May. The resident pastor, Rev.
Mr. Waldo, being quite ill, he had invited Father Ballou to
take charge of the morning meeting. He gave a hearty address of welcome to all the attendants, and an invitation to
both clergy and laity present to occupy the time as profitably
as possible. The meeting through the day was one of much
fervor. Mr. Whittemore took a conspicuous part in the
services.

A conference at Woburn followed, May 16. It was much
like the one at West Cambridge, and was well attended.
Mr. Whittemore was unable to be present. On May 30,

there was another conference at Waltham. Rev. E. A. Eaton, the resident pastor, made an address of welcome. The attendance through the day was good. Father Ballou, Mr. Whittemore, and others of the ministers, were in their happiest moods, and the laymen seemed to have much freedom of speech. Mr. Whittemore writes: "We set down this occasion as one of the most profitable we have ever enjoyed."

In June of this year, the Massachusetts Convention held its annual session in Plymouth. It was a well-attended and happy meeting. The Occasional Discourse was delivered by Rev. L. Willis. Stirring conferences were held. Mr. Whittemore writes of the meeting: "The place of meeting was the spot where the Pilgrim Fathers first came when they fled from religious oppression in the Old World, to enjoy unmolested their rights of conscience in this wilderness home. Since their day how had this home changed! How had bigotry and error receded before the irresistible power of religious freedom and heavenly love! The friends of our cause in this place are among the strongest and best. The religious feeling in the place was in our favor. This was manifest in the numbers of other sects present at our meetings. At our conference on Thursday evening, Rev. Mr. Briggs, colleague of Rev. Dr. Kendall, of the Old First Church, addressed the audience in some very happy remarks, commending the spirit manifested in the meeting, and assuring us of his desire to meet it with a corresponding spirit of charity."

On Wednesday, June 21, the Universalist Church in Saco, Me., was dedicated. Mr. Whittemore preached the sermon. From this place he came to South Reading, and attended and took part in a very spirited conference meeting there held on the 22d. A church was recognized. Seven candidates were baptized by Rev. S. Streeter, who wisely and earnestly advised them. The members of the church, about forty in number, were then addressed by Mr. Whittemore, who extended the hand of fellowship to them through their pastor, Rev. J. H. Willis. Father Streeter's words at the communion service were very appropriate. After the silence during the distribution of the elements, he remarked, Earth has no scene like this: how calm, how sweet! The best feelings of our nature are called into exercise here. How we long that all divisions throughout the world should come to an end! He referred to the heavenly rest hereafter. What countless hosts will commune there! He spoke of the great hosts on Bunker's Hill a few days before. They all became wearied, and trumpeters and harpers were worn out and went home. But all will be rest in heaven. None will tire: there will be no fainting, but renewal of strength, as souls wait on the Lord. Mr. Whittemore gave a glowing account of the meetings.

He was present at the recognition of a church in Winchester, N.H., on the 1st of July. He preached twice on Sunday. Twenty-four presented themselves for baptism. "A severe thunder-storm," writes Mr. Whittemore, "prevented our reaching Warwick to preach a lecture, of which notice had been given."

The twentieth session of the Rockingham Association was held this year in August, at East Kingston, N.H. Mr. Whittemore writes of it: "Going into the meeting-house the first afternoon, we found it filled with ladies; a great contrast from the congregation that assembled at the service of the Association in 1828, at Kingston Plains, when but one lady was present, — Mrs. Barnard, of South Hampton. An awning was fixed at the side of the church, under which seats had been placed. One window at the side was taken out, and the speakers stood in the opening thus made. The meetings were of great interest. At the first evening conference, references were made to the fact that it was in East Kingston, in 1834, that the conference meetings of this Association began, which excited no little speculation at the time in our religious journals. We could not forget our beloved brethren, T. F. King, A. L. Balch, and William C. Hanscom: all of them now in glory; all of whom were present at that meeting, and took an active part in the exercises." Discourses were preached during the two days by Rev. J. M. Austin. Rev. J. G. Adams, and Rev. Sebastian Streeter. At the close of the last sermon, Mr. Whittemore gave a brief history of the Association from its first meeting in 1824.

In September of this year, Mr. Whittemore, in company with Rev. H. Ballou, visited Akron, O., to attend the United States Convention in that place. Editorial letters in the *Trumpet* give interesting descriptions of their journey. They visit Niagara for the first time, and are guests of General Whitney, at the Cataract House. Mr. Whittemore's views of Niagara are vividly drawn. Of the view from the tower on the Terrapin rocks, he writes : —

" What a scene above ! what a scene below ! Down came the mighty waves, chasing one another as if in an eager race for some desired goal, maddened by being interrupted by rocks that refuse to move ; now contracting, now expanding, now rising, now falling, lashed into foam ; increasing their impetus every moment ; roaring with deafening energy ; and then going over the smooth shelf in one unbroken sheet. All this at one glance ! The sheet, seemingly for fifty feet after it goes over, is a beautiful variegated green ; but then it begins to jet, as we have described at the American fall, only with greater effect. It seems as if this was the grand thoroughfare of all the waters of heaven above and earth beneath. Here they hold their jubilee ; here they sing their everlasting anthem, — 'the hand that made us is divine;' they rest not until the pæan is closed; and then they grow quiet, and smilingly pass away. Such was the view from the tower. We went away weakened by the excitement, and humbled by the awful majesty of the scene."

Of Father Ballou's impressions at Table Rock, on the Canada side, he writes: "Father Ballou is not easily moved; but, when he came to Table Rock, he stood in amazement. And, when we were urged to get back over the river before dark, he said, 'How can I go away?' He said his thoughts were like those of Peter on one occasion: 'It is good to be here; let us build tabernacles, and dwell on the spot.' A prism was handed him, from which he could see the rapids, fall, and chasm, in colors ineffably glorious. 'O my soul!' 'Glory to God!' were his exclamations. Such a sight our eyes shall never behold again, unless we come here to realize it."

A Sunday was passed in Buffalo, where both the ministers preached. Passing up Lake Erie to Cleveland, they went by carriage to Akron. The Convention meetings were largely attended. The church was filled; and a spacious tent, belonging to the Campbellites, placed beside it, contained from 1,500 to 2,000 persons. Sermons were preached, on Wednesday and Thursday, by Rev. J. A. Gurley, Rev. W. S. Balch, Rev. H. Ballou, Rev. T. J. Sawyer, and Rev. T. Whittemore. Other services were held after our visitors had departed, until the following Sunday evening. Mr. Whittemore writes: "When Father Ballou appeared in the congregation front of the pulpit, many of his friends of former days, who had emigrated from New England to the Western country, came up to take his hand, and make inquiries concerning his health. We saw whole families advance, and, shaking hands with him, burst into tears. The scene was truly moving."

On his return from Ohio, Mr. Whittemore preached in Rochester, Auburn, and Troy, N.Y.

On Sunday, Nov. 4, after preaching during the day at Hingham, on his way home a somewhat serious accident befell him, of which he writes : " We started on our return in a carryall, sitting on the back seat, wrapped in a cloak, a man in front having charge of the horse. Descending a hill in Weymouth, just on the edge of the sea, the shafts got disengaged from the axle-tree, and of course the horse was freed from the vehicle. Thus left to itself in descending the hill, the carriage soon gave a turn to the right, and ran off the bank about twelve feet, plunged to the shore, struck on one side, turned over upon its roof, and went down upon the other side. In the whirl it got completely reversed. We could comprehend nothing for a few moments ; and, when we could once more think, we found ourselves standing in the carriage exactly on the top of our head. With some effort, we emerged through the frame, from which the glass had been broken out by the fall, and thanked God that neither we nor our companion, so far as we could judge, was dangerously injured. The horse stood patiently in the road, a quiet spectator of the scene. We righted the carriage, gathered up the fragments, and rode home. To-day (Monday) we feel severely the effect of the fall. Had there been a fence, or even a timber laid along on the edge of the road, the carriage would not have gone over the brink, and no damage of any importance would have been done. We shall put measures in train to obtain reparation."

As a new year begins, the watchful journalist makes a call upon Universalist parishes to see to their financial standing, and relieve themselves from debt. He cites the instance of Rev. T. J. Sawyer, pastor of the Orchard Street church, in New York, who, seeing that there was a floating debt of about

$4,700 upon it, told the members of the parish that they must reduce his salary, if necessary, although he hardly met his expenses as it was. They took the hint wisely, and immediately raised enough by subscription to relieve themselves from embarrassment. He asks: "How are other committees of societies? are they watchful? The judicious commander of a vessel never lets many days pass without sounding his pumps to learn whether his vessel leaks. So ought the committee of a society to do. They ought to say, How are we getting along? Is our income equal to our expenses? Are the subscriptions paid in? Is the pew-tax collected promptly? Has the pastor received his salary regularly? The pastor can hardly preach well if he is obliged to be in debt himself. How can he preach faithfulness to others if he is delinquent? And, even if he should summon courage to do it, his people would at least *think* of the proverb, 'Physician, heal thyself.' Let every society put its minister into the situation to keep out of debt."

Conferences open again; one at Marblehead, Jan. 11, largely attended and quite fully reported in the *Trumpet*. Ministers and laymen took a lively part in the meeting. Another of equal interest was held at Lynn on the 24th. The audiences filled the large Town Hall. A third in Danvers on Feb. 14, was of the same spirit, and proved edifying to the many attendants. Mr. Whittemore was present at each one of them, and signified by speech and prayer and songs of praise his high enjoyment of the occasions.

In an editorial article about this time, Mr. Whittemore writes very freely respecting the absurdity of singing, as offerings of praise, many of the hymns written by Watts and others on the horrors of endless punishment. He is noticing what the compilers of the "Psalmist," a new Baptist book of hymns, say, that "hymns intended for devotional purposes should express *joyful* emotion;" quoting Scripture in support of the statement.   He accepts the statement as true and just, and proceeds in the light of it to show how utterly repugnant to all good Christian taste and feeling such lines as these must be when put to music and sung as offerings of praise to the God of all grace : —

> "Tempests of angry nre shall roll,
>   To blast the rebel worm,
> And break upon his naked soul
>   In one eternal storm :
>
> .   .   .   .   .
>
> Cursed be the man, for ever cursed,
>   That doth one wilful sin commit ;
> Death and damnation for the first,
>   Without relief, and infinite, &c."

And he raises the question : " If these things are not fit to be sung, are they fit to be preached?   When the Baptist clergyman preaches a sermon on endless misery, where is he to find an *appropriate* hymn?   Here is a difficulty which, perhaps, Messrs. Stow and Smith did not anticipate.   Can it be expected of hearers that, while the roaring of the fiery sea is yet resounding in their ears, they will be able to sing with the spirit and understanding also some sweet stanza, like the following : —

> ' When all thy mercies, O my God,
>   My rising soul surveys,
> Transported with the view I'm lost
>   In wonder, love, and praise.'

" We come to the conclusion that the design of banishing the doctrine of endless torture from the choral service of the church originated in that strong aversion which is springing up in the public mind to the doctrine itself; and that it is but a part of a great reform which will eventually exclude that doctrine, not only from the choir but from the pulpit. 'And let all the people say Amen.'"

Mr. Whittemore was present at the meeting of the Massachusetts Convention at Worcester, June 5 and 6; but it does not appear that he preached on the occasion. He speaks of the meeting as "an agreeable and happy one." Of the closing communion service he writes: "A large company was present, both of those who took part in the ordinance and those who witnessed it. The exhortation of Father Streeter before he gave the benediction was one of the most affectionate, subduing, and faithful we ever heard from his lips on any occasion."

To complaints occasionally made by other sects, and perhaps by some Universalists, that the *Trumpet* was "too warlike," the editor takes occasion to reply: "Too warlike! Not at all, brother. Does not the *Trumpet* war against sin? against error? Can we be too warlike in this sense? We must contend earnestly for the faith once delivered to the saints (Jude 3). This must always be done in a right spirit. The weapons of our warfare are not carnal. Hatred, revenge, malice, dishonesty, rejoicing in iniquity: these weapons we must not use; and God helping us we will not. But the weapons for our use are those with which the apostle arms the Christian soldier. The loins must be girt about with truth; we must bear the breastplate of righteousness; our feet must be shod with the preparation of the Gospel of peace; we must have the shield of faith and the helmet of salvation. We must put on this armor of God; and must wrestle, not with flesh and blood, *i.e.*, not against men, but the evil principles of men, — 'principalities, powers, the rulers of the darkness of this world, spiritual wickedness in high places.' We acknowledge that we have erred; and, in view of the vastness of the object at which we have aimed, we have done too little. We will strive to do more, and to prove ourself, ' a good soldier of Jesus Christ.' He is ' the Captain of our salvation.' "

In August of this year, Mr. Whittemore made a tour to the White Mountains. Letters in the *Trumpet* give a lively account of it. His brother ministers and others made up a party of ten or twelve. They took the railroad conveyance to Concord; thence by stage to Centre Harbor, N.H. Next morning the ascent of Red Hill was made. "It was a clear morning," he writes. "Our party was ready at the time, — consisting of Brothers Ballou, of Medford; Adams, of Malden; Fay, of Roxbury; Coffin, of Centre Harbor; four lay brethren and the writer. We had also an excellent guide in the son of Hon. Benning M. Bean, our host. We took carriage four miles to the point where we left the road; and then, turning abruptly into a pasture, the horses were secured and we began the ascent. There was much pleasantry in the company, and many a wise speculation was uttered whether a man of 220 pounds weight could drag his body up. This made us anxious, as we had had little experience in climbing mountains. One of the company suggested that it was wise to put the heavy man behind in the ascent, and in front in the descent, that if he should fall and roll down the mountain, the lives of the others might be preserved.

"Without jesting, it was a severe effort. The thought occurred painfully to the mind, if it be thus laborious to ascend Red Hill, what must it be to ascend Mount Washington? That is yet to be tried. Stopping awhile at the cottage of ' Mother Cook,' we came to the summit after another trial of our strength. Of the scene from here, we can give no adequate description. Red Hill seems a standpoint thrown up by nature in the midst of a vast amphitheatre of mountains. The sublime and beautiful are in the prospect.

In the east, the Ossipee Mountains, with their broad dark features, frown upon us. In the north-east, far away in the distance, are mountains in Maine, and much nearer the far-famed
Chocorua, the scene of a thrilling fiction. The Sandwich
Mountains lift up their shaggy forms in the north, as though
forbidding all progress in that direction; in the north-west,
are the mountains of Thornton and Campton; in the south-
west, Kearsarge and Monadnock; in the south, the Gunstock
mountains in Gilmanton. Squam Lake beneath us was
bright as molten silver; and to the south lies one of heaven's
brightest smiles, Lake Winnipiscogee.

"We prepare to descend. Who cannot *go down* a mountain? We commenced upon the run, for we were a little
chilly. We jumped with pleasure four or five feet at a leap
when we began the descent; but near the close had to manage our steps very cautiously. As we write this account on
the following day at noon, the muscles of the legs are so sore
that common walking, and the rising from a chair even, is very
painful." After the descent from Red Hill, the party were
glad to meet, as one of their number, Rev. E. H. Chapin of
Charlestown.

In a letter from the Notch House near Mount Washington,
he describes their journey from Centre Harbor. His sketches
of the scenery in this region are admirably made. On the
9th of August, the first ascent of the party to Mount Washington was made. They went, a few on foot, the rest on
horseback; Mr. Whittemore taking a horse with a friend.
The summit was gained, but they were environed by clouds.
They could see but a few rods in any direction. The guide
furnished them with a substantial dinner. They endured
cheerfully the disappointment of having no prospect in the
far distance, and, in due time, made their long descent. One
of the company, Rev. C. H. Fay, walked to the summit and

back, a distance of about eighteen miles, without much apparent fatigue. All bewailed their failure to enjoy a fair weather prospect from Mount Washington.

Sunday came. It was a delightful day without. Religious services were held at the "Notch House." Rev. E. H. Chapin preached, and prayers were offered by Mr. Whittemore and Rev. J. G. Adams. Another ascent was made on Monday. Clouds were floating about the mountains, and a snow and rain storm met them at the summit of Washington. But soon the clouds broke, scattered, and rolled above and afar, and the grandest views they could have desired were before them. Mr. Whittemore walked up and down the mountains, was not greatly fatigued, and thought he could have done the same thing the next day.

The party visited the Franconia Range on Monday. Passing through Bethlehem, they met the Hutchinsons with other singing friends there, who were on their way from Littleton to the White Mountains. The journalist writes: "They were just on the point of leaving when we came up; but, at our earnest request, they gave us a couple of songs. Nine of them were seated in the coach, and they poured out for us a strain of music of thrilling interest. They concluded with the song called the 'Old Granite State.' It was so rich, so pure, so chaste; it had such strains of touching melody and melting harmony; it was so tender, filial, fraternal, replete with such just sentiments, and we were so well prepared for it by what we had seen and the state of our own feelings, that we can say, with perfect accuracy, that never in our lives did music so charm us."

They visited the attractions in the Franconia Range, including the "Old Man of the Mountain," and spent the night at Littleton. From this place Mr. Whittemore and others of the company passed round through Haverhill to West Rumney, N.H., where a meeting was held in the Universalist church on Friday evening. On Saturday morning, the party divided into smaller fractions. Mr. Whittemore preached the following Sunday in Concord, N.H.

CHAPTER VIII.

1844–1847.

AGED 44–47.

Paige's Commentary — Rev. T. Parker and Unitarians — A Gloucester veteran — Conference at Medford — Temperance festival at Acton — Denunciation, and Answer to it — U.S. Convention in Boston — Mr. Emerson on Swedenborg — Temperance and some mistakes of its friends — Protest of Universalists against American Slavery — Evils of Fiction-writing — Massachusetts Convention at Hingham — Proposed Reform Association — Miracles and Magnetism — 37 Cornhill — U.S. Convention at Troy, N.Y. — Remarks on Convention work — Boston Association in Malden — Home Missionary work — Statements of Rev. Dr. Pond, and Remarks — Criticism of *Christian Reflector* and Reply — A Western editor on Theological Institutions, and Reply.

In September of this year (1844), the first volume of the Commentary on the New Testament, by Rev. Lucius R. Paige, was published by B. B. Mussey, 29 Cornhill, Boston. It was a work needed by the Universalist public, and since its issue the succeeding volumes to the completion of the Books of the New Testament, with the exception of the Apocalypse, have proved the whole series to be a valuable contribution to the literature of the Christian church. On the appearance of the first volume, in an editorial notice Mr. Whittemore says: "Of the manner in which the Commentary is executed, we feel it our duty to say that, in our judgment, it will reflect credit upon its author, as well as upon that class of Christians to which he belongs. It manifests much learning, deep study, an earnest desire after truth, independence of mind far removed from any thing like self-confidence, or an overweening attachment to preconceived opinions, slavery to the opinions of any man or sect; in fine, it is the fruit of a candid, unbiased, intelligent, persevering study of the Scriptures for many years. No person will fail to see the characteristic modesty of the author. He states the opinions of those from whom he differs in all their force, and proposes his own perspicuously and decidedly, yet in a becoming manner." Other very favorable notices of it were given in the religious journals of the day.

Mr. Whittemore was not present at the session of the United States Convention in Baltimore, in September of this year. A report of it was given in the *Trumpet* by Rev. C. H. Fay. On the 16th of October, he was in New London, Ct., and preached a discourse at the Recognition of the Universalist church in that place, of which Rev. T. J. Greenwood was then pastor. He was present at another conference meeting in Waltham, Dec. 11. It was a large gathering of ministers and laymen, many of them from neighboring churches, and proved to be a meeting of deep enjoyment on the part of the attendants. On Jan. 25, 1845, another meeting of the same character was held in East Lexington.

In the *Trumpet* of Feb. 2, Mr. Whittemore, in a notice of the excitement in the Unitarian churches in consequence of the influence of Rev. Theodore Parker's opinions, and especially of the proposal of Rev. James F. Clarke to exchange with him, gives thus plainly his views of Mr. Parker and his ministry : —

" For ourselves, we believe Mr. Parker's opinions to be decidedly *deistical*. We acknowledge that he has all the right to the promulgation of his opinions which we have to the promulgation of our own. We then proclaim our opinion that the views of Mr. Parker are subversive of the Christian religion ; that, if he is right, there is no Christianity : it is gangrened at its vitals ; it is gone. Mr. Parker has denied the truth of the Gospels ; he has preached that the statements of the Evangelists have to him ' but a low degree of historical credibility ; ' that they have mingled with their story puerile notions and tales which it is charitable to call absurd ; that they have possibly represented Christ as teaching what he did not teach ; that the Saviour was frequently mistaken, and that other Christs still greater are to come ; that the pretended miracles of Christ are ' myths and fables ; ' that there is no certainty of Christ's resurrection, and that the account of his subsequent history is impossible.

" With Mr. Parker we have no acquaintance. We accord to him all the rights we claim to ourself ; we would abridge him of no liberty : but we must say that, holding as he does the opinions above described, he is not a *Christian* minister. In this remark we mean nothing against his character ; we would detract nothing from his reputation as a man of eloquence and talent : but he can no more be considered a Christian than Paine or Taylor. We might as well expect a man to live with his head stricken from his body as Christianity to live if the sentiments of Mr. Parker should become general. While we express these opinions, we also express the hope that no measures may be adopted towards him but those of kindness. While he denies the theory of Christianity, let us meet him in its spirit ; for Jesus ' had compassion on the ignorant and those who are out of the way.' "

On Feb. 3, the venerable William Pearce of Gloucester passed from this life in the ninety-fourth year of his age. He was one of the early friends of Murray, and helped to sustain him through the trials of his ministry in that place. In a long and interesting obituary notice of him, Mr. Whittemore thus speaks of his last interview with him in 1842 : —

"We tarried, as we had long been accustomed to, at his house. He delighted to talk on religion. He would sit for a long time and converse on this theme. His whole heart was in it. His eyes now sparkle with joy, and are now suffused with tears. He speaks of Murray, and of the joys, sorrows, pleasures, and privations which the early Universalists of Gloucester realized. We asked him about his faith. 'My faith,' said he, 'is as strong as ever — never weakened — no, sir, founded on a rock — the gates of hell cannot prevail against it.' He was evidently much absorbed in meditation, and would give vent to his feelings in quotations from the Scriptures. '*Every* knee *shall* bow, and *every* tongue shall confess. Does this not mean ALL? Yes, EVERY ONE. He will not forsake his own work; he cannot hate himself. Are we not Christ's? Our life is hid with Christ in God. Who hid it? God. Who can take it away? None. God cannot change. Here am I, going on to ninety-one, near my earthly end: but I am ready, blessed be God; he is my support, and though I walk through the valley of the shadow of death, I will fear no evil.'"

A conference was held in Medford on the 12th of February, in which Mr. Whittemore took part with much earnestness of feeling. There was a good attendance, although the day was unpropitious.

The 20th of February finds him at the public-house of Mr. Tuttle, in Acton, Mass. The occasion was a congratulatory one on the part of the friends of temperance. The proprietor of the house had resolved to keep it clear from the evil of liquor-selling for one year, at the end of which time he was satisfied of the wisdom of his course, in which opinion his fellow-citizens agreed with him; and, as an expression of their good-will towards him, proposed that a public supper should take place at his home. It was largely attended; and after the feast at the table, other exercises followed. Mr. Whittemore made an address to the company, in which, after a brief reference to the occasion, he spoke of the evils of intemperance; the blessings of temperance; present obstacles to the temperance reform: the pernicious nature of the rum-selling business; that it is opposed to the public good; is not an honorable calling, like that of the carpenter, mason, tailor, blacksmith, etc.; that many of the dealers are themselves ashamed of it; that they devise means to hide the real nature of the business from public observation; that it is the duty of the State to guard the public good, &c. After speaking with strong effect for fifty minutes, he was followed by others, who indorsed the sentiments that had been uttered. Rev. Mr. Frost of Concord, Rev. Mr. Dyar of Stow, Rev. Mr. Woodbury of Acton, Dr. Bartlett and Mr. Bowers of Concord, and Mr. Bean of Warner, N.H., were the other speakers. Temperance songs were sung between the addresses. Mr. Whittemore writes: "It was fully proved on that evening, that there can be a free flow of social feeling, wit, pun, and merriment, without wine or any alcoholic stimulant. It seemed to us that we never saw a happier company. Crowded as the hall was, we could not see that a single person left until all the exercises were concluded, at about half-past ten. Persons of all religious sects were there, and one common impulse seemed to possess their souls."

In the *Trumpet* of March 8, there is a notice by the editor of an opposer, who takes occasion to denounce said journal, in these expressive terms: —

"Mr. Whittemore: I say down with the *Trumpet*. It is an infamous publication. It has done more hurt than you could do good, if you should be converted to-morrow and live until you are one hundred years old. You are a God-defying sinner, and you will go to hell. I hope you will be forsaken by your subscribers. Your paper is a scourge. Down with the *Trumpet!*" To this lively tirade the trumpeter replies: "These seem to be days of 'cursing and bitterness.' The vials of fury are poured out on our head. Thank God, we will bear it without flinching, and say of these opposers, so full of wrath, 'Father, forgive them, for they know not what they do.' We have never harmed them; but their errors we hate, as God is said to hate a lying tongue and a froward heart. We regard the doctrine of endless misery as the great abomination of the age; the support of all priestcraft. No reforms can succeed well while this doctrine stands. If it be true, capital punishment is right, slavery is right, war is right, every other kind of sin is right. It was to oppose this doctrine, and priestcraft, and the designs of ardent sectarians, that the *Trumpet* was established nearly seventeen years ago. We gave it that name because we intended to 'sound an alarm in Zion.' By God's blessing, we have not swerved: we have adhered to the original design of the paper.

"And now our opposers cry, 'Down with the *Trumpet!*' Well, let us see them put it down. We know that the sound of it is unwelcome to them; but how will they stop it? that is the question. It is said to be an *infamous* publication, and why? Because it tells the plain truth. Truth always has been infamous, if we may believe errorists. The editor is said to be 'a God-defying sinner,' and is told that he shall 'go to hell.' It is a small matter to be judged of man's judgment. Those who express these threats cannot execute them. They are empty words, especially in this land of liberty. This opposer hopes we 'shall be forsaken by our subscribers.' Yes, but the hope of the hypocrite shall perish. Whether we shall be forsaken by our subscribers is a question for *them* to settle, and not for *him*. We are not yet forsaken, and publish a *few* papers now, after enduring the maledictions of our opponents for seventeen years. We think there is room enough for us to occupy a little longer."

It does not appear that Mr. Whittemore was present at the Rockingham Association this year, which was held in Brentwood, N.H. A good report of the meeting is given in his paper of Sept. 6.

The United States Convention of Universalists held its annual session this year (1845) in Boston. It was a great occasion, and there was a very large attendance. On Thursday morning, Sept. 16, — the steamboats from Maine and the trains from New York arriving so early that neither the *Trumpet* office nor Mr. Tompkins's store was open, — Cornhill on each side was well lined with delegates and others who were in waiting. School Street church was filled and running over with the multitude that had come to hear the Occasional Sermon by Rev. E. H. Chapin. It was repeated in the afternoon to another crowd in the Warren Street church. Meetings were held in different churches in and about Boston. Conference meetings of deep interest were also held. The communion service was observed on Thursday afternoon, at the First and Fifth churches. A largely attended meeting was held in the School Street church, on Friday morning, for the discussion of certain important subjects connected with the welfare of the denomination. Educational and reform interests, and the instrumentality of the press in the dissemination of Christian truth, were the main topics considered. The last resolution discussed and passed, but with a single "Nay," was the following on slavery, presented by Rev. Henry Bacon : —

" *Resolved*, that a Committee of five be appointed to prepare a solemn, earnest, and plain Protest against American Slavery, and, when prepared, to present it to every Universalist clergyman in the United States, for his signature ; respectfully requesting those who are not willing to sign it to give a reason for refusing; and when it has been fully circulated, and they have waited a reasonable time for answers, they shall publish the Protest and signatures, with the reasons offered by those who do not sign it."

The Committee chosen were, — Rev. Messrs. H. Bacon, E. H. Chapin, L. R. Paige, S. Cobb, and S. Streeter.

Mr. Whittemore says of this last meeting, that it was the best of the four days. "It must have an influence very much to be desired on our Academies, on Theological learning, on the Theological School at Clinton, on the Universalist press, and on the efforts of Universalists to aid in the philanthropic measures of the age. There was no radicalism, no come-out-ism; all was reasonable, Christian, affectionate, and patriotic. Thus closed the services of the four days. May God sanctify the whole to all who were present. Let the truth prevail over all the earth; and let all the people say ' Amen !'"

Two hundred and ten ministers were present at the Convention.

The installation of Rev. W. H. Ryder as pastor of the Universalist Church in Nashua, N.H., took place on Christmas day this year. The installation discourse was by Rev. A. A. Miner. Mr. Whittemore preached in the evening.

Mr. Whittemore speaks with approval of some parts of Mr. R. W. Emerson's lecture on Swedenborg, particularly that statement in it respecting the impossibility of the existence of pure malignity. Mr. Emerson had said of the Swedish seer: "He believed in devils, objective devils. But that pure malignity should exist is a contradiction. Goodness and being are one. To deny this is atheism, the last profanation. Old Euripides, pagan as he is, may teach us that ' goodness and being with the gods are one ; he who imputes evil to them makes them none.' Yet Swendenborg admits no return for the sinful spirit. At death its condition is fixed and final. If man were an azote, or a salt, or an alkali, he might never change, and it would be best that he should not. But he is a spirit and is never stationary. Must and lees will work themselves clear, carrion in the sun will purify itself, and turn into flowers and clover ; and with man, wherever he is found, — in brothels, in prisons, on the gallows, — the tendency is always upward." "This," says Mr. Whittemore, "is sound philosophy ; it is the basis of Universalism."

In the *Trumpet* of Feb. 1, 1846, Mr. Whittemore has some more plain words in reference to the Temperance cause, and the attempts of those called orthodox Christians to monopolize its work, and have special guardianship of its interests. Dr. Edwards, a somewhat prominent orthodox temperance lecturer, had been affirming that the great object of the temperance reform was not to save men from being drunkards here, but from being made for ever miserable hereafter. As Mr. Whittemore thus understands the matter, he says : "We have no sympathy with such a design. We will do every thing we can for the cause of temperance, but nothing to build up orthodoxy. One great reason why the orthodox took ground against the Washingtonian Reform was, because it was begun and carried on without their aid. The six men who formed the original Washingtonian Society in Baltimore, and who thus commenced a moral movement that gave an impulse to the cause of temperance which it never will or can get over, were men independent of all sects. It was this which turned many of the orthodox clergy and others of their churches against this reform, and led them to stigmatize the reformed drunkard who undertook to be a lecturer as 'a gutter graduate,' and expect his downfall and return to his cups. The cloven foot of orthodoxy was never more plainly seen than in the position it assumed in regard to Washingtonianism. We urge on Universalists the duty of maintaining their devotion to the great and glorious cause of Temperance. Fail not, flinch not. The cause belongs to no sect: it belongs to the world. No man has any right to exclude his neighbor from its benefits or honors. We say, then, to Universalists, ' Pray on, fight on.' "

The " Protest against American Slavery," signed by 304 Universalist clergymen, appears in the *Trumpet* of April 18 of this year. It was copied into other denominational papers. These reasons are stated as the basis of the Protest : —

1. Because slavery denies the eternal distinction between a man and property, ranking a human being with a material thing. 2. Because it does not award to the laborer the fruits of his toil, in any higher sense than to the cattle. 3. Because it trammels the intellectual powers and prevents their expansion. 4. Because it checks the development of the moral nature of the slave ; denies him rights and thereby responsibility. 5. Because it involves a practical denial of the religious nature of the slave. 6. Because it presents an insurmountable barrier to the propagation of the great truth of the Universal Brotherhood, and thereby most effectually prevents the progress of true Christianity. 7. Because the essential nature of Slavery cannot be altered by any kindness, how great soever, practised towards the slave. 8. Because the long continuance of a system of wrong cannot palliate it, but, on the other hand, augments the demand for its abolition. 9. Because we would in all charity remember that peculiarities of situation may affect the judgment and moral sense ; still, we must not forget that no peculiarity of situation can excuse a perpetual denial of universal principles and observations.

Reasons for not signing the Protest were sent to the Committee appointed to prepare it, and these are published in connection with the Protest itself. About forty different reasons, in substance, were given, most of them calculated to elicit the liveliest discussion, and some of them evincing a lack of earnest attention to the vital merits of the question. One was especially noteworthy, because of its apparently indifferent and implicit reliance on the divine decrees! It runs thus: "As God works all things after the counsel of his own will, he has permitted the blacks to be enslaved by the American people, and works that slavery according to his will, and has not influenced me to act in the matter; and my not being a free agent, I cannot sign your Circular."

Mr. Whittemore was one of the signers of the Protest. The tone of it was every way creditable to the church which sent it out, and was one of the influences that helped to effect the downfall of American Slavery.

In one of two editorials, Mr. Whittemore speaks with much freedom and earnestness on the trashy fiction sent forth at the time from the press, and having so large a circulation among ready readers throughout the land. As a Christian minister and journalist, he gives a timely utterance on this subject: —

"It is much to be lamented that our periodical literature has fallen so low in this country. Science is an old and stale affair. Morals, history, in fact every thing that is *real* seems to have lost its power to interest: the community and the world are gaping after fiction, fiction. Hence by far the greater part of the periodicals of our country are given up to this species of writing. Novels from France, Germany, Sweden, England, Scotland, Ireland, and almost everywhere else, are brought over, and fairly (or rather unfairly) flood the country. In addition to fictions imported, are to be mentioned those of a domestic origin. All the love-sick boys and girls, and old maids (as we should think), have taken up the writing of stories, almost all of them beginning, progressing, and ending in love. There is need of great reform in these matters.

The papers which are given up to such publications are the very bane of youthful society, and for the amount of damage which they do are to be classed with the grog-shops. They are most of them downright impositions on the community. They vitiate the public taste, and, besides being destitute of truth, have sometimes the effect to excite feelings that lead the young astray. We advise fathers and mothers to keep a good lookout as to what their children read."

The Massachusetts Universalist Convention held its annual session this year in Hingham. Among other business of importance, the following resolution was introduced by Rev. C. H. Fay, and, after being discussed by the mover and others, was adopted : —

" *Resolved*, That this Convention recommend to the Universalists of New England, to form an association to be known as the New England General Reform Association, which shall meet annually in Boston during 'Anniversary Week ;' having for its object the collection of such statistical information relative to the various reform movements of the age, as illustrates not only the progress of Christianity as we understand it, but the best means of promoting and applying it."

A Committee of twelve was appointed to carry into effect this resolution ; viz., Revs. C. H. Fay, T. Whittemore, E. H. Chapin, H. Ballou 2d, J. G. Adams, S. Cobb, A. A. Miner, J. M. Spear, B. B. Mussey, Esq., T. A. Goddard, A. Mudge, A. Tompkins.

At the first meeting of this Committee, preparations were made for the first public meeting of the Association in May, 1847. Committees on a Constitution, of Arrangements for the meeting, on Resolutions, and on a Circular to the public, setting forth the objects of the Association, were appointed.

Little reverence had our brother for that class of reformers who thought they saw in some modern discoveries a clearer interpretation of the miraculous powers affirmed in the New Testament than the world had hitherto known. One of this class gives publicity to his views in this strain: "It is more than probable that the key to the miraculous powers exercised by men in all past time is found in the wonderful discoveries of animal magnetism. If the evidence of Messiahship rests on miraculous power, the moment that the discovery is made that the so-called miraculous power is a faculty appertaining to developed man, at that moment the seal is broken, the proof of Messiahship is lost." In noticing these statements, he calls upon those who have faith in them and are experimenting in animal magnetism to try and see what they can effect in the new line of miracle-working, and thus show their faith by their doings. "Let us see," he writes, "the power of magnetism in working miracles. True, we cannot understand how *animal* magnetism can operate on the rock, or on the sea, or on loaves and dead fishes; but we ignorant creatures who know nothing about *philosophy* perchance do not understand all these matters, and need to be instructed. Let some magnetizer or magnetized strike a rock and cause the waters to gush out; let him calm the billows of the sea; let him feed thousands of hungry persons to satiety with a few loaves and fishes, and gather up afterwards twelve baskets of fragments. Do let us see something of this kind. Do not, gentlemen, philosophers, keep all these things to yourselves.

"But hark ye, readers! If these men attempt this, we will tell you how they will succeed; somewhat as did the ' vagabond Jews ' of whom we read in the 19th chapter of Acts. God had wrought special miracles by the hand of Paul, so that he healed men of their diseases, and calmed the madness of the mind. Then ' certain of the vagabond Jews ' took it upon them to do the same things by calling over the name of the Lord Jesus. There were seven sons of one Sceva, a Jew, who tried their hands at it ; but neither of them, not even the *seventh son*, was able to succeed. They said to the mad man, ' We adjure you by Jesus whom Paul preacheth.' Oh the hypocrites! thus to crowd themselves into Christian company. What did they care for Jesus whom Paul preached? Even the madman knew they were a set of impostors ; for he said, ' Jesus I know, and Paul I know, but who are ye?' And then he fell upon them and overcame them, so that they fled out of the house naked and wounded.

" Let some of our philosophers who tell us that the miracles of Christ were wrought by animal magnetism, try to work miracles like his by that power, and they will suffer as much chagrin as did ' the vagabond Jews.' "

During the latter part of Mr. Whittemore's life as an editor and publisher, his office was at the stand since known as the " Universalist Publishing House," 37 Cornhill. It was a place where much active business was done ; a place where all visitors, all sects, and especially those of the Universalist faith, were made welcome, and where our church clergy were exceedingly glad to congregate. The proprietor of the establishment had a welcome word and hand for all. Whether from city or country, from near or far-off places, those who came were easily made to feel themselves at home. Few of our common faith residing in New England could enter the office without receiving a recognition from him. He had preached to them, had conversed with them in their own towns, had shared the warm hospitalities of their homes, had held business conferences or mingled with them in the social walks of life. He had a pleasant or witty or tender word for all.

The ministers' meetings at the office, most largely attended on Mondays, were among the very strong attractions at

Cornhill. Most of those living in the neighborhood of Boston, and usually some from other and distant places in or out of Massachusetts, would be present. And the conferences then and there held were often highly enjoyable. Knotty theological problems were encountered and discussed; the latest attacks on the common faith criticised; church duties proposed and debated; historical reminiscences brought up, persons, and anecdotes of them called back from the past and re-enjoyed. Breezy talk generally abounded. The logical sharpness of a Ballou; the spicy parish relatings of a Streeter or Skinner; the strong argumentative sentences of a Cobb; the racy witticisms of Chapin, Starr King, Ballou 2d, Paige, and the Trumpeter himself, were often parts of the Monday morning programme, and all alike enjoyed by others of the neighboring ministers and laymen, or by fresh visitors from more remote residences, who would be sure to take away with them most agreeable and lasting remembrances of these interviews.

Opposite 37, Mr. Abel Tompkins for a long time kept his bookstore; a home for all representatives of Universalism, equally welcome to the fraternity with that of the *Trumpet's* editor. Here the first Universalist Sabbath-school paper was published, and the "Ladies' Repository," and the sweet "Rose of Sharon," whose fragrance yet lives in many a memory. Conferences like those already described were often enjoyed there also. Mr. B. B. Mussey's publishing-house and bookstore was also near, where visitors to these other houses always found a cordial reception from the gentlemanly and generous proprietor. Cornhill is still an attraction to Universalists, and long may it be; but it must grow greatly in interest to be more attractive than in those tenderly remembered and felicitous days of the past.

Another journey to the United States Convention. This

time it is at Troy, N.Y. A full and pleasantly descriptive
account of the passage from New York city up the Hudson
is given in an editorial letter. The Convention opened with
a Sabbath-school meeting on Tuesday. An Address in the
evening on Sunday-school work was given by Mr. Charles F.
Eaton of Boston. Discourses were preached by Rev. Asher
Moore (Occasional), Rev. E. M. Pingree, Rev. O. A. Skinner,
Rev. E. H. Chapin, Rev. D. Skinner, Rev. H. Bacon. Excellent conference meetings were held, in which Mr. Whittemore took part. The Universalist Historical Society had
several interesting and satisfactory meetings, and a collection
of fifty dollars was taken for the purchase of books.

In his comments on the Convention, Mr. Whittemore takes
occasion to signify his very strong desire that the Convention
should adhere more closely to the work for which it was
formed, and not allow so much of its time to be frittered away
in the discussions of topics foreign to this design. "The
Convention was formed, as we understand it, to effect a one-
ness of interest in the order throughout the United States.
Has this been done? Have the interests of the denomination
throughout the country been consolidated? We think not.
Another object of this Convention was, to communicate
useful information in regard to the denomination in all sections of the United States; and it is made the duty of each
State Convention to forward to the general body, in some
form, information respecting the condition and prospect of the
cause within its limits. This was done for several years after
the organization of the Convention. The Reports sent in
1835 were models of what ought to be done. But this important duty is now wholly neglected." He is suspicious that
" Reform" topics as they come in, have a tendency to make
less important the other work for which the Convention was
organized.

The Boston Association was held this year in Malden. Among other resolutions passed was one offered by Rev. J. G. Adams, that a Missionary Society be established within the limits of this Association, immediately. Messrs. Whittemore, E. H. Chapin, and A. A. Miner were appointed a Committee to prepare a Constitution of a Home Missionary Society. Rev. W. R. G. Mellen delivered the Occasional Discourse.

A letter appears in the *Trumpet* of Nov. 1, from the distinguished English Baptist divine, Rev. Robert Hall, of date April 30, 1821, in which is acknowledged his perplexities in regard to the doctrine of the eternity of punishment. In his notice of the letter, Mr. Whittemore says: "Mr. Hall does not seem to have believed in endless misery, but to have *acquiesced* in it. That is the term he used. 'I acquiesced in the usual and popular interpretation of the passages which treat on the future doom of the finally impenitent.' As to the supposed arguments offered by Mr. Hall in favor of the doctrine in question, we refer our readers to the works of Rev. John Foster. In his letter to a young clergyman he answers them all. Mr. Hall moreover says that belief in endless punishment is never proposed as a term of salvation. He further states that the evidence on which the doctrine of endless suffering rests 'is by no means to be compared to that which establishes our common Christianity; and therefore the fate of the Christian religion is not to be considered as implicated in the belief or disbelief of the popular doctrine.' We commend the sentiments of Mr. Hall to the serious consideration of our American Baptists."

He also notes with gratification the statement of Rev. Dr. Pond of the Bangor Theological Seminary, who says in an article in the *New England Puritan*, — in reference to the wide prevalence of the opinions of Swedenborgians, Universalists, and Unitarians: "It has come to this, that when the doctrines of divine sovereignty, of total depravity, of the consequent necessity of regeneration, of a general judgment, and of the endless punishment of the wicked, are plainly preached, and the most positive language of Scripture is quoted in proof of them; there are not a few in our congregations who are ready to say, 'All this may be so or may not be so; there are different opinions in regard to these points; these passages of Scripture are variously interpreted, and who can tell how much or how little is to be depended on?'" Mr. Whittemore regards this as an admission from an unquestionable source, that the leaven of divine truth is working in many of the orthodox churches.

The *Christian Reflector*, a Baptist journal of Boston, takes occasion to speak of what it considers the "Universalist Estimate of Revivals." He asserts that they vent their malignity when they hear of the outpouring of the Holy Spirit on the churches and the impenitent; that they cannot endure the scenes of primitive times, of Pentecostal and other revivals; to have the heavens "drop down from above," and the skies to "pour down righteousness." To this Mr. Whittemore replies: "We should be glad to see 'an outpouring of the Holy Spirit, on the churches and the impenitent;' but we believe that many persons use these phrases who little understand the true meaning of them. Moreover, there are few things less like 'the outpouring of the Holy Spirit' than a partialist excitement called a revival. 'The scenes of primitive times' we should be glad to see repeated on the earth; but the revival on the day of Pentecost, and other revivals under the preaching of the apostles, were not produced by the preaching of endless torments, but by the preaching of the love of God. If the Baptists would only convert people as they were converted in the days of the apostles, we would join with them in heart and hand. We pray fervently, let the heavens 'drop down from above,' and the skies 'pour down righteousness;' but we also pray, 'Deliver us, O Lord, from fanaticism, falsehood, priestcraft, and deceit.' Will the *Reflector* understand *now?* or will it accuse us again of being inimical to revivals of pure religion?"

During these days when Mr. Whittemore and many of his brethren were advocating so strongly the setting up of institutions for the better education of the Universalist ministry, he is called to encounter that kind of opposition to this work which some other sects have realized in the first stages of their growth in this country. In the instance now noticed, it is that of a minister in the West, a man of good natural ability and editor of a Universalist journal. He has read an appeal made by Rev. S. R. Smith to the ministers of the Universalist Church, that one hundred of them, if possible, subscribe one hundred dollars each (making a sum of ten thousand) towards the founding of the proposed literary and theological institution. The appeal was a reasonable and manly one.

But the Western editor did not thus regard it. He was not in favor of " the elevation of the Universalist ministry," not deeming it consistent with the spirit and character of the Christian ministry to elevate the clergy above the laity, as that course had always created a religious aristocracy. " Give the people the New Testament," says this sturdy opposer of theological institutions, " and they can learn from that all theology necessary for them to know without having to pay a self-created aristocratic priesthood. Such expensive church lumber is altogether unnecessary. Give the people the New Testament; let them study it themselves, and they can know as much of its doctrine as a priest can tell them."

It is for Mr. Whittemore to answer such intolerable rant. "In the name of common sense," he asks, " who ever desired to ' elevate the clergy above the laity in any' other sense than to fill their minds with knowledge, that they might be competent to elevate the people? How can the people be elevated unless the teachers are? There are in our land, in the West we suppose, as well as in the East, institutions to fit men to be teachers of academies and common schools. Why does not our brother apply his logic here? ' What! elevate the teachers above the people? Has not this always created an aristocracy?' Such is his logic. A teacher must know more than those he is to teach. Why does our brother preach if he cannot teach the people any thing? And which is the most aristocratic, to qualify a minister so that he can really elevate the people, or to let him keep on preaching and receiving support as a clergyman when he can teach them nothing at all? Who cannot see that our brother's position is unsound? The truth is, people need no other religion than is embraced in the New Testament. But there are many helps to the understanding of that book; and a class of such men ' duly and truly prepared,' humble, faithful, honest teachers, will be blessings to society."

CHAPTER IX.

1847–1849.

AGED 47–49.

Too lively — A visit South — Reform Association — J. Victor Wilson — Dr. Bushnell — Rockingham Association at Brentwood, N.H. — U.S. Convention at New York — John M. Edgarton — Duty of an editor — Andrew Jackson Davis and his Revelations — Boston Association at Lynn — Extra Session at Cambridgeport — Anti-Sabbath Convention — Commentary on the Apocalypse — Reform Festival — Purity of the Ministry — Rockingham Association at Epping, N.H. — Ignorance of Universalism — Boston Association — Christian Progress — Too controversial.

OUR brother's *Trumpet* had been called too warlike. Now the complaint comes that it is too lively; that is, that its strains are not solemn enough, that there is something altogether too cheerful in them. The editor pleads not guilty. "It is true," says he, "we do not write as though we stood on the brink of endless despair. We discard all the repulsive features of Calvinism. We keep the good of that system, and cast the bad away. We believe that God is good; that virtue is happiness; that heaven is the state of the pure and rational soul; that all men are the offspring of God; and that he will finally overrule all things for good. Why then shall we not be cheerful? Why may not the *Trumpet* sound a joy-inspiring note? God calls upon us to rejoice before him. The saints of old used to shout aloud for joy. Heaven is full of joy, especially when sinners are saved. One of the judgments denounced against Rome, in the Apocalypse, which was to be regarded as a proof of her downfall and her sadness, was that the voice of the *Trumpet* should be heard within her borders no more. (Rev. xviii. 22.) We live not in the city of spiritual Babylon; but in the holy city of New Jerusalem; and we will, agreeably to the injunction in Psalm xcviii. 6, ' with trumpet make a joyful noise, before the Lord the king.' ' Blessed is the people that know the joyful sound.' "

In May of this year, Mr. Whittemore visited Fredericksburg, Va. He gives, in letters in the *Trumpet*, a very interesting account of his journey. It is full of descriptions of places and of historical reminiscences. He tarried awhile in New York city to attend a Convention called to consider the educational interests of the Universalist denomination. He listened to a discourse of deep interest to him and others, from Rev. T. J. Sawyer, on German Rationalism, — a timely and able effort. He spent a day in Baltimore; visited Washington and Mount Vernon. Of the tomb of Washington and its occupants, he writes: "On the lid of the sarcophagus is wrought the arms of his country; and the only epitaph (but how expressive!) is the one word, ' *Washington.*' What significance! Volumes could not have told more. And on the other coffin, ' Martha, consort of Washington.' The gratitude of his country has been irrepressible; monuments have been reared; statues have been carved; counties, cities, and towns have adopted his name; the capital of the nation is itself Washington; but, after all, the man, the illustrious man, adorned with the highest virtues of our race, is, and for ever will be, his own monument. All the means by which the memory of great men has been perpetuated in times past are superseded by him. His name must live for ever."

Washington, the national capitol there, and other buildings, are particularly described in these letters. He preaches in the Universalist church in Baltimore on the Sabbath, and then returns home. Reviewing his very pleasant journey, he takes occasion to pay a tribute to "home, sweet home." "Our gardens do not come into bloom so early as those in Virginia, but it is 'home' notwithstanding. Boston is our native city. We love the air of Boston, even its cold north winds: they make men rugged. We love its business character, its free schools, the development of mind in it, its good order, its liberality of religious sentiment, its enterprise, its cleanliness. True, our domicile is not within the city bounds, but it is just the other side of Charles River, in one of the sweetest, most quiet, and orderly villages in Massachusetts. Cambridgeport for ever!"

During the absence of Mr. Whittemore in Virginia, the first meeting of the Universalist Reform Association was held during "Anniversary Week" in Boston. Addresses were offered on the following subjects; viz., on Peace, by Rev. J. G. Adams; on Criminal Reform, by Rev. J. M. Spear; on Temperance, by Rev. A. A. Miner; on Human Freedom, by Rev. S. Cobb. The first Festival (breakfast) at Washington Hall, in Bromfield Street, was an occasion never afterwards forgotten by those who attended it. Richard Frothingham, Jr., of Charlestown, presided, who introduced the intellectual repast admirably. He was followed by the ministers, C. H. Fay, A. A. Miner, J. G. Adams, S. Cobb, H. Bacon, E. H. Chapin, H. Ballou, S. Streeter, E. Thompson, J. S. Dennis, J. M. Spear, and P. H. Sweetser, Esq., of South Reading. The speakers were in their happiest moods, and under their strongest inspirations. Mr. Chapin's speech was a torrent of eloquence; the venerable Ballou's, an uplifting benediction. It was a grand inauguration of the Reform Association. Mr. Whittemore regretted his absence from it. The excellent report of the Festival in the *Trumpet* was from the pen of Rev. T. Starr King.

In the *Trumpet*, of July 3, there is recorded the sudden death of a young man (J. Victor Wilson) of more than ordinary promise, who had elicited on the part of Mr. Whittemore much interest in his behalf. He was employed in the publishing office for some time, and was the author of the work entitled, " Reasons for our Hope ; or, the Bible a Universalist Book ; " a work which shows that he had great industry in the study of the Scriptures, and a peculiar faculty at the classification of proofs. The little work had quite a large circulation, and deserves a place in the Christian Church henceforth.

It was in this year that the tract on " Christian Nurture," afterwards enlarged to a small volume, from the pen of Rev. Dr. Bushnell, of Hartford, Ct., appeared. The tract was approved by the Committee of Publication of the Massachusetts Sabbath School Society. It was declared by some to be a most valuable work. Upon examination, however, by the Unitarians, it was found to contain many very reasonable thoughts and doctrines on the subject of human nature ; and, if carefully examined, it was seen to conflict directly and broadly with the doctrine of total depravity. The Unitarians expressed their admiration of the tract. This caused a re-examination of it on the part of the orthodox, and it came under condemnation. Even the committee who had examined and approved it now withdrew their approbation, and had the tract suppressed. But this only served to increase the demand for it, and it soon came to be read extensively, and is now regarded with much favor by many of the more advanced thinkers in the orthodox ranks, and by Christians of liberal views generally. It was the beginning of a series of volumes which afterwards came from the able pen of Dr. Bushnell, and which have served to modify and change in no small degree the old puritanic theology of New England. Mr. Whittemore, of course, took particular notice of the flutter occasioned in certain quarters by the discovery that the new tract was in contradiction of some of the Calvinism of the past.

In August, he is present again at the Rockingham Association. It was held in Brentwood, N.H., this year, and was largely attended on both days of the session. Four or five discourses were preached, one by Mr. Whittemore, and conferences were held. Mr. Whittemore closes a notice of the meeting in his paper, by noting the different kinds of Universalists in the county of Rockingham, and fervently exhorting them to union and work under the one great Master and Lord.

The session of the United States Convention this year, in New York city, was one of great interest. One of the largest Sabbath-school meetings yet known at any session of this body was held in the Bleecker Street church, and an Occasional Address given by Rev. J. G. Adams. The Occasional Sermon before the Convention was delivered by Rev. H. Ballou, D.D. Mr. Whittemore writes: "It was pronounced by many of the clergy the most powerful discourse ever delivered by that distinguished man, to which, so far as our knowledge goes, we do cordially agree. We can give no epitome of this sermon that will give the reader any competent idea of it." His topic was, "The Responsibility of Universalists in the Position they now hold before God and the World." It was listened to with intense interest in that long hour, and has been doing its work in our churches ever since. Discourses were preached in different churches, and conferences of unusual interest held. On Friday, there was an Educational Convention in the Orchard Street church. It was there voted that a general agent be appointed to solicit subscriptions, to the amount of $100,000, for the erection of college buildings.

In the *Trumpet* of Oct. 9, Mr. Whittemore very tenderly notices the death of Mr. John M. Edgarton, of Shirley, Mass., a brother of Mrs. Sarah C. E. Mayo. He was in expectation of entering the ministry at the time of his decease. His intimate friend, Rev. T. Starr King, writes of him: "His mind was of the first order. To great acuteness of thought was united an expansive view of every subject which he treated; and very few have ever possessed in such harmonious union those qualities of intellect so rarely conjoined, — metaphysical exactness and philosophical breadth. His style of composition was admirable, and would have given him a high rank among the cultivated writers of the day. At this time, when the great need of our denomination is men of education and commanding intellectual power, we feel that the Universalist public have sustained in his death an almost irreparable loss."

In an animated article on the "Duty of an Editor," Mr. Whittemore makes this plea for the press: "What is the duty of editors? We reply, to set their faces like a flint against the prostitution of the press. The press! A noble engine! The lever that moves the moral world! In the hands of good men, how useful! In those of the bad, how dangerous! The conductors of the press should be men of ability, of good judgment, of good morals, of uncontaminating thoughts. They preside at the fountains at which all the people drink; and would you have the fountains poisoned? The public does not seem to be aware of the responsibility of editors, and the immense power which they wield for good or for evil over the destinies of the republic. If any men ought to be held to a strict accountability, it is they. We talk of the influence of the pulpit. One newspaper, with a circulation of five thousand, has the influence of fifty clergymen; for such a paper is read by at least fifty thousand persons. When its articles are copied into other journals, its influence may be doubled and trebled. We hope Universalist readers will hold their editors to a strict accountability; and if they find the tone of their press wavering, or speaking in any way to foster corruption, or division, or political party spirit, or any thing that is not for the good of man and the advancement of the Gospel, let it be promptly discountenanced. Whatever other sects may have, let Universalists cherish a pure press."

In these days there appeared a bulky volume, purporting to be " Revelations " from a higher sphere than that of the earthly, coming through Andrew Jackson Davis. A few Universalist ministers were quite forward in giving it a welcome, professing to regard it as a spiritual light in advance of all others that had yet appeared. Rev. T. J. Sawyer, then of Clinton, N.Y., gave the book a pretty sharp notice, and made some expositions of the cordial reception it had met with by those professing to be teachers of Christian Universalism. Mr. Whittemore indorses Mr. Sawyer's opinion of the work. Speaking for himself and others near him, he says: " We believe the book to be an infidel publication; and that, if our ministers who have accepted it as a new and higher revelation from heaven have fully considered what they are doing, there is no Christian faith in them. We hope the time will come when the Universalist denomination will not be the receptacle of every strange thing under heaven." Mr. Davis, in after years, gave it as his serious conviction that Spiritualism (which his " Revelations " advocated) had been relied upon altogether too much *as a religion;* thus verifying these criticisms to which we have here alluded.

The Boston Association held its annual session this year in

November, at Lynn. The first day was given to business, the last to public religious services. The important business, however, seemed to have been left until the last day. A very vigorous discussion came up in reference to the faith necessary to constitute a person a Universalist. There seemed to be an impression among a large number of the ministers and lay delegates that it was time to define what Christian faith is, in order to meet the exigencies of the times. The main question seemed to be, whether a man ought to be sustained as a Christian clergyman who sets aside the peculiarly divine character of Jesus Christ, and the account given of his miracles in the Scriptures, and of his resurrection, the greatest miracle of all. It was thought that a person who did not believe in the resurrection of Jesus could not be in faith a Christian; and no one who disavows miracles can believe in his resurrection. There had been such signs of defection among certain self-styled reformers, that it was deemed necessary for the Association to define the ground on which it stood. And there was an evident readiness for this step on the part of the attendants at that meeting.

The subject was discussed with much ability on Thursday; but there was not time to come to a definite conclusion. The Association, therefore, adjourned to Cambridgeport, there to hold an extraordinary session on Wednesday, the first day of December.

This session was well attended, and a very deep interest was evinced in its proceedings. Rev. A. A. Miner was Moderator of the meeting, and Rev. E. Fisher, Clerk. The Resolution presented at the former session at Lynn, and reported again at the present one, was the following, offered by a committee appointed for the purpose : —

" *Resolved*, That this Association express its solemn conviction, that, in order for one to be regarded as a Christian minister with respect to faith, he must believe in the Bible account of the life, teachings, miracles, death, and resurrection of the Lord Jesus Christ."

A minority report by one of the Committee was offered, as follows : —

"*Resolved*, That the articles of faith adopted by the General Convention of Universalists in 1803 are sufficient for all practical purposes, as it respects the Christian belief."

The first question before the meeting at Cambridgeport was the unfinished business at Lynn; viz., the motion to set aside the Resolution offered by the committee, and substitute the minority report. At the beginning of the discussion, a motion prevailed, by a large vote, that no person should speak more than fifteen minutes at a time; nor more than once, if any other wished to speak: a wise resolution, which prevented long and tedious speeches.

The discussion was pertinent and animated. The chief speakers in favor of the Resolution offered by the majority of the Committee were, — Rev. Messrs. E. Fisher, L. R. Paige, S. Cobb, T. Whittemore, T. D. Cook, C. H. Fay, H. Ballou 2d, J. G. Adams, H. Ballou, A. A. Miner. Those in advocacy of the minority Resolution were, — Rev. Messrs. J. W. Hanson, J. Prince, J. M. Spear, E. Thompson.

Mr. Whittemore, in his remarks, said that "he wished no other rule than what we have in the Profession of Faith made in 1803. But he did not want this Profession to be put to a perfidious use. He was perfectly satisfied with the Convention's Profession, if it were received in the same sense in which the Convention uttered it. We have no right to put an utterly different sense on that Profession from that which the Convention put upon it, and then claim that we believe it. This was doing by the Profession what some men did by the Bible: they made an entirely different book of it from

what was originally intended, and then claimed to be believers in the Bible. We must receive the Bible in its true
and proper sense; in the sense its different authors attached
to it. Here are men around us who are unwilling to receive
the Bible account of the life, teachings, miracles, death, and
resurrection of Christ. How then, in any true sense, can
they be said to receive the Convention's Profession of faith?
Is it to be supposed for one moment that the Committee who
drew up the Convention's Profession forty-five years ago,
believed as some do who oppose the main resolution here to-
day? Is it to be supposed that Zebulon Streeter did not
hold to the Bible account of Christ? Could this be said
of George Richards? or of Walter Ferris? or of Zephaniah
Lathe? Those four men were the Committee who drafted
the Convention's Profession, in connection with one other
individual; and it is a remarkable fact that the individual
referred to (the only surviving member of the Committee
appointed in 1802) was here present with us this day; and
the hand of that very individual drafted the Resolution which
some of the members of the present Association were seeking
to thrust aside. Was there, then, any contradiction between
the Convention's Profession and the Resolution of the Committee here to-day? None at all; they both agreed in spirit:
but the latter was brought in to guard the former against
misuse. Which was the most likely, that our venerable
Father Ballou would best know the real intent of the Convention's Profession of Faith, or those men who have been known
among us at the best but five or six years? If, therefore,"
said Mr. Whittemore, "the business should take such a form,
that he should be required to give a direct vote on the Committee's Resolution, he should certainly vote in the affirmative."

By a previous vote, the discussion was to close at half-past four o'clock. The Resolution of the Committee was sustained by a very large majority of the clergy and laity. Some of the few who voted for the minority Resolution affirmed that they did so, not because of their doubts of the Bible account of Christ, his works and his life, but because of their scruples as to the propriety of making this new statement at that time. That the movement was an exceedingly proper one, however, has been the conviction of by far the greater part of our churches and congregations of professed Universalists to this hour. It was a wise, timely, honest, and faithful utterance on their part against the loose German Rationalism and speculative free-thinking and doubting then so rife in New England and elsewhere; and in affirmation of their faith in the Christ of the New Testament, and his Gospel of Universal Grace and Salvation. Mr. Whittemore, some weeks after this decision at Cambridgeport, writes in the *Trumpet*: "Most of the laymen who come into our office—of whom there are many at this season of the year—speak with very high approbation of the late meeting of the Boston Association. All who express their opinions say to us, 'Stand by the Bible, Brother Whittemore: we shall never get any thing better.'" Again: "We did not know before the depth of the reverence for the Scriptures which the great body of Universalists entertained. We knew that great efforts had been made to spread false notions in regard to the divine character of the New Testament; and although Universalists from the beginning had been led to believe that the Bible is the Word of God; although they were so taught by Murray, Winchester, Barnes, Streeter, Richards, and others, — we did not know that the efforts of certain men to undermine our confidence in the Bible had been almost altogether *without effect*. Yet such seems to be the fact. The great body of the Universalist laity have proved their soundness in respect to the Bible."

In February of this year (1848), there appeared in the newspapers a call for an Anti-Sabbath Convention by Messrs. Garrison, Parker, Wright, Foster, and others, prominent anti-slavery men and advocates of reform. Mr. Whittemore gives in his paper an account of the meeting, which was held two days in the Melodeon; a meeting which he considered as designed to destroy "all reverence and all regard for the Sabbath as a day of sacred rest." There was not a unanimity of opinion on the part of those who had called the meeting. Rev. Theodore Parker introduced a series of resolutions expressive of a belief that the habit of assembling on the first day of the week, though not a sacred day, for the purposes of spiritual and moral instruction, was not amiss. The leaders, however, would not tolerate this idea. The whole platform objected to it. The Sabbath could never be broken down if people were encouraged to go to meeting on that day. On the second day, a vote was passed that none should speak in the meeting except such as were opposed to the Sabbath. Mr. Whittemore thus states his opinion of the meeting : "The whole affair of an Anti-Sabbath Convention strikes us as a most melancholy illustration of the folly and cruelty of all measures professing to have the public good in view, which are not based on the principles of the Bible, and are not conducted in the spirit of Christianity. Here are men professing to be special friends of the poor and the advocates of the oppressed, laboring with malignant energy to destroy that day of rest from servile labor, which is the poor man's richest earthly boon, and without which he must be exposed to unremitting toil ; and to deprive the community of the consolatory, improving, and elevating influences of the Sabbath, by shutting up the places of prayer and religious instruction, and destroying all special observance of the day as a season for assembling even for moral and intellectual improvement.

Such is Infidelity." Again, he says: "We wish to have it distinctly understood that we have no sympathy with the anti-Sabbath movement. There are rum-holes enough open now on Sunday; enough men riding about the vicinity of Boston, from one hotel to another, on that day; enough fighting, and other species of wickedness, without asking the Legislature to open the gates and let a full flood of wickedness in upon us. We speak not of the *intent* of the anti-Sabbath men, but of the unavoidable *effect* of their labors."

Another valuable work appears at this time from the pen of Mr. Whittemore. It is his Commentary on the Apocalypse, or Revelation of St. John. Much of it had appeared from time to time in the *Trumpet;* but its publication in book form gave to the Christian public a new and very instructive volume on this closing part of the New Testament, which had so tasked the wits of commentators as they had searched for its meaning. This new expositor makes his commentaries very plain, comparing Scripture with Scripture, and showing the great resemblances in the imagery of the Apocalypse and that used by Daniel and other Old Testament writers. It met the warm approval of the Universalist press; as one of our church editors wrote: "We did not suppose it possible to render the high-wrought imagery of this book so plain. Mr. Whittemore's commentary will give a new interest to it; and while it will rescue the book from the hands of visionaries and enthusiasts, who have imagination without judgment, it will cause it to be studied by the thoughtful, and those who value the Word of God for the rational and useful instruction it imparts."[1] Rev. Dr. Paige declined writing a commentary on the Apocalypse, because he wished that of Mr. Whittemore to accompany his own work on the other books of the New Testament.

<hr>

[1] Rev. O. A. Skinner.

The *Trumpet* of June 10, contains a lively editorial report of the second Reform Festival, held by the Universalists, in Boylston Hall, Boston, during Anniversary Week of this year. There was a large company at the tables. Mr. B. B. Mussey was President, and made a very appropriate and fervent opening address. The principal speakers after him were, Rev. A. A. Miner, Rev. J. G. Adams, Richard Frothingham, Esq., Rev. H. Bacon, Rev. Dr. Ballou, Rev. L. C. Brown, Mr. Charles Marsh, and Father Ballou, who used those striking words that were so remembered afterwards: "Changes are not always improvements : we must not forget the first principles of truth. We use the same numerals now that were used of old, and the first principles of numeration and multiplication still hold good. We do not forsake them. We find use for the same sun, moon, and stars now which people used to see thousands of years ago. Don't throw every thing behind you. Do not suppose that you are going to *surprise your Maker* by any operation that you can perform !"

The speech of Rev. E. H. Chapin was a fitting one to conclude the series. He was in his happiest vein. Exhorting to hopefulness in the work of reform, he spoke of the little drummer in McDonald's division, when that celebrated General passed the Splugen with his forces. "Into one of the vast fissures, the little drummer fell as they were marching along. There was no hope of deliverance for him ; but he kept on beating his drum as though nothing had happened. Let us be faithful to our duty. Humanity is on a grand movement to victory. Let us beat our march well ; and if we meet with obstacles, with dangers, let us beat on, for *we shall come off victorious at last !*"

Wise and thoughtful are the words of the editor on the "Purity of the Ministry :" —

"There are other indispensable qualifications for the ministry, but purity stands above them all. A bad clergyman will do more harm than twenty good ones can counteract, just as one incendiary can kindle more fires than a whole town or city can extinguish. Bad men of good talents are the most dangerous men in the world. They are somewhat like insane persons with fire-arms. It has fallen to our lot some three or four times, in the course of our public life, to see men of good, yea, even of splendid talents, who were dishonest. They would find their way easily into the affections of others, who were generally honest themselves, and therefore unsuspecting. When once the bad preacher gets enthroned in the affections of a church or congregation, it is very difficult to give him up. They admire his eloquence, are captivated by his winning ways. They hear evil reports concerning him, but they cannot believe them. If they believed them, they would not sustain him for a single hour. But all seems improbable to them. It is so different from his preaching, from his professions, and his public walk, that they cannot believe the evil spoken of him. When they go to him with these matters, he will always have some explanation on the tip of his tongue, for his mind (perhaps from long practice), will be familiar with all kinds of pretexts, expedients, and tergiversations. He will have some way to turn, some excuse to give, which will serve his purposes for the time. But this state of things cannot long be. There must be a *dénoûment*, an end. Sin, by the decree of God, can have no long triumphs. But in the case of a pastor, the consequences will often be lamentable. All the members of the society will not get their eyes open at once. Some will honestly take the ground that he is a bad man and must vacate his office; and others with equal honesty will believe that he is innocent and ought to be sustained. And so divisions come, and societies have thus been shaken and rent.

" The pure and impure will suffer together, because all will be suspected. 'Whom can we trust?' will be the inquiry. But let it be remembered that bad ministers furnish no argument against the genuineness of religion. These men are not bad because they practise the religion they recommend to others, but *because they do not.* It is not their religion, but their *want of it* which makes them wicked men. Let it be borne in mind, too, that where there is one minister who falls there are one hundred who do not; and if you denounce the whole, you make ninety and nine innocent persons suffer for the sins of one man."

Mr. Whittemore is present at the Rockingham Association, this year, at Epping, N.H. The weather during the meetings was excellent, the discourses were highly acceptable to the hearers, and the conference meetings very enjoyable. Mr. Whittemore preached the last afternoon. He says of the session that it partook more of the former character of the meetings of this body than any session of recent years.

He was unable to attend the United States Convention which met this year at Hartford, Ct.

In one of his editorials, we find these truthful thoughts on the ignorance of the Universalist faith so prevalent even among the professed lovers and advocates of the Christian religion: " Ignorance is the great foe of Universalism. This doctrine will be fully embraced by every person who fully understands it. It is so agreeable to reason, to the Scriptures properly interpreted, and to the benevolence of the human heart, that to be believed it needs only to be understood. The most of those who reject it are deceived in regard to the character of the doctrine. There is wide-spread misrepresentation. We ask the privilege of explaining our own doctrine. We do entreat most earnestly of the community that they will not receive the misrepresentations of our enemies as pure

Universalism. How can a man be qualified to explain Universalism who never read a book on the subject nor heard a lecture designed to illustrate it? And yet is it not true that a large majority of the opponents of Universalism at the present day never avail themselves of any means to become acquainted with that doctrine? Ignorance is the cause of all opposition to this sentiment. However wise the opponents of this doctrine may be in other respects, they are certainly ignorant of the doctrine itself. It was said of old, ' the world by wisdom (or philosophy) knew not God.' So we say, the world by wisdom knew not Universalism. Men who stand highest in worldly wisdom may be the greatest fools in regard to religion. The ancient Greeks were very wise men; but to them Christianity was foolishness. They were ignorant where they needed the highest wisdom. The way to convert men is to instruct them. Let every means be used to spread abroad a knowledge of the truth; and when the happy time shall come that knowledge shall cover the earth as the waters cover the sea, the truth shall be known, believed, loved, and rejoiced in by the whole intelligent creation. Amen."

Mr. Whittemore was Moderator of the Boston Association which met this year with the First Society in Lowell. Four discourses were preached, and a social conference held. The clerk of the session reports: " The business of the Association was very harmonious; and, although that part of it referring to a subject of discipline was of an unwelcome nature, it was met and disposed of in a spirit of brotherly kindness and courtesy becoming professors of the just and merciful doctrine of the Gospel."

In an editorial on Christian progress, he writes: " It is the duty of men — of Christians — to go forward. But let us understand this matter. What is meant by going forward?

If real improvement, then let us move on. We confess that to go forward is very desirable; but if a man be on the wrong road, with his face the wrong way, then the more he goes forward the worse it is for him, and for all who are led by him. The Calvinist may say, Let us go forward; and may lead his votaries farther into the darkness of his gloomy religion. This in his view is progress. On the other hand, the Rationalist cries, Let us go forward; and he leads men farther into the mysteries and fog of his so-called Rationalism. The Atheist calls on men to go forward; and he would lead them to doubt every thing, believe nothing, and sink down to a level almost with the brute creation. All are for progress. Progress is an enchanting word. It has a peculiar music for the ears of young men. This class are always wise. They know many things; but there is one thing they do not seem to know, and that is, that they are not so wise probably now as they will be by and by.

"Real progress is desirable, — progress towards the truth and in the truth. The pathway of the truthful and just is always increasing in brightness. We wish to make progress in the faith of Universalism. We would increase in the knowledge of the sacred Scriptures. Here we find a wisdom so great that the wisest men never went beyond it. Are we told that it is conservatism to stand by the Bible? It is, and a very salutary conservatism too."

He is addressed by a correspondent who avers that the *Trumpet* is too controversial. He replies: " In the beginning of Christianity, the disciples were commanded to defend it, to ' contend earnestly for the faith once delivered to the saints.' This was necessary, because it was continually attacked. It was worthy of being defended. Universalism is, in many respects, in the situation of Christianity at the outset. It is little understood; it is violently opposed; its friends are few compared with those upon the other side; the wealth and worldly power are principally in the hands of its enemies; and all kinds of unjustifiable means are resorted to to put it down. Shall we, then, permit the truth to be sacrificed? or shall we stand up manfully and defend it?

"We have taken our ground. We shall defend the truth. It must be made known. It has many feeble friends who follow it, as Peter followed his Master after the latter was arrested, 'afar off.' The power of sectarian influence is so strong, that many perhaps who secretly believe in Universalism do not openly avow it. Shall *we*, then, be faithless? Surely not. Therefore, our paper for the present must be controversial. Gladly would we cease the shrill warlike sound, and utter tones of sweetest harmony. The time will come when the truth will not be opposed, but that time is not yet. The *Trumpet*, however, will not be wholly controversial. There are other things to be done. Fields are to be cultivated and harvests to be gathered in. The first settlers of our country found time to till the ground, although they had to work with the implements of agriculture in one hand, and of defence in the other. We must not fail at any time in the midst of the warmest conflicts to inculcate and practise the Christian virtues."

CHAPTER X.

1849–1851.

AGED 49–51.

The Railroad President — Visit to Bath, Me. — Anniversary Week —
Massachusetts Convention — Universalism dear to Universalists —
Religious Insanity — Visit to the West — U.S. Convention at Cincin-
nati — Fugitive-slave Law — Notice of book — Visit to Montpelier, Vt.
— Boston Association — Bibliotheca Sacra — Controversy — Sugges-
tion to stop preaching, and Reply — Letter of Rev. John Foster —
Anniversary Week and Reform Association — Speech — Revivals,
how regarded — Massachusetts Convention in Milford — Sabbath at
Medford — The Bible and Creeds — Execution of Dr. J. W. Webster
— U.S. Convention in Buffalo, N.Y. — Niagara — Address before
Samaritan Society — Rev. J. Wesley and Dr. A. Clarke — Women's
Convention at Worcester — Death of Rev. M. Rayner — Professor
Stuart and his Opinions.

IT was in the year 1849 that Mr. Whittemore's connection
with the railroads of Massachusetts commenced. "One
hundred millions of dollars had been invested in railroads in
that State. The roads first built were prosperous, such as
the Lowell, the Worcester, the Fitchburg, the Eastern. This
fact increased the railroad mania; and, because the railroads
which had a terminus in Boston were good property, it was
hastily concluded that all others would be. Due allowance
was not made for the greater cost of building railroads among
the mountains, sometimes crossing rivers at every mile, the
roads being left therefore exposed to destructive freshets.
Neither was due allowance given to the fact, that, unless a
road should have a profitable *through* business, the farther it

was extended into a sparsely settled country, the smaller its business must be. That the railroad mania has been a benefit to the whole country there is no doubt, albeit it has been decidedly the reverse to those at whose expense the interior roads were built. These different lines of interior roads were pressed on to completion, with subscriptions to their capital stock altogether inadequate to the expenditures. It was soon found that railroads could not be built without large amounts of money. Many persons became fearful of loss, and hesitated, and some at last refused to pay for the shares for which they had subscribed. These things threw the executive officers of these boards into great embarrassments. They had either to stop the works as they were, and thus sink all they had invested, or they had to raise money by extraordinary means. The roads became greatly in debt. They were obliged to borrow money; and, as their paper was mistrusted, they had to pay high commissions to individual indorsers.

"A crisis had come; and certain of the large stockholders in the Vermont and Massachusetts Railroad applied to Mr. Whittemore to allow himself to be run as a candidate for a seat at the board. This was done for the avowed purpose of changing the character of the board almost entirely, and the proposition produced a great opposition from the friends of the old directors. The new ticket, however, prevailed by a large majority. This happened in February, and in the course of the following summer the former president resigned, and Mr. Whittemore was elected in his place. The new board had great difficulties to overcome, — land damages to be settled, a series of suits in the courts, buildings to be erected, a branch road to be finished; and they also found the corporation floating on a sea of debt, on which it was doubtful how much longer they should be able to keep it afloat. The new

board scanned all these matters carefully, and were not long
in coming to the conclusion that upwards of a million of
dollars must be raised, and that the best way to raise the sum
would be by the issue of bonds secured by the mortgage of the
road. This measure was carried through, and bonds to the
amount of $1,100,000 were issued and sold at a sacrifice of
from twelve to twenty per cent. This measure gave great relief for the time. Great care had been exercised in the expenditures on this road ; every effort was made to increase its
business, and, so far as possible, to get a remunerative price
for it. Mr. Whittemore took a deep interest in aiding the
project of a tunnel through the Hoosac Mountain, at North
Adams, Mass., which would remove the last objection to a
through road from Boston to Troy, N.Y., *viâ* Northern Massachusetts, — twenty miles shorter than the Western Railroad,
and with but slight grades. While the subject of a loan for
this object was before the Legislature of Massachusetts, in
the spring of 1851, Mr. Whittemore wrote many articles in
aid ; the chief of which was his pamphlet entitled, ' A Letter
to a Boston Representative,' &c. If this tunnel should be
made, that part of the Vermont and Massachusetts Railroad
between Fitchburg and Greenfield — fifty miles — would constitute a very important part of the line. With the aid of a
careful and untiring board of directors, Mr. Whittemore conducted the corporation through a series of trials which seemed
at first almost utterly overwhelming." [1]

In May of this year (1849), Mr. Whittemore visited Bath,
Me. He preached there on Sunday. He writes : " The first
service we attended was that of the dedication of two children
of a gentleman, the husband of a young lady formerly of the
society in Cambridgeport. The family seemed happy to see
the face of their former pastor once more. On returning to

----

[1] Sketches of Eminent Americans.

Brother Brooks's house (the pastor's), we were gratified to find that Father Stetson, of Brunswick, had arrived. He had travelled on foot ten miles to attend the meeting. The good old man was formerly an orthodox clergyman of the straitest sect, and, as such, was settled in Plymouth, Mass. He tasted the bitter cup of woe which his belief prepared for him ; and, after suffering indescribable agonies of mind, he was delivered by being brought to the knowledge of the truth of Universal grace, — a mercy for which he has never· since ceased to praise God. Brothers Dillingham, of Augusta, and Bailey, the Missionary in that State, were present. A church was recognized and the Lord's Supper observed. During the visit, a little son of the pastor, Elbridge Streeter, was dedicated."

Anniversary week again in Boston. The third meeting of the Universalist Reform Association was held. The day was very rainy, but the audience was quite respectable in numbers. An able report was read by Rev. Henry Bacon. It took a wise and comprehensive view of the whole field of Christian reform. The Festival at Boylston Hall was a very enjoyable one. Four hundred were at the tables. Thomas Goddard, Esq., presided. Mr. Whittemore was present, and was called upon to address the company, but declined because of the lateness of the hour.

The Massachusetts Convention of Universalists held its annual session this year in Salem. Mr. Whittemore offered the following resolutions, which were discussed, and finally passed : —

" *Resolved*, that capital punishment is opposed to the spirit of Jesus and his Gospel.

" *Resolved*, that it is our duty to sympathize with all who suffer, especially with the victims of violence, if living, and, if dead, with their friends ; but we do not see that capital punishment has had any influence in restraining violence, nor do we believe it is the best means for that purpose.

" *Resolved*, that we regard capital punishment as essentially wrong ; and we will pray and work for its abolition."

He was chosen to report the condition of the cause of Universalism in Massachusetts at the next session of the United States Convention.

In an article entitled, " Universalism beloved of Universalists," Mr. Whittemore notices a statement of Rev. Dr. Bellows, that union between Unitarians and Universalists can never take place on the doctrine of universal salvation, in any popular sense of that phrase ; a doctrine, he (Dr. Bellows) adds, " which every day's experience, every day's progress in spiritual science, in the knowledge of the intellectual and moral constitution of man, will make less true and less interesting, until it becomes an unmeaning phrase."   Mr. Whittemore remarks : " Does Mr. Bellows suppose that such a state of things will ever take place?   Does he think that Universalists are losing their attachment to the great doctrine that all men are in the hands of a kind Father, who is training them all, by various means of trial and discipline, for the enjoyment of purity and happiness?   If he has such a notion, he is suffering under a self-formed delusion.   There is not the slightest prospect of any such thing.   We do not believe that there ever was a time when the doctrine of the final holiness and happiness of all men was more precious in the eyes of all Universalists than it is at the present moment.   We are desirous of living in union with all sects of Christians ; but we can never purchase union with any sect under the heavens by the surrender of what we believe to be God's truth.   Give up Universalism !   What shall we have in its stead?   If we could find any thing better, we should think it true ; but there can be nothing better.   Therefore we have the highest evidence that it is the doctrine of God. Besides, what an inauspicious moment in which to give up the doctrine! Give it up at the very moment when the evangelical sects are coming to believe it; when some of the greatest scholars, the profoundest philosophers, the most eminent divines in Europe, are avowing their faith in it! How can any one suppose such an absurdity? If Dr. Bellows has any hope of promoting a union between Universalists and Unitarians on the ground of renunciation of the distinctive doctrine held by the former, he may as well dismiss that hope now as at any future time, for it never will be realized."

In noticing a statement of the *Congregational Journal* of New Hampshire, that some of the inmates of the insane hospital of that State " were the dupes of Millerism, cheated not only out of their estates, but of their intellects, by a delusion as prevalent as it was absurd;" Mr. Whittemore asks: " And who were the abettors of Millerism? It is an undeniable fact that the clergy called ' evangelical' were willing to make use of that delusion for the purpose of getting up revivals, and filling up their churches with members. Generally they were wise enough not to commit themselves fully and entirely; but still they did not at the time pronounce Millerism an error. They were willing to have it preached; they opened their meeting-houses readily to Miller and his disciples; they ,said they did not know but it might be true; it was *best to be prepared*. And in this way, without committing themselves, they gave Miller countenance, and made use of his theory to excite the people for the purposes above named. Had the Congregational, Baptist, and the Methodist clergy taken a decided stand against Millerism, it would have been comparatively a harmless thing. Miller could have produced but little or no excitement. They gave him countenance; they supplied him with hearers; they furnished him with inflammable material, and were glad to see him set it on fire, because they hoped to profit by the excitement. But now that the deception has profited them all it can, they cry out against it with loud voices, and denounce it as one of the delusions of our times."

Mr. Whittemore was a delegate to the United States Convention, which met this year in Cincinnati, O. His engagements in and about Boston were so many at the time, that he would not have undertaken the journey had he not believed that it was his absolute duty to go. He left Boston on Thursday, Sept. 27, and was four days on his way to Cincinnati. His letters descriptive of the journey, in the *Trumpet*, were full of his observations made while on his passage. He presided at the meeting of the Universalist Historical Society, on one of the days of the Convention, and presented its claims to the congregation at the taking up of a collection for the benefit of the Society's library.

His conservatism as an American citizen is sorely tried about these days. He always deemed himself a "law and order" man, and had never joined the radical abolitionists in their peculiar measures in opposition to slavery in the Southern States. But a crisis has now come, calling for a free expression of his mind in reference to some of the extreme movements of the slaveholders to sustain "the institution." The Fugitive-slave Law has been enacted by Congress, and all persons in the non-slaveholding States are called upon to use their endeavors to sustain it. He has no disposition whatever to do any such thing. And thus he discourses in one of his editorials : —

" It is due to ourselves, to our readers, and specially to our readers in the Southern States, that we express the public feeling of the North in regard to the law for reclaiming fugitive slaves. We hold, in the language of the Declaration of Independence, 'that all men are created equal, that they are endowed by their Creator with certain unalienable rights; that among these are life, liberty, and the pursuit of happiness.' This certainly did not mean to exclude a certain part of mankind from the possession of these rights; it was meant as the assertion of a great and wholesome political truth, the basis of our Independence. The question of slavery is one of great difficulty. We suppose it is conceded on all hands that it is a violation of the natural laws of man; but how is this country to get rid of it? That's the question. As it respects that question, we know not what to do, nor what advice to give, except that the subject should be discussed dispassionately.

"But the new law, — the Fugitive Slave law, — unlike any other we have before had, has created a new sore. It is unjust to our Southern brethren to hide the fact that it has roused a spirit in New England which has scarcely been paralleled since the times of 1770 and 1775. It is regarded as highly unconstitutional. It sets aside, it is said, the writ of *habeas corpus*, — that great guardian of personal liberty; whereas the Constitution of the United States declares (sect. ix. part 2) : 'The privilege of the writ of *habeas corpus* SHALL NOT be suspended, unless when, in cases of rebellion or invasion, the public safety may require it.' We have not a copy of the law at hand; but, if it sets aside the writ of *habeas corpus*, it surely *is* unconstitutional. Should it be said that the writ of *habeas corpus* is not designed for the protection of slaves, as they are not citizens, we reply that the question pending is, whether the person arrested *is* a slave; and at any rate he has a right to the benefit until it is proved that he is a slave. If the writ of *habeas corpus* is suspended, what man is safe? A free man — black, mulatto, yellow, or some other color — may be seized. He is hurried before a commissioner.

Some person swears he is a slave. The writ of *habeas corpus* has no effect. He cannot stay proceedings; he has not the right, under the new law, to have the question of his liberty settled in the State of which he may truly be a citizen; and he is hurried off the Lord knows where.

"In what we now say, our object is to show the state of public feeling which this law has created in New England, New York, and, perhaps, in all the Free States. Public meetings have been very generally holden. Among the colored population, of course, a determined resistance to the law is contemplated. They say that under this new law there is no protection for them; and they will resist seizure unto death. If they slay the marshal of the district, they say, in defence of liberty, they certainly shall be held in Massachusetts for trial; and they would run the risk of a trial for murder in Massachusetts, under such circumstances, sooner than to be carried off into slavery. But the excitement is by no means confined to them. Men who have never interfered with the subject of slavery are aroused on this new movement. The churches and their ministers are. The Northern men who voted for this law will find it very difficult to maintain their political standing among the people.

"The religious periodicals of all the sects will speak in unmistakable terms against this law. These extracts (a number of which he has given) will show most conclusively the feeling of which we have spoken. The cause of Anti-slavery is greatly strengthened by it."

In a notice of a book announced in the West, to be entitled, "The Doctrine of Future and Endless Punishment logically proved in a critical Examination of such Passages of Scripture as relate to the Final Destiny of Man;" by Rev. R. N. Coon, he cannot resist an inclination to say of the author: "We think Mr. Coon is going up the wrong tree. Why does he take to the tree of damnation? Why does he not choose the tree of life?"

In November, he visits Montpelier, Vt., for the first time. On his way by Bellows Falls, he notes with minuteness the places and scenery which come under his observation. Of Montpelier he writes: "It is embosomed among the hills. Come from which quarter you may, you must descend to find the village.   We had business at the State House, and one of the first men whom we met in the building was our friend and brother Rev. Eli Ballou, the Universalist clergyman of this region, and editor of the *Universalist Watchman*. The Onion or Winooski River runs through the village. The principal streets are State and Main. The State House stands on the first named, towards the western terminus of the village. It was the first object we saw on going in; and waving above the dome was the State flag.

"We visited the Legislature, — both branches. It was a dignified body; not one whit below the Legislature of Massachusetts. We had occasion to avail ourself of the kindness of the Librarian and Secretary of State, both of whom sought to promote our objects with as little discomfort to ourself as possible. There are in this State upwards of forty preachers of the Reconciliation; and if twelve illiterate fishermen, aided by the power of divine truth, could fill Jerusalem with their doctrine, what may not these forty do in Vermont, if they shall be truly faithful to their Master?"

The Boston Association was held this year at Beverly. Mr. Whittemore was present during some of the meetings, and speaks of the sessions in terms of strong approval. He gives in his paper the names of the ministers who were present, and also of those who were not present, stating the causes of their absence. Most of these causes are marked "unknown." Some were, "illness," "business,"

" teaching."   One of the reasons assigned was, " exceeding love of home."

He congratulates the conductors of the *Bibliotheca Sacra,* a popular orthodox monthly, for an able article he had just been reading in its pages, on the retributive justice of God in the present life.   He considers the article an evidence of advancement towards the truth as the Scriptures affirm it. Of this inflexible justice, this article in the monthly says: " It links together human crime and human suffering, the vices and the miseries of men, so that the one shall follow the other unvariably, as sound and echo pursue each other along the mountain side.   There is with it no respect of persons, no taking of bribes.   With its whip of scorpions it pursues the wrong-doer, whoever he may be, wherever he may go; tracks him into every obscurity, finds him out in the deepest retirement and the darkest night; overtakes him in his swiftest escape, and like the terrible avenger pursues and hangs over him wherever he takes his way."   This is precisely what Universalists had been constantly preaching, and what many of the so-called orthodox teachers seemed to have overlooked in their eagerness to make the fear of endless punishment an inducement with men to secure their salvation.

Again he speaks in defence of Christian controversy, induced to do so by an article in the *Christian Secretary* deprecating it.   " Controversy is not what we love.   We prefer peace rather than war.   The ear drinks in the smooth and soothing notes of concord, rather than the smart and startling alarm of the war-trumpet.   But with all our love of peace we must not cry ' peace, peace, when there is no peace.'   If we see the enemy approaching and give not the alarm, we must suffer the *anathema maranatha.*   As much then as we love peace, we shall hold out no white flag to the enemy; we shall make no compromise with error; we shall 'contend earnestly for the faith once delivered to the saints.' The Christian course is a warfare. The Christian has a helmet, a shield, a breastplate, a sword. He must wrestle or contend, not merely with flesh and blood, but with principalities and powers and spiritual wickedness in high places. Let those who feel the weakness of their cause deprecate controversy; we should expect them to do so: but the true servant of Jesus will be ready always to contend for his Master's honor. The time has not come to lay our armor by. We say to our soul, in the language of the poet: —

> 'O watch, and fight, and pray,
> The battle ne'er give o'er;
> Renew it boldly every day,
> And help divine implore.'"

On a suggestion made to him to "stop preaching Universalism," he writes: "'Well, Mr. Whittemore,' said an opponent a few days since, 'when shall you stop preaching Universalism?' Stop preaching Universalism! said we, — what should put that inquiry into your head? Never, sir, while we live, never. Look round the land, sir; do you not see one hundred persons preaching the doctrine of endless misery where you find one faithful disciple of Jesus preaching good tidings of great joy to all people? And is *this* the time to cease preaching Universalism? No, sir; and we say to all who believe that doctrine, Preach it; sow it among the people till all the fields are green, and the waving grain of truth betokens a glorious harvest."

The letter of Rev. John Foster, a distinguished Baptist divine, was republished in this country about these days. It disavowed the doctrine of eternal punishment in the strongest terms. Mr. Foster was a man who could not be easily set aside or excommunicated, so strong a hold had he on the respect and affection of the sect to which he belonged. The Universalists, of course, welcomed his Letter; and Mr. Whittemore thus speaks in reference to it: —

"It was a severe blow to our partialist brethren when the works of Rev. John Foster, the celebrated English Baptist, were republished in this country, without the excision of such parts as assaulted the doctrine of endless punishment. Many good men believe that this doctrine is not taught in the Sacred Scriptures. For this reason among others they do not preach it. God is love, and as he is love, he cannot be the author of interminable pain to his offspring. The doctrine of endless punishment has been very generally believed in the church; but since the reformation, under the labors of Martin Luther, there have always been found some men, who were bright and shining lights in the world, who would not believe it, but who were obliged to express great doubts whether such a doctrine could be true. We might name among them Bishop Newton, Sir Isaac Newton, Dr. Barrow, Jeremy Taylor, Jeremy White, Dr. Samuel Clark, Dr. Samuel Johnson, Dr. David Hartley, &c., and in later times Robert Hall and John Foster in England, and Jung Stilling and a thousand others in Germany. The doctrine of endless torture is destined to fall, like a ponderous error, to the ground. Like some old dilapidated tower, it already trembles, and gives warning of the coming crash. Let it fall. We invite our Baptist brethren to read the Letter of John Foster on endless punishment; and, if consistent with their feelings, we would recommend them to publish it in the form of a tract for gratuitous distribution. They have hitherto done so much harm by preaching the doctrine referred to, that it is surely time for them to seek to do something to counteract it."

Anniversary Week comes again, and the Reform Association has its place among the attractions of the occasion. The meeting was held in the School Street church. There was a large gathering, and a Report of much interest was read by Rev. Henry Bacon. Peace, Temperance, Anti-slavery, Anti-capital Punishment, and Prison Discipline were the themes presented and ably discussed. Speeches followed from Rev. Messrs. H. Ballou 2d, E. Thompson, M. Goodrich, T. Whittemore, S. Cobb, A. A. Miner, W. H. Richardson, O. H. Tillotson, and J. G. Adams. Mr. Whittemore said (among other things) : "I am happy that no speech shall exceed ten minutes. I do not feel encouraged in regard to the cause of Anti-slavery. It is at this time the all-absorbing question throughout the North. The other subjects embraced in the Secretary's Report are very important; but the Anti-slavery cause for its vast influence, for its intimate connection with our national peace and prosperity, does, in its immense interest, like Aaron's rod, swallow up the rest. But I do not feel despondent. We have now a state of things we have never seen before. I cannot have the buoyancy of feeling which has been manifested by my brother Thompson, who has so recently sat down; indeed I feel more as if I were at a funeral than at a wedding. The cause of Anti-slavery was never in so bad a condition as at this moment. I do not refer to the late riot at New York, but to the position recently taken by the greatest of our Northern statesmen. He has forsaken the cause of universal freedom at the very moment when we need his aid the most; when most we are inclined to lean upon him, he has withdrawn his shoulder from us. Oh if that man, instead of what he has done, had stood firmly by the cause of human rights, what a pillar of defence would he have made! how would he have enshrined himself in the heart of every philanthropist throughout the world! how well then might this vexing question of Slavery have been sealed and settled permanently for our country! We had hoped that Slavery would be extended no more; that we might say to it 'hitherto shalt thou come, but no farther; and here shall thy proud waves be stayed.' But we are destined to disappointment, and now we can see no barrier to prevent its extending South and West for a long time.

"But we are not left wholly without consolation. The cause we have espoused is just; and though our great men abandon it, it remains just. Slavery is a great wrong, and nothing can make it right. What is wrong must sooner or later die. It must be a curse to those who promote it, and none can even connive at it without guilt. It is lamentable that this great matter is so completely in the hands of mere politicians." He spoke at some length very earnestly, when he was apprised by the chair that his ten minutes had expired, and he took his seat.

The Festival at Winthrop Hall, Tremont Row, was largely attended, and was richly enjoyed by the company. Mr. William H. Richardson, Jr., of Malden, presided, and made a very appropriate opening speech. He was followed by Rev. Messrs. E. G. Brooks, T. B. Thayer, H. P. Cutting, H. B. Soule, T. Starr King, J. Boyden, John Moore, S. Streeter, Hosea Ballou, Hon. Richard Frothingham, and others. Father Ballou was in his happiest mood. Speaking of reform, he said: "This work of reform has gone on so effectually, that even the old God himself in whom the theologians used to believe, has got reformed. He is so changed that the old clergy, if they were to hear him described now, would not know him! The old divinity is gone. Our heavenly Father has become our *real* Father. The work is going on: it will go on to the end and prosper." The speeches were interspersed with appropriate songs and hymns.

"Are we the enemy of revivals?" is a question which he attempts to answer in an editorial. "When men ignorant of religion are brought to understand and believe it, religion is revived; and when disciples increase in knowledge and faith, religion is revived. Paul exhorted the Colossians to hold fast their connection with the head (Christ), 'from which all the body, by joints and bands having nourishment and knit together, increaseth with the increase of God.' This is the true spiritual increase,—the true revival of religion in the hearts of believers. The disciples said to Jesus, 'Lord, increase our faith.' 'And the Lord make you to increase and abound in love one toward another, and toward all men, even as we do toward you' (1 Thess. iii. 12). This was a prayer for a revival of religion. When sinful men break off their sins and turn to righteousness; when believers grow in grace and in the knowledge of God; when the practical duties of religion are more strictly attended to, we have surest evidences of a true revival of religion.

"Who will not pray, in view of such a blessing, 'O Lord, revive thy work'? But how blind are the great body of professors of religion to the beauty of this subject. To them a revival of religion is a mere increase of zeal, an increase of sectarian feeling, of bitterness towards other sects, an increased fear of endless damnation, an increased excitement,—especially among young persons,—crying, 'What shall I do to be saved?' which means, 'What shall I do to be saved from the pains of hell for ever?' Call you this a revival of religion, and an acceptable work of the Lord? Is there more love in the times of these *sectarian* revivals than at ordinary times? We all know there is not. We describe a true revival as a revival of religion; but a false revival we call a revival of sectarianism. Here is the difference: the one aims at the good of man, the other at the aggrandizement of sect;

the one is promoted by the influence of truth, the other by false doctrine; the one is carried on by addressing the reason and conscience of men, the other by addressing their fears. For these reasons, we have aimed for many years to put the public on their guard against spurious revivals of religion, so called. There is much false religion in the world. We have never denied the benefit of pure religion. We have prayed and labored for its advancement; and we will continue to pray, ' Thy kingdom come, thy will be done on earth, as it is done in heaven.'"

The Massachusetts Convention held its session this year (1850) in Milford. Mr. Whittemore preached the Occasional Sermon. He writes of the session, that it was largely attended by the people, that at all the services the house was full. "The conference meeting on Thursday evening was rich, spiritual, free. In the hymns, every one seemed to sing with the spirit and the understanding also. It was a sublime chorus of praise. Too much cannot be said of the hospitality, politeness, and attention of the members of the Society. Every house was thrown open, and, upon every door-post was written, ' Welcome.' The Society is enjoying a season of high prosperity under the labors of our young and energetic brother, Henry A. Eaton."

" A Sabbath at Medford," is one of the recollections which he notes in August of this year. " While the Universalist Meeting-house in Medford is undergoing repairs, the Unitarian and Universalist congregations worship together in the Unitarian house. This arrangement was brought about by the kind offer of the Unitarian Society. The clergymen sit in the pulpit side by side; the Unitarian pastor (Rev. John Pierpont) preaches in the forenoon, and the Universalist in the afternoon. They interchange services in the devotional parts. How vividly this brings to mind the language of the Psalmist, ' Behold, how good and how pleasant it is for brethren to dwell together in unity'! It became our duty to preach in Medford, in the Unitarian pulpit, two or three weeks ago, on exchange with Rev. H. Ballou 2d, and we had for our coadjutor Rev. Mr. Fuller, of Manchester, N.H., who had exchanged with Rev. Mr. Pierpont on that day. It was not in our power to be present in the morning, and we lost, therefore, the pleasure of hearing him. He offered prayer in the afternoon, and listened to our discourse. The audience was large and attentive, embracing many of the principal men of the town. We selected for our subject the nature of false and true worship; and we preached precisely as we should have preached anywhere else. The people heard as if they loved the word spoken. It was the doctrine of the Bible that touched their hearts. May God bless the Unitarian parish in Medford, and their faithful and devoted pastor; and may they grow not merely in numbers, but in the better sense of increase in grace and in the knowledge of the truth. And may the Universalist church, under the charge of that good man, Rev. Hosea Ballou 2d, profit by the lesson of liberality and Christian kindness which their brethren have set them."

Of "The Bible before all Creeds," he writes, significantly: "Men have great attachment to their creeds. *I believe*, with the most of men, is a fixed position, from which it is very difficult to remove them. We go for the Bible. This is, in our view, the highest authority; above reason, but not against it; above all philosophies, all creeds, all fancies. The Bible is the sun; the creeds are the clocks which men have invented by which to denote the hours of the day. The sun we know is sure; but clocks may be out of order, and may not denote the true time. When there is a sensible variation between the sun and the clock, which shall we follow? Shall we undertake to regulate the former by the latter? Surely we ought to believe the sun against the clock, and not the

clock against the sun. So we ought to believe the Bible
against the creeds, and not set up the creeds against the
Bible. Now, God says in his word, that he will 'gather
together all things in Christ;' that 'unto Jesus every knee
shall bow, and that every tongue shall confess that Jesus
Christ is Lord, to the glory of God the Father.' The creeds
deny this; which shall we believe, the Bible or the creeds?"

The execution of Dr. John W. Webster for the murder of
Dr. George Parkman, of Boston, calls forth a new protest
against capital punishment from the pen of Mr. Whittemore.
He is replying to an article from the *New York Express*, vindicating the gallows, and especially in reference to the case of
Webster. He doubts the favorable effect of the gallows in
deterring men from crime, and denies that blood for blood is
the requirement of the divine law as revealed under the Christian dispensation. Of the olden utterance, "Whoso sheddeth
man's blood, by man shall his blood be shed," he asks, "Is
this a command, or is it a prophecy of what should happen
among men? Perhaps it may be said that the Jewish law
denounced capital punishment on offenders ; and, as *that* was
a divine law, it shows that capital punishment was just. So
it was in that age and among the Jews. But is the Jewish
law in force now? Are *we* under the law? Was not the law
done away in Christ? If we are under the law, then ought we
to punish disobedience to parents, and even the trivial offence
of picking up chips upon the Sabbath-day, *with death*. Now,
as no one would contend for this, we see full well that we
cannot comply with the terms of the Jewish law. We say
again, *we* are not under the law, but the Gospel.

"Does the Gospel sanction capital punishment? If so,
we will yield the point. Does the Gospel demand an eye for
an eye and a tooth for a tooth, or life for life? Does the
voice of the Gospel say, Hang the murderer? Did Jesus

pray that his murderers might be hung? Did he approve the request of his disciples when they wished power to call down fire from heaven to consume his enemies? Did he order the Pharisees to stone the woman taken in the act of sin, — a sin punished with death under the law of Moses? No, Jesus never uttered a syllable that would justify the punishment of death."

The United States Convention held its session this year in Buffalo, N.Y. An account of his journey thither is given in the *Trumpet.* Between Albany and Buffalo, the railroad passengers were detained by the conductor, who affirmed that they could go no further, as the engine had given out, and that they must wait until another could come from Buffalo to take them on. An indignation meeting of gentlemen passengers was held. The engineer had gone to bed, and refused to be seen. The passengers had no faith in the pretence that an engine was coming from Buffalo to relieve them. They applied to the officers of the Attica & Buffalo Company, and in the morning its president appeared, on his way to Albany. Finding that his accommodation train loaded with passengers had been lying at Attica since two o'clock in the morning, he set himself earnestly at work to relieve them. He expressed his exceeding sorrow for the disappointment, and offered to make any satisfaction in his power. It was finally agreed that he should pay to each single passenger three dollars, and to each gentleman and lady five dollars, for the expense, fatigue, and disappointment they had suffered. Thus ended the disagreeable affair.

The Convention at Buffalo was well attended, and the business and devotional meetings were of much interest. Resolutions in reference to the death of Rev. Stephen R. Smith were adopted, and a committee of three appointed to tender in person, to the family of the departed, the sentiments of the Convention.

During this Western visit, Mr. Whittemore takes occasion to visit Niagara again. He gives a vivid description of the Rapids, and of the Falls on the American side, as seen from Goat Island. "The precipice, as far as the eye can reach, is about 160 feet. No mortal eye ever saw the bottom, or mortal hand ever sent down a measuring-line. Probably the depth of water below the reach of human sight is as much more. But call the depth of the fall 160 feet, for such it appears to be. Now imagine a branch of a river nearly a quarter of a mile in width, driven along with unlimited fury, and precipitated from such a height; and what would be the scene? How would the sheet look as it rolled over the shelf? How, as it began to expand and separate into particles, forming a million jets, and every one of these a thousand more, being received into the boiling receptacle, — an immense volume of foam white as the purest snow? What would be the roar of this concussion of water, air, and rocks? No one can imagine it; and you only stand still in amazement, fixed to the spot." On his return home, he delivered an evening lecture in the Universalist church in Buffalo.

The "Female Samaritan Society" held its thirty-third Anniversary on Sunday evening, Oct. 27, in the First Universalist Church in Hanover Street (Rev. S. Streeter's). Mr. Whittemore gave the discourse on the occasion from Matt. xxv. 40: "Inasmuch as ye have done it unto one of the least of these my brethren, ye have done it unto me." A collection of $120 was taken.

Of John Wesley and Adam Clarke, two celebrated English Methodist divines who had been suspected of having strong tendencies to Universalism, he writes about this time: "A writer, at the foot of a letter, sends us one or two quotations from Clarke's Commentary, to show that its author believed in the salvation of all men. We are fully of the opinion that

Dr. Adam Clarke was not a Universalist. A Universalist is one who believes in the ultimate holiness and happiness of all men. Clarke, it is well known, advocated the doctrine of endless misery. There is no proof that Clarke ever *intended* to profess faith in the salvation of all men; but on the contrary he has defended very explicitly, though with sophistical reasoning, the endless continuance of sin and torture. The truth on this subject seems to be this: Clarke, although a professed believer in endless misery, frequently lays down those principles from which the doctrine of Universalism unavoidably flows. The same was the case with John Wesley; and in fact it has been so with a great many others. But they should not be called Universalists unless they intentionally avowed their faith in Universalism. All we can in good conscience say of them is, that although they professed to believe in endless misery, yet Universalism is a doctrine so congenial to benevolence and good sense, that they could not avoid laying down the principles from which that blessed doctrine flows."

It was in the autumn of this year, that a Convention of women was held at Worcester, Mass., to take into consideration the subject of " women's rights." It was a new movement, and, of course, not a very popular one with the multitude. To many wisely thinking persons in other respects, both men and women, it was an action entirely out of place on the part of the " gentler sex." It was a movement then in its incipient stages, and very startling to many cautious and conservative minds. Mr. Whittemore was among the number who saw it in this light, and could not resist the inclination to give the Worcester Convention a notice expressive of strong dislike as to its intentions. He says of the meeting: " We scarcely know who was present. Some distinguished female talkers were there, whose husbands at home must have had a time of heavenly stillness during their absence. This is the only good, so far as we can see, that will ever grow out of the Convention. Judge not the women of Massachusetts by this motley assembly. The women of Worcester had a right to assemble, for aught we know, and had also a right to express their opinions as to any burdens under which they labored; but they had no right to speak in behalf of all female humanity. There are thousands and tens of thousands of good, honest, sober-minded women in Massachusetts who will not thank their sisters who assembled at Worcester for presuming to speak in their behalf." He copies a well-written article from the *Christian Inquirer* (Unitarian) on the same subject, and taking similar views to those expressed by himself.

How far his opinions on this question of Woman's position and work might have been modified by time and observation, we are, of course, unable to say. We have a right to conclude, however, that he would have weighed the arguments offered by the new reformers with his usual force of discrimination, and perhaps have seen reason to modify or change some of his prejudices against the movement as a whole. We remember that in subsequent years he manifested a deep interest in the public advocacy of the Gospel by women, and was most pleasurably exercised while attending the ministries of one of them (Mrs. Jenkins), whose addresses in our pulpits and churches in New England were at the time so very acceptable.

The *Trumpet* of Nov. 30, contains a notice of the death of Rev. Menzies Rayner in New York city. He has been mentioned before in this biography. He came from the Episcopal into the Universalist Church, and had been pastor in Hartford, Ct., Portland, Me., and Troy, N.Y. He lived during the last of his life with his children in N.Y.; but continued to preach as his services were called for until a little time before his decease at the age of seventy-nine. Mr. Whittemore writes of him: "For his age he was a man of vigor. He would walk into the country, five, six, eight, or ten miles, upon a Sabbath morning, perform the duties of the day and walk back again at night. To the last he was an open, consistent, candid Universalist. While strength lasted, he was ever ready to preach the word. He was a Christian, — no rationalist, no half-believer. He was a man of acute logical powers, — keen, sagacious, remarkably apt and pungent. His society was prized by all his friends, for the sound judgment he had in Scriptural matters, and for the fund of knowledge and entertainment he possessed."

Mr. Whittemore notes the statements of Professor Stuart of Andover, in the *Biblical Repository*, respecting the many doubters of the doctrine of endless punishment to be found outside the Universalist fraternity, and even in orthodox churches. "There are," says the Professor, "minds of a very serious cast, and prone to reasoning and inquiry, that have in some way come into such a state, that doubt on the subject of endless punishment cannot, without the greatest difficulty, be removed from them. Can heaven itself be a place of happiness for them, while they are conscious that a husband or a wife, a son or a daughter, a brother or a sister, is plunged into a lake of fire from which there is no escape? With the great mass of thinking Christians, I am sure such thoughts as these must, unhappily for them, be acquaintances too familiar. That they agitate our breasts as storms do the mighty deep will be testified by every man of a tender heart, and who has a deep concern in the present and future welfare of those whom he loves. It would seem to be from such considerations, and others like these, that a belief in the *future* repentance and recovery of sinners has become so wide-spread in Germany, pervading even the ranks of those who are regarded as serious and evangelical men in respect to most or all of what is called orthodox doctrine, saving the point before us. Such was the case also with some of the ancient fathers; and such is doubtless the case with not a few of our day."

Mr. Whittemore says: "It should be remembered, in regard to this extract, that it is an apology for those Universalists who do not avow their faith; whose breasts, like the Professor's, are agitated by the doctrine of endless torture, as storms agitate the mighty deep, but who keep their suspicions as to the falsity of this doctrine to themselves. There are *thousands* of such persons connected with orthodox congregations!"

CHAPTER XI.

1851–1852.

AGED 51–52.

Sickness — Spirit Rappings — The name Universalist — Services at Milford, Mass. — The Papal Church — Anniversary Week — Festival — Editorial Chair — Rev. D. Thom of Liverpool — U.S. Convention in Boston — A Preacher for England — What is New-England Theology? — A Journey — Layman's Letter — College Trustees' Meeting — Rev. O. Dewey's Lecture — Death of Rev. W. Balfour — The new College — Mrs. Soule's Letter — Visit to Washington and other Places — Memoir of Rev. W. Balfour — Lawrence, Mass. — Proposal to Dr. Edward Beecher — Anniversary Week — Festival Speeches — Massachusetts Convention at Plymouth — Illness of Rev. Hosea Ballou — His Death — Criticism on Rev. Walter Colton.

A SEVERE attack of erysipelas kept Mr. Whittemore for a few weeks confined to his house. The supervision of the *Trumpet* devolved upon good and ready helpers. Medical skill and watchful home care soon enabled him to resume his work; on doing which, he says to the readers of his paper: "I am permitted once more to take my pen to address you. I have been brought low by sickness, — a sickness the most severe of any that I have yet known. My mind is still weak, although I am improving, and I write with an unsteady hand. The last four weeks have been strange weeks to me. Much of the time I have lain in a stupor, and when roused my mind was filled with the strangest conceits. My face swelled to a frightful size and was hideous to behold. I have gained strength very slowly, and feel very anxious to return to my duties. I trust soon to come to you again in the columns of the *Trumpet* 'in the fulness of the blessing of the Gospel of Christ.'"

Of his experience in sickness, he says: "In our lucid moments, during our late confinement, we had abundant opportunity to reflect upon the nature and tendency of the doctrine we had preached. It appeared to the soul a glorious doctrine. Nothing can be so rich in sickness and death as a strong faith in Universalism. The fact which predominated in our mind was, that it is God's word. We could rejoice that we had defended this doctrine. It seemed to us at one time that an angel spoke to us, and said, ' You have done well, — as much as one could do in the same length of time ; you have preached much, written much in favor of the truth ; well done, good and faithful servant.' This was one of the happy illusions that came over the mind while it was weakened by disease. Now that we are getting strong again, we shall return to our work. We have no new doctrine to propose. Our faith in Universalism is as strong as ever. We say with great fulness of feeling, ' Give us Universalism in health ; Universalism in sickness ; Universalism in life ; and Universalism in death.'"

His mind is exercised of course in reference to the " Spirit Rappings" now rife in the land. Facetiously and soberly he writes : " It is needless for us to say that we have no faith in this thing. The reason is, we have never heard the rappings. Either there are no spirits where we are accustomed to be, or else they do not rap. It may be asked, why do you not go and see the young ladies to whom or by whom the spirits rap? For two reasons : 1. We object to running after spirits ; and 2. We object to running after the young ladies. The spirits can come to us much easier than we can go to them. If they are really spirits, they can pass a distance of a thousand miles in the twinkling of an eye. If we should set out to go after them, and they should seek to keep away from us, we could not catch them. We shall not attempt, therefore, to run after the spirits. But, if they will come where we are, we shall be very happy to see their antics and hear their rappings; and they shall be accommodated in the best room in our house, if they will not break the furniture.

"As to the young women, there is something suspicious. Cannot the spirits communicate without the aid of young women? Would not young men do as well? or old men? Cannot the spirits communicate directly with the inquirer, without the intervention of a mediator? We do not understand these things. We strongly suspect there is humbug somewhere. We may not be able to point it out; but if every thing is honest what is the need of a third person in the case? If we were going to consult the spirits, we should request the young ladies to retire; and we would attempt ourself to call the 'spirits from the vasty deep.' If they would not come, we would tell them that we had a poor opinion of them.

"Where have these spirits been until now? Horace Greeley told us that the world had not been sufficiently enlightened for the spirits to visit it until recently. Enlightened! The darker the world, the more need of light from the spirits. They would let their light shine in a dark place, if they were from heaven. We ask for an interview with the spirits without the aid of the young women."

"The name Universalist" is a topic to which he directs special attention.

"Some think the name Universalist an improper one. We think otherwise. We know of no one that will better express the greatness and goodness of our sentiments. Universalists are not Partialists: Universalism is not Partialism. Any system which confines salvation to a part of mankind, or which teaches that a part of mankind only will be saved (from whatever cause their want of salvation may arise) is *part*-ialism. The name is proper; and is no disgrace, unless the doctrine itself which is described by it is a disgrace. On the contrary, the doctrine which teaches the salvation of the whole world, — of all men, — of the *universe* of human beings, is *Universalism*. It is a glorious idea; ' God in Christ, reconciling the world unto himself.' God-like! Christ-like! heavenly! angelic! The will of God, the death of Christ, the joy of heaven, the hopes of angels, are all in favor of Universalism."

On the first of May of this year (1851), there were services of great interest to the Universalists of Milford, Mass. The new church edifice was dedicated; the venerable Father Ballou, just passed his eightieth year, preaching the sermon with apparently the vigor of youth. The new pastor, Rev. Henry A. Eaton, was installed, the sermon by Mr. Whittemore, from 2 Cor. iv. 1 : " Therefore, seeing we have this ministry, as we have received mercy we faint not." In the evening, a church of Christian believers just formed was publicly recognized; sermon by Rev. O. A. Skinner. The Fellowship of Churches was given by Rev. J. G. Adams.

He takes occasion just now to speak of Catholicism, in noticing an article in another Universalist journal, deprecating the indiscriminate abuse which Catholics seem to be receiving from most Protestant sects. " Universalists," says this journal, " whose motives for supporting their religion are so often impugned, should learn to look with charity upon the motives which attach others to their peculiar views." Mr. Whittemore writes: " Catholics are entitled to all the privileges enjoyed by other sects, and no more. Catholicism is one form of Partialism, and is rapidly increasing in this country, not by making new proselytes, but by the immigration of foreigners. So far as Catholicism is an error, it should be exposed, like all other errors. We have resolved to oppose all error, wherever found, without respect of persons. Catholics should not be attacked in a bad spirit, any more than any other sect. A bad spirit is the worst religion a man can have. If we cannot oppose error in a good spirit, we had better not oppose it at all.

"We confess that we are afraid of the Catholic or (as we prefer to say), the Papal religion. We are afraid of the order of Jesuits, who are insinuating themselves into every part of the country. Nursed in the midst of the scenes of the Inquisition; believing that it is right to lie, defraud, and even to commit murder, for the support of the Papal religion, — sworn to be enemies to all who are not friends to the Catholic church, — we deprecate their increase in this country. Their spirit is most intolerant. The past and present are full of evidences of this statement. But we see little to choose between Papal Partialism and Protestant Partialism. Protestants, however, have not been nursed in the lap of the Inquisition; they have no Jesuits, no Dominicans, no trained bands for secret service, ready to peril character and life for the cause they have espoused. We have no doubt that there are Catholics of an excellent spirit among us; but this fact does not alter the general character of the Papal religion. We repeat, that we lament its increase among us."

Anniversary Week brings the Reform Association together again. The business meeting was held in the Warren Street church, Rev. O. A. Skinner, pastor. The Secretary, Rev. H. Bacon, presented an admirable Report. It alludes to the efforts of woman to exalt her sisterhood, and to the contemptuous sneers with which the movement has been met; gives valuable information and statistics in regard to capital punishment and the Temperance Reform, on the vice of gambling, and on the substitution of arbitration as a substitute for a resort to war. "The monster evil, American Slavery," is handled with vigor, and dealt with justly. The Secretary's definition of conscience, as given by Daniel Webster in his own words, and in such glaring contrast to his advice to Northerners to obey and execute the Fugitive-slave law, is simply withering.

The Festival was held in Central Hall, Milk Street. Hon. Israel Washburn, Jr., of Maine, presided, who made a stirring opening address. He was followed by Rev. John Moore, of New Hampshire; Rev. T. Starr King, in one of his happiest efforts; Rev. H. Bacon, Rev. A. D. Mayo, Rev. Eli Ballou, of Vermont; P. H. Sweetser, Esq., Rev. Mr. Gaylord, W. H. Richardson, Jr., Rev. J. W. Hanson, and others. Mr. Whittemore writes of the occasion: "Very unexpectedly to ourself, we were called away on the previous day, and it was impossible for us to be present. It was the first annual dinner we have not attended since the festivities commenced. It was a great privation to lose not the eatables (for those we can get anywhere), but 'the feast of reason and flow of soul.' The occasion is spoken of as one of the most sparkling and exhilarating the Association has ever enjoyed."

The present of a new "Editorial Chair" from the American Chair Company, Troy, N.Y., is the occasion of a note of admiration in view of its convenience and perfectness. "It is an admirable piece of workmanship. The frame is of iron, finely wrought, presenting a light and beautiful appearance, and rolling on substantial brass castors. The seat and back are stuffed with the best of hair, and covered with purple plush; they rest on eight cast-steel semicircular springs, and so revolve on a pivot that the person seated in it seems almost suspended in mid-air, in a delightful position, and can whirl about in readiness to face either friend or foe, from whatever quarter he may come, with an extended hand and a benevolent heart for either."

In the *Universalist* for July, 1851 (an English publication), Rev. D. Thom of Liverpool, a believer and preacher of the doctrine of Universal Salvation, takes occasion to state his opposition to some of the opinions of American Universalists, and express his regret that these opinions are getting such hold upon the public mind in this country. In reply to his statements, Mr. Whittemore writes: " We do not think Dr. Thom has described correctly the Universalism of America : he certainly has not described Universalism as we hold it. He says, ' Human ·free will, conditional salvation, and a mere moral change of sentiments and conduct, substituted for God's sovereignty, the finished work of Jesus Christ, and the new creation of the conscience by divine truth and love, are now the idols of American Universalists.' Suffice it to say that this is not Universalism as we hold it. But if the Universalism of the United States were to be correctly described, Dr. Thom does not hold it. He is a Trinitarian ; and the great body of American Universalists are not Trinitarians. He is a believer in the Calvinistic doctrine of the atonement, and we are believers in the Scriptural doctrine of the atonement. That is the difference in reality. We lament that Universalism has never been presented in England in its true form. The Relleyans have gone down. Men of sound sense, who understood the Scriptures, cannot be made to receive that system. It lived for a time, and then died out. The Universalism of Winchester and Vidler and Richard Wright has been swallowed up in Unitarianism. Universalism, as it exists in the United States, has never been known in Britain. . Mr. Thom's form of Universalism never will prevail. It has as yet shown not the slightest signs of progress.   But in our judgment, if the opinions of the American Universalists were to be preached in Great Britain by preachers of the right talent, it would find a ready access to many hearts."

The United States Convention again held its annual session in Boston.   There was a full attendance.   It was a time of much excitement in and around the city on account of the Railroad Jubilee, or grand *fête* which the city gave to the people and rulers of. Canada, on the event of the connection of Boston Harbor with Quebec and Montreal by means of railroads.   Meetings were held in the different churches of the city.   The Occasional Discourse was delivered by Rev. Eli Ballou, of Vermont.   Stirring conferences were held, and a meeting of much interest in reference to the proposed literary institution preceded the other meetings, on Tuesday afternoon.   Father Ballou preached at the First Church, in Hanover Street, on Thursday P.M.   The communion service followed.   There were two hundred and twenty ministers present.

There is a desire at this time, which finds expression in the *Trumpet*, that a preacher be sent out from America to England to proclaim the Gospel of "glad tidings."   One thousand dollars are offered by one person for this purpose, and contributions from others are solicited.   Rev. A. C. Thomas seems to be the person unanimously designated to go on this mission. Mr. Whittemore is warmly in favor of it.   Arrangements were subsequently made which resulted in the proposed mission on the part of Mr. Thomas.

" What is New England Theology?" is a question asked by the *Congregationalist* of Oct. 31.   A grave question, Mr. Whittemore thinks, and one which it would puzzle the questioner to answer.   "Orthodoxy has changed so much that scarce any two agree what it is.   The Old School say it is one thing, and the New School say it is another. It seems, however, that there is this agreement among them, that they have 'a common standard of judgment.'" "But what is this?" asks Mr. Whittemore; "the Bible? oh no! The Bible forms no part of New England Orthodoxy. It is conceded by all, says the *Congregationalist*, that the writings of Edwards exhibit the true type of New England theology. The writings of Edwards; not the writings of prophets and apostles.

"But we declare, on our part, that the Orthodox party in New England do *not* follow Edwards, how much soever they may profess to do so. They dare not preach and write as Edwards did. The *Congregationalist* itself dare not publish, as its own sentiments, certain extracts which we can send its editors from Edwards on the subject of endless torture. Will they do it? Let Dr. Beecher, or Dr. Storrs, or Mr. Dexter, or Mr. Clarke, signify a willingness to publish what we shall send him from Edwards on the subject of endless torture, adopting the sentiment as his own, and extracts shall be forthcoming which will make their flesh shrink upon their bones. They undertake to say that Edwards is the true type of their theology! The idea is ridiculous!"

He is called to make a journey — partly ministerial and partly secular, as we judge from the record — to Troy, N.Y. He notes, among other things, the swiftness of the travelling, considering the places he visited and the distances between them. He left Boston on Saturday, Nov. 8, at 8 A.M.; arrived at Springfield — 100 miles — at 11; had an hour and a half for consultation with the President and Superintendent of the Connecticut River Railroad; was in Albany at $5\frac{1}{2}$, and in Troy at 6 P.M., — 206 miles from Boston. On Sunday, he preached twice in the Universalist church in Troy (Rev. J. C. Waldo, pastor), on the occasion of the reopening of the church after extensive repairs.   On Monday morning, he started for Saratoga Springs; "passing over almost the very ground at Stillwater where the armies of Gates and Burgoyne had their fierce struggle in the war of the Revolution, and also within a short distance of the place at Saratoga where the British army capitulated. Leaving this point," he writes: " We passed on through the villages of Fort Edward and Fort Ann (both celebrated in the early wars of the country), to Whitehall, at the southernmost part of Lake Champlain.   This is the first time we had ever seen the waters of that lake.   But we had no time to tarry, and immediately took a new train, and started for Castleton, Vt., and thence to Rutland, where we arrived at about eleven o'clock.   Thence we passed through Clarendon, over the summit at Mount Holly, and down through Ludlow, Proctorsville, and other places, to Chester, where we had the misfortune to be obliged to sit in the cars two hours and a half, waiting for the up-train, which had been detained by an accident on one of the freight trains. The road clear, we rushed on again for Bellows Falls, with a speed that was designed to redeem as far as possible the lost time. At six o'clock, we were in Keene, N.H, and at seven, in Fitchburg, Mass. We passed up on Tuesday to Athol, and thence returned to Boston in the afternoon. If this were not riding enough for three days, let those who think so get astride a streak of lightning, for that is the only way in which they will be able to beat it."

An aged layman of Middlefield, Mass., writes him : " I have always received your paper with a great deal of pleasure, and of late with a thankful heart. I have received more information and real knowledge from reading the *Trumpet* since I began to take it, than from all the preaching I have ever heard, and I am now in my seventy-second year. Being blind, I have been led by the blind, whether my leaders have been in the ditch or not. One thing I know, that I have been there; but you, my dear sir, have helped me out. Your paper has been refreshing to me; and, as I have received it weekly, I have not suffered much with drought. The college, the missionary enterprise, and the tract movement, will be as great helps to our blessed cause as any thing that has yet been done. God grant his blessing on all that may be done for the advancement of the truth as it is in Jesus." Mr. Whittemore remarks: "There, we would sooner have the gratitude of this old man, for the benefit we have conferred upon him, and the happiness we have poured into his soul, than all the praise that the enemies of God's truth could confer upon us."

The trustees of the new college held a meeting in Boston, in November of this year, and were greatly encouraged by the prospects of the institution. They found that the plan of subscription was legally drawn, that rising one hundred thousand dollars were subscribed, as stated by the executive committee at the meeting in September, and that the terms of the subscription had been fully complied with; so that every subscription is legal. The treasurer was required to give bonds satisfactory to Messrs. Oliver Dean, Sylvanus Packard, and O. A. Skinner. "It is probable," says Mr. Whittemore, "that the location will be selected by the first of January next. All hearts are cheered!"

During this autumn, a course of lectures on "the Problem of Human Destiny" was given at the Lowell Institute in Boston, by Rev. Dr. Dewey, of New York. Mr. Whittemore thus writes of them: "The breathless attention of the great audience which has listened to the beautiful passages and the refined eloquence of the speaker, is creditable to the cultivation and taste of the citizens of Boston. The theologian, the moral philosopher, the student of the history and nature of man, have here found some ingenious solutions of intricate and abstruse questions, and many suggestions which may assist to ' vindicate the ways of God to man.'

" Nevertheless, we confess to some degree of disappointment in these lectures. Their title led us to expect something which has not been accomplished, nor attempted. A philosophy which would lead the fainting soul to the grave, and there leave it to grope its way through the dark valley of the shadow of death, is incapable of solving ' the problem of human destiny.' He who would solve this problem, who would exhibit to us the design, the plan, the purpose of heaven in the creation, must look far beyond the narrow boundaries of the grave : he must tell us whether we are the heirs of the promises of God, and whether these promises rest upon the immutability of his counsel. Nothing less than this will satisfy the cravings of those who have fled for refuge to lay hold upon the hope set before us. The soul wants ' an anchor sure and steadfast.' Give us but this, and philosophers may speculate as they please ; and if some of the ways of Providence wear a frown, and present mysteries we cannot penetrate, we will rest on our assurance that all will be well at last."

The *Trumpet* of Jan. 10, 1852, records the death of Rev. Walter Balfour of Charlestown, Mass., of whose conversion and entrance upon the ministry of Universalism the readers of this memoir have already been informed. His age was seventy-six. He was one of the most sincere and faithful of Christians. His funeral was private. On the Sunday succeeding it, Mr. Whittemore officiated in the Universalist church there, and delivered a discourse on the life and character of the beloved and respected man. A large congregation was in attendance. In the same number of the *Trumpet*, the death of Professor Stuart of Andover is recorded. The agency which the Professor had in the conversion of Mr. Balfour to Universalism, made notable to many the nearness of the time of their departure from this life. Mr. Whittemore announces at this time his intention to issue a memoir of Mr. Balfour.

The site of the new College is announced in the *Trumpet* of Jan. 17. " It is at length determined, we understand, to locate this institution on Walnut Hill, so called, in Somerville, though the line of the town passes across the hill in such a way that the building probably will be erected in Medford. The trustees had so far determined the matter that the institution should go either to the place chosen or to Franklin, Mass. It was a nice point to decide. Now that we learn the vine is to be planted, and where, let it be nurtured, let it be watered freely, that it may grow and shed its blessings all around."

Mr. Whittemore about this time notices, with much tenderness and fervor of feeling, a letter of Mrs. Caroline A. Soule, widow of Rev. H. B. Soule, who suddenly departed this life at Rome, N.Y., not long previous. The letter was written to Rev. J. M. Austin, editor of the *Christian Ambassador.* It was a soul-stirring affirmation of living faith in the great Gospel of the Reconciliation. " A religion," she writes, " that could come to me as ours has come, in this, the sudden and awful dispensation of my Father, I know will never fail to strengthen and comfort me. Death ! it seems now that it were but a little thing to die ; for God and heaven are at death's portals. My brother, preach Universalism ; write it, live it, feel it, — never faltering, never failing. It has changed my tears into smiles, my bitterness into joy ; and what it has done and is doing for me, it will do for thee, for thine, for all. Strengthened, comforted, assured by that, I can take up my cross, — and oh, it is no light one, I assure you ! Five little ones — the youngest but a babe in my arms, the oldest having seen but seven summers — look up to me as their all on earth. My road will be a rugged one, I know, let sympathy

and friendship smooth it as they will.   But I do not faint nor
fear."

Mr. Whittemore's heart responds to her appeal.   "Let professed preachers of Universalism take note!   Hear this voice
of the widow.   We *will* preach this Gospel.   It is that of the
living God, the God of all consolation.   Better than all mere
human creeds or philosophies, is Universalism.   A doctrine
that can so comfort the soul in the season of the darkest ad-
versity, so lift the soul heavenward, *must be of God*.   We say
to the widow, and we say to all, ' Acquaint now thyself with
God, and be at peace : thereby good shall come unto thee.' "
He regarded the whole letter " as an extraordinary production."   Rev. T. B. Thayer, of Lowell, wrote to him respecting it: "I confess I have never been more moved by any
thing in my life.   I desire to thank that bereaved woman for
the witness she has given.   I took the letter into the pulpit
with me yesterday instead of a sermon, and read it to the
people, with such comments as you know must have flowed
from it.   It was more to them than any sermon of mine could
have been, and did them far more good."

Mr. Whittemore writes from Washington, D.C., under date
March 2.   He had preached in Hartford, Ct., on the Sabbath
previous.   He describes his journey to the capital, and places
in it, the Smithsonian Institute, the Capitol, the unfinished
Washington Monument.   Desiring to enjoy the extensive view
to be taken at its top, he writes: " With the foolishness of
a child we resolved to climb to the top, and take a view.   The
only means of access were the ladders used by the builders.
Up we climbed, stopping at each plank to view the stones and
take breath.   But the descent.   It was more fearful than the
ascent.   Suppose (thought we) a man should become faint up
here on this ladder.   The very thought caused a cold sweat!
the knees that bore us shook! the arms trembled! and glad

enough we were when we reached the ground. We could not take a firm step for several hours. We went to see the President, but he was engaged with his cabinet. We repaired to the Capitol, and held very pleasant interviews in the Senate Chamber with Governor Davis and Mr. Sumner of our own State; and in the House, with Messrs. Thompson, Davis, Rantoul, Appleton, Duncan, and others. As our business with these eminent men had nothing to do with Universalism, we will not describe it here." He says at the close of his visit: " We must say that we had rather spend a month here than in any other city or place in the United States which we have ever visited."

From Washington, he went to Fredericksburg, Va., where he notes and describes a Virginia spring; thence to Baltimore and New York, up the Hudson River, and home by the Hudson and Berkshire, Vermont and Massachusetts, and Fitchburg Railroads. " No place like home " is again realized.

The Memoir of Rev. Walter Balfour, by Mr. Whittemore, is issued in May. It is a volume of 224 pages; " a book for the people," as its author states.

A visit to Lawrence is recorded. " We rode to Lawrence through Andover. On arriving at the Merrimack River, we learned that there was no crossing for carriages, and were obliged to leave the horse on this side, and cross on foot on the viaduct of the railroad. On the other side, we joined a friend waiting with a chaise, who took us to the church. It happens to us, almost every time we go to Lawrence, that a text is placed in the pulpit for us to explain; and on entering, on Sunday morning last, we found the following note : —

" ' Mr. Whittemore, — Will you please to preach from the following passage of Scripture this morning : " And the smoke of their torment ascendeth up for ever and ever; and they have no rest day nor night" (Rev. xiv. 11).' Instead of preaching from this text in the morning, we gave notice that we would do so in the afternoon; and a very large congregation came together to listen to the services, and they did *listen*. Owing to the great heat of the day, we found ourselves much fatigued by the exertion. It did not, however, prevent our return to Cambridge after the service. The ride was pleasant. The fields were all green; the trees were blossoming; the woods were fragrant; the brooks and rivers glowed in the sunlight; the birds were singing; in fine, it was such a day as filled the heart to overflowing with devout gratitude to God."

Mr. Whittemore proposes to Dr. Edward Beecher, pastor of a Congregationalist church in Boston, an exchange of pulpits. He urges his reasons for this invitation. One is, that he belongs to a family who have exercised great freedom of speech and independence of action; another, that such a step might help Universalists and Congregationalists to a better understanding of each other's opinions. " Calvinists say that they are misrepresented by Universalists; and we on our part say (and I fully believe the declaration is true), that our opinions and interpretations of Scripture are misrepresented — perhaps without due reflection — by Calvinists. An exchange of pulpits between the two will do much to obviate these evils. If the proposition I now make should be acceded to on your part, let it be understood that each is to declare his doctrines without reserve in the pulpit of the other. I should be exceedingly happy to have such an opportunity; for I sometimes suspect that Calvinists in all cases do not know what are the creeds of their own churches. You shall have the same privilege, and you need not be in the least afraid that our darkness will put out your light. Will this give offence? To whom? Not to those who have the right spirit. If I have been correctly informed, there are some Universalists who are communicants in the church of which you are pastor. They will not be offended, but gratified. A member of your church called to see me a few days since, and avowed himself a Universalist. He said that it was known to you that he was. How many such there are in orthodox churches I do not know. Professor Stuart speaks as though there were many. I am not a pastor, Doctor; but I feel perfect confidence that if you accede to this proposition for an exchange, I can procure for you a Universalist pulpit in this city; and your services can be repaid by the services of the pastor in whose pulpit you preach, or by my own."

Dr. Beecher is not inclined to accept the invitation. He objects that the proposal should have been made in the paper instead of having been privately offered. He says: "I feel no need of such a discussion. If I supposed that the principles and practices of my denomination on this subject were wrong, I should not hesitate to free myself from their influence. Believing them to be true, I have no desire to be free from the truth. I therefore respectfully decline your offer. I am, however, in favor of a full and candid investigation of the points at issue between us; and have already, in a course of evening lectures, taken occasion to state my views. I propose still farther to pursue the subject, giving public notice of the time and place; and I extend a cordial invitation to your readers to be present, and hear and judge for themselves. Regarding with deep interest the welfare of your denomination, it has been and shall be my aim in such discussions to avoid whatever may produce misunderstanding and hostility, and thus prevent the full results of fair and candid reasoning."

Mr. Whittemore answers, in substance: "You say, dear Doctor, that you are in favor of a full and fair investigation of the points at issue between us. This is very well: I am happy to have you avow it. Now, the principal point at issue between us is that of the endless punishment of a part of the human race. Are you in favor of a full and fair investigation of that point? You say you have already taken occasion, in a course of evening lectures, to state your opinions on certain of those points. But, dear sir, please to remember that you give Universalists no opportunity to reply to what you say. The very fact that you avow your desire to have my readers listen to your lectures, because you wish them to judge for themselves, lays you under an obligation to let them hear both sides when they come to your church; for how can they judge safely without hearing both sides? What should you think of a jury who should be ready to render a verdict after having heard one side only? Or, what should you think of a party in a cause who should be unwilling to be confronted face to face with his opponent? Now, as you are so deeply friendly to Universalists; as you are willing they should know the truth; as you are seeking to edify them; as you invite them to your church, — will you not open your pulpit? Or, if you cannot do that, will you not allow some Universalist clergyman a foothold upon your pulpit stairs, to notice what you may say; that if you preach the truth, we may rejoice with you; 'and if you should happen to defend an error, we might point it out.'

"If you cannot do this, my clerical friend, will you do what you ask me to do? Will you come with your church and congregation to one of our churches? Your honored father said, twenty years ago, that all he wanted was ' an open field and fair play.' I hope that all this talk about fair play is not mere talk. If it is right for you to invite our people to your church, it is right for us to invite your people to our churches; and if it is right for you to expect our people to accept your invitation, it is right for us to expect yours to do the same thing. I do now invite you, your deacons, your church, your congregation, one and all, to come. You, Doctor, believe in free ageney; and I join with you in that belief so far as to say that you can come *if you will*. Now, Doctor, *will* you come? ' The Spirit and the bride say, Come. And let him that heareth say, Come. And let him that is athirst come. And whosoever will, let him take the water of life freely' (Rev. xxii. 17). Will *you* come? I hope I am not calling ' spirits from the vasty deep.' So far as it is possible for man to do it, we will give you the water of eternal life, without any admixture of the *toxicum* of eternal death. Signify that you will come, and I will use my best endeavors to obtain a Universalist meeting-house as near yours as possible; and a large part of it, if desired, can be set apart, especially for your congregation. ' Whosoever will, let him come.' "

" Anniversary Week" this year is thus comprehensively reported by the editor through his *Trumpet*, of June 5 : —

" The great week has passed, and it has been indeed a great week. At its close, almost exhausted in body, but strengthened and quickened in soul, we sit down to report to our readers ' that which we have seen and heard.' Oh that they could all have been there! Such zeal in the cause of truth, such faithfulness, such a spirit of self-sacrifice, such a determination to persevere in all that is good, we have never seen among our brethren before. At certain times it seemed like the ' day of Pentecost fully come.' The glow of heaven seemed to dwell upon the brethren; they were filled with power from on high; and spake as the Spirit gave them utterance. The speaking was of the most useful and effective kind; and it must do good. Those who have listened to it cannot resist its power. These remarks are especially true of the addresses at the Festival on Thursday afternoon. Brothers Cobb, Hosea Ballou, Miner, Case, of Bath, Me. ; Tillotson, of Manchester, N.H.; Dennis, of Attleboro; Chapin, of New York; E. A. Eaton, P. H. Sweetser, B. B. Mussey, T. S. King, and others, — spake as they never spake before. Brother Chapin never made an address equal to his address on that occasion; and we are almost tempted to say, no other man ever made such an address. King's, too, was neat, beautiful, powerful. Father Ballou was singularly appropriate and happy, and Tillotson, whom we never heard address a Boston audience before, took the house by storm. There were probably about five hundred persons at the tables, — ladies and gentlemen, — a third of them, perhaps, clergyman and their wives. We dare not encourage any one to believe that the Universalists will ever have another meeting in Boston in all respects equal to it."

The Boston *Bee* said of Mr. Whittemore's speech at the Festival: " The Old Bay State was complimented in a neat sentiment. Rev. Thomas Whittemore was called upon to respond, which he did in a most witty manner. He paid an eloquent compliment to Rev. Mr. Chapin, whom he and all Bostonians were always glad to see. The speaker referred to Faneuil Hall as the ' Cradle of Liberty,' and then went on most humorously to consider it as a cradle. Mr. Whittemore was the occasion of much amusement. Anecdote, wit, philosophy, were delightfully blended."

The Massachusetts Convention held its session this year in Plymouth. It was well attended, and the meetings were of much interest. "Only one thing," writes Mr. Whittemore, " occurred to mar the perfect felicity of the occasion; viz., a report which reached the town of the sudden sickness of Father Ballou, which proved afterward not to have been without foundation." Mr. Whittemore and Rev. H. Ballou 2d, presided at the communion service on the last afternoon of the session.

On Monday of the next week after the Convention, June 7, the Rev. Hosea Ballou departed this life. It was a startling announcement to the Universalist public: it was an event causing a deep sensation wherever personally or by reputation this distinguished and now venerable man was known. A "father in Israel" had indeed fallen; but full of honors as of years. When the announcement of the event was made at Cornhill, the Board of the Home Missionary Society was in session. Surprise and sadness brought its business to a close. An impressive silence was broken by the emphatic utterance of its chairman, Mr. Mussey, "Let me die the death of the righteous, and let my last end be like his."

Mr. Whittemore writes in concluding a notice of the life and character of this eminent man: "For myself, I acknowledge that I feel most deeply the loss of this steadfast friend. I mourn not for him, but for myself. To me he had been a father. He found me in my early manhood, and drew me out from seclusion. He taught my lips to pray. He turned my attention to the ministry, and sought and obtained the means to support me when I had not a cent with which to help myself. He has been the earnest, steadfast friend of my wife and children; my teacher to the day of his death; a man of whom I have learned more concerning God and the Divine Word, and the relation between God and man, than I have learned from any other human source. How can the event of such a man's death transpire without exciting in me extraordinary sensations? And yet I am not inconsolable. When I reflect upon what he was, upon the length of his life, upon the great measure of good he accomplished, I cease to mourn. And now, although there never will be, for there never can be, another man to me like Father Ballou, I will be reconciled. And I will close this brief sketch with the words of Job, — ' The Lord gave, and the Lord hath taken away ; blessed be the name of the Lord.' "

He has a sharp but just criticism upon a short article from the pen of Rev. Walter Colton, an Episcopalian Chaplain in the United States Navy. The article appeared in the *Sailor's Magazine*, a pretended unsectarian publication.

" Universalism among Sailors. — A Universalist was once appointed a chaplain in the navy, and reported for duty on board one of our ships fitting for the sea. His creed very soon became known to the sailors, and was freely discussed in their messes.

" ' If we are all so good that we are going to heaven,' said an old tar, ' what's the use of overhauling one's sins? it only gives a man a bloody sight of trouble for nothing.'

" ' If we are all on the right track,' said another, ' and must bring up at the right port, what is the use of preaching and praying about it?'

" ' If we trust this doctrine, and it don't turn out to be true, there 'll be hell to pay,' exclaimed a third.

" These sentiments were shared in by the whole crew, and soon became known to the newly appointed chaplain, who was wise enough to resign his mission."

Mr. Whittemore says : " Probably this narration is solely fictitious. The Episcopalians have so long enjoyed the honors and emoluments of chaplaincies on ship-board, that they feel almost as if their rights were invaded if a clergyman of another sect is appointed. A Universalist was appointed we believe ; and this fact gave rise to the attempted witticism. However, we will suppose the story all to be true ; what is the just inference?

" 1st. That sailors are not Universalists. They are believers in endless misery, and are profane and wicked. They think ' there 'll be hell to pay,' if Universalism don't turn out to be true.   This is the language which naturally grows out of such a faith.   These sentiments, says Mr. Colton, were shared in by the whole crew.

" 2d. The great fault of the article is, it represents that there is nothing for man to be saved from except endless hell-fire. No salvation from sin ; because if we are all ' going to heaven at last, what is the use in overhauling one's sins.'   According to this the only motive to goodness is the hope of escape from endless burnings.   No other salvation is needed.   People who believe this ought to pray, ' Lord, save us from endless burnings : we need no other salvation.'   Salvation from sin is nothing : all we want is to be saved from endless burnings. Such is the character of the prevalent orthodoxy of our country, whether of the Episcopal or any other form."

CHAPTER XII.

1852–1854.

AGED 52–54.

U.S. Convention at New York — Mr. Higginson's Sermon — A Question asked and answered — Should Universalists be aggressive? — Site of Tufts College — Life Sketch by Rev. T. J. Sawyer — Sonnet — Foot-notes — Irish Repartee — Death of Rev. Edward Turner — Anniversary Meetings — Reform Festival — Mr. Whittemore's Speech — Rev. Theodore Parker — Rev. Dr. Sharp — Laying Corner-stone of Tufts College — Stale Joke noticed — Spiritualism — Rockingham Association — Preaches in New York — Dr. E. Beecher's "Conflict of Ages" — Boston Association — Controversy among Brethren — Mr. Whittemore on Future Punishment — Remarks — Professor Maurice — Dr. Ballou visits Europe — Anniversary Week — Excitement — Festival: Mr. Whittemore's Speech — Letter from Rev. T. Clapp — Orthodoxy of the past and present — U.S. Convention in Philadelphia — E. Kingston, N.H. — Warren, Mass. — Attack of Paralysis — Hard Work — Expostulation of Friends.

THE session of the United States Convention was held in New York city this year. At the first meeting in Metropolitan Hall, three thousand persons were present. A mass meeting of great interest was held there on Wednesday morning (of the second day) ; and there were services in five or six churches (including Brooklyn and Williamsburg) at other times. Mr. Whittemore preached in Brooklyn, on Thursday evening, at the close of the session.

He notices at this time a published sermon by Mr. T. W. Higginson, minister of the Free Church in Worcester. It was preached by the author at his own installation. Mr. Higginson's sentiments were similar to those of Rev. Theodore Parker; less definite in theology, however. Mr. Whittemore makes brief extracts from the sermon, and objects to the manner in which Mr. Higginson speaks of the Bible. "In our opinion he has no faith in the Bible. His system, if it may bear that name, lays the axe at the root of all revelation. We do not see why he may not consider himself, according to his theory of inspiration, as much inspired as Paul was; and perhaps he does. He would have men discard the Bible and trust in themselves. Like the infatuated seaman, he would throw the compass and all astronomical instruments overboard, and then cut the cable, and set sail, without any sight of the heavens or the land. Where would he bring up except on the rocks of infidelity? For our own part, we shall not follow Mr. Higginson's advice. The very religion which he recommends to men as the sum of all good (viz., love to God and love to men) is the religion of the very Bible which he seeks to undermine. In fine, we regard Mr. Higginson, not as a planet, revolving around the Sun of Righteousness, according to fixed laws, and ever reflecting the central light; but as a meteor, that sparkles for a little time, and then goes out to be seen no more." Mr. Higginson afterwards gave up his ministry as a religious teacher, and his congregation in Worcester was scattered. He has since been somewhat eminent among the literary writers of our land.

"Who Believe It?" is a question asked by Mr. Whittemore in the November 6th issue of his paper: "Within one fortnight, we were conversing with a gentleman who is a stated attendant at one of the orthodox churches in Cambridge. He said 'he trusted in the goodness of God.' He 'felt that he was in the hands of a Father, who cannot afflict willingly, and who will overrule all things for good.' 'Well,' said we with some surprise, 'what becomes of your doctrine of endless misery? How do you get along with that?' 'I don't have any thing to do with it,' he replied. 'But' (said we), 'your minister preaches it.' 'That's his concern,' said he, 'and not mine. I don't believe it,' he continued; 'I believe that God is good; that's my confidence: he will do all things well; he cannot forsake the work of his hands.'

"We believe that two-thirds of the people who attend what are considered orthodox meetings are like this man. They do not believe the doctrine of endless punishment. If the clergyman preaches it, that is his concern, they think. They go to the orthodox meetings for very different reasons than because they have strong faith in orthodox doctrines: many go because it is fashionable; some because their wives or daughters wish to go there; some because they dislike to break away from a circle of old friends; some because they own pews; some because they love the minister as a man; some because the society is the chief one in the town, &c. How few go because they believe the creed. Talk about the vital power there is in orthodoxy! If it had had nothing to sustain it but its own essential power, it would have died out long ago. It is sustained in many places merely by the fact that it is the fashionable religion. *That* is its vital power, its saving efficacy. It is the religion of the many — the rich, the leading men in society. Were it not for all these things, how long would it live?"

"Should Universalism be Aggressive?" is another question claiming attention. There seems to be but one side to it, as Mr. Whittemore regarded the subject. He says: —

"The sermon preached recently before the General Convention of Universalists in New York was objected to by some as being aggressive in its spirit. If this was the fact, it should not be regarded as an objectionable feature. Shall a preacher of the Gospel hold up a flag of truce to sin and error? Shall he parley with false doctrines? Shall he say to those who defend them, 'We will let you alone if you will let us alone?' 'We are merely going to maintain our ground, and if you do not trouble us we shall not trouble you.'

" Primitive Christianity was aggressive. Jesus was aggressive. He did not come into the world merely to share dominion with the adversary. But he came to assault the kingdom of darkness, and claim every child of Adam as the purchase of his blood. He attacked error and sin. He did not act merely on the defensive. In his Sermon on the Mount, one of the earliest he ever preached, he denounced the old and venerable errors of the Jews, honored from old time by the faith, affection, and reverence of the people. Jesus when on earth felt it his duty to be aggressive. So did his apostles. When his resurrection was known, did they not carry the war into the very centre of the enemy's field? They pursued a straightforward course. They could suffer, but they would not temporize. Paul regarded the Christian enterprise as a conflict, and told his brethren what armor they must put on.

" Has the necessity for the aggressive plan of operations passed away? No, indeed. There are now strongholds to be pulled down, and high things that exalt themselves against the true knowledge of God. Let the preacher have his own style, but let him be faithful to the cause of Christ. Let him remember that the world belongs to Christ; that error has no right in the world; that, however venerable and gray by age it may be, it should be thrown down, because it exalteth itself against the true knowledge of God."

Of the scenery as viewed from the hill where the new College is to have its place, Mr. Whittemore says : " Mingling in the panorama are sea and land, the city and the country, beautiful villages and detached and elegant buildings, vessels

of war and vessels of commerce, steamers, railroads with
trains continually passing, bridges, viaducts and excellent
roads, spires of churches pointing to heaven on every
side, monuments and public buildings, farms, gardens,
hills, valleys, graceful lawns arrayed in living green, — in
fact, every thing that can please the eye of the true lover
of nature."

In the *Trumpet* of Dec. 25, a Biographical Sketch of Mr.
Whittemore, by Rev. T. J. Sawyer, is copied from the *Universalist Miscellany*. It was written four years previous.[1]
Some foot-notes are added, in which Mr. Whittemore gives
an account of certain matters which the original sketch did
not contain. Of his connection with the Cambridge Bank
and other secular interests, he writes : " I take the occasion
to say that I have never permitted any thing to interfere
with my duty to the cause of Universalism. Associated as I
am with men of all creeds, mixing with them at Temperance
conventions, railroad meetings, &c., I never sacrificed for

[1] Accompanying the above-mentioned Sketch of Mr. Whittemore's
life, by Rev. T. J. Sawyer, is the following sonnet to the preacher, by
Mrs. C. M. Sawyer, which we place in this volume : —

THOMAS WHITTEMORE.

Man of most rare and unrelaxing zeal, —
  Pressing still onward in the path of truth,
  Thy manhood's prime fulfilling all thy youth,
In its full ripeness heralded, — the seal
Of faith is on thy life; thy years reveal
  A brave unflinching heart; an earnest love
  For God and truth, which weighing far above
All baser motive thy strong mind could feel,
  Have sped thee on, thy ofttimes thorny way,
  And shed their light o'er many a darksome day.
On then, nor falter! let thy path be trod,
  What time thy Maker grants thee yet with eye
  Upturned, and reverent heart; then shalt thou die,
When comes thy summons, blest of man and God!

once my religious principles. I never cringed to any sect. I have always loved the cause of Universalism ; and, although I am changeable like other men, I have no fear that I shall ever love any other doctrine. Whenever men see fit to refer to my religion, as they sometimes (but not often) have done, I defend it. I will not introduce it out of place ; but if others introduce it I will defend it. A stockholder once referred to my Universalism at a railroad meeting, and got up a laugh. I replied to him that since he had introduced Universalism I wished to say that, if some railroad men *whom I knew* were not saved on the principle of divine grace, they never would be saved at all ; for they certainly never could be saved for their *good works ;* and this turned the tide altogether against the individual who had alluded to me.

"My life has been an exceedingly active one. I went West for a larger field in 1827. If I had then removed, I should have gone to Cincinnati and commenced the *Trumpet* there. My neighbors, the members of the society in Cambridgeport, and my oldest sister especially, over-persuaded me not to leave New England. My dear wife was willing to follow the fortunes of her husband, but perhaps was pleased (though she kept it to herself) when she found I was not going. I have never done so much business that I could not have done more. My business is my pastime. Once in a while there may have been a pressure, and my feelings may have got excited, like the waters in a freshet, when the river gets suddenly obstructed ; but, in a little time, the current would clear the obstruction away, and every thing would flow on again as smoothly as usual. The secret of doing a great deal, is to do it in an easy and orderly way. In the midst of my labor I have taken much bodily exercise. Although my weight has uniformly been 210 or 215 pounds, except when sick, I walk, as a general thing, five miles a day. The owners of the Cambridge omnibuses are not much the richer for me."

In these foot-notes to the Memoir by Dr. Sawyer, he records the following instance of repartee on the part of an Irishman, which he deemed too noteworthy to be lost. It was very seldom that Mr. Whittemore was outdone in an encounter of this kind : —

" As to wit, I recollect an instance in which I found the wit of an Irishman altogether too quick for me. I had been appointed President of the Vermont and Massachusetts Railroad, and was up in an interior town, in 1849, looking about, when I discovered two Irishmen loading a platform car with chestnut rails, with which the road was being fenced. They threw the rails with great violence on the cars, and I thought they were doing damage. I spoke to them as kindly as possible, ' Men, do not throw those rails so furiously.' They evidently did not know the new President, for one raised his head and asked, ' Who in —— are you?' I did not wish to hurt the man's feelings, and therefore I did not let him know who I was. They abated their violence for a few moments; but soon got at it again as badly as before. I spoke again, ' Men, I asked you not to throw those rails so violently.' The same arch fellow lifted his head with a comical mixture of fun and face, and belched out the profane retort, ' You go to ——.' I replied with all the formality I could command, ' No sir, I shall do no such thing : I never was there in my life, and, more than that, it's the last place I should wish to go to.' ' Ah !' said Pat, wagging his head, ' perhaps it's the *last place* you iver will go to !' It was a shrewd thrust from a Catholic, for he holds that some will escape from future punishments after having suffered them for a time ; but Pat thought there was no hope for me. The place he named, he supposed was the last I should go to. I never let him know who he was addressing; but spoke to the fence contractor to prevent their abusing the cars."

In his paper of March 5, 1853, he announces his intention of preparing the biography of Rev. Hosea Ballou, containing a full account of his life and writings. His design was subsequently carried out. Four volumes of the Biography were issued, which included quite a comprehensive history of Universalism in America during the lifetime of this eminent man.

The death of Rev. Edward Turner is noted in the *Trumpet* of March 19. He was one of the early preachers of Universalism, and a man of marked ability. His chief settlements as pastor had been in Charlestown, Mass., Portsmouth, N.H., and Charlton, Mass. Mr. Whittemore writes of him: "His sermons were marked with clearness of thought and a happy purity and sweetness of expression, and never partook of severity towards any sect. His delivery was not impassioned; but gentle, persuasive, and winning. These qualities gave him a high standing in the denomination."

In a brief notice in the *Trumpet* of March 19 of this year, of Governor Benjamin Pierce, of Hillsboro', N.H., he mentions the following fact: "The Governor was a noble-minded man, — open, free, candid, who would not have hid his religion from the world for all the persecution that bigots could bring upon him. His house was often — indeed, so far as his wishes were concerned, always — open to the preachers of our glorious faith. On one occasion, Rev. Sebastian Streeter preached in Hillsboro'. Governor Pierce had some friends of distinction at his house; and the Universalists, we believe, were to hold their meeting in a hall. The Governor attended service with the Universalists. The preacher said to him, 'Governor, I did not know that I should see you here to-day, as you have distinguished visitors at your house.' 'Sir,' said the Governor, 'I serve my God first of all, and my fellow-men afterward.' This was a case of living up to the dictates of conscience which ought not to be lost upon us."

The May Anniversary meetings come again, and Mr. Whittemore makes a full and fair record of them. A spirited Home Missionary meeting was held on Tuesday at School Street church. The Reform Association met at the same place on Wednesday. Reports were read, — one by Rev. E. A. Eaton, on Juvenile Offenders, and another by Rev. J. S. Lee, on Temperance. The Massachusetts Sabbath School Association also held its session on Wednesday afternoon and evening. Resolutions on Slavery and Peace were discussed and passed in the Reform Association meeting on Thursday morning.

The Festival was held in Faneuil Hall on Thursday after-noon. Mr. Charles F. Eaton presided, and made a pertinent and stirring opening address. Speeches were subsequently made by Revs. Messrs. L. Willis, John Moore, E. H. Chapin, T. Whittemore, A. A. Miner, C. H. Fay, J. G. Adams, and others. To a sentiment offered in memory of the honored Ballou, Rev. A. A. Miner appropriately and eloquently responded. Chapin again raised and thrilled the assembly. Mr. Whittemore, in his address, gave a brief history of Faneuil Hall and its founder, and comprehensive notices of the worthies whose forms are speaking there on the painted canvas. In conclusion, he raised the question, "Why are we, the Universalists, in Faneuil Hall to-day? I reply, we come here by permission of the authorities of Boston; and I wish you all to join me in showing thanks to them for the kindness they have shown us. We have properly come here because *we* are the sons of liberty. We are all the friends of *independence;* we seek to establish spiritual freedom; we preach a truth which has the power to set men free: 'for if the Son shall make you free, you shall be free indeed.' Let it be known on this day, that John Murray used to preach in this hall; the mysterious winning preacher, who first turned the attention of the town of Boston to Universalism. And there is still another reminiscence which belongs to this place: Thomas Handyside Peck, one of the earliest of the friends of Murray in Boston, lived but a few rods to the south of us, between Faneuil Hall and State Street. He was the honored father of the honored mother of our present distinguished fellow-citizen, Thomas Handyside Perkins, who once informed me that his mother cherished to the last moments of her life the sentiments she derived from Murray. We may properly meet in this hall, because we are, or ought to be, the true liberty party. What right should we have to be here if we were any thing else? I should as soon expect to see a body of British tories convened in this hall for a festival, as a gathering of men who are not of the go-ahead liberty party. Let us press forward. We are not afraid of light; let us see all there is, for it cannot lead us wrong. Let no man be cramped or hoodwinked. We drive even the horses now without blinders. We must aim to progress: we must go on unto perfection."

He notices Rev. Theodore Parker again in the *Trumpet* of July 2, and objects strongly to what he considers the deistical sentiments of Mr. Parker. In a notice of two sermons published by him, Mr. Whittemore speaks of the statement made in one of them that Christ taught the doctrine of eternal punishment. "I am ready to believe," says Mr. Parker, "that Jesus taught, as I think, eternal torment." Mr. Whittemore says: "Christ taught nothing of the kind, and it is strange that Mr. Parker knew no better. There is not a passage in either of the evangelists which when properly interpreted will show that Christ taught eternal torment, but *the contrary.* We are astonished at Mr. Parker's statement. He tells some truths; he utters some apt sayings; but he is sadly out of the way in his opinion of Christ's sayings."

He thus notices the departure by death of the distinguished Baptist divine of Boston, Rev. Daniel Sharp, D.D.: "Our venerable neighbor and friend whom we all so deeply loved, is gone! We shall see him no more on earth. Dr. Sharp was a Baptist; but, whatever he was in his ecclesiastical associations, there was one thing in him which rose above every thing else, — he was a Christian. He was one of the most dignified, urbane, and remarkable of our city preachers. No one could see Dr. Sharp pass, even if a perfect stranger, without being prompted to ask, *who* is that? Ease and dignity were beautifully combined in him. No man could be more meek; none more respectful of the rights of others. We had occasion once to address him by epistle on the subject of baptism, making certain inquiries we desired to have answered. We shall never forget the tenderness, cordiality, and respectful character of his reply. It added strength to the conviction we had before, that he was a true man."

Tuesday, July 19, was a day long to be remembered by the friends of Tufts College. The corner-stone of the first edifice was laid, with appropriate religious services, on the forenoon of this day. Mr. Whittemore thus records it: "A special train left Boston at nine o'clock. On arriving at the hill, it was found that Mr. Yale, of Boston, had spread a very large awning, under which seats had been prepared for the ladies. Three American ensigns floated from the top, at proper distances from the canvas, and equidistant from each other. A part of the walls of the college had been built, and a section of the freestone laid, at one of the corners, some fifteen feet in height. The day was delightful, the tent screened the people from the rays of the sun, and no one suffered from heat. The people kept coming until the services were half through; and we are confident that there were upwards of a thousand present; some thought fifteen hundred, or two thousand. There was a great crowd."

At a quarter-past ten the services commenced. Mr. Whittemore (Vice-President of the Board of Trustees) presided, in absence of the President, Dr. Oliver Dean. The Scriptures were read by Rev. T. J. Greenwood, and prayer was offered by Rev. H. Bacon. Two original hymns were sung: one by Mrs. N. T. Munroe, the other by Mrs. Mary T. Goddard. Rev. A. A. Miner delivered the address; Rev. H. Ballou, D.D., President of the College, laid the corner-stone; Rev. W. H. Ryder offered the concluding prayer, and gave the benediction. Social greetings were enjoyed by the multitude after these services were ended.

To one of the stale jokes on Universalists about their views of the devil, Mr. Whittemore deems it his duty to apply in answer a brief editorial admonition: " We said, two or three weeks since, that we were about to publish a sermon of our own writing, from the text, ' Resist the devil and he will flee from you.' On this the editor of the *Cambridge Chronicle* (printed in the city where we dwell) remarks: —

" ' The editor of the *Trumpet* notifies his readers that he is to publish one of his own sermons, from the text, " Resist the devil and he will flee from you." Brother Whittemore, we think, must have received some new light; for we have always supposed, from the tone of his paper, that there was no devil to resist. We would suggest whether it would not be better to wait till cooler weather; for *fleeing* from old Cloven-foot about these days would be dreadfully hot.' "

The *Trumpet* editor replies: " We have seen no new light on the subject referred to. It is the editor of the *Chronicle* who needs the new light. He says he always supposed we held that there is no devil to resist. Therein he was in *dark-ness*, for we never held any such thing. He then suggests that we had better wait for cooler weather, ' for fleeing from old Cloven-foot about these days would be dreadfully hot.' Fleeing! We said not one word about fleeing from him. A droll way, indeed, would it be to *resist* the devil by running away from him. When the Irish soldier boasted that his regiment made a glorious resistance to the enemy, he was asked how they did it. 'Och, upon my soul, sir, we *run away* from them.' The *Chronicle* is evidently confused in its ideas."

A subscriber desired an expression of his opinions on spiritualism, as his mind was much exercised on the subject, which was eliciting so much attention at that time. Mr. Whittemore very readily and candidly replied: " The truth is, we have no knowledge to communicate. If we turn to our own experience on the subject, we find that it has been very small. No spirits ever appeared to us, either good or evil. We have heard very little of the rappings, and seen very little of the writings. We have put ourself in the way of getting knowledge, but it did not come. We have been to see those who were called good mediums; but it happened, unfortunately, that, whenever we were present, the manifestations were not as they were said to have been at other times.

" But we are far from saying that the whole matter is a deception. We have no doubt that many honest people believe in the spiritual manifestations. We do not believe that these persons are all dishonest who profess to have held communion with the spirits. That there may have been artful and designing men and women engaged in these matters who have professed things not true, we have no doubt; and the same fact is true in regard to religion. Men are hypocrites in re-

ligion who profess much that is not true; but we do not condemn all religion on that account. It is going too far to say
that all who profess to have held communion with spirits are
dishonest. But, let it be remembered, it does not prove that
the spirits of the departed produce the rappings merely because honest persons sometimes think so; for honest persons
are sometimes in error.

"We are waiting for light; but perhaps we shall not get it
in this world. There are many mysteries yet to be revealed.
Perhaps, in the course of future examinations, it will be proved
that the spirit-rappings, so called, are produced by natural
causes now unknown to men. While the subject remains in
so much doubt, we suggest to all to cultivate charity. No
one has yet obtained perfect satisfaction on either side; and
those who are the most confident in their assertions are, perhaps, least to be depended upon. We say again, then, cultivate charity. 'Let every man be fully persuaded in his own
mind.'"

The thirteenth session of the Rockingham Association was
held this year in Atkinson, N.H. The attendance was good.
A funeral discourse on the death of Captain John Bassett, of
Atkinson, was delivered on the morning of the first day by
Rev. T. J. Greenwood. Mr. Whittemore preached a spirited
discourse on the last afternoon to a large audience. A social
conference in the evening closed the session.

On the Sabbath succeeding this meeting of the Association,
Mr. Whittemore preached in the pulpit of Rev. Mr. Chapin's
church, in New York city. The day seems to have been one
of much enjoyment to him. On Monday, he had a very
agreeable meeting with his ministering brethren and others,
at the *Ambassador* office, in New York. He afterwards visited
the Crystal Palace, and gives a very full account of his observations there, in his paper.

A new book appears at this time from the pen of Dr. Edward Beecher, of Boston ; son of Dr. Lyman Beecher, and pastor of one of the orthodox churches in the city. It is entitled, " The Conflict of Ages ; or, the Great Debate on the Moral Relations of God and Man." The author of the work, finding himself unable to defend the doctrine of endless punishment on the old grounds, has, in this work, sought out a new way of doing it. Mr. Whittemore, in an editorial article of some length, reviews the work. We present a few extracts from it. Speaking of its author, he says : " He maintains that orthodoxy, as it has been taught, has been like a steamer, the wheels of which revolve in opposite directions, the pilot of which, therefore, cannot control it, and which does nothing but sail in a circle. He affirms that there is a constant theological conflict between the different parts of the orthodox creed, and between different schools of their divines : that the principles of honor and right in man are the same in nature as the same principles in God ; that God is bound by these principles ; that if God gave existence to men with a nature radically depraved and corrupt anterior to any desire or choice of their own, with full power to do evil and none to do good, and then placed them under the all-pervading influences of corrupt social systems ; and, in addition to all this, subjected them to the tremendous and delusive power of malignant spirits, fearfully skilled in the work of developing, maturing, and confirming original native depravity, — if God did this, we cannot (says Dr. Beecher) say that he has fulfilled towards his creatures the demands of honor and right, as these principles have been implanted in ourselves by him.

" Here, then, is the conflict. Orthodoxy, as it has been taught, outrages our moral sense : it is opposed to the sense of honor and right which God has given us. Orthodoxy teaches us to love our enemies, and yet teaches us that God hates them. Thus one wheel of the steamboat revolves in one direction, and the other in the opposite, and therefore the vessel cannot go ahead. So with orthodoxy: it cannot go ahead; it cannot prosper. Orthodox sects may advance, build churches, multiply numbers; but the dogmas, the creeds, remain the same confused mass, confusing all who seek to understand or to explain them. Such is the CONFLICT which Dr. Edward Beecher has developed."

Mr. Whittemore goes on to show that this conflict which Dr. Beecher has just discovered, was seen and described by Universalists long ago; that all the principal advocates of our faith have taken a similar view with him of its contradictions and absurdities. He says, again: " Dr. Beecher's book has grown up out of the conviction on his part, that orthodoxy must be readjusted, or else the world will take refuge in Universalism. It gives to orthodoxy the severest blow it has ever had, considering the quarter from whence it comes. The family of Beechers are doing a great work in renovating the old Calvinistic creed. They seem to be digging away the foundation of orthodoxy. They inherit the propensities from their venerable father, who was himself the son of a black-smith in Connecticut, and who has learned to deal many a hard blow. Dr. Lyman Beecher departed from orthodoxy twenty-five years ago in several important respects. We hope the good work will go on. The doctrine of endless misery is destined to fall. It is a horrid doctrine, and *must* come down. It is the Bastile in theology, and the public are shouting, ' Raze it to the ground! Let it no longer disfigure the fair city of the New Jerusalem!'"

The Boston Association this year held its annual session in Danversport. Mr. Whittemore was chosen Moderator. The Occasional Sermon was delivered by Rev. T. B. Thayer.

Mr. Whittemore preached on the afternoon of the second day of the meeting. The clerk of the session, Rev. C. Damon, says of the discourse: " The preacher took for his text, Acts xvii. 18 : ' He preached unto them Jesus and the resurrection.' And that which the apostle preached unto others was on this occasion preached faithfully unto us. It was a pure Gospel sermon : the words spoken to us were spirit, and they were life. The preacher closed his discourse, of which I will not attempt an epitome, by exhorting his brethren in the ministry not only to preach ' Jesus and the resurrection,' but to take heed that they preach the *same* ' Jesus and the resurrection' which was preached by the apostles ; and depart not from the purity of the Gospel and the simplicity that is in Christ."

During the years 1851–54 much controversy was carried on respecting the doctrines of the Divine Sovereignty and Human Agency, Future Punishment, and No Future Punishment. Rev. Messrs. T. J. Sawyer, J. M. Austin, and T. Starr King were among the principal writers in advocacy of the doctrine of future punishment, and Mr. Whittemore, Rev. I. D. Williamson and others of those who denied that evidence existed in the Scriptures of the extension of punishment into the future or resurrection state. The *Universalist Quarterly* came in for a share of criticism on the part of Mr. Whittemore for its apparent departure from the " distinctive" Universalism of the past. The controversialists on each side were keenly alive to the topics in hand, and there was even a suggestion that a new paper might be started in Boston in advocacy of a Universalism that would give more prominence to the doctrines of human agency and future punishment. In reference to such a movement, Mr. Whittemore writes : " We merely say, that as we conduct the *Trumpet* according to our best ability and our conscientious convictions of duty, and as we defend in its columns what we fully believe, we cannot change our course, even if fifty new papers were threatened to be set up alongside of us. A man who publishes a paper merely for the sake of a party is worthy only of defeat. We cannot change our course until God changes our opinions. The Bible, and the Bible only, has made us what we are. If the old Bible should be withdrawn by proper authority, and a new one be set up in its place, we do not know what might then happen; but, as it is, we must walk in the good old way."[1] The new paper, however, did not appear.

Mr. Whittemore, in all his controversial course, manifested the strongest interest in contesting the doctrine of the punishment of souls after death, or in connection with their rising into the future life. He was evidently wedded to the opinions of the elder Hosea Ballou on this subject. The professed ground of his objection to the doctrine of future punishment was, that he did not find it revealed in the Scriptures. He asked for the passages of the Bible that others regarded as evidences of it; and, when these were presented, he had another explanation of them. When questioned philosophically or analogically on the subject, he deemed such queryings of little consequence compared with what the Scriptures affirmed. His views were, as stated by himself (in 1845) : "1. That there is an immortal state ; 2. That that state is a happy one ; and 3. That in describing the resurrection into that state, Jesus and the authors of the New Testament books speak of one resurrection for all men ; it is the resurrection from THE DEAD. What it is to me it is to all; all are raised, so far as we can learn from the sacred writers, to the same condition." These opinions he was ever ready to maintain through his ministry, giving no countenance to the

<hr>

[1] *Trumpet*, Feb. 18, 1854.

doctrine that character in the present existence could affect the spiritual life in the future beyond death. In one public utterance, however, recorded as having been made by him, he thus speaks of the work of Christ with souls. The text was 1 Tim. i. 5. Alleging that Christ's work shall go on to its accomplishment, he said: "But when? No man can tell. Will all enter heaven when they die? For himself, he doubted whether even the best Christians were fitted to enter at once on the joys of heaven. He would speak with great caution as to the conditions of the future life, immediately succeeding the present. The future, he believed, would be an advance for all. He could not undertake to say that all would be equal in virtue and happiness. He had been greatly misunderstood on this point. It was enough for him to feel sure, beyond all doubt, that the Universal Father will for ever seek the good of all."[1] This was coming nearer than was usual for him to the allowance that possibly all souls would have their different means, spiritually speaking, of entering fully into this resurrection life, — this enjoyment of a sinless immortality. "The conditions of the future life *immediately succeeding the present*," — respecting these he did not seem to have definite opinions. "The future, however," he believed, " would be an advance for all." Precisely what his brethren believers in future punishment, discipline, or instruction would affirm as their convictions respecting the future life.

The controversy on this whole subject was carried on for years with great ability, in which Mr. Whittemore's opinions were questioned by some of the clearest and soundest minds in the Universalist church. And they are questioned still, and will be. But one thing is to be remembered to his credit touching this controversy.

[1] Quoted by Rev. E. G. Brooks, *Universalist Quarterly*, July, 1877.

Strongly as he adhered to his own opinions respecting the future life, he opposed all attempts to bring alienation of feeling or divisions among professing Universalists on this account. He had witnessed in the early days of his ministry what he regarded as an unjust division caused by the Restorationists, and could scarcely free himself from the effects of that experience. Yet he lived on terms of closest friendship with those who differed widely from him on this point, and was unyielding in his convictions and affirmations that all were to be accounted as Universalists who believed in the great saving work of Christ with all souls, whatever their differences as to the methods by which they might enter upon the life of final freedom from sin and its effects.

It is not, of course, the intent of the writer of this biography to take up this controversy in these pages. A few fraternal words, however, involving both sides of it, may not be out of place. Among Universalists, the leading advocates of the doctrines of future punishment and of no future punishment have been equally sincere and earnest in their work for the Gospel. Mr. Whittemore, in his way of working, was apparently as deeply interested in the religious life of the Universalist Church as was Dr. Ballou, his estimable co-worker. Their conflicting opinions in reference to punishment in the future life did not lessen their anxiety for the spiritual advancement of the Church which they both so worthily represented. The same may be said of others whose differences of opinion were in substance the same. That there were those calling themselves Universalists, accepting the doctrine of an instantaneous change from a sinful life here to a sinless one hereafter; and who, regarding all sin and punishment as necessarily connected with the body, were little inclined to bestir themselves to the work of religious action and spiritual life here, choosing rather to await the "glorious transition" hereafter, is true; and that such were often a reproach to the cause of Universalism is equally true ; just as some Calvinists, deeming themselves sure of future salvation by God's electing grace, have contented themselves with a kind of spiritual apathy in respect to the world's present religious needs.   Such, however, are not fair representatives of any living Christianity.   Such are not of Universalism.   That always signifies present spiritual life and salvation; never puts off this work; believes and affirms continually that obedience is its own reward, and that here or hereafter, in this or in any other life to come, the one thing needful to the highest realization of our highest spiritual being is, " holiness unto the Lord."   So have preached in the past, and so preach now, all true believers in the Universalism of Jesus, whether they confine the punishment of sin to the present life, or extend it into the future.   Differ as truthful souls may, and do, in reference to time or eternity wherein the punishment for sin shall be meted out, they all agree to the pre-eminent need of that greatest of all inducements to righteousness, — the blessedness of the righteous life itself; the inducement which Jesus himself had to do the will of his Father ; by which the angels that " excel in strength " above are moved, and which all Christian believers will more and more realize to be the true one, as they advance in the Divine life in this world, or in any other which they may enter. " We love him because he first loved us."   The words in Francis Xavier's hymn express it : —

> " Then why, O blessed Jesus Christ,
>   Should I not love thee well ?
> Not for the sake of winning heaven,
>   Or of escaping hell.
>
> Not for the hope of gaining aught,
>   Nor seeking a reward ;
> But as thyself hast loved me,
>   O ever-loving Lord ! "

There is no practical Universalism higher than this; there never need be.[1]

The dismissal of Professor Maurice from King's College, Cambridge, England, is noticed at this time by Mr. Whittemore. He says: "This very learned gentleman has raised the envy of his inferiors by his rare talents, and roused the fury of bigoted Episcopalians by the liberality of his views. Dr. Jelf, the Principal of the College, entertaining fears that the Professor had doubts of the strict eternity of punishment, has deposed him. It is not certain that he will remain deposed; for the case may be carried into higher courts, and the sentence of Dr. Jelf be reversed. Professor Maurice is certainly not liable to expulsion from the College for a disbelief of the doctrine of endless misery. That doctrine forms no part of the Thirty-nine Articles, if we may believe some of the most reliable authorities of the English Church. Dr. Henry More, Dr. Thomas Burnett, Sir Isaac Newton, Archdeacon Paley, John Hey, Norrissian Professor of Divinity at Cambridge, England; Dr. Thomas Broughton, Dr. Thomas Newton, Bishop of Bristol; James Brown, D.D.; Rev. Francis Leicester, A.B.; Rev. John Brown of Sidney Sussex College: all these divines, and some of them eminent dignitaries of the Established Church, rejected the doctrine of

---

[1] "'What must I do to be saved?' we should cause it to be understood, is a question which we have, every one of us, to ask with profound solicitude. Not, What shall I do to insure rescue from the wrath of God and perdition in hell?—as one is rescued from deserved hanging, or from drowning; but, What shall I do to be saved from sin and its darkness and absence from God? What shall I do to become pure, unselfish, Christ-like, thoroughly good, superior to temptation, and growing in freedom from sin? This is the grand question—not particularly with reference to the present, not particularly with reference to the future; but with reference to the everlasting Now in which we are always living, and always shall live, and because holiness alone is life, and any lack of harmony with God is spiritual poverty, death, and woe."—*Rev. E. G. Brooks, D.D., in "Our New Departure,"* p. 111.

endless misery; and a part of them received and defended enthusiastically the doctrine of the final holiness and happiness of all men. In the original Forty-two Articles of the Church of England, the doctrine of Universalism was condemned; but when the Articles were revised in the reign of Elizabeth, and reduced to thirty-nine, the condemnation of Universalism was omitted. From that time they have remained unchanged."

He speaks of his much-loved friend, Rev. Dr. Ballou, President of Tufts College, now on the eve of his departure for Europe. "It is his intention to visit England and also the Continent. He will view much of the beautiful scenery which he has long desired to feast his eyes upon; and likewise make himself acquainted with whatever it may be of interest for him to know of the highest literary institutions of England and Germany. He should tarry longer than two months in Europe, especially if he intends to ascend to the highest peak of Mont Blanc. The best wishes of many thousands of true friends will go with him."

As Anniversary week approaches, the *Trumpet* sounds a call to the fraternity to come to the Festival at that time. "The entertainments of the day, we trust, will be excellent both for the outer and the inner man. There will be no lack of speakers from all the New England States, New York, &c. Come to Faneuil Hall, — come to the Cradle of Liberty; come to the Annual Festival of the true-hearted; come one, come all! and years hence you will have it to say, ' I was at that great Universalist Festival in Faneuil Hall, in 1854.'"

Anniversary week came; and, taken altogether, it was one of the most remarkable ever realized in Boston. Let Mr. Whittemore describe it: "It was the week of the religious anniversaries, when almost the entire body of the clergy of New England, of all sects, were in Boston. They will carry home with them, and infuse into the hearts of their parishioners, the feeling which pervaded our city. It is estimated that there were two thousand clergymen present from all parts of New England. They came to consider the matters which respect the different denominations. During all the time they have been here, Boston has been under martial law, in effect, for the purpose of awing down public sentiment, and enabling one Colonel Suttle, of Alexandria, Va., to carry off one negro, *whom he claimed to own*, as he owns his horses or his swine. This lesson has been taught in the presence of all the clergy of New England ; and will be repeated and reiterated in all their pulpits. The people everywhere will have their story, not only in their papers, but from the burning lips of their pastors, in words that will enter their hearts. On the very spot where the citizens of Boston were shot down by British troops, on the 5th of March, 1770, stood the hired soldiery of the nation, backed up by the military companies of Boston, with guns loaded and bayonets fixed, to murder the men and women of Boston, if they did not permit Colonel Suttle to *drag away his negro*. A description of this event will go to every part of the land. There could not have been a more favorable time for educating the people of New England, and quickening the Northern pulse."

The Festival at Faneuil Hall was all that Mr. Whittemore had anticipated, and more. One thousand were at the tables. Hon. Francis B. Fay presided. Addresses were made by Rev. Messrs. Ryder, King, Whittemore, Laurie, Eaton, Mellen, and Maxham ; and B. B. Mussey and P. H. Sweetser, of the laity. The atmosphere was surcharged with the spirit of aggression against the Fugitive-slave Law. A few timid ones expressed the hope that no allusions would be made to the out-of-door excitement ; but they might as well have expected utter indifference on the part of a multitude feeling the

throes of an earthquake beneath them. Mr. Whittemore's
speech was full of it. He spoke of the press and its great
influence ; of the present gathering and its fraternal significance ; and then of Faneuil Hall, " where liberty was once
rocked, but where it would *never go to sleep !* " What followed
was to have been expected.

" Sir, I have thought much of Faneuil Hall during this
week of excitement. How can we get through the day without speaking of the violation of the moral sense of the community which has been realized? Sir, as I was coming from
Cambridge this morning, I met one of my good neighbors
who said to me, ' Now, Brother Whittemore, you will not say
any thing about the Fugitive-slave Law in Faneuil Hall to-
day?' Said I, ' My friend, I do not know as I shall speak
at the hall ; but if I do, I promise you in regard to the Fugitive-slave Law, that I shall not say *one word in favor of it.*'
Sir, how can we avoid speaking of it? We are *thinking* of
it, and we should all of us be monuments of falsehood if we
did not speak. I am not in favor of the mob spirit ; I counsel not treason ; I lament the blood which has been shed ;
but I cannot respect the Fugitive-slave Law. God grant
that it may soon be blotted from the statute-book. It does
the South no good ; in matters of property, it has not been
one dime's advantage to them ; and it is only an irritation to
the North, — a source of pain, disquiet, and agitation. I
can have some kind of respect for the government officials
who seek to enforce the law, if they only do the business
judiciously ; but I have none for the man who comes slave-
hunting, or those who *volunteer* to assist him in his business."

After a witty and sarcastic allusion to Mr. Suttle, comparing him with the serpent mentioned in connection with the
Garden of Eden, he proceeds : —

"But I turn once more to Faneuil Hall. It is a glorious place. Sir, our affections will cluster around it as long as we live. But if this place be glorious, what shall we say respecting the Court House to the county of Suffolk? It has been made a Bastile, a prison. It is not owned by the United States, but by the county of Suffolk; and the United States government have hired three or four rooms in it, not for the purpose of a prison, but for the holding of their Courts. Henceforth that building will be as infamous in the history of our country as Faneuil Hall is glorious. It is less difficult for me to respect the officers of justice, who were called on to perform a legal duty, than the men who *volunteered* in the business, or engaged in it for the sake of gold. I counsel no mobs, no treason; but I am not obliged to respect a slave-catcher; and least of all am I obliged to respect a man who, for gold or for any other reward, volunteers his aid in such a cause.

"On the other hand, a man who comes forward at his peril, and neither for gold nor honor, but for the sake of humanity, offers to defend a poor stranger, a negro, claimed as a slave, who is ready to do every thing that can be legally done to save him, I honor that lawyer; and such a man is Richard H. Dana, Jr., Esq. (Intense cheering.) Honor to him and honor to his colleague in this duty! Sir, their labors were unavailing; but a grateful public will not forget them. Richard H. Dana is the honored grandson of Chief Justice Dana, who was on the bench of the Supreme Court at the time the great case of John Murray against the First Parish in Gloucester was decided. It was the first case under the Third Article of the Bill of Rights of the Constitution of 1780, — the first construction of that Article, and was altogether in favor of Murray, and of religious liberty. But, Mr. Chairman, I have spoken too long. Let us do all we can in a legal and honorable way to prevent the repetition of the odious scenes which our eyes have beheld the past week. Spare us, spare our wives and children, such excitement. Let us petition Congress to repeal the law; and let us do all we can as good citizens, prudent men and Christians, to save our good old Commonwealth from the disgrace under which it lies."

A letter from Rev. Theodore Clapp, of New Orleans, to Mr. Whittemore, appeared in his paper of July 8, in which certain queries proposed by Mr. Whittemore respecting slavery are answered. Mr. Clapp was an able preacher of Universalism in the South, and was supposed to have strong sympathy with the Southerners in reference to their "peculiar institution." Mr. Clapp's reply was very candid and hopeful. He stated in his letter that the most prominent and influential men of the South with whom he had conversed on the subject had expressed their opinion that slavery would in the order of God's providence come to an end. The following passage from his letter is worthy of a place in these pages : —

"A year or two before his death, Hon. John C. Calhoun spent several weeks in New Orleans. I saw him often. and had lengthy conversations with him on the subject of slavery. Do you know that he was a decided Universalist? He said that it was a sufficient refutation of the doctrine of endless misery, that it is incomprehensible; for a righteous law-giver would never ordain a penalty which his subjects could not understand. On one occasion he spoke to me in nearly the following words: 'Slavery cannot live long in the United States. It will have run its race by the end of the next one hundred and fifty or two hundred years. Slave labor is too expensive to last long. According to an eternal law of heaven, in the long run the most expensive and unpropitious forms of labor must be everywhere superseded by the least costly and most efficient.' The good rising above the evil: this is the philosophy. The Hon. Henry Clay, when in New Orleans, expressed to me the same opinion with Mr. Calhoun concerning the end of slavery, and also the duration of future punishment. I wish I had space to tell you what he said about the Parable of Dives and Lazarus. The whole South are kept from espousing the cause of Liberal Christianity, partly through the fear that it involves ultra-abolitionism."

In noticing an accusation, in an orthodox journal, that Unitarians as a sect are running down, Mr. Whittemore says: "We leave our Unitarian brethren to defend themselves in regard to this matter. We affirm, if the orthodox flourish as a sect, their religion is dying out as a principle. Where is the orthodoxy of the past century? Gone. Where is the orthodoxy of President Edwards? Gone, irrecoverably gone. The orthodoxy of the Beechers, of Bushnell, of Dr. Park, of Amherst and Andover, is not the orthodoxy of Griffin and his associates. As a principle, orthodoxy is trimming itself to the state of the times. The Old South stands where it did a hundred years ago; and Park Street rests on its first foundations: but do the people who worship in those places *believe* as they used to? No: many of those persons are known to believe in Universalism, if their own private confessions may be relied on. Their assent to the creed is mechanical, formal, with great mental reservation; and is no more to be taken as a proof of real faith on their part, than the confession of Galileo was a true index of his faith when he renounced the doctrine of the earth's diurnal revolution. His mental reservation was, ' It moves still.' And so the mental reservation of many persons may be greatly unlike their creeds. How can *the people* be expected to believe these creeds, when it is very doubtful whether the priests believe them themselves?"

In September, Mr. Whittemore attended the United States Convention in Philadelphia. He was called to speak on several public occasions during the session, and makes a very spirited report of the Convention's doings in the *Trumpet.* He also administers a proper reproof to a Philadelphia newspaper editor who undertook to criticise the Occasional Sermon before the Convention by Rev. T. B. Thayer. The sermon was very timely and acceptable to most of the hearers of it.

He visits East Kingston, N.H., in October. Services are held on the Sabbath in the church there. He seems to have realized great enjoyment in them. "The day was warm and clear, and the attendance greater than we had expected. In the afternoon, chairs were brought in from the houses near and placed in the aisles. We preached the Gospel as revealed in the word of God, — plain, unadulterated, Scripture truth. The people drank it in as a thirsty man receives cold water. It was upwards of twenty years since we had preached in that house. We remembered the days that were gone."

On Saturday, Oct. 21, he went 'to Warren, Mass., a town upon the Western Railroad, seventy-three miles west of Boston. He had engaged to preach there on Sunday. The day was clear, the audience large, and he seemed in his usual health and spirits. While engaged in the services of the forenoon, he perceived that his left hand was numb. In a moment more he found that the feeling of numbness was increasing upon him; and a sense of insecurity came over him, which caused him to be on his guard that he might not fall. In this way he went through the services of the forenoon and brought them to a close. He came down from the desk with some little difficulty, and informed his friend with whom he tarried of his condition. A carriage was proffered to take him to his quarters, but he thought walking would be beneficial.

The hour of the afternoon service having arrived, he again went to church, against the suggestions of some of his friends, but he said he should persevere. He thought a "pulpit sweat" would be a benefit. He was secretly aware that he might die in the pulpit before the service should close; but he would be no more likely to die in preaching than in sitting still. If God saw fit he should die in the pulpit, he could only say Amen. He went to the church, therefore, and conducted the services through to the end, preaching one hour from John iii. 36. At the close of the service, physicians (Drs. Warriner and Carpenter) were called, who rendered all the assistance in their power, attempting by depletion to remove the cause of the disease. On Monday morning, Sullivan Cowee, Esq., attended him to the cars, and thence to his own home in Cambridgeport. He was confined to his chamber for some weeks, when his feebleness gradually left him, and he was able to resume his duties as usual.

He thus accounts for his illness, in answer to the expressed solicitude of friends in his behalf: "All our brethren suppose that the attack was brought on by too much labor. If we allow this, — although there might have been other causes, — we then ask, what kind of labor is most deleterious? That we have done a great task during the last ten months is undoubted. The labors that tax the mind are the hardest to bear, and the most destructive to the nervous energy. To us it seems singular people should suppose that attention to a kind of business which is almost a relaxation, — that a daily walk to the depots in Boston and Charlestown, and a journey once a week to Fitchburg, or Brattleboro, or Greenfield, or some other place, would bring on a paralysis. No, it is the working of the mind — the pushing of the pen; the searching after materials and facts, and the painful duty of reading proofs that has done it. What part of our duties,

then, shall we strike off? Do our advisers say, give up the
Trumpet? write no more books? No; but they call on us
to give up that which affects *the mind* the least injuriously of
all. We are willing to subsist on scanty food, to walk five
miles per day, all of which we can do; but we cannot resign
our labors for the *Trumpet* and the cause of Universalism.
To resign the latter labors will excite us more than to perform them. Our thanks to all who have tendered us their
advice."

CHAPTER XIII.

1854–1857.

AGED 54–57.

Tufts College — Dr. W. E. Channing — Rev. John Moore — A Friend's Approval — Wesleyan Methodists — A Correspondent — Professor Stuart — Unitarians and Parkerism — Mr. Clark's Telescope — Anniversary Week — Festival; Mr. Whittemore's Speech — Installation of Rev. H. Jewell — Revivals under Edwards and Whitfield — Unqualified preachers — Opening of Tufts College — Mr. Whittemore's Address — Rockingham Association at Brentwood, N.H. — U.S. Convention at Middletown, Ct. — South Hampton, N.H. — Death of Rev. H. Bacon — Anniversary Week — Speech at Reform Meeting — Massachusetts Convention at Haverhill — Sandown, N.H.— Lowell, Mass.— Progressive Christianity — First Anniversary at Tufts College — Connecticut Convention at New Haven — Preaches in Carver, Stoneham, Franklin, Plymouth, and Worcester, Mass., and Kingston, N.H.— Visit to Concord, N.H. — Commentary on Book of Daniel — Dedication at Malden — Rev. Mr. Finney.

MR. WHITTEMORE pleads for Tufts College. To be prosperous, it must be supplied, fed, strengthened. Five thousand dollars are needed for a library; $100 each for fifty men. "We have already paid in our full subscription of $1,000, and shall be happy to join with forty-nine others, to make up the $5,000 referred to. Then, two or three professorships must be founded, on not a smaller basis than $25,000 each. Who will give the telescope? A superior telescope has just been given, by one man, to Amherst College, at a cost of $1,800. When the telescope is obtained for Tufts College, who will build the observatory? We hope that many will learn to give while they live."

Noticing a statement in one of the papers that Dr. W. E. Channing was a Universalist, he takes occasion to state the truth respecting it. "We are confident that this is a mistake, unless Dr. Channing changed his opinion greatly at the close of his life, of which there is no proof. In his discourse on sin, future punishment, &c., he says: 'I have spoken of the pains and penalties of moral evil, or of wrong-doing in the world to come. How long they will endure I know not. Whether they will issue in reformation or happiness of the sufferer, or will terminate in the extinction of his conscious being, is a question on which Scripture throws no clear light. Plausible arguments may be adduced in favor of both these doctrines. On this and other points, revelation aims not to give any precise information, but to fix in us a deep impression that great suffering awaits a disobedient, wasted, immoral, irreligious life.' This is not Universalism. It is the spirit of doubt, darkness, and fear. Dr. Channing did not know but a large portion of mankind would be annihilated!"

An account of the death and burial of Rev. John Moore, of Concord, N.H., appears in the *Trumpet* of Feb. 17, 1855. Mr. Moore dropped dead suddenly on his way to his home in Concord. He was one of the noblest of men and most faithful of ministers. Not long before his death, he was nominated for governor of the State by one of the political parties. It was afterwards found that he had not resided long enough in the State to be eligible to the office.

His friend and brother in the ministry, Rev. A. C. Thomas, writes Mr. Whittemore: "How you manage to get through with so much work is a mystery to me. I only know that multitudes will be refreshed by the waters you have drawn, after the wheel is broken at the cistern."

He has very serious queryings as to the consistency of the Wesleyan Methodists who had seceded from the Episcopal

Methodists on the ground of their opposition to slavery. They supposed themselves to be participators in the sin of Slavery by remaining in the communion of the old church. As the Wesleyans claimed more liberality and benevolence than the Episcopals, Mr. Whittemore is surprised that they are not more consistent with themselves. But what do they do? Mr. Whittemore says: "In framing their new discipline, we see, they introduced the doctrine of endless misery into their Articles of Faith, — a doctrine the most repulsive to a benevolent heart of any that could be named. Call you this growing more liberal, more benevolent, more merciful than the Old Church? It seems to us to be less so. How does it happen that men who are so deeply moved by the spectacle of slavery on earth embrace, with so much enthusiasm, the doctrine of *endless slavery* in the world to come. According to their doctrine, the Almighty is the greatest slave-holder in the universe. There is no relief from his cruel bondage. He afflicts willingly and grieves the children of men. Slavery, wherever it exists, is wrong. There is no circumstance under which in itself it is right; it is wrong now, wrong for ever; we are opposed to it utterly, both in this world and the next. But the Wesleyan Methodists, who profess such a horror at slavery on earth, seem to go far beyond the Episcopal Methodists in vindicating the doctrine of endless slavery in hell. It seems to us that 'they strain at the gnat and swallow the camel.'"

A highly esteemed correspondent had written respecting the great controversy on divine sovereignty and human agency: "The arguments on various sides of this subject remind me of a puzzle I have seen, which was cut out of a thin square piece of board. The problem was to put the right-angled, scalene, and truncated triangles all together, to form a complete square. Many would succeed in arranging a square, but they would leave out some of the pieces. So in this problem: it is easy enough to make a plausible theory by leaving out a part of the pieces. But that is not the way to come at the truth. Let us hold to the facts, even if we lose our theories; for the facts will hold us at last." To which Mr. Whittemore replies: "All I ask of you is to admit that nothing ever took place which God, on the whole, intended should not take place. Admit this, and you may put together 'the right-angled, scalene, and truncated triangles' as you please. I will not interfere with that at all. But, if you deny my proposition, you are lost; I am lost; we are all lost; Universalism is a fable; and our faith in God is all a deception. To that length you and I will never go."

Mr. Whittemore learns that a Memoir of Professor Stuart, late of Andover Theological Seminary, is to be published; and expresses a strong wish that the fact that he was mainly instrumental in bringing about the conversion of Rev. Walter Balfour to Universalism be distinctly stated therein.

He notes a blow aimed at Parkerism by the newly elected Professor at Harvard University on the Plummer foundation, who says, speaking of a sermon of Rev. E. K. Buckingham (Unitarian) in defence of the Scripturalness of Unitarianism: "It strikes us, however, that all such defences are rendered completely futile and nugatory, so long as preachers among us are recognized as regular ministers of regular Unitarian parishes (and are accepted and welcomed on exchanges with Unitarian pastors) who deny the authority of the Scripture itself, reject the idea of a Mediator, sneer at the word redemption, criticise Christ's personal character, prate about Pauline misconceptions, and tell their congregations and Sunday schools that many parts of the Old and New Testaments are fables, while sin is only an imperfection in which Jesus himself participated! While we joyfully assert the

devout character and tendencies of a portion of the sect, we
have facts to sustain all these intimations. For ourselves, we
will not be compromised by being associated with an irrever-
ence and an infidelity which disgusts us by their conceit, as
much as they wound our sensibility and insult our understanding." Mr. Whittemore adds: "We learn from this
that Mr. Huntington has an utter detestation of the class
called Parkerites. He believes the system of Mr. Parker
to be a rank infidelity, bearing merely the appearance of
Christianity. And we must confess, in all honesty, that we
do not think Mr. Huntington's judgment is incorrect. Let
every thing bear its true name."

After enjoying a telescopic view of the moon, he writes of
it, and of the maker of the instrument through which he
looked: "On the evening of the 22d of May, we had the
most pleasant and satisfactory view of the moon that any
man probably ever enjoyed. We have a neighbor in Cambridgeport (Mr. Alvin Clark) who manufactures telescopes.
He is a genius. Besides being a first-class painter of portraits, and keeping a room in Boston for that purpose, and
having as much business of that kind as he can possibly do,
he spends his mornings and evenings at Cambridge in the
manufacture of glasses. At present he is engaged in making,
or rather he has just finished, an object-glass of large dimen-
sions, for an English astronomer of note, Rev. W. R. Dawes,
of Kent county. On the evening in question, the glass was
done, and was mounted on a rude frame, with a pine box instead of a tube; and the artist kindly invited us to call and
see the moon. She was in her first quarter; the atmosphere
was in the most favorable condition; and the new object-
glass was elevated to receive her rays. The view was exciting. Along the line which separates the enlightened from
the dark portions, the objects were very distinct. Spots of

light off in the dark field showed that certain high objects there, caught the sun's rays, while the parts by which they were surrounded were in darkness, just as high mountains on the earth are tipped with the light of the sun in the morning, while the regions at the base are still in the dark. There are unquestionably mountains in the moon. Other parts appeared to be marked like deep pits of a circular form, which seem to indicate that internal fires have raged in the moon, and that the lunar surface has been disfigured by immense volcanoes. One large field of light was coming into view, as if the light of the sun was spreading itself upon some vast plane.

"We have no doubt that the object-glass will be received by the English astronomer with high pleasure, and that he will regard it as the most valuable one of its size he ever saw. Mr. Clark is a gentleman of modest pretensions; but he will bring honor not only to himself by his attainments, but to his country. He is the discoverer of several new double-stars, which have been reported to European astronomers, and which will undoubtedly appear in the next catalogues which shall be published."

Mr. Whittemore is this year, as usual, involved in the interests of Anniversary Week in Boston. It is a week of many meetings. The Universalists have their share of them. The Home Missionary and Sabbath School Associations had meetings of much interest. The Festival was in Faneuil Hall again. Edwin Howland, Esq., presided and made an inspiring introductory address. Good and grand speeches followed, by Dr. Ballou, Rev. S. Cobb, J. W. Hanson, E. Fisher, M. Gaylord, T. Whittemore, and E. H. Chapin. The last-named was in his happiest vein. Mr. Whittemore's address was a string of contrasts. His wit was running over in the beginning, making many facetious allusions to certain friends around him. Then, apologizing for his neglect of preparation for want of time on short notice, he took the interior of Faneuil Hall for a theme. Walls, pillars, portraits, busts, all were "hailed" and honored; and the distinguished ones of the past there represented, aptly and eloquently apostrophized. Then came a tribute to the press, especially the Universalist press, including an amusing account of his first subscription for the *Universalist Magazine*, published by Mr. Henry Bowen. After a complimentary notice of Tufts College, he made a very touching allusion to his serious illness during the past year, and to the sudden death of Rev. John Moore of New Hampshire. "He was serene in life, resigned in death, and leaves to his heirs and to us all the inheritance of his virtues and his good name. Let us like him be faithful, striving for union, knowing but one Universalism, one work, and one life. And the God of peace will bless us."

On Thursday evening, June 27, Rev. Henry Jewell was installed as pastor of the Second Universalist Society in Lynn. Mr. Whittemore preached the sermon from Rom. xv. 29. "And I am sure that when I come unto you, I shall come in the fulness of the blessing of the Gospel of Christ."

The Massachusetts Convention held its session this year in the First Church in Lynn. Mr. Whittemore officiated as Chairman. The Occasional Sermon was delivered by Rev. N. Gunnison.

A Sunday in June is spent at Tyngsboro, Mass. He writes of the visit: "It was twenty years since we preached in that town. A new race had sprung into being, the middle-aged had become old men and women. But heaven and earth looked young as ever; the sun, the green fields, the smiling river, were still in perfect youth. Sunday was a lovely day, and *we had the people*. The Universalist meeting-house was

full, and there were no services in the other churches.   We
preached the Gospel according to our poor ability, and exhorted the people to love and to good works."

In an editorial in his paper of July 21, he speaks somewhat
at length on " Revivals in Former Times" in New England,
under the preaching of the senior President Edwards and
Rev. George Whitfield. " Mr. Edwards was in the height
of his influence, and in the midst of religious excitements,
when Mr. Whitfield came to New England. He soon threw
the Northampton divine into the shade. While Edwards
could get up one revival, Whitfield could get up twenty.
There was a great difference in the two men. Edwards was
a man of great natural ability, and his mind was stored with
the fruits of thirty years' close application to study; but
Whitfield had little to recommend him except his orator-
ical powers. As shallow rivers make the loudest noise in
their course, so Whitfield for a time attracted the more
attention.

" President Edwards saw the extravagances into which the
inhabitants were falling, and made an effort to deaden the
flame which he had kindled. The devil, he said (he always
had a remarkable familiarity in his language in regard to the
devil), was always most active in times of revival. The
times when ' the influences of the Spirit of God abound are
those in which *counterfeits* also abound [an evident allusion
to Whitfield], the devil being then abundant in *mimicking*
both the ordinary and extraordinary influences of that
Spirit.'

" Mr. Whitfield's work caused much division in the churches.
He did more to split the country into sects than any other
man. A writer of that day speaks of the fruit of the revivals
then carried on as being ' spleen, bigotry, and uncharitableness.' He enumerates, among other evils those excitements

had produced, ' an enthusiastic, factious, censorious spirit, — a vain, conceited temper;' 'children teaching their parents or ministers;' 'low-bred, illiterate persons settling difficult points of divinity better than the most learned;' 'conversions spoken of with the same air as common news;' 'churches full of contention, and crumbling into sects;' 'ministers, instead of endeavoring to strengthen each other's hands, using party names, — Arminians, Antinomians, — and treating each other with bitterness and severity.' Such were the revivals of a hundred years ago. And do they not bear a strong resemblance in their effects to many of the revivals of the present day? Do we not now have spleen, bigotry, and uncharitableness; an enthusiastic, factious, censorious spirit; a vain, conceited temper; churches full of contention, and ministers treating each other with bitterness and severity? How unlike the religion of the Lord Jesus!"

He has some sensible sayings in reference to " Unqualified Preachers." He thinks that Universalists have suffered somewhat from the non-qualification of ministers : —

" Universalists were obliged in former times, perhaps, to receive into their fellowship any who offered themselves, if they were believed to be earnest Christians. But we are not under that necessity now. Our cause is not now in its incipient stages. We have a few clergymen who, instead of helping the cause onward, are impediments. Some destroy societies. This is not always because the preacher needs literary qualifications, — such deficiency is bad enough, — but there are other things which make a preacher useless.

" What, then, is to be done? The standard of ministerial qualifications must be raised. The clergyman should ask himself, Am I doing good? Am I serving the cause of truth? Are my labors profitable? Have I left every society of which I have been pastor better than I found it? If not, brother, —

if on the whole you are obliged to answer these questions in the negative, — think what you ought to do. It is a pity for a man to be dull of apprehension in such things. But it may be said in reply, that, if our advice be followed, the present number of our clergymen will decrease. Well, let it decrease. Is the strength of our clergy in its *numbers* merely? What should we think of a man who, if asked, ' Why, sir, do you remain in the ministry?' should answer, ' Only to swell the numbers!' Fifty competent clergymen are better than five hundred of the opposite class."

Tufts College was opened on Wednesday, Aug. 22. It was a day of gladness; bright and beautiful without, and inviting a large attendance at the Hill. The college edifice was thrown open, and free access given to the roof, from the top of which one of the most delightful of prospects could be enjoyed. The building was thronged, — entry-ways, stairs, and every other place where there was the least opportunity of hearing or seeing. The procession moved (if it could be called a procession in such a crowd) from the south-west basement to the great chapel, when music was given by the Germania Band. Then followed a prayer by Rev. Henry Bacon, of Philadelphia. Another strain of music followed, when the Vice-President of the Board of Trustees, Mr. Whittemore (the President being absent), proceeded to install the officers. He spoke as follows : —

" Dr. Ballou, and Gentlemen Professors : The noble eminence on which this edifice stands is covered with unusual beauty this morning. We see an immense gathering of our friends from regions near and distant, every face beaming with smiles. They have come here, sir, to witness the opening of this infant institution, and the installation of yourself as President thereof, and your colleagues as professors in the various departments.

" Our thoughts naturally turn to-day to the origin of Tufts College. It grew out of a want which we had long felt. You and I remember, sir, the efforts that were made by our fathers for the founding of a school in which the young could be educated without being subjected to sectarian influences, or brought under bondage to creeds. We have known, too, the necessity of literary culture among young men aspiring to the Christian ministry. We have known the disadvantages under which they have labored who have entered the sacred office without competent preparation. I do not deny, Doctor, that the great qualification of a preacher is from above ; it consists in an ardent love of the Gospel, an irrepressible desire to preach the same to suffering, dying men ; and in a sanctification of the soul by the power of the truth as it is in Jesus ; it consists in a consecration of all the powers to God, leading us to look to his will as the supreme law of our lives, and to say, with the converted Saul, in the first outburst of his piety, ' Lord, what wilt thou have me to do ? ' Without these qualifications all others are vain. But even with these, a preacher of the best intentions, without proper literary culture, will constantly find himself under embarrassment, and the benefit of his labors will be greatly abridged. We have seen all this, and felt it in that class of Christians to which we belong. I know that, in the apostolic days, God prepared his servants in every respect for their duty. He left nothing in the matter of preparation for them to do ; they needed not to contemplate the form of language they were to use, for God would breathe upon their lips at the very moment when required the words they should utter. But God does not qualify his servants in this manner now. He does not work miracles except when miracles are necessary ; and the ministers of the Gospel may as well expect now to be able to heal the sick, to open the eyes of the blind, and to raise the dead, as to have the other qualifications of the apostles which God miraculously bestowed upon them.

"It was a conviction of these truths, and a deep sense of the wants of our branch of the church, that moved to action the individual whose name this College bears. His great heart throbbed with deep pulsations to answer our wants. He owned this noble eminence from which a panorama incomparably beautiful may be seen, — an eminence near the capital of the State, that the students of the College may avail themselves of the lectures and other literary advantages which are furnished freely there, — an eminence swept so constantly by the sweet winds of heaven, that sickness, or weakness of mind or body, can never originate upon the spot: he, happily for us, I say, owned the hill, and he said to us, take it; 'set it apart for your use,' baptize it with the influence of Christianity; consecrate it to religion and science; beautify it; let wisdom, as of old, cry from the high places, 'Whoso seeketh knowledge, let him turn in hither; forsake the foolish and live, and go in the way of understanding.'

"Our brethren in regions near and distant contributed of their worldly wealth to aid in establishing this institution. The Commonwealth has given us a charter, conferring upon this College all the literary advantages, powers, and privileges which the most favored institutions enjoy; and with an object so noble as ours, if we do our duty well, she will not let the College suffer. We owe a great duty to the donors. To carry out their designs we have erected this building, — the main College edifice, — and have commenced the erection of others which are to stand around it.

"Still farther to carry out the designs of these donors, we have selected you and your colleagues to take charge of the department of learning. We have chosen you because we have confidence in you; and we trust you come here, gentlemen, with a hearty good-will, not for your own good, neither for honor, nor for wealth, but to establish this institution, and build it up, and make it useful. We have chosen you, because you are a man of great hope and faith, and you will be called to exercise the full measure of both. We have not placed you here that we may turn and leave you. You are still to share our sympathies, and to be sustained by all the aids we can render. There is not a man or woman standing on this hill this morning, whose responsibility will not be increased by the opening of the College and the installation of the officers. The institution does not belong to the few, but to the many."

After speaking very emphatically upon the necessity of connecting Science with Christianity in our literary institutions, Mr. Whittemore concluded by saying : —

" With this expression of my sentiments, I proceed, Dr. Ballou, to place the institution under your care. In consequence of the absence of the President of the Board of Trustees, Dr. Oliver Dean, of Franklin, Mass., the duty devolves on me. In behalf of the donors, in behalf of the Board of Trustees, I welcome you, sir, to your elevated position ; I welcome your colleagues to the heads of their different departments. Permit me to say, sir, if you meet with the success your merit deserves, it will be all we can ask. We know the family to which you belong ; we know your long-tried devotion to the truth. We believe we may anticipate a prosperity here, which shall justify the application of the words of the prophet : ' There shall be a handful of corn in the top of the mountains, the fruit whereof shall shake like Lebanon.' "

President Ballou made a brief reply, and afterwards proceeded to deliver an elaborate address, the subject of which was, the general influence of colleges on the literature of the country, on the academies and schools, and on the churches through its ministers. Thanks were then rendered by Rev. E. Fisher, of Dedham.

After the services of installation, there was a gathering of the multitude under a great tent erected on the college grounds, where an excellent and ample repast was enjoyed; after which, President Ballou gave a brief address of welcome; appropriate sentiments were offered, and speeches were made by Rev. O. A. Skinner, Rev. A. A. Miner, Rev. E. H. Chapin, B. B. Mussey Esq., and Rev. T. B. Thayer. An appeal for funds was made, and about $4,000 subscribed by the company present.

The Rockingham Association held its session this year in Brentwood, N.H. It was well attended. Rev. T. J. Greenwood preached the Occasional Sermon, and Mr. Whittemore addressed the assembly on the last afternoon of the meeting. Rev. S. Streeter followed him in a very animated and inspiring exhortation. "This Association," writes Mr. Whittemore, "taken altogether, was thought to be the richest that has been holden for several years."

The United States Convention was held at Middletown, Ct. The Occasional Discourse by Rev. T. J. Sawyer, D.D., was eminent for its ability, appropriateness to the time, and loyalty to Christian Universalism. His words respecting American Slavery, as Mr. Whittemore reported, "were absolutely cauterizing." Mr. Whittemore preached on Thursday morning, and Rev. E. H. Chapin in the afternoon, after which the communion service was observed. Mr. Whittemore says of Mr. Chapin's discourse, "Others may say what they please: *we* think the orator went beyond himself." The *Middletown News*, a secular journal, said of the Convention: "The sermons were as eloquent and finished theological discourses as we have ever heard. They appeared to be addressed to the understanding, and produced a profound and lasting impression on all present. We noticed that several of the leading members of other denominations in the city were in constant attendance at the public exercises."

A Sunday at South Hampton, N.H., is noted. There is a large attendance from adjacent towns, and it was an enjoyable occasion to the preacher. He writes: "The text was, 'Let us go on unto perfection,' and most attentively and feelingly did the people listen. It seemed like good old times truly. On the same day, Brother Spaulding, of Methuen, preached at Kensington, only a few miles distant; and Brother Jewell, at Danville, which was quite near in another direction. We think some good was done that day for the truth in old Rockingham."

On the 19th of March, 1856, Rev. Henry Bacon, pastor of the church of the Messiah, in Philadelphia, departed this life. He was born in Boston in 1813, and was educated religiously, a Universalist. He was a man of great mental activity, a close student, ready writer, easy and rapid speaker, fervent in his public ministries, and a pastor of rare merit. He had been settled in East Cambridge, Haverhill, and Marblehead, Mass., in Providence, R.I., and in Philadelphia, Pa. Funeral services were held in the last-named place, and in School Street Universalist church, Boston, on which occasion a discourse was delivered by H. Ballou, D.D. An interesting account of the life and character of the lamented and honored minister appears in the *Trumpet* from Mr. Whittemore.

Business with the Trustees of Tufts College, and other engagements, prevented Mr. Whittemore from making his own reports of the meetings on Anniversary Week this year. But his paper is quite full of the record. Prayer-meetings of much interest were held in the Universalist churches in Boston; the Sabbath School Union and Home Missionary Societies had their sessions; and the Reform Association was held in the School Street church. Frank B. Fay, Esq., presided. The Report on Peace, by Rev. T. D. Cook, elicited strong discussion on non-resistance and war, in which Mr. Whittemore took part. He would not justify the spirit of war, but would justify self-defence. "If others will let us alone, we have no occasion to engage in war. But if robbers enter his house with an evil design upon himself or his family, he believed resistance justifiable. In such resistance, he did not exercise the spirit of war. Did Charles Sumner possess the spirit of war, when he rose to defend himself from the attack made upon him?" An able Report on Slavery was made by Rev. W. R. G. Mellen. Resolutions on Temperance were discussed and passed.

At the Festival in Faneuil Hall, Mr. Fay presided. In his opening address, he gave lively sketches of the Festivals in years past. He was followed by speeches from Rev. Messrs. W. H. Ryder, C. H. Leonard, E. G. Brooks, C. H. Fay, E. H. Chapin, A. A. Miner, Professor Drew, and Dr. T. K. Taylor. Rev. Mr. Brooks's speech was one of great power. He alluded to the infamy which in our Congress halls had just fallen upon the name of Brooks (the Congressman who assaulted Mr. Sumner), and said, "I wonder these walls didn't hiss at it!" He nobly vindicated *the name* from the reproach so lately cast upon it. Mr. Chapin was as electric as ever. His personal allusions to friends in the hall were admirable. He spoke of Mr. Whittemore as "railroad wise and theologically steadfast; with the sovereignty of God in one hand, and love and fellowship for men of every name in the other." Of the hall itself, he said, "If he had but four breaths to draw, he would wish to draw one in the air of home and sacred duty; the second in the gorge of the White Mountains; the third on the broad and heaving sea; and the fourth sniff he would have out of old Faneuil Hall." All the addresses were of the highest order. Dr. T. K. Taylor responded in a very appropriate speech to a sentiment recognizing "the Laity of our denomination."

The Massachusetts Convention held its session this year in Haverhill. A Sunday School Convention was held at the same time. Sermons were preached by Rev. Messrs. Laurie, Miner, and Whittemore. Of Mr. Laurie's sermon Mr. Whittemore writes: "It was well written, and delivered in an excellent spirit; but many of the brethren took exceptions to the statements thereof. On a motion to render thanks for the sermon and ask a copy for the press, there was a very spirited debate, and the resolution did not pass without an amendment, declaring it to be the opinion of the Convention, that the sermon did not express the convictions of the Universalist clergy on the subject, 'Ministers preaching on the Reforms of the Day.' The feelings of the Convention had been greatly aroused by the murders, rapine, and destruction of the property of the settlers in Kansas, and also by the fact that one of the Senators of Massachusetts had been knocked down on the floor of the Senate Chamber, and the State been thus deprived of one half her constitutional representation in that body. The other sermons spoke an additional voice against such aggressions, and there is no doubt—there can be none —that Brother Laurie himself would approve them." The communion service was observed at the close of the last day.

On Sunday, June 8, Mr. Whittemore preached in Sandown, N.H. He had not been there for nearly nine years. The hill on which the church stands was covered with carriages from neighboring towns. He writes: "It was an opportunity to do good, and we sought to improve it. We have not been so wearied by a Sunday's services for a long time. We urged it upon the brethren to unite with Freemont, Brentwood, and Kingston, and get a faithful and talented man to live among them."

"A Sabbath in Lowell" is recorded. Mr. Whittemore preached to large congregations in the First Universalist Church. The pastor, Rev. T. B. Thayer, was not in good health, and had suspended his labors for a season. Mr. Whittemore rode from home and back in his carriage, fifty-four miles, beside preaching, on the same day.

Of Senator Sumner's speech in the Senate of the United States, on the 19th and 20th of May, for which he was stricken down by a son of South Carolina, he says: "It has been published by John P. Jewett & Co., Boston; also in Cleveland, Ohio, New York city, and in many other places. Edition after edition has been called for. It is going into every family in New England, the Middle States, and all the great West, to be read by males and females, parents and children, who never would have seen it but for the present excitement. The assault on Mr. Sumner has created this unparalleled call for his Kansas speech. Thus we see that the violence of man subverts itself. Brooks's gutta-percha cane has done more for freedom in Kansas than Sharp's rifles. He did not intend, however, to produce such a result."

There was much talk in these days about "Christian progress" and "progressive Christianity," occasioned by the somewhat pretentious radicalism that had shown itself in some of the "liberal" churches. Mr. Whittemore takes occasion to say on the subject: "We hear much said in our day about *progressive* Christianity. For our part, we do not believe in a progressive Christianity. We believe in Christianity just as it came from its divine Founder. It was perfect as it fell from his lips, and as it was illustrated in his life; and it needs to be no better improved, nor is it possible it should be. Why then do we talk about *progressive* Christianity? Is not Christianity good enough? Has it not always been good enough? If men had in all ages clung to Christianity, and not receded from it, would they not at this day be purer in life and in faith than they are? Can men improve the character of Christ? his precepts? his doctrines? Vain presumption. If they would try to improve *themselves* instead of trying to improve Christianity, they would be engaged in a far more useful work, and in which, perhaps, they might be successful.

"While we do not believe in a progressive Christianity, we do believe that Christians should aim at progress in themselves. They should 'grow in grace and in the knowledge of Christ.' The knowledge of Christianity among men may increase; nations that know it not may be brought to see it and believe: but Christianity itself has no change. Heaven and earth may pass away, but God's truth abides."

The first anniversary meeting at Tufts College was held on Wednesday, Aug. 20. It was a meeting heartily enjoyed by a large company. Dr. Ballou presided, and addresses were made by Professor Marshall, Drs. Sawyer, Chapin, Paige, and Mr. Whittemore. The latter remarked that he rose with reluctance. He said he had long ago promised never to make a speech on the same day that Chapin spoke; and now he had nothing to say, for he could add nothing new to what had been already offered. He merely congratulated the friends of the College upon the encouraging prospects before them, and contrasted the prospect now with that which was presented at some of the earlier meetings of the Trustees, when the path before them seemed dark and discouraging, and they looked at one another as if they would die of famine, and were obliged to put their hands into their pockets to save the enterprise from failure. He could not help imagining that the thunder we heard to-day was God's voice approving

of our work.   The donations and pledges given here to-day
were magnificent, and served as an assurance that the enterprise would not go down.   It would go down to future gen-
erations, and that is the only way in which it ever will go
down.

Large contributions to the College were made on this occasion, and Mr. Packard (one of the most generous donors)
stated that there was represented at that gathering more property than existed in all New England at the time when Harvard College was commenced.

Mr. Whittemore attended in August the Connecticut Convention held at New Haven, and preached during the session.
This visit kept him away from the Rockingham Association.

In September, he attended the annual meeting of the
Cheshire County Association at Winchester, N.H., and met
several ministering brethren younger than himself whom he
had never seen before.   He preached on the last afternoon
from Rom. vi. 1, 2.   " After.the sermon," he writes, " the
Lord's Supper was administered to a large body of believers.
Brothers Whittemore and McCollester officiated at the table.
It was a solemn, happy occasion.   We all renewed our vows,
and pledged ourselves and all our talents to the cause of Universal grace.   One old father was in the assembly (Doolittle,
of Winchester), who was born in 1767, four years before
Father Ballou, and who knew Father Ballou all his life long.
This aged man came forward at the end of the communion,
and gave us his hand, saying, ' Brother Whittemore, this is
one of the happiest days I ever saw in my life.   I bless God
that I am able to be here.'   The benediction was pronounced,
when the friends went slowly and reluctantly away."

During this same month, we find him doing the work of an
evangelist on different Sundays, in Carver, Stoneham, and
Franklin, Mass.   He is unable to attend this season the

United States Convention, which holds its session in Erie, Pennsylvania.

In a notice of " The Editor's Labors," he records his work on three Sundays in October. "On the first Sunday, we preached in Plymouth, the old Pilgrim town. The Universalist church stands almost on Forefathers' Rock, on the site of the original burying-ground ; and probably right beneath our feet the bones of some of the first settlers, and perhaps even of some of the native men of the forest, were mouldering. Public worship was well attended all the day. On the second Sabbath we were at Worcester. It was a bright day. The pastor (Rev. J. G. Adams) was sick, and was not able to reach the church in the forenoon. The house was well filled. We are happy to believe that this society is in a very prosperous condition. One or two members [perhaps only one] have become disaffected because the preacher's expressed opinions on certain subjects of high national interest do not agree with their own. Liberty to think and liberty to speak is natural to every man born in New England. Brother Adams is from New Hampshire, the land of democracy. The Gospel is free, the pulpit is free, and where the Spirit of the Lord is there is liberty."

Another Sabbath was spent in Kingston, N.H. " We were quartered beneath the honored roof of Dr. L. S. Bartlett, grandson of Governor Josiah Bartlett, — a signer of the Declaration of Independence. A gloomy night was succeeded by a most lovely day ; one of the happiest Sabbaths we ever spent in the county of Rockingham. An urgent request came for us to appoint a Sabbath when we would preach in Rye, a town on the sea-coast. Oh that we had the strength we used to have twenty years ago !"

He visits Concord, N.H., in November, and preaches in the Universalist church there ; the pastor, Rev. J. H. Moore, having been ill for some little time. He writes : " Our first duty on Sunday morning was to call on Brother Moore. He bore the marks of acute disease ; but was so far recovered as to be seated in the pulpit with us during the services. The church edifice here we think the handsomest one in Concord, and perhaps in New Hampshire. The audience, we are told, fills the large edifice respectably. We consider the society to be strong."

He thus announces his intention to bring out another commentary : " The book of Daniel is the Apocalypse of the Old Testament. The editor of the *Trumpet* has desired for quite a long time to attempt a commentary on that book, but has been dissuaded hitherto by the expostulations of ministering brethren, who fear that he is taking too much upon himself, and may provoke another attack of paralysis. Why should it do so, if we can do the work calmly and take pleasure in it? What is life worth, if we cannot be active and make good use of our time? Are we to account ourself dead while we live? We should be more likely to die if we should sit down and do nothing, than if we should calmly, carefully, and usefully labor in the great work of expounding the Scriptures, and defending the great doctrine of the Gospel. We will at least *begin* the commentary on Daniel, and publish it in sections on the first page of the *Trumpet*, as we published at first the commentary on the book of Revelation. We know not how far we may go. The first number may be looked for soon."

The new house of worship belonging to the Universalists of Malden was dedicated on Thursday, Jan. 1, 1857. An excellent discourse was delivered by Mr. Whittemore from Micah vi. 6 : " Wherewith shall I come before the Lord, and bow myself before the high God?"

Sunday, Jan. 11, was spent by Mr. Whittemore in Portsmouth, N.H. In the absence of Rev. Mr. Patterson, he preached in the Universalist church. He speaks of the occasion as one of much enjoyment, and gives a very favorable account of the condition of the church and of the faithfulness of its pastor.

He takes occasion to notice the ministry of Rev. Mr. Finney, who has been delivering a course of " revival" lectures in Park Street church, Boston. The *Traveller*, a secular paper of that city, represents Mr. Finney as " portraying the horrors of an eternal death, by representing the pangs through which mortals pass during the few brief minutes of gasping, agonizing suffering that precede physical death, as prolonged through the endless ages of eternity." " How unlike Jesus!" writes Mr. Whittemore. " Find a passage like this if you can, in all the words of Christ, spoken either to saints or sinners. Nothing like it ever passed his lips, in a single instance, so far as we can learn from the Bible. Mr. Finney seems to delight in tormenting mankind. It is his vocation. If he cannot torment them, he has no success. He is one of those preachers who drive men to insane asylums. All this is done for sectarian purposes, — to sustain partialist churches, and maintain the partialist clergy. For this selfish object do they rouse the worst fears of men. They are like the captain of a ship, who should torment his passengers all the voyage through with fears of a shipwreck at last. ' Oh, you will never reach the desired port ; you will all be lost ; you will be thrown upon the rocks ; your bodies will be washed up on the sands of the country to which you go !' Who would submit a ship to the command of such a man? Who would sail with him? And yet these preachers are somewhat like him, but far worse. They seek to make men unhappy ; they are the tormentors of mankind. God forbid that we should believe them."

CHAPTER XIV.

1857–1858.

AGED 57–58.

Keeping up with the Times — Applications to preach — Woonsocket, R.I. — Anniversary Meetings — Address — Eight Days' Labor — Commencement at Tufts College — Address — Visit to Connecticut and the West — Niagara again — First Visit to Chicago — Springfield, Ill. — U.S. Convention at Chicago — Various kinds of Universalists — Conference at Roxbury — Barnstable — Conference and Funeral at Salem — Conference at Worcester — Visit to Rockport, Mass. — Conference at Lawrence — Middleboro, Mass. — Book of Rev. C. F. Hudson — Conference at Cambridgeport — In Milford, Mass. — Address of Rev. E. T. Taylor — The Religious Revival — Interest of Universalists in it — The true Interest urged — "Too Much Zeal" — Visits to the "Black Sea" in Boston.

"KEEPING up with the times," is a subject which Mr. Whittemore considers in a brief editorial article. The complaint is often made, "You do not keep up with the times. What does this complaint mean? Up with the times? Do you mean that we do not run after every new thing? that we are not easily moved from the strong foundation of the Gospel? If you mean this, then we do not keep up with the times. But if you mean that we do not receive all truth in the love of it, — truth that is new to us, as well as that which is old, — you do us injustice. We keep our mind wholly open to conviction. Let the light of heaven shine. We will not object, if, like Saul, we should see a light above the brightness of the sun. Let old things pass away, as they accomplish their purposes, and let all things be made new. But

truth can never pass away. There can be no new truth.
Truth may appear to us to be new, because we have not seen
it before; but it is old truth, after all. The stars are shining
just as brightly before they rise in the eastern horizon to our
sight, as they shine afterwards. But they seem to us to begin to shine at that moment, because we had not seen them
before. So truth is bright before we see it; it is old before
we hear of it. It seems to rise and fall to men; but it neither
rises nor sets, and seems to do so only from the mutations
of earthly things.

"We have seen many theories rise and fall. Like meteors
they appear in the sky, shine for a brief space, explode, and
go out in darkness. We are on our guard against such theories. We wish to be steadfast, immovable, always abound-
ing in the work of the Lord. We have no ambition to chase
every new phantom. But every *truth* we will receive. If in
this way we do not keep up with the times, it is because the
times are wrong. We are not over-anxious to be conformed
to the present manners. Christianity was a separate thing
from the popular systems of religion that prevailed in its day;
and Christians were a peculiar people. As for us, we will
seek to follow Christ; to abide by the divine word, keeping
the mind open to all truth."

In May of this year, he writes: "We have received this
spring several applications to preach, to which we have not
responded affirmatively. We may name Kingston, East
Kingston, Weare, and other places in New Hampshire, and
several places in Massachusetts. We have a very strong
desire to go, — a desire so strong that it is almost uncontrolla-
ble. But reason and prudence for the present say No. Still
we hope to go out a little to visit our friends in the country.
No man has stronger friends than we have, nor more of them.
God bless them all."

On Sunday, May 1, Mr. Whittemore preached in Woonsocket, R.I. More than twenty-one years had passed since he had been there. He writes: "The society is now steadily prosperous under the care of Rev. John Boyden. We used to preach much in this vicinity in the first year of our ministry. All our old feelings were called into life by seeing the people whom we used to address in A.D. 1821. We took the hands of many of them. Woonsocket is the place in which Hosea Ballou closed his earthly ministry. The society is well established."

Mr. Whittemore is again at the Anniversary meetings in Boston. He takes part in the discussions, and is called upon to speak at the Festival in Faneuil Hall. He spoke to this sentiment: "*Our Course* — steady, but sure, like the course of the true light which shineth more and more unto the perfect day."

Mr. Whittemore said, by "our course" he presumed was meant the course of the Christian denomination which we represent. He was glad that there was no boasting in the sentiment about our progress, — no glorification; our course had been steady, not fitful, not unnaturally rapid, but sure, like the course of light which shineth brighter and brighter unto the perfect day. "At first a slight glow appears in the east; then the light shoots up into the heavens; the glory increases until it reaches its noonday splendor. Excitements, called revivals, sometimes take place, which are moral whirlwinds, earthquakes, conflagrations. They are designed to quench out truth. People say, Your sect does not increase like ours; see what numbers are running after our gods. Yes, and so numbers ran after Nebuchadnezzar's god in Babylon. We know that wildfire will run over a country much faster than civilization. A whirlwind will knock down a thousand orchards while you are rearing one. All this is to be expected. A conflagration will destroy a town in much less time than it took to build it up. But the whirlwind, the earthquake, the fire, do not betoken God. He addresses us in the 'still small voice.' If you doubt whether our cause is progressing, compare it now with what it was a few years ago." Mr. Whittemore here gave a lively and very acceptable account of his own experience in this respect, and related some striking and amusing anecdotes of the older clergy, and closed with a most fervent exhortation to those of his own church, in the present time, to be as faithful, self-sacrificing, and devoted as were the fathers. Chapin's speech on the occasion was a stirring trumpet-blast.

In his paper of June 20, "Eight Days' Labor" is a subject of record. "Thursday, June 4. We left Boston for Fitchburg, fifty miles, where we spent the forenoon, and returned home at the close of the day.

"Friday, 5th. Went once more to Fitchburg, and returned.

"Saturday, 6th. Attended to editorial and other duties in Boston, and, at 5 P.M., started for Lawrence, where we shall preach to-morrow.

"Sunday, 7th. Preached through the day in this city.

"Monday, 8th. Returned to Boston. Attended to various duties during the day.

"Tuesday, 9th. Started once more for Fitchburg. Remained here until 1.30 P.M., when we left Fitchburg for the Vermont and Massachusetts Railroad. Arrived at Brattleboro at 4.40. Spent the time here in various duties until next day.

"Wednesday, 10th. At 10.30 passed over the Vermont Valley Railroad to Bellows Falls. There took the Rutland and Burlington Railroad, and passed up to Cavendish, where we found the Green Mountain Association of Universalists in session.

" Thursday, 11th. Preached before the body here named, and in the evening went to Proctorsville, and spent the night with Rev. Warren Skinner.

" Friday, 12th. Left Proctorsville at 7 A.M., and arrived at Cambridgeport, about 130 miles, at 3 P.M."

The meetings at Lawrence and Cavendish are spoken of as having been highly enjoyable.

At the dinner on the day of Commencement at Tufts College, Mr. Whittemore presided by request of President Ballou, who stated that, feeling exhausted by the labors of the last few days, he feared that, should he attempt to preside on this occasion, he might disturb them rather than add to their pleasure. He would therefore call on Rev. Thomas Whittemore to preside in his stead.

Mr. Whittemore thought it exceedingly cruel that the President after informing the company that he did not wish to disturb them, should call up a person who would be more likely to do so than any one present. He welcomed all the company to the scenes of the day, especially the ladies, — who had before smiled on the prospect before them, — the clergy, and all friends of the College. This was the first Commencement at Tufts College. True, the graduating class was small; but every thing was small in its beginning. Harvard University had but six graduates at its first Commencement, and for some years after not any. The Trustees of Tufts College were fully satisfied with the talents of the young men who graduated. He complimented the President upon the success that had attended his labors and his fitness for the position he occupied, and in conclusion invoked the blessing of God upon the institution, its founder, and friends, congratulating the former and the donors upon the success of the glorious enterprise, which had been inaugurated through their efforts. He spoke four minutes.

After Mr. Whittemore left home, on the 26th of August, he was absent between five and six weeks. He greatly enjoyed the Connecticut State Convention held at Stafford. Passing on West, he visited Niagara; and the Sabbath found him there. He writes: "We worshipped God in our own heart, in the solitude of the chamber, and in the deep groves of the surrounding woods. We listened to hear the floods sing his praise. Deep sounded unto deep; and, as the solemn anthem was pealing, the breath of praise seemed to rise from the abyss like incense from the censer of the great heart of nature. Never before had we such a sense of the vastness of God's power. We wonder not that the Psalmist considered all nature to be animate; and called upon the winds, the hail, the snow, the floods, the vapors to praise the name of the Lord. When we look back upon that Sabbath, it is with feelings of deepest reverence."

Crossing Suspension Bridge at Niagara, he passed through Canada to Detroit; thence to Chicago and Milwaukie. Of Michigan "city" he writes: "The part of it through which we passed was distinguished for sand-hills, repair-shops of the railroad, old cars, old rails, old wheels, and all that sort of thing. There must have been some part of the city we did not see, or it would not be called a city." His first appearance in Chicago is rather humorously described: "We are at the depot. On emerging from the cars, we looked up to the roof. The structure — the immense trusses — amazed us. The floor of this depot seemed almost as large as Boston Common: I am sure it was as large as a part of it. But what a noise! men must be hired here on purpose to make a noise. I am confident they would not make so great a noise if they did not expect a reward for it. Every one speaks with all his might, as loud and as rapidly as he can. Some are crying the names of steamboats, their points of destina-

tion, and hours of departure; others vociferate the names of
hotels, setting forth some favorable characteristic of each.
Some cry, 'Hack!' others, 'Omnibus line this way, sir!'
'Dis way, Master!' 'American House!' 'Tremont House!'
'Deutsches Haus!' 'Richmond House!' 'Hôtel du Peuple!'
all, all mixed in one grand Babel. We bore it well, until one
rude fellow laid hold of us who seemed determined to have us,
until we asked him, 'could he lend us ten dollars?' when
he instantly forsook us as a man having no cash!" His
description of Milwaukie is well given.

He visits Chicago again, and thence goes to Springfield, Ill.,
where he preached on the Sabbath. In this neighborhood, he
visited the relatives of Mrs. Whittemore. Leaving Springfield,
he returned to Chicago, and attended the United States Convention which was held there. The meetings were very fully
attended, and Mr. Whittemore preached during the session. On
his return from Chicago to the East, he visited Niagara again.
Two accidents occurred here which seemed to imperil the lives
of Mr. Whittemore and his company. One was, the breaking
of an iron on the carriage as they were descending a dangerous place near the edge of a precipice; the other was, their
coming near a railroad-crossing when a locomotive was close
upon them. They escaped all injury, and had new occasion
for thanksgiving to the Providential Guardian of his children
amidst the dangers of life. In a day or two he was at his
own home again.

There could hardly be a more explicit or comprehensive
statement than this, in one of his editorials, entitled "Various
Kinds of Universalists." "Reader, what kind of a Universalist are you? There are different kinds, such as theoretical
and practical, zealous and frigid, those who understand the
system and those who understand it not. Here are six kinds
in this brief enumeration. Reader, to which of these kinds

do you belong? Of all kinds, frigid, theoretical Universalists are the worst; and we are sorry that there should be any such. A person should be at once a practical, zealous, understanding Universalist. Understand the doctrine ; study it ; read books and sermons carefully, and particularly the Bible. Read your denominational journal. Fill your mind with knowledge on this subject. When you understand the doctrine, act it. practise it. Do every thing as a Universalist ; remember in every thing that you are such. It will make you hate profaneness and cursing and bitterness and wrath and anger. Be zealous, and not lukewarm. Be not a doubtful Universalist. You will be an example to others ; and you must be just such a Universalist as you wish them to be."

A conference of much interest was held at Roxbury, on Wednesday, Oct. 14. It was called "to consider the need and the means of awakening and developing more spiritual life and religious feeling in our order." Mr. Whittemore was present, and made some very practical and fervent remarks on the occasion. Rev. W. H. Ryder, pastor of the Universalist Church, presided.

A visit to Barnstable, in November, is noted. He was welcomed there by Deacon David Parker, formerly of the First Universalist Church in Boston. The place of public service was the Town House. "A crowd of carriages was around it, and scores of persons were waiting for the hour of service. We entered the house," writes Mr. Whittemore, "unhappy, because unwell. But the occasion, the singing, and other circumstances, soon gave a better tone to our feelings. We preached to a congregation who gave us a fixed attention for the truth's and not for the speaker's sake. In the afternoon, we had a slightly increased congregation, so that the brethren seemed cheerful and grateful to see that so many had come together to worship God in Barnstable Town House."

He was called to attend the funeral of Deacon N. Frothingham, of the Universalist Church in Salem, Mass. The Deacon was an aged and honored believer in the Abrahamic faith. Fifty years before his death, he had welcomed Rev. John Murray to his house, and obtained him to preach the Gospel of a world's salvation in Salem. He took his own family Bible to the place of the meeting, from which book Mr. Murray read his text. The volume was preserved ever afterwards as a relic of that event. The Deacon stood very high in the estimation of his fellow-citizens. The funeral was at the church, where a conference for the day had been appointed. This was its first service, — a solemn and impressive one. Rev. S. Ellis, Rev. E. G. Brooks, and Rev. Dr. Thompson, of Salem, took part in the service. Mr. Whittemore was called upon to deliver the address, in the absence of Rev. S. Streeter, of Boston, who was kept at home by illness. The conference exercises were held in the church in the afternoon. Mr. Whittemore writes of the meeting : " We are confident it will do good. It was devotional, animated, evangelical, experimental, practical."

A conference largely attended, and of deep interest, was held in Worcester, on Wednesday, Dec. 16. It opened with an address by Rev. Russell A. Ballou, on " The Inward Christian Life," which was followed through the day and evening with many addresses of ministers and laymen. Dr. Alonzo Hill (Unitarian), of Worcester, was among the speakers. Mr. Whittemore made some very timely and earnest remarks on family devotion, urging it upon all who had not yet given attention to it.

A visit to Rockport, Mass., is noted in the *Trumpet.* " Nearly a quarter of a century had elapsed since we visited this town. The weather on Saturday seemed to threaten a storm; but Sunday was clear and bright. There were two services. Large audiences were in attendance. We looked in vain for our old friends, whom we knew years before. They were almost all gone. Those who were then young men, and whom death has spared, are now advanced in life; and such as were then fathers have nearly all passed away. The society here has been afflicted with a frequent change of pastors."

A conference at Lawrence is attended by Mr. Whittemore, on Wednesday, Jan. 20, 1858. The meetings were all edifying, as Mr. Whittemore reports them; growing in interest through the day and evening. The opening address by Rev. Sumner Ellis, was on the development, the manifestation of the spiritual life. Many speakers followed, Mr. Whittemore among them. He speaks in strong terms of the evening service. "For fifteen years," he writes, "we had not enjoyed a meeting like this. The Spirit of the Lord was there. It was the house of God, the gate of heaven. We need not state who led in prayer, for all prayed. Clergymen and laymen testified of the value of the Christian religion. A Methodist brother gave us his experience, and uttered interesting reminiscences of the Universalist preachers whom he used to hear in his youth. He loved, he said, the spirit of this meeting. He felt that the Spirit of Christ was here. At the later part of the meeting, the speeches were ruled down to five minutes in length. Nine o'clock came, but we were not ready to part. One after another rose, until at last the whole services were closed by prayer, about thirty minutes past nine."

A Sabbath was spent in Middleboro', Mass., Feb. 7. "The meeting was held in American Hall, — a very large room, — at the principal village called the 'Four Corners.' People came in from neighboring towns, and a large number of the citizens of Middleboro' gathered together. The afternoon meeting was very full. We preached A.M. from Acts xxviii. 22, and P.M. from Heb. x. 23. In the evening, we went to the north part of the town, and delivered a lecture in a large new school-house. More than could be accommodated with places to stand were present. Excepting the excessive labor, we enjoyed a very happy day."

In his paper of Feb. 20, Mr. Whittemore notices a book which had been before the public for some little time, entitled, "Debt and Grace, as related to the Doctrine of a Future Life," by C. F. Hudson. The volume attracted much attention because of its author's advocacy of the doctrine of the annihilation of the wicked in opposition to that of eternal punishment. It is notable, too, on account of the ability of its author, and his very clear and strong arguments against the doctrine of the endless torment of the " finally impenitent ;" and because, moreover, it was regarded as a kind of oracular utterance on the part of the more scholarly advocates of the "Second Advent" theories. Mr. Whittemore writes of the book : " We have not been so well pleased with it as we expected we should be by the notices we saw of it in some of the public papers. The author has been an orthodox clergyman ; but he was troubled with the doctrine of endless punishment. He could not reconcile it with the justice and mercy of God. His brethren learned that he expressed his doubts on that point, and withdrew their confidence from him. He then became a free man, *i.e.*, somewhat free and somewhat in bondage. Although he saw some of the difficulties attending the doctrine of endless sin and misery, yet he did not see clearly the way out. He halted at the doctrine of annihilation. This latter doctrine, it is true, is a favorable modification of the theory of endless sin and pain : but it is not the true 'theodicy,'—to use our author's favorite word; it is not a sufficient vindication of the Divine justice. Mr. Hudson has been somewhat of a student, but he has not studied the facts nearest to him. He has been so busily engaged in looking after comets, that he has not seen the familiar constellations, nor Venus, Jupiter, Saturn; no, nor even the Sun. The great theodicy, Universalism, he scarcely seems to know has existed at all in this country.

"To a person who has slightly gone over the field of ecclesiastical history to see what Christian writers have said on the great subject of reconciling theology with the justice, wisdom, and goodness of God, Mr. Hudson's book may appear to be a very valuable one. But it is deficient in many important points. One of its points of principal value is the history it gives of the doctrine of annihilation. But Mr. Hudson failed to learn that there was such a class of people in the United States as the Universalists. Is not this a singular fact? He does not give a sufficient notice of the great 'theodicy' of all, the doctrine of the final holiness and happiness of all men. This result is the only sufficient justification of God in the permission of sin, pain, and sorrow in our world. Important as it is, it is passed over slightly in Mr. Hudson's book. Notwithstanding this expression of our opinion, we do not deny that the book is a valuable one; but it is valuable more in an historical point of view than for any excellence it has as a vindication of the divine government."

A conference was held at Cambridgeport on the 17th of February. It opened with an address, presenting the leading theme of the day, by Rev. J. G. Adams, of Worcester,—"Religious Culture in the Family." Speakers were ready and earnest in their addresses. The theme was taken up again in the afternoon, Rev. W. H. Ryder making the opening address. There was an evening meeting of much interest, a large number of persons, ministers and laymen, taking part in it. Mr. Whittemore spoke frequently during the services, and offered a very fervent prayer. The remarks of Rev. L. R. Paige in the evening, on the "Excellency of the Hopes and Consolations of the Gospel," were very impressive. "Forty-six years ago," he said, "I brought with me to this city a young family, apparently more likely to survive me than I to survive them. They, and others afterwards added, are departed, and I am left. During my residence here, I have followed six members of my family to the grave. However they may have seemed to others, they were very dear to me; and, as blow succeeded blow, and limb after limb was severed from me, my heart was filled with bitterness. Yet in all these afflictions I have found that 'God is our refuge and strength, a very present help in trouble.'" Mr. Whittemore pronounces the meetings "spirited, pleasant, and profitable."

Another conference was held in Milford, Mass., on the 10th of March. It was a meeting of unusual interest, because of the vital character of the topics discussed, the number and variety of the speakers, and the deep feeling which pervaded the services. The morning exercises were opened by a very able and searching discourse on "Growth in Grace," by Rev. M. Goodrich of Pawtucket, R.I.; which the pastor of the Milford Church, Rev. J. R. Johnson, pronounced "an admirable production, sound in doctrine and forcible in spirit." Other speakers followed, Mr. Whittemore among them. In the midst of his first address, he discovered in the audience Father E. T. Taylor, of Boston, the Seaman's Preacher, sitting in one of the pews in the broad aisle. He exclaimed: "I am truly happy to see Father Taylor. I congratulate the audience on the fact of his presence. You will have spiritual refreshment before you leave this meeting, I am quite sure."

This was during the afternoon service. Father Taylor was present in the morning, and had spoken then, to great acceptance. But as Mr. Whittemore was not then present, he plead for an opportunity of listening himself to the veteran preacher. "He was impatient to hear him. Father Taylor, it is true, is a Methodist; but we love him almost as well as if he were a member of our own body. Father Taylor arose in his pew and said, 'I had my opportunity in the forenoon, brother. It will not be proper for me to consume any more of your time.' But to this Mr. Whittemore replied from his place, 'Yes, I heard that you gave the people large draughts of the water of life this morning, Father Taylor, but I was not here, and did not get one drop of it.'

"Father Taylor came into the broad aisle. He is now verging towards seventy years; his head is gray; but his eye is full of fire; his voice is strong; his soul has great energy; and yet he is at times exceedingly tender and affectionate. He said that he felt like a little child. [He had not spoken but a few moments before the audience were in tears.] I find that I know but little about you and your church, my brethren. I am almost ashamed of myself that I did not know you better. Such a meeting as this I have seldom attended. It draws my heart towards you. The grace of the Lord Jesus Christ be upon you!" He had thought much, he said, as to the best way to gain certain individuals he had known. He had tried many ways to reach them. Prayer, said he, is a good thing, but prayer did not always accomplish the object. He was afraid of dry prayers. They did little good. You were not sure to reach the heart by such prayers. He spoke of the benefit of praise, issuing from a sense of God's love, God's mercy and forgiveness, — his reaching out after the sinner to draw him back to heaven, as we reach down after a drowning man. Sometimes, said he, when I cannot get my men (the

sailors) to pray, I reach them by getting them to praise God.
God asks man to offer unto him the sacrifice of thanksgiving.
It is impossible to mingle in praise without melting the heart.
When we get men to praising God, said he, they will begin
to serve him.

From this train of thought, he turned to relate a few incidents in the lives of young sailors whom he had known.   One
concerning Edward ———— was inexpressibly tender and
affecting.   Edward had a pious mother; she loved him,
doated upon him.   There was a thrilling incident of his
coming home one very dark night, when the mother had
promised to put a light in the window, to guide him to the
house.   The narration was given admirably.   No one who
was there that afternoon will ever forget the " light in the
window."   It became a metaphor for religion in the family of
Edward's mother.   Edward went to sea, and the affectionate
mother died during his absence.   She left her dying word for
her son.   She left him by bequest her old Bible and the stand
on which it lay.   " Tell Edward, when he returns," said she,
" that I am gone home, and he will remain in this dark
world."   [The style of the preacher was so touching here
that tears flowed freely in all parts of the house.]   " Tell him
to follow after me ; to come where I am gone, and beseech
him not to forget the *light in the window*.   And when he
passes through the dark valley of the shadow of death," said
the dying woman, " he shall see on high the light in the window of the house not made with hands, where I shall be
waiting for him."   " We cannot," writes Mr. Whittemore,
" pursue this description : we can do it no manner of justice.
A theme so rich, in Father Taylor's style, is insipid when we
undertake to repeat it.   He told other incidents in the lives
of some of his sailors.   At last he closed by lifting his eyes
and hands to heaven, and invoking with tremulous voice a

blessing on his dear brethren with whom he had enjoyed the pleasure of meeting on that day. It was some time before the attention could be turned from this address to other parts of the service."

During this year, there was a wide-spread religious interest in all parts of the country. The various Christian sects shared in it; the Universalists among them. As an observer and chronicler of passing events, Mr. Whittemore could not fail to have a strong interest in the whole movement. He speaks freely in reference to it, and expresses an earnest desire that his own church might share in its blessings, and that all the churches might be able to discriminate between the genuine and spurious, the false and the true. We append some of his reflections on the whole subject : —

" There is said to be a great revival of religion now in progress all over our land. That there is a great *excitement* is indisputable. There will be some chaff among the wheat, perhaps a good deal of chaff, but there will be some wheat too. We are in favor of revivals of pure and undefiled religion. We pray for more love of God, more love of truth, more love of Christ, more faithfulness to him in our heart; more zeal among Universalists; less coldness, indifference, worldly-mindedness. We would rejoice to see a true revival of religion reaching from one end of our land unto the other. We may speak of the community in three points of view: 1st. As having true revivals ; 2d. As having false revivals; and 3d. As having no revivals at all. There are no revivals at all when every thing is dull, indifferent, dead. This is like a treacherous calm at sea. It cannot always last: if it did the waters would stagnate. Such a state of things is more likely to end in a destructive storm, which we describe as a false revival, where every thing is thrown into disorder; a wild excitement reigns, and perhaps great harm will be done.

A true revival is when hearts are warmed **anew** by the love of God; when the Saviour's love is shed abroad in our **hearts**; when saints are quickened into a higher degree of life, and sinners are turned from the evil of their ways; when Christians of different sects love each other more; when there is less contention, less bitterness in one sect towards another. Some persons think they love God, when they love chiefly their sect; they hate others; and this is nearly all the religion they have. But this is not the spirit of Christ's religion. Universalists desire a revival of Christ's religion; more brotherly kindness, more charity. We pray God to preside over the revival now in Boston, and conduct it to a good end; purge it of every particle of unholy feeling, and make it glorious in holiness and love. Then there will be more justice, more benevolence, more humanity among us. Universalists will aid in all good revivals, and discountenance all bad ones. The Lord gave the Universalists of Boston a new dispensation of life last autumn. In that sweet conference meeting in Roxbury, on the 14th of October, we felt that the work had begun with us; and it has been going on ever since. From that time to this it has not ceased among us. But yet Universalists are far below what they ought to be. We must go up higher; we must rise from mountain to mountain until we stand on the highest peak."

In concluding a sensible article on the "Philosophy of Revivals," in which he vindicates the Universalists against the unjust accusation of their being opposed to them, and showing how ready many of them are to aid in the work of religious awakening and Christian life, he speaks thus faithfully and pointedly in reference to those professed Universalists who take but little or no interest in such manifestations of their faith. His words are worthy of being remembered by all who read them.

"We have thus given our own mind on revivals of religion. On the whole we approve of them. There is much that is bad in them: there is much that is good. The principal difficulty of which we have to complain is that Universalists do not participate in them as they ought to do. Would to God that every Universalist Church and Society could have a time of refreshing at least once a year. We need it. If we had it, our churches would not remain as stagnant and dead as some of them now are. Why are they so backward? Why is church organization so much neglected among us? Why are some of our churches so cold and even dead? They have a name to live only. Some of them never knew what a revival is. They are moral graveyards: the dead are buried there. Some of them have not admitted a score of members for years. They never have prayer-meetings, nor, in fact, any other kind of church meetings. They go to the communion table once in a while, but seem to act as though they would as soon omit it as not. We lament this state of things. We had rather see the wildfire than such coldness. We would that there might be kindled a fire once in a while like that which the old hymn pleads for: —

> 'Come, Holy Spirit, heavenly dove,
>   With all thy quickening powers;
> Come, shed abroad a Saviour's love,
>   And THAT shall kindle ours!'

Oh for such a revival among our people! The love of God can convert sinners, and nothing else can do it so well. We have the love of God in our doctrine: we long to see the effects. 'Come, Lord Jesus, come quickly!'"

And once more, in a brief article entitled "Too Much Zeal:" "One of the strangest conceits that ever entered a mortal brain is the fear expressed by some of our brethren that the Universalists will become too zealous. It is almost an impossibility for a Christian Universalist to have strange fire upon his altar. Universalism itself is the safeguard. There is small danger of wildfire with Universalism. We wish our alarmists would look out upon the Universalist denomination, and see which we are most in danger from, coldness or zeal? *Beyond all question* it is the *former*. We sometimes feel when we visit certain Universalist societies as if we were with Dr. Kane in the arctic regions. The expression of the belief that Universalists are in danger from too much zeal will make some of our iceberg saints feel very happy in themselves. Good Lord, quicken us! "

There was a section of Boston called the " Black Sea." It had borne that name for a long time, because it had been a place of infamy. Abandoned men and women, drunkards, gamblers, harlots, thieves, congregated there. They kept shady and quiet by day, but emerged from their dens and went to their dancing-halls by night, and set their nets to catch the unwary. The revival in Boston had reached that locality. A prayer-meeting was instituted and held every day in one of the dancing-halls, a large room that would contain one or two hundred persons. Mr. Whittemore was strongly induced to visit the place, and take part in the religious exercises and in reclaiming the wandering. We present his account of his first visit there.

" Little did we know what we were to enjoy. We expected to be received with coldness, if received at all; but the impulse to go was so strong, we could not, or at least did not, resist. The first day on which we were present, one of the redeemed harlots spoke. She avowed her hope that she had turned once for all from the impurity of her ways. She felt that she could not be taken back again into Sodom. She had escaped; she had been longing to escape; and now the crisis had come, and she determined with all the resolution she had (feeble it might be) to do wrong no more. She was a young woman of talents, of personal beauty, and evidently of great decision of character.

" We said to ourself, Shall Universalists see *such* a revival going on in Boston and take no part in it? It must not be that we hold back."

At the first meeting, Mr. Whittemore was a silent spectator; but his soul was deeply moved. A few days after he went again, and took part in the exercises. He spoke of the need and excellency of the true religious life, and his words seemed very welcome to all present. Of the third meeting which he attended, he writes :—

" Father Taylor was there (the same who was at Milford), and we had another opportunity to grasp his hand. He did not know that we had been in the meeting before. We want to hear your voice, said he : this is a free meeting. Rev. Perez Mason (the City Missionary) presided. He sings, prays, and talks readily. We made an address on the intrinsic value of religion. Religion consists in love to God, and love to man, and in a good life.

> ' More needful this than glittering wealth,
>   Or aught the world bestows.'

" We turned to those who professed to have been converted. We said, ' Have you enlisted under Christ for a day? or have you given yourself to him for a life service? Shall you ever fall back into sin.' There was much weeping. It called to mind the words : —

> ' Were not the sinful Mary's tears
>   An offering worthy heaven,
> ' When o'er the faults of former years,
>   She wept, and was forgiven.'

" Whether these converts will fall away or not, we do not positively know ; but if men make no efforts to convert sin-

ners because they *may* fall away, we shall never do any thing
for sinners.   In a private conversation with Father Mason,
he said, ' His duty was to lift the fallen on to their feet.   He
did not know but they would fall again; but if they did we
must lift them up again.'

   " One layman prayed (we were all kneeling), with great
solemnity, that sinners might be saved *now ;* they needed
salvation *now ;* salvation from sin, from darkness, from un-
belief, from evil ways of drunkenness, from cruelty *now.*   He
prayed for the inmates of the dark holes of infamy; for cruel
husbands infuriated by rum who abused their wives and
children; he prayed for the tempted, the fallen, the polluted,
and abandoned.   He prayed in some respects like a man who
believed in endless punishment; but there was much in his
prayer that was lovely and of good report.   We responded
at the close, heartily, ' Amen ! '

   " A brother rose (a perfect stranger to us).   He said he
was from Charlestown.   He had brought to the meeting a
poor fallen brother, he said, — a seaman, a Swede, for whose
salvation he felt the most fervent desires; and he wanted
him to be regarded as a special subject of prayer that day.
The old seaman was deeply moved.   His emotion must have
begun before he entered the room.   Father Mason knelt down
with him, and said, ' Let us all pray for this man.'   He
offered a very fervent petition; so fervent and striking, that
it penetrated to the soul of every one present.   The Swede
trembled, wept, ejaculated promises of amendment, hoped
God would forgive him.   We were all kneeling.   How could
my soul refrain from praying?   It was not I that prayed,
but the soul that dwelt within me.   I prayed for the success
of such efforts to save souls from sin.   I prayed for the continuance of the revival.   ' Amen ! ' ejaculated Father Taylor,
' Amen ! '   I prayed that God would show us far greater

things than we had yet seen.   ['Bless the Lord!']   I prayed that God would continue the revival until all the haunts of sin should be broken up; until every sinner should bathe in that fountain which had been opened for sin and uncleanness. ['Glory to God!']   I prayed that God would open the windows of heaven and pour us out a blessing until we should not have room to receive it.   ['Amen! Hallelujah!' shouted Father Taylor. 'This is surely the millennium!']   At the close of the service, we shook hands with many who had entered the new life."

CHAPTER XV.

1858–1859.

AGED 58–59.

Anniversary Week — Speech — Orange, Mass. — Visit to Vermont — Commencement at Tufts — Review of Rev. T. Starr King — The Old Testament — Visit to Norway, Me. — Rockingham Association — Fitchburg — Vermont Convention at Bethel — Connecticut Convention at Granby — Universalism conducive to Purest Piety — U.S. Convention at Providence — Sippican, Mass. — Hinsdale, N.H. — South Acton, Mass. — Conference in Boston — In Roxbury — Woman Preaching : Mrs. Jenkins — Nomination of a Minister for Congress — New Bedford — Lawrence, Mass. — Methuen — Conference at Mattapoisett — At Worcester — Sabbath in Lowell — Rockport — Marblehead — Lynn — Dr. Ballou's Notice of Mr. Whittemore — Manchester, N.H. — Dedication Sermon at Cambridgeport — North Bridgewater, Mass. — Annisquam — Interesting Incident — Visit to Milford, Mass. — Palmer — Southbridge — Salem — The Main Question — The Doctorate.

ANNIVERSARY Week in Boston was one of unusual interest this year. The meetings of the Universalists were well attended, and the conference and prayer meetings were especially impressive. The Festival in Faneuil Hall was again a success. The exercises were of a high order. Lieutenant-Governor E. Trask presided. Addresses were made by Rev. Messrs. T. B. Thayer, A. D. Mayo, B. M. Tillotson, A. C. Thomas, T. S. King, T. Whittemore, and Governor N. P. Banks. Mr. Whittemore's speech was as humorous, pathetic, patriotic, and varied as ever. In his allusions to Universalism and the American Revolution, he was quite happy. "Universalism and the Revolution," he said, "began to rise together at North End, the glorious old North End of Boston. They were rocked together in the same stormy days, in the cradle of American Liberty. Universalism has been rising like the leading star, like the true church, clear as the sun, fair as the moon, and terrible as an army with banners. The banner of Universalism is love. Let that banner be lifted up. I see it borne aloft, pure, white, steady; and I read the inscription thereon, 'Hope for every soul,' for every creed-bound, affrighted, crushed soul, hope!

"So shall it be ere long, we trust, with the banner of our country. It shall symbol yet the true idea of the Declaration of Independence, 'all men are created free and independent.' I look forward to the time when our flag shall wave in unsullied glory, not over smoking ruins, not merely at the masthead of our battle-ships, not merely on bloody fields, not merely from the parapets of our forts. I look to a higher victory. I look to great moral achievements, for I shall see parties overturned and overturned, until the best shall at last arise; and I shall see that national banner floating out, not only from the dome of the Capitol, but from the dome of the Temple of Justice, the highest glory of the nation and of the world. The stars and stripes and the white banner shall be seen together, the one floating in the wind, the other upheld by steady hands, over slaves redeemed, sinners converted, cruel statutes abolished, Kansas happy and free, the people united, and the North and the South one.

"Before I close," said he, "I must say a few words in regard to the localities of the Revolution in the vicinity of Boston. Our societies are established almost in the very places where the forts, the strong places of defence against tyranny, stood. At the base of Bunker Hill, you have a society, whose pastor, although a Scotchman born, has many high regards for his adopted land. Two societies are there in Cambridge, the headquarters of Washington during the siege of Boston. Thus we see the resemblance between the moral and political revolutions of those days. At Roxbury, where there was one of the most important points of defence in the old war, you have now a noble society under the charge of our excellent brother, Rev. W. H. Ryder. At Dorchester Heights (South Boston now), there is a society, under the pastorship of Rev. W. W. Dean, who is seeking by his wise labors to aid in driving sin and error out of the city altogether. Would that these evils might be put on board their respective crafts, go out of the harbor, and never be heard of more. In the city itself, you have a host of good men, like the true patriots of 1775, who gave the adversaries of liberty great disquiet, and were ever active in the good cause. At Somerville, there is also a society, under the pastorship of Rev. G. H. Emerson, devoted to the great idea of universal love, standing almost on Prospect Hill, a point of great interest in olden time. And on another of those eminences, the spot where the troops of Burgoyne were quartered after they were brought prisoners to Massachusetts, stands now that young but noble institution, Tufts College. Truly we may say, Faneuil Hall and Universalism, — the Revolution of the Country and of its Religion simultaneous." He concluded his speech with a strong plea for Tufts College, and expressed it as his belief that this was the last anniversary he should ever attend in Faneuil Hall. A few weeks afterwards he wrote: " It seems to us that we never shall cease talking about the enjoyments of Anniversary Week. It was the week of weeks. We shall never see another like it on earth."

Mr. Whittemore was not present at the Massachusetts Convention, which held its session this year in Quincy.

The Universalist church in Orange, Mass., was dedicated on the 16th of June. Mr. Whittemore was present, and gave the Address to the Society.

The last of June, he journeyed to Vermont, and attended the Windham Association at West Halifax. He preached on the last afternoon of the meeting to a very large congregation. The journey to him was highly enjoyable.

He was at the Commencement exercises at Tufts College, July 14. He presided at the collation, and made a short but very encouraging speech in reference to the present condition and prospects of the institution.

Sometime this year, Rev. Dr. Nehemiah Adams, of Boston, had delivered a discourse in advocacy of the doctrine of endless punishment. Rev. T. Starr King, pastor of the Hollis Street (Unitarian) church, invited the Doctor to repeat the discourse in his pulpit, which he consented to do. Mr. King forthwith replied to it, in two discourses, which were soon afterwards published. In a notice of his reply, Mr. Whittemore expresses his strong dissent from some of the statements advanced by Mr. King; especially declarations like these: "I do not find the doctrine of the ultimate salvation of all souls clearly stated in any text, or in any discourse that has been reported from the lips of Christ. I do not think we can fairly maintain that the final restoration of all men is a prominent and explicit doctrine of the four Gospels; but all the principles glow there, vivid as the sunlight, that are required to give us the most consoling trust in God through eternity, and the most cheering hope for man."

In reply to these statements, Mr. Whittemore writes: "With the utmost good-will to Mr. King, we feel obliged to declare that we object most decidedly to these statements of his. They may be his opinions: we are quite sure they are not ours, nor those of Universalists in general. In fact, they are not those of all Unitarians; for there are scores of the latter who hold that the doctrine of the final, universal happiness of men is a plainly revealed doctrine of the Word of God." He notes the eagerness with which the (orthodox) *Recorder* takes up this admission of Mr. King, and asks him how he can dare hold and advocate a doctrine which he fails to find in the Gospels? Against these statements of the Hollis Street pastor, Mr. Whittemore gives his convictions in reference to the teachings of the New Testament on this great subject, — the salvation of all souls.

In an article in the *Universalist Quarterly* for October, 1858, Mr. Whittemore reviews the two discourses of Mr. King. The review is very tender in spirit, because of the kind regard of the writer towards the author of the discourses; but it is at the same time very plain and searching. In answer to the question, "Is Universalism Revealed in the Four Gospels?" he shows very plainly that the whole drift of the Gospels is in the direction of this idea. The Samaritans learned from the instructions of Jesus himself that he was "indeed the Christ, the Saviour of the world" (John iv. 42). They knew nothing about the matter except what they learned from him. He affirmed, moreover, that "all things," — meaning all intellectual beings — had been committed to his care, and that he should labor for their welfare, and would suffer no one to draw them out of his hand. "All things are delivered unto me of my Father" (Matt. xi. 27). "The Father loveth the Son, and hath given all things into his hands" (John iii. 35). "All that the Father giveth me shall come to me" (John vi. 37). "And I, if I be lifted up from the earth, will draw all men unto me" (John xii. 32). The drawing of all men to him was just as sure as the fact of his being lifted up from the earth on the cross. Other proofs from the Gospels and Epistles are brought forward to show

how Christ spoke of the extensiveness of his work of salvation, and how the Apostles understood his mission with man. His quotations from the Apostles, and his whole review, seem to us decisive. He differed from his younger brother in his estimate of the importance of the textual evidences of Universalism, and of making its distinguishing truth prominent in all his teachings; as also in his preference for the Universalist Church above all others as his " chief joy " and most constant home. But he held in very high regard the rare talents of this loyal soldier of the Cross; and had he lived to witness his subsequent ministry, would have been, with many others, thankful for the noble work he wrought in the cause of human enlightenment and regeneration.

" A young preacher" asks Mr. Whittemore the question, " How do you treat the Old Testament in your pulpit communications?" Mr. Whittemore replies, in substance: —

" I believe the Old Testament to be a sacred book, an important part of the Bible. It always pains me to hear any one, especially a minister of the Gospel, speak irreverently of the Old Testament; and more especially if that preacher be a professed Universalist. Jesus never expressed any disrespect for the Old Testament, but, on the contrary, he always spoke of it with reverence. We do not deny that the Old Testament was better fitted to the condition of the Jews than to our condition. Jesus never found fault with the Jews for believing too much in Moses; but he frequently found fault with them for believing too little in him. ' For had ye believed Moses ye would have believed me; for he wrote of me. But if ye believe not his writings, how shall ye believe my words?' Hence he said to them, ' Search the Scriptures; for in them ye think ye have eternal life; and they are they which testify of me.' Moses and the prophets prophesied of the coming of Christ: ' We have found him of whom Moses in the law and the prophets did write, Jesus of Nazareth, the son of Joseph' (John i. 45). 'And beginning at Moses and all the prophets, he expounded unto them in all the Scriptures the things concerning himself' (Luke xxiv. 27). Our Lord was in the habit of quoting distinct passages from the Old Testament, — passages which announced the most important truths. While I seek to be Christ-like, I cannot fail to cherish a deep respect for the Old Testament. Paul cherished a profound respect for it. He writes to Timothy: 'From a child thou hast known the holy Scriptures, which are able to make thee wise unto salvation.' At Thessalonica, he reasoned much with the Jews 'out of the Scriptures.' Apollos, we are told, was 'an eloquent man, and mighty in the Scriptures.' He 'mightily convinced the Jews, and that publicly, showing by the Scriptures that Jesus was the Christ.' Let our young inquirer regard the Old Testament as it was regarded by Christ and the apostles."

He makes a visit to Norway, Me. He preached there on a Sunday, in the Universalist church, to a very large and deeply attentive congregation, most of whom had never heard him before. He enjoyed the day highly. In the evening of this day, he delivered a lecture at Paris Hill, in the Baptist church. The Norway society is the oldest of the order in Maine. Its first meeting was held in 1798.

This year the Rockingham Association was held in Kingston, N.H. It was very fully attended, and the congregations occupied two churches, — the Universalist and Methodist. The Methodist clergyman was very cordial, and was in his pulpit with our ministers during the services. On the afternoon of the last day, Mr. Whittemore preached in the Universalist church. He writes: " We think Christianity gained something in the hearts of the people by the influence of this meeting. It was, taken altogether, one of the greatest meetings ever held by the Association. It seemed as if the times of twenty years ago had come back again."

While in attendance on the Union Association in Fitchburg, in August, Mr. Whittemore was called, as a railroad officer, to take part in the celebration of the laying of the Atlantic cable. It was an occasion of much excitement in the place. There was a large assembling of people, and addresses were made by Colonel Ivers Phillips, A. Crocker, J. J. Piper, and P. E. Aldrich, Esqrs.; Rev. Mr. Brooks, and Judge Bishop. Mr. Whittemore was called upon, and spoke very earnestly and to great acceptance, for fifteen minutes. In closing, he reminded the foreign population that they were now to live within five minutes' communication of father and mother, and brother and sister, at home. They had come to this country to live with us. We must all be friends, and forget all national antipathies, and all religious differences, and live together as brethren.

Mr. Whittemore preached during the session of the Association in the Universalist church. During the last services, a church was publicly recognized, and the communion service, observed. He regarded the meeting as one long to be remembered by those who attended it.

He journeyed to Vermont, through Keene, N.H., where he spent a little time in attention to railroad matters. He then attended the Vermont Convention, in Bethel. Soon after his arrival, he was taken quite ill; and, failing to recover, reluctantly resolved to return to his home. It was a great sorrow to him, for he had anticipated a rich season at the meeting.

Soon after this, he was able to attend the Connecticut Convention, in Granby. The audiences increased so that it was resolved to hold the meeting on the second day in a grove near by. An appointment had been made for Mr. Whittemore to preach there, but he feared to expose himself to such a trial of his strength just at that time. He preached in the church in the morning, and the meeting was held in the grove in the afternoon. Rev. C. H. Fay, of Middleton, was the preacher there. Mr. Whittemore was present, and deeply enjoyed the occasion. The sermon was able and appropriate, and was followed by the communion service. It was to Mr. Whittemore something entirely new, this service in a grove. "A table had been constructed in front of the rostrum, on which the elements were laid. Mr. Whittemore was invited to preside at the service. All were invited to keep their places. The air was perfectly serene. Appropriate remarks were offered. It was such a spectacle as we never saw before, and probably shall never see again. A communion service beneath the broad, illimitable sky! But all was subdued and pleasant, and the closing hymn went up to heaven in a chorus of three or four hundred voices."

Of the encouragement given by Christian Universalism to the purest piety, he says: "A doctrine so congenial to piety and benevolence as to engage all good men to pray that it may be true cannot have a bad influence. We allow that it may be misunderstood and perverted, and then the good influence of it will be lost. The grace of God of old was turned into lasciviousness; but who would argue from it that the natural tendency of divine grace was evil? A New England divine, who made himself quite eminent by his opposition to Universalism twenty-five or thirty years ago, allowed that the tendency of that doctrine on a good man was salutary. After stating that the effect of this doctrine on a *bad* man was unfavorable, he is very particular to add, ' but that the belief in Universalism would have the same effect on those who are born of God, we have never said; much less that if we believed it we would by all means live in all manner of sin in this life.' The same divine, in a published discourse that came out in 1818, after a most fallacious argument designed to show that the wicked would encourage themselves in sin by this sentiment, says (and let all observe his words) : 'I speak not the language of the *pious* soul, who knows the comforts of religion, and rejoices in his liberty as a child of God, being set free from sin and the power of Satan ; but of those who know nothing of that comfort and liberty, and who delight in the drudgery of sin, and hug their chains.' Unfortunately for his argument, he adds : 'These are the people who mistake *in every thing.* They call evil good and good evil ; they put darkness for light and light for darkness, bitter for sweet and sweet for bitter.' We should expect that Universalism would be misunderstood by such people. How can it be otherwise? If they call good evil, how can we expect that they would make a proper use of such a good doctrine as that of which we have spoken? It would of course be the contrary doctrine that they would consider good, on the reverend gentleman's own rule. He acknowledges just what we have always asserted, that Universalism is a doctrine congenial to piety."

The United States Convention was held this season in Providence, R.I. It was an occasion of great interest. The Occasional Sermon was by Rev. G. S. Weaver, of St. Louis, Mo., and gave great satisfaction. Many other discourses were delivered, and most attractive and impressive conferences held. Services were in both churches. Mr. Whittemore writes of the meeting: "For high spiritual power, it was like the great meeting in Boston on the 29th of May last. The silent prayer on the last evening, when the immense assembly bowed before God, not uttering a word ; when not the slightest sound or motion or breath was heard, — never was any thing more impressive. When the silent prayer was ended at the pronunciation of ' Amen,' by Brother Balch in the desk, a brother began the Lord's Prayer aloud from the broad aisle, and the more than a thousand people, every one (so far as we could discover), joined in, audibly, word for word, to the end, and at the close responded out of the very depths of their souls, not loudly, but sincerely, such an Amen as only a thousand souls together can utter. We are speaking of the meeting we attended; there was another great meeting at the same hour. We bless God for that last meeting in Providence. It was hard to leave it. It seemed as if the people could not go away. It was half-past ten before the last ones left the house."

A Sunday in Sippican, Mass., is greatly enjoyed; including a prayer-meeting of unusual interest in the evening.

In October, he attended a conference of the Cheshire Association, in Hinsdale, N.H. He preached twice on the occasion, and took part in a very demonstrative and enjoyable conference at the conclusion of the session. In the same month he passed a Sabbath in South Acton, and preached in a new hall there, which was densely crowded. Scores were standing around the windows. In the afternoon, a ladder was raised to the top of the piazza, and settees were placed on that, and the windows were opened, so that the outsiders might hear. He had not preached in the town for more than twenty years.

On the 14th of this month, a spirited conference was held in the First Universalist Church in Boston. Mr. Whittemore was present. Rev. R. A. Ballou delivered an address which invited much discussion, because it involved the doctrine of religious awakening and culture in the future life, for those who knew not the blessings in the present existence. The remarks were all in the fraternal spirit. Mr. Whittemore made a sweet and stirring speech. Father Taylor, the seaman's minister, was present. Being invited to speak he said that he had enjoyed many things in this meeting. He had been in Universalist conference meetings before. He remembered that precious meeting at Milford very vividly. But he never went to any meeting with the full intent beforehand to say he approved of every word he should hear; neither did he expect the people to approve every word he should say. He had been greatly pleased with certain parts of the address: it came from a Christian's heart; but there were some things new to him. He spoke tenderly and in a loving strain, but objected somewhat to the idea that men had got to mend up their characters when they reached another world. He thought they had better do it here, down here in the workshop, and not up in glory. Be saved *now*, for now is the time. Every thing was said kindly. The harmony of the meeting was not in the least disturbed. Rev. Mr. Ryder spoke in explanation after Father Taylor closed. Mr. Whittemore made another address in the evening, and closed the meeting with prayer.

He attended a Conference in Roxbury, on Wednesday evening, Oct. 20. He entered with great earnestness into the exercises, speaking twice during the evening. He concludes a notice of it with the exclamation, " What a series of happy meetings have we enjoyed during this month of October! "

Woman preaching is coming into favor with him. He says of Mrs. L. A. Jenkins, of Central, New York: " This lady has been winning golden opinions in Williamsburg, N.Y. We had the opportunity to hear her speak in Providence, R.I., before more than a thousand persons at the time of the great gathering there. She made a deep impression upon us. We shall throw no obstacle in her way. She is possessed of great talents. Let her follow the dictates of her own conscience. She will perhaps visit New England in a few weeks with her husband, and some of our societies will have an opportunity to hear them declare the Gospel. We have no doubt that she can be instrumental of much good." Again he remarks: "We believe her efforts are highly favorable to the cause of pure religion, and it is our duty to say so to the world."

In noticing the nomination of Rev. John A. Gurley of Cincinnati, Ohio, for Congress spoken of as a minister's "promotion," he objects to the expression. "Call you this promoting ministers? To take a man from the sacred desk and put him into the Congress of the United States? We have a high respect for John A. Gurley, but shall never think that he has been *promoted* by going to Congress!"

He preached in New Bedford on Sunday, November 28th. The day was stormy, but the church was filled with hearers. A good conference in the evening was highly enjoyed by him.

In December, Mrs. Jenkins, the preacher, made her first visit to Massachusetts. Mr. Whittemore and wife accompanied her to Lawrence, where she was to preach. The Sabbath was a stormy and wintry one ; but a large congregation came to greet the preacher. Mr. Whittemore took part with her in the services. He writes of her, as she appeared on the occasion : "There was an utter absence of all attempt at show. She read the fourteenth chapter of the Gospel according to John. It was done distinctly, tenderly, in not a loud voice ; but she was heard with ease at the remotest parts of the house. Everybody was listening. The cadences were well preserved, the interrogations exceedingly well given, and the dialogistic parts were recited almost as if two persons were talking to each other. Her topic for discourse was the Fatherhood of God. Her sermon was written and lay before

her. At times she read, and at times she spoke extempo-
raneously to all appearance. If we speak of the sermon
according to the impression it made upon us, our words will
be regarded as scintillations from a heated imagination. We
have no desire to write one eulogistic sentence, any further
than an exact statement of the facts will be such. It was
one of the most effective, tender, instructive, truthful discourses on the paternal character of God that we had
ever heard. We did not hear her in the afternoon, as
we were obliged to go to Methuen to fulfil our own appointment."

While in New England, Mrs. Jenkins preached two Sabbaths in Lawrence, two in Medford, one in Lowell, and one
in Manchester, N.H. Her husband also preached in different
places. She preached in the evening in several towns not
here named. Mr. Whittemore writes of her visit: " The
peculiar fact of a lady-preacher helped to draw large crowds
to hear her in many instances, — the greatest probably in
Lowell and Manchester, who if they came from curiosity, went
home in admiration of her talents, and softened and humbled
by the power of her discourses. We are glad she has come
to New England." He afterwards writes: " All our early
impressions were against woman's appearing in public as a
speaker. We supposed a woman could not do it, unless she
were bold, masculine, and presuming, and that was the very
class, we thought, who, for the credit of their families, ought
to stay at home. We are now sure that a woman can speak,
can preach, can pray, in the pulpit, without throwing off her
womanly dignity and modesty."

A conference was held at Mattapoisett, Mass., in December. The ministers and laity from other places were present,
and the occasion was one of unalloyed enjoyment to Mr.
Whittemore, who, took an active part in the exercises.

Another conference was held during this month in Worcester, which Mr. Whittemore attended. Mrs. Jenkins preached on the occasion. Rev. C. F. Hudson, author of "Debt and Grace," and "Doctrine of a Future Life," took part in the meeting. It was one of rich enjoyment.

A Sabbath is passed by him at Lowell in this month. He preached in the First Church, and Mrs. Jenkins in the Second. Both churches were filled, and the last named was running over. Mr. Whittemore had a brief but very affecting interview with Rev. T. B. Thayer, who was at that time lying very low in consequence of a severe accident of which he had been the subject. The event occasioned great anxiousness on the part of the many friends of the suffering one, and great was the joy when he came up from his long prostration to his place and work in the ministry again.

The first Sabbath in January of the new year (1859) was spent by Mr. Whittemore in Rockport, Mass. The day was exceedingly pleasant, and large audiences greeted the preacher. He writes: "We never before saw such a concourse in Rockport. This is to be attributed in part to the labors of the settled pastor (Rev. J. H. Farnsworth), who for the year past has been steadily bringing the congregation up in its numbers. The society embraces many of the best men and women, and young men and women, in the town. We love them for their integrity, temperance, good order, and devotion to the Christian cause."

He preached in Marblehead on one Sabbath in this month. He had not preached there since 1841, when Rev. Henry Bacon was pastor of the society. His visit made him very happy. Although the wintry weather was forbidding, his congregations were large. "Such a sea of faces!" he writes: "Such attention! It excited us; we preached more than an hour on the character of God as the standard of moral excellence." A Sabbath of much enjoyment was soon after passed with the Second Society in Lynn.

A notice of the " Autobiography " of Mr. Whittemore, by Rev. Dr. H. Ballou, appears about this time in the *Universalist Quarterly*. The description of Mr. Whittemore which it contains is so well drawn, that we give it a place in these pages : —

" From about the year 1825 to the present, — the period usually allotted as the term of a generation, — no man's name has been more familiar to the Universalist denomination than that of Thomas Whittemore; after excepting the late Hosea Ballou, no other person is so generally known. Possessing in a most extraordinary degree the faculty of reaching the popular mind ; making himself understood by every grade of hearer and reader ; speaking the language of the people, and speaking to them with a directness and familiarity which always arrest attention and awaken sympathy ; and possessing a fund of humor which perpetually gushes out, and for the time, and despite even of prejudice, compels a friendly feeling ; he is, by the consent of friend and foe, the people's man, above any other in our denominational history. Add to this the fact, that for nearly thirty years he has preached as an itinerant about thirty-seven hundred times, and thus been brought into personal intimacy with brethren in numerous localities ; and the further fact, that during nearly all of his professional life he has been the industrious editor of a journal which, if not reaching a large number of readers, has circulated over a much larger territory than any other advocating the same cause. These things, both personal and circumstantial, account for the notoriety which has made the name and character of Mr. Whittemore more widely and intimately known than that of any other Universalist minister."

The last Sunday in January was spent by Mr. Whittemore

in Manchester, N.H. The day was wintry. He writes
of it: "In the afternoon, we addressed the greatest number of people we ever saw in Manchester. One lady was
introduced to us who said she was a member of the Methodist church, but she was a Universalist, she said, in heart
and soul. The Methodists loved her, and when she asked a
dismission they were unwilling to let her go. They love her
still, and she loves them; but she loves Christ and the Gospel above her chief joy. She goes regularly to the Universalist church. The sermon in the afternoon was just one
hour and thirty minutes in length."

Mr. Whittemore preached the sermon at the dedication of
the new Universalist church-edifice in Cambridgeport, on
Wednesday P.M. December 26, 1859. The pastor and ex-
pastors were in the pulpit together.

He preached in North Bridgewater (now Brockton), Mass.,
on the 13th of February; had large audiences and a very
agreeable day. On the last Sunday in the month he preached
at Annisquam. Winter's trials attended him. His ride of
six miles after leaving the comfortable cars at Gloucester,
is thus spoken of: "The ride to Gloucester was well
enough; but when we had to take a seat in a coach on wheels,
for a ride of six miles in a dark evening, up hill and down,
through drifts of snow, the wind howling, the driver suffering,
and the poor horses scarcely able to pull the coach, it was a
very different matter. We called all our religion and philosophy to our aid, but that act did not make our feet warm.
It was the longest six miles we ever rode." A safe and
pleasant home was reached at last; the next day was greeted
with sunshine, and the preacher had a happy interview with
large congregations. On the 20th of this month, he preached
in Middletown, Ct. On the last Sunday he preached in
Danvers, Mass.

In the *Trumpet* of April 9, he relates an interesting incident which came up in his ministerial experience. He preached on a certain Sabbath in a town in Massachusetts, on the Parable of the Sower. His aim was to describe the effects of the sowing of the truth in the minds of different persons. If the seed of love be sown in the receptive heart, it will produce the happiest effects, and bring forth the largest fruits; " some sixty, some thirty, and some a hundred fold."

" In the course of the argument, which I extended to some length, I happened to cast my eyes at the singers, among whom I saw a person of forty years, perhaps, in plain but cleanly apparel. He was giving earnest attention to the preaching, — so far as he could under the emotion he manifested; and I observed, in the moment my eye was fixed on him, that he shed tears profusely. His countenance indicated a feeling of mingled grief and joy. The circumstance passed from my mind, until, at the house where I dined, a person came in whom I recognized as the same individual. He extended his hand, and while I was exchanging salutations with him, he burst out in audible grief, and left the room. He shortly came in again somewhat composed, and dined with the family, speaking but few words, and those betraying his emotion. I did not see him after he left the table, at that time, though I saw him often afterward.

" When he had retired, I inquired of the lady of the house the cause of his grief. ' Formerly,' said she, ' this individual was a man of very irregular habits. He was a tippler, an idler; careless of his family, and still more careless of himself. Every one gave him up as lost for this world, and regretted that a person of such good natural sense should become so abandoned. At last,' she continued, ' he commenced to attend the Universalist meetings, and to read the books and papers of that denomination. His neighbors — generally

Methodists — drew from this fact an argument to prove that Universalism was agreeable to the depraved heart. But there soon commenced a very great change in his character. His rashness and irascibility passed away, and his disposition seemed to be softened and moulded anew. He became patient and meek and kind. He left his cups entirely (and this,' she said, ' was more than two years previous), and became a sober and industrious citizen. It seems almost impossible,' she added, ' for him to forgive himself for having sinned so long against infinite, unmerited, and unchanging goodness. When he first came among us, we hesitated to receive him, and believed he could not be a Universalist; but his conduct soon made us all proud of him, and he is now universally respected. Whenever any preacher comes here who speaks particularly of God's love to us, even when we are sinners, and the duty this imposes on us to love one another, he cannot restrain his feelings; and this,' said she, ' I apprehend was the cause of his emotion to-day, which excited your attention.' Here was an instance of the natural influence of the love of God as revealed in the Gospel. When it is said that Universalism is licentious, I always think of the case now described."

He visits Milford, Mass., in April. "We called," he writes, " at the house of Mr. Newell Nelson, the Town Clerk in 1821, when we lived in Milford; who, on one Sabbath-day, posted conspicuously upon the front-door of the church in which we preached the following notice: ' Marriage is intended between Rev. Thomas Whittemore and Miss Lovice Corbett, both of Milford.' Brief as this notice was, it led to very important results. Mr. Nelson is now about seventy-five years of age. Leaving him, we rode to Hopedale, and called on Rev. Adin Ballou, and spent a half-hour with him very pleasantly, talking principally about old times. His amiable wife was the daughter of one of our steadfast friends (Perly Hunt, Esq.), who joined in marriage the parties named in the preceding publishment. From Rev. Mr. Ballou's house, we went to Mr. Elliot Alden's, where all our party joined company again. Thence we all went to the venerable mansion of Mrs. Corbett, Mrs. Whittemore's mother. The old lady will enter her ninety-third year on the 4th of May. She is in excellent health, good spirits, memory and hearing very good for a person of her age. She believes every thing will take place just as the Lord decrees. She will live all the days of her appointed time until her change come. Her life has been far above the medium purity of mortals."

He preached in Palmer, Mass., on Sunday, April 10. The place of meeting was a hall in a public-house. It was filled to inconvenience. Hearers were there from many neighboring towns. He writes: "A large number of very sincere inquirers after truth were present. Several ladies tarried after the benediction to assure us of the deep interest they took in the cause; and to promise that each one in her town would do all she could to spread the knowledge of the great and glorious doctrine they had heard that day."

The next day, Mr. Whittemore went to Southbridge, preached in the evening, and enjoyed a conference afterward. "After service," he writes, "we had a few words with every person who remained in the house; words of advice, recollections of old times, and of the fathers and mothers who had passed away."

A Sunday of great interest is spent in Salem, Mass. From eleven to fourteen hundred persons were supposed to be present in the Universalist church. Quite a number were from the Unitarian congregations in the place.

In a brief article entitled, "The Main Question," he writes: "'What is the *main question* with you Universalists?' said a

Partialist to me a few days since. ' Is this it, whether materialism or immaterialism be true?' 'No.' 'Whether there is an intermediate state?' 'No.' 'Whether men will be punished after death?' 'No.' 'What is the main question with you, then?' 'This is it,' I replied, ' *whether all men will eventually be saved?*' 'But,' said he, 'that is the ground of the Restorationists.' 'We are all Restorationists,' I answered ; ' we admit of no distinction. All Restorationists are Universalists, and all Universalists are Restorationists. There is no room for distinction.' 'But,' pressing his question still further, ' is the *Trumpet*,' said he, 'a Restorationist paper?' 'Yes,' said I, 'in the proper sense of that term. We do not hold to making division among Universalists. In that sense we are not Restorationists ; but, in regard to the eventual salvation of all mankind, we are so. We prefer, however, the name Universalists. It is the name Relley bore, and Murray, and Winchester, Adam and Zebulon Streeter, and the General Convention from 1785 to the present time. The name was good enough in former times, and it is good enough now. We are UNIVERSALISTS, believers in the universal love of God, and the universal salvation of men. We pray that we may defend this doctrine by a good life as well as by good arguments.'"

In a friendly letter received from his venerable brother in the ministry, Rev. Russell Streeter, of Vermont, Mr. Whittemore humorously refers to the title of "D.D.," with which he had not long before been honored:[1] "I thank you, dear brother, for the kind wishes you express in my behalf. I will always excuse you for not calling me *Doctor*. I have no conscientious scruples about the matter. I never used any effort to gain this distinction. The next day after it was conferred, I happened to fall in with a number of friends conversing together

[1] By Tufts College.

upon the sidewalk in State Street. They all saluted me as 'Doctor.' 'Ah, Doctor, I wish you much joy.' 'Doctor, I congratulate you.' 'Doctor, permit me to take your hand,' &c. I replied by saying, 'Gentlemen, do forbear, do forbear; for you know we have to take these things *by degrees.*'"

CHAPTER XVI.

1859–1860.

Aged 59–60.

Anniversary Week — Festival in Music Hall — Father Taylor's Speech — Mass. Convention in Milford — West Boylston — Palmer — Norwich — Biddeford — Thoughts on his Ministry — The New Massachusetts Convention — Martha's Vineyard — Dedication at South Reading — Westford — Stoughton — Weymouth — Doctrinal Sermons — Wareham — Norfolk Co. Association — Rockport — U.S. Convention in Rochester, N.Y. — New York *Independent* on Universalism: Call for Discussion — Rev. Adin Ballou: Reciprocal Words — Visit to Boxboro', Mass. — Abington — Marlboro' — What begets Love to God — Visits Maine — Westmoreland, N.H. — Hinsdale — Several Sundays — Roxbury — Claremont, N.H. — Sabbaths at Home — Lowell: Illness in the Pulpit — A Question Considered — Adherence to his Faith — Rev. C. F. Hudson — Anniversary Week — Advice of Family and Friends — *Versus* Tobacco — Forefathers' Rock — Newport, N.H. — Isles of Shoals — Vermont Convention in Cavendish — Agrippa's "Almost" — U.S. Convention in Boston — Three Ways to Live.

Anniversary Week this year brought attractions of more than usual interest to the Universalists, as well as to others. There was much activity in most of the meetings. Sabbath-school and other conferences began with the week. Home Missionary and Reform Meetings were held, Mr. Whittemore taking part in most of them. The Festival in Music Hall was very fully attended. Latimer W. Ballou of Woonsocket, R.I., presided, and made an admirable opening address. Rev. S. Cobb followed in a sensible and pointed speech, responsive to the sentiment "Universalism and the Universalist denomination, — an embodied spirit and a spiritualized body." Rev. Messrs. Patterson, Adams, A. Moore, and E. H. Chapin, followed; and the meeting had a new inspiration in the presence of Father Taylor of the Seamen's Church. He was called upon for a speech, and responded to a welcoming audience. His words were characteristic. "He was exceedingly pleased to be here, and pleased with the cause by which he got here. It was by Dr. Whittemore, the lungs and breath of the great *Trumpet*. And if it depended on Brother Whittemore to keep the blast and music going on earth, he hoped he would be kept a good while out of heaven yet. He had made up his mind to go to heaven with the brother. (Applause; Messrs. Taylor and Whittemore shaking hands amid much laughter.) If the reason was honestly asked, he would honestly say, because he saw no way to help it. Brother Whittemore had stuck close to him twenty years, and could not be shaken off. Therefore he had made up his mind to it, and was much pleased with the idea. He was pleased, too, with all he saw before him, and right down pleased with himself. He spoke of the care which Providence had taken of him through his long life. He had wandered far, preached among men of all nations, and did not know that he had ever been designedly injured. The Lord had cared for him always, and he was thankful." He concluded by saying: "It was by their fruit that we should know men. He himself was waiting for the fruit of his labors. He had not been in the habit of judging others. He might get a *skiving* for being so happy in this company to-day, but he cared little for that! He believed that the children of God everywhere knew their Father, and so he was glad to be here. He saw another brother yonder with whom he expected to go to heaven; and, to make short metre, he believed that we might all go to heaven together. A hope of heaven, a glorious Father, and a blessed Redeemer, was for all of us."

The Massachusetts Convention held its session this year in Milford. A charter obtained from the State Legislature providing for the Sabbath School Association, Massachusetts Convention of Universalists, and Universalist Home Missionary Society into one corporate body, to be called the "Massachusetts Universalist Convention," was presented and adopted. Mr. Whittemore was present and took part in most of the meetings, especially those of conference and prayer.

On Sunday, May 29, he preached for the first time in West Boylston, Mass. He writes of the meeting: "At the ringing of the second bell, the people began to gather from Worcester, Old Boylston, Northboro', Berlin, Sterling, Holden, Rutland, and Oakham. The church was filled, and we must give the people the credit of listening very earnestly. The larger congregation came in the afternoon. We preached on 'the fountain of living waters.' A stranger came up as we reached the threshold at the close of service: 'Sir,' said he, extending his hand, 'I thank you. I live in Holden. I attend the Baptist church. It seems to me that I never really heard the Gospel before. My soul is full; I am satisfied; I have drank of the living water.' We went back to Worcester a very happy man, believing that we had done much good that day. In the evening, we took part in the conference meeting in Worcester."

In June of this year, he visited Palmer, Mass., Norwich, Ct., and Biddeford, Me., as a preacher. In Palmer there was a large gathering. In Norwich, the Quinebaug Association held its session. Mr. Whittemore preached a sermon on the occasion of the admission of new members to the church in Norwich. The meetings here were all deeply interesting. At Biddeford, there were large assemblies; persons being present from nine or ten of the surrounding towns.

The words of the apostle to Timothy strike him with force. "But watch thou in all things, endure afflictions, do the work of an evangelist, make full proof of thy ministry. For I am now ready to be offered, and the time of my departure is at hand. I have fought a good fight; I have finished my course; I have kept the faith" (2 Tim. iv. 5–7). "We have thought much of these words, and have aimed to catch their spirit. Paul believed that he was near the end of his life. He was like a man arrived nearly at the end of his journey. He looked backward and forward. He could say, 'I am now ready to be offered.' How few can say that! We have been thinking of this matter. Are we ready? That is the main point. Dr. Watts has well described the experience of Christians. God does not permit us to know *when* we shall die. We must therefore be always ready. O thou Holy One that inhabitest eternity, grant us thy presence in that solemn and mysterious hour, and all will be well. Come, Lord Jesus, to our help. Leave us not alone; support and succor us when nature fails.

> 'Oh! if my Lord would come and meet,
> My soul would stretch her wings in haste;
> Fly fearless through death's iron gate,
> Nor feel the terrors as she passed.'

"But let not the thoughts of death drive wholly away the thoughts of life. We must know how to live, as well as how to die. We must 'watch in all things;' we must 'endure afflictions;' we must 'do the work of an evangelist;' we must 'make full proof of our ministry.' Then shall we be able to say, 'I have fought a good fight.' Every Christian soldier has to fight; but it must be a *good* fight, a proper warfare. He must have on 'the whole armor of God.' He must take those weapons which 'are not carnal, but mighty through God to the pulling down of strongholds, and every

high thing that exalteth itself against the knowledge of God.'
So much for the good fight. He must keep the faith. We
sometimes flatter ourself that if the Lord hath made us steadfast in any thing it is in 'keeping the faith.' There is one
faith above all others that is worthy to be called 'THE faith.'
I have nourished it; I have loved it; I have defended it.
And it has nourished and blest me. Let me not be presuming. May I add the rest of Paul's words, 'Henceforth
there is laid up for me a crown of righteousness'? I have
taken great comfort in the work. So much have I experienced, and I cannot lose it. The laborer is entitled to his
reward. My work is with the Master. If men despise me, I
will think of him. Let me aim only to be useful, to be steadfast. So much of my life having been already given to the
cause of Christ, and a fragment only remaining, let me not
spoil that. Let me go through triumphantly!" Such is
"The End in View" upon which he meditates.

He is not pleased with the newly formed Massachusetts
Convention. He is not satisfied with having it made a corporation, — a "close corporation" as he terms it. He is
suspicious that all the action respecting it has been unconstitutional. "We do not believe," he writes, "that this change
in the form of the Convention has been brought about fairly,
even if it has been brought about at all. It is a forced state
of things. The proposed change was pushed through indis-
creetly. No proper pains were taken to give previous notice
of what was about to be done. There was not a proper
brotherly feeling and open-heartedness concerning the matter.
There was, we suppose, a good deal of secret caucusing
among those who were determined to push it through at any
rate. This will be pardoned among politicians; but among
brethren who have hitherto professed to love each other, it
was hardly to be expected." This was a free and honest

expression of opinion on his part. He had, however, as fair an opportunity to give the whole subject a thorough discussion as any other member of the old or new Convention. But he seemed inclined to withdraw himself from any active participation in the discussion, when he saw that quite a majority of his brethren were disposed to favor the new movement.

In July he visited Martha's Vineyard. He preached there on the 17th. He writes of the visit: "We ran out of the harbor of New Bedford into Buzzard's Bay, thence directly across the Bay to Wood's Hole in Falmouth, and thence to Holmes' Hole on Martha's Vineyard. We spent Saturday evening in visiting an aged father of our faith, Samuel Daggett. He is in his ninety-sixth year. His reason is clear and good, his voice is strong, and his faith is very firm. He has lived just such a life as Micah describes (ch. vi. v. 8). He said that, although so old, he should come to hear us preach on the following day, if he had his usual health, and we saw him in the church. Our services on Sunday were holden in the Orthodox church, which was kindly opened for our convenience. We preached on important Gospel themes, and the people listened with great attention. They were animated by the presence of a large number of worshippers. The Lord be praised for the spiritual enjoyments of this day."

On Thursday, July 28th, the Universalist church in South Reading was dedicated with appropriate services. Mr. Whittemore offered the dedicatory prayer. On the following Sunday, he preached in Westford, Mass. He writes: "In the Unitarian congregation here are quite a number of persons who believe in Universalism; and they requested the use of the meeting-house for several Sabbaths, which was granted. Two or three of our preachers had been there this season, before our own visit. The Unitarian pastor was present, and also an aged gentleman (once a preacher), Mr. Abbott. He sat in the pulpit through the day. The great bulk of the Unitarian congregation were present; and none, we believe, stayed away through prejudice. We felt it our duty in the afternoon to give a distinct sermon on some of our leading views. Excepting our bodily weakness, we enjoyed the day greatly."

A Sabbath is spent at Stoughton, Mass. "We felt," he writes, "a deep sensation in entering the pulpit. It was the very spot on which we were ordained as a minister at large, in the month of June, 1821. Thirty-eight years have since rolled away; and yet we live to preach the Gospel. The thought filled the soul with deep solemnity and gratitude. At the close of the afternoon sermon, we referred to old times; spoke of the departed fathers of the society; made reference to the long, faithful, useful pastorship of Rev. M. B. Ballou (who was present all the day); and besought the sympathy of the people for Brother Dennis, their pastor, who is unable for a time to perform the public duties of his ministry. He is a talented, useful, spiritually-minded pastor. The young men here take an interest in the society. We are looking to one of them as a young man who is yet to adorn the sacred desk. We shall not cease to pray that his heart may be inclined to the ministry. He has preached two or three times to great acceptance."

A Sabbath in August is passed in Weymouth, Mass. There was a large attendance. In the afternoon, Mr. Whittemore writes: "They listened with great attention to a sermon of more than an hour's length. Towards the close, the speaker faltered, being suddenly seized with sickness and pain. Brother Hawes, from North Weymouth, who was in the pulpit, at once rose, and conducted the service to the end. Gratitude compels us to say that, as soon as we reached our lodgings (at Brother A. B. Wales's), every aid was rendered that good judgment and attention could bestow. We did not suffer for any considerable length of time; and now (Monday morning) are in good preaching order."

The "Importance of Doctrinal Sermons" comes up for consideration. He is very clear and decided on this point. He writes : " The cause of Universalism has been injured by telling the people that *doctrinal* sermons are of little or no importance. What are doctrinal sermons but sermons in exposition and defence of THE TRUTH? And is not truth important? Christianity is the highest style of truth ; and shall not *that* be taught to the people? We conjure you, readers, whoever you are, to say no more against doctrinal sermons. Do you say, ' We want the precepts of the Gospel, the morality of the Gospel' ? But how can you have the precepts, the morality of the Gospel, unless you have the Gospel itself preached? And how can you have the Gospel preached if you have no doctrinal sermons?

" There are two things you may rely upon, viz. : First, if the doctrines of the Gospel are not preached, the people will not understand them ; and, if they do not understand them, your congregations will not be rooted and grounded in the faith. How can you have the unity of the faith, if the doctrines to be believed are not preached? If you do not have a unity of faith, you cannot have the knowledge of the Son of God ; you will not become perfect men ; you will not come unto the measure of the stature of the fulness of Christ, but will be ' carried about with every wind of doctrine, by the sleight of men, and cunning craftiness whereby they lie in wait to deceive.' If a congregation be not rooted and grounded in the faith, they cannot stand. A breath of eloquence has drawn them together, and a breath of eloquence will disperse them. Second, if the doctrines of the Gospel are not preached, the souls of the people will not be fed. Man's animal wants are not his only wants, nor his highest. He has a moral, spiritual nature. This is no farce. Every man knows it to be true. 'Man,' said the great Teacher, 'cannot live by bread alone;' i.e., by mere food for the body. His spiritual nature must be fed 'by every word that proceedeth out of the mouth of God.' The soul cannot be fed without the Gospel: the Gospel is the best of all food, emphatically called 'the bread of life.' Those who have it once want it again. 'Lord,' said the disciples, 'evermore give us this bread.' The great truths of the Gospel, then, must be preached, or the societies will die. Chapin, our great moral preacher so called, is also a great doctrinal teacher. How have we had our souls fed by his sermons on the Christian doctrines; on the resurrection; on the providence and faithfulness of God; on the goodness of God as his chief glory; on the salvation of all men as the crowning work of the divine mercy. Those who think that Chapin preaches not Christian doctrine make a great mistake."

He was in Wareham, Mass., a Sunday in September. Here he preached long discourses to the congregations, for which he apologizes; but it does not appear that the hearers were dissatisfied on this account. He writes: "We are determined to persevere in the attempt to shorten our sermons, until we get them down to a reasonable length. Speaking in public is a hard habit to alter." During this same month the Norfolk County Association met at Canton, Mass. Mr. Whittemore was present, and preached a sermon on the recognition of a church in Canton. The rite of baptism was administered to about twenty persons by the pastor, Rev. H. Jewell. He visits Rockport, also. His stage ride from Gloucester was one of anxiety to him. "A strong north-east storm was raging. It grew worse and worse, and the prospect was dubious. Darkness had set in, the wind howled, and seemed as if it would blow passengers and driver from the top of the coach. We had a seat inside, where there were nine other full-grown men and women beside ourself (*we* are small) ; but we believe there were ten or a dozen on the top of the coach. Without accident we arrived at Rockport. A good friend was in waiting to receive us. An ardent welcome on such a night is doubly a welcome. The waves were rushing upon the rocks in frightful force ; the roaring of the storm was heard from all directions ; and, after we were in bed, we felt the house flinch from the wind, and tremble as though it were afraid. The trees were frightened, also, and threw their great arms about in desperation. On Sunday morning, the disturbance of nature began to lull. The back-bone of the storm was broken. A gleam of hope sprung up that, possibly, we might be able to hold a meeting. By noon the sun broke through the clouds. Omitting the forenoon service, we preached in the afternoon and evening. We went into the town in deep gloom, and came out in gratitude and hope."

The session of the United States Convention was held this year in Rochester, N.Y. Mr. Whittemore had a lively experience in getting there, and a mingling of displeasure and happiness during the meeting. He gives a vivid description of the noisy scene at the Rochester Depot on their arrival. The first Sabbath-school meeting gave him little or no satisfaction, because " its main business seemed to be to make officers. The debates were not at all interesting, and seemed to have very little to do with the subject of religion. Religion was what *the people* went to Rochester after." Mr. Whittemore preached during the session. He enjoyed in a high degree the conference meeting on Wednesday evening ; and, in speaking of his interest in the faithful women who gave in their testimony on the occasion, he seems to have found an increased interest in this exercise of the gifts of the sisterhood. His written words are quite an improvement on certain expressions made by him years before on the Women's Convention in Worcester. Of the conference he says: " To say that it was a spirited meeting is but a poor description of it. To us, who had met but few of these Universalists ever before, it was a very precious opportunity to hear them speak, and commune with them on the subject of the great salvation. Among others, Mrs. Cobb and Mrs. Jenkins spoke with much power. There was a great desire to hear Mrs. Jenkins, not only on the part of those who had heard her in other places, but those who had not. She, however, made no long speech. She spoke clearly, tremulously, experimentally, and eloquently. She never puts herself forward." He asks why other sisters present, capable of addressing the meeting, did not make their voices heard. " They might have added much to the interest of the meeting. Why did they not offer prayer? or speak a few words to their backward sisters on the subject of religion? With the exceptions and omissions here named, this conference was a very good one. A lady who said she was from Vermont made a very acceptable address. Several speakers were strangers to us. One avowed himself a member of one of the Presbyterian churches in Rochester."

The New York *Independent* (an orthodox journal) takes occasion to speak of the prevalence of Universalism in orthodox churches, among the orthodox clergy, and the literati of our country; and very wisely concludes that this fact is not to be disregarded " by those who believe that the doctrine of eternal retribution is taught in the Scriptures, and has a vital place in the moral government of God. No subject can be more important for pulpit instruction than this. We are glad to learn that some pastors in this city and elsewhere are taking up the doctrine of retribution with earnestness and thorough discussion. We need to hear again the voice and argument of an Edwards, a Bellamy, a Taylor, upon the law and government of God." To which Mr. Whittemore replies: "Thank God that Universalism is to be discussed. Send us no boys. Give us your strong men, — men who have high characters for intelligence and learning. Come forward! you will find the Universalists all ready for the conflict."

A notice of Mr. Whittemore's *Trumpet* appears in the *Practical Christian*, a Restorationist paper edited by Rev. Adin Ballou. In former years, the two editors had been hostile to each other on account of the differences between the Restorationist party under the lead of Rev. Paul Dean and others, and the larger body of those who would be known as Universalists. Alluding to their former antagonisms, Mr. Ballou says: "Since then we have scarcely alluded to our old opponents as such. Meantime the seceding Restorationist Association was dissolved by· a concurrence of adverse circumstances, and we have since worked in the world as an independent Practical Christian. Thus our opponent and his coadjutors triumphed ecclesiastically over our Restorationist secessional movement; but theologically and morally we believe the victory was on our side, and that ultra-Universalism has lost ground ever since. Be this as it may, Dr. Whittemore adheres tenaciously and faithfully to the doctrines of his youth, and we dissent from him as radically and inflexibly as ever. We also differ widely from him on some points of Christian, civil, and social ethics. Yet there is not a particle of enmity, bitterness, or unkindness between us. He has called on us in the most friendly manner; and, wherever we chance to meet, we greet each other with mutual salutations of peace and good-will. Time and labor, sickness and the afflictions of life, are marking us both for our great change, and the time cannot be distant when we must test the realities of the spiritual world by actual experience. Our respective errors will perish. Our respective truths, with all that has been right and good in us, will be immortal. 'So mote it be.' May we both forgive and bless, as we hope to be forgiven and blest. And may the last years of both of us on earth be our best."

Mr. Whittemore manfully and cheerfully reciprocates these good, plain, but fraternal, words. He first has a few spicy remarks on Mr. Ballou's use of the term, "ultra-Universalism." "There is," he says, "no such thing. Universalism in itself, as taught by Winchester, and the other fathers, was ultra. Salvation could not be extended beyond it, and hence there is no need of such a distinction as *ultra* Universalism. The great fact which makes me a Universalist is my belief in the *eventual* resurrection and happiness of all men. Nothing else can make me a Universalist. I may have views on minor subjects, in which I differ from some Universalists; but those views are not what make me a Universalist. Whether others are quietly sliding down into a kind of indefinite Restorationism, they can tell better than we; but we are not sliding at all. 'I have trusted also in the Lord, *therefore I shall not slide*' (Ps. xxvi. 1). I have always held myself ready to renounce every error; and even if I had defended it for a long time and with great energy, and had become convinced it was not true, I would renounce it at once as publicly as I had defended it. If any man wishes me to believe in future punishment, let him give me a 'thus saith the Lord.' I reciprocate cheerfully the kind things Brother Adin has said. If I ever felt unkindly to him, all that feeling is gone for ever. I remember the old Restorationist controversy, and the part

I took in it. Probably I was not always prudent. I was easily excited: perhaps I said some things rashly; but I had no long lasting hatred. My great object was to do all I could to save the denomination as a unit. 'If a few will go off, then let them go; but let us keep the denomination united,' I said. The same wish, I know, thrilled in the good heart of Father Ballou, and Dr. Ballou, with whom I was associated more than with any other men. It was no more than we ought to have felt or done. In closing, I reassure Brother Ballou that I reciprocate all his friendship. We have both lived beyond the heat of youth. Our heads are gray. May the Lord preserve him. We shall meet in heaven, where no jarring interest shall be known, but where all shall arrive at the perfection of their being."

"A glorious meeting" in Boxboro', Mass., on the last Sabbath in October, is recorded. Hearers were present from seven or eight neighboring towns, "fifty singers made excellent music," and the preacher seems to have been in his happiest mood. He visits Abington also. There was a large attendance, although the day was rainy. "One old gentleman," he writes, "who came over with his daughter and grandchildren from Bridgewater, and who, In his early days, used to listen to John Murray, could not sustain his emotion. It is the Gospel which takes such hold of the people's hearts." In December, he preached one Sabbath at Marlboro', Mass. "The meeting-house here," he writes, "is not large, and the audience filled every pew, and all the aisles, the gallery, and every place where a person could stand or sit. We preached the truth, we are sure, for we declared the Word of God. We have not for a long time enjoyed a Sabbath more richly than this."

To the question, "What will beget a Love of God?" he thus gives answer about this time: —

" Christian, we have one question for you to answer. Would not all your high hopes be realized, would not your most fervent prayer be answered, if all men were brought to love God with the whole soul? Yes, oh yes! you answer. Stand then at this point, as one from which you will never swerve. But how will you bring men to love God? We know that the beloved apostle said, ' We love him because he first loved us;' thereby showing that a knowledge of God's love to man is the cause of man's love to God. But we will say nothing about that now. Do you think that the preaching of the doctrine of endless misery ever made one soul love God? It is impossible. No man can say, I love God because he will make me endlessly miserable; or, because he will make my wife, or my children, my parents, or brothers, or sisters, or any of my fellow-creatures, endlessly miserable. It is impossible, utterly so, that men should love God for such a reason. Suppose we put this doctrine where Jesus certainly did not put it, — we mean into connection with the commandments, — would it give the commandments increased force? Let us try. ' Thou shalt love the Lord thy God with all thy heart, and with all thy soul, and with all thy mind,' *for God will torment his creatures unmercifully for ever.* Would men be any more likely to love God or to love their neighbor for such a reason? We may answer with the utmost certainty, No. Jesus gave men reasons why they should love God. ' GOD LOVED THE WORLD,' and gave his Son to die for it, all poor and sinful as it was. ' God is rich in mercy' [not in wrath], and loved us with a ' GREAT LOVE,' even when we were dead in trespasses and sins. Blessed be his name. This is the doctrine that will make men love God."

In December, he visits Auburn and Portland, Me. It was Christmas Sabbath when he preached in Auburn. The day was clear but intensely cold, the thermometer at 23° below zero. "We had a large number," he writes, "even for a calm and fine day. The house was admirably trimmed in honor of Christmas; and a well-trained choir was in the orchestra." In the evening, the house was densely crowded. The next day, he went to Portland, and preached in the Universalist church there in the evening; thence home.

On the evening of the last day of January, 1860, Mr. Whittemore visited Westmoreland, N.H., and attended a festival there, given by the Universalists in the place, under the pastoral charge of Rev. S. H. McCollester. He made an address on the occasion, of much interest to the assembly.

Another festival calls him at Hinsdale, N.H. It was opened by exercises in singing and speaking by the Sabbath-school children. "The little orators," he writes, "were frequently applauded." These services were of an unusually high character in a moral point of view. Rev. Mr. Matterson (Methodist) and Mr. Whittemore followed with addresses. Then came the table entertainment, at which a gustatory scene is opened, as Mr. Whittemore gives it. "It would have done any spectator good to have seen Rev. Mr. Matterson and Brother Whittemore with their huge bowls full of oysters, sitting side by side upon the elevated platform, smiling, talking, swallowing, and once in a while uttering a pleasant story. They both wished very much that Father Taylor, of Boston, had been there."

"Several Sundays," and his doings in them, are noted in the *Trumpet* of Feb. 18. On Jan. 8, he was in Providence, R.I., at the Second Universalist Church. On the 15th, he was in Milford, Mass.; on the next Sabbath, in East Cambridge, in absence of the pastor of the church, Rev. H. W. Rugg, who was in ill health; on the 29th, in Haverhill, Mass.; and on the 5th of February, at East Boston.

Of the second Sabbath in February, he writes: "It was

our happy lot to spend this day in Roxbury, Mass., with the church just left without a pastor in consequence of the removal of Rev. W. H. Ryder from them to Chicago. It was a satisfaction to us to stand once more in the town where we commenced our ministry in the year 1820."

He is much pleased with his first Sabbath spent in Claremont, N.H. It was at a new opening of the church after repairs upon it had been made. The day was inauspicious on account of the weather, but the attendance was large. He writes: "It was a somewhat painful service. The house was very warm, and we feared a repetition of the fainting scene of the preceding Sunday, at Manchester, N.H. Our strength, however, did not utterly fail, but we went to our quarters exhausted." He notes the changes that had taken place in the society, especially by death; and of the efficiency of the Sunday school in keeping up its vitality. He speaks with much tenderness of Father Abraham Fisher, who was for so many years a constant attendant on the church services, and of his excellent wife, who gave the bell in the tower to the society. Of the best helpers of the society at the time of his visit, he says: "They are not men of gold watches and moustaches, but men of industry, honesty, economy, temperance, patriotism; solid farmers, honest merchants, and the like."

Two Sabbath services are lost to him in April, because of illness and confinement at home. Congregations in Concord, N.H., and Acton, Mass., are thus disappointed. His reflections are: "We are not worn out; our work is not done, we think; we speak reverently: but while the Lord has any thing for us to do we shall live."

On the second Sunday in May, Mr. Whittemore officiated in the First Universalist Church in Lowell, Mass. The pastor, Rev. J. J. Twiss, was present. In the afternoon the ordinance of baptism was administered to about a dozen children; by Mr. Whittemore to the child of the pastor, Mr. Twiss, and by the latter to the remainder. After the baptism, Mr. Whittemore commenced a discourse from Matthew xviii. 2, 3: "And Jesus called a little child unto him," &c. While in the midst of the discourse, the preacher was over-come with sudden illness, which compelled him to call upon Mr. Twiss, the pastor, to finish the discourse, which the latter did, taking it up at the point where Mr. Whittemore left it, and carrying it through to the satisfaction of all present. Mr. Whittemore recovered so as to address the congregation before the close of the service. He expressed the hope that he might soon be well again. He thought that for danger to life, this attack was not to be compared to the one experienced by him in Warren, Mass., in 1854. He advised his friends not to be alarmed.

In a consideration of the question, "Which is the best view of God?" he writes: "Our Saviour gave this direction to his disciples; ' Be ye therefore perfect, even as your Father which is in heaven is perfect.' Many descriptions have been given of God's character. We will now note only three: —

"1. It has been said that God from all eternity, without regard to faith, works, or conditions, elected a part of mankind to everlasting life, and reprobated the remainder to endless suffering. The elect he loves, bestows blessings upon them in this life, and will grant them endless happiness in the next. The reprobate he hates: if he bestows on them any good thing here, it is only to aggravate their final dreadful doom. How would the character of a man appear who should thus deal with his children? Yet this conduct should be imitated by all who verily believe that God conducts thus.

"2. It has been said that God loves all men, and has made salvation possible for all; but at the same time has given

men an ' agency' which he fully knows will hinder the salvation of many.   Let a man conduct thus.   Let him profess
to love all his children, and to desire the continuation of their
lives ; at the same time let him give them food which he
knows they love, in which he has mingled so much poison
that he knows it will destroy the lives of one half the number.
This would be God-like, if the conduct of God be such as
has been represented.   But, God-like or not, such conduct
would be rewarded by our magistrates with hanging.

" 3. It has been said that God loves all men ; is good unto
all, and his tender mercies are over all his works ; that he
bestows all the good men enjoy in this life ; and not only
desires, but will assuredly accomplish the everlasting salvation
of the whole human family.   Let man imitate this character.
He need not hate any one.   His benevolence may extend not
only to all his own family, but to the whole human race ; and
by exercising this benevolence he imitates God.

" Reader, which character, think you, should man imitate
to become holy?   Think of these things.   Remember, it is
your duty to become perfect, even as your Father in heaven
is perfect."

In his first number of the new volume of the *Trumpet*
(June 2, 1860), he writes of his faith : " We always preached
Universalism. .We thought it a glorious doctrine when we
began, and we think so now.   We rejoice in what we have
done.   We look back from the stand-point of threescore
years, and devoutly thank God that we never, in a single instance, preached any thing adverse to Universalism.   True,
we have sometimes made mistakes, and are far from being a
perfect man, but we rejoice that in our whole ministry we
never felt the slightest temptation to swerve from that great
doctrine, which is the truth as it is in Jesus."

He is particularly inquisitive as to the anxiousness of Rev.

C. F. Hudson to disseminate his theological opinions in reference to the endless destruction (or annihilation) of a part of the human race. He has announced a new book entitled "Christ our Life," the object of which is to prove, not so much that Christ *is* our life, as that a part of the human race shall be endlessly and radically destroyed. "What is it," he asks, "that makes this theme so sweet to Mr. Hudson? If he were at work for Universalism, we could easily account for his zeal, for then what he would reveal, it would do mankind good to know. But who is to be benefited by being befogged on the subject of destruction? Will the sick and the dying be any happier if they receive Mr. Hudson's doctrine of destruction? Certainly not, for there is no comfort in it. Mr. Hudson became sick of the doctrine of endless punishment, and sought a remedy for that doctrine. But his favorite theory leaves men in darkness, doubt, and despair. It is unworthy of God."

It is a lively Anniversary Week again in Boston. Mr. Whittemore took part with great earnestness in the meetings that were held by the Universalists. The prayer and conference meetings were of high interest. Three thousand Sabbath-school children and their teachers held a meeting in Tremont Temple. The Festival at Faneuil Hall was one of the highest order. Horace Greeley, Esq., of New York, presided. He made a timely and noble address; and was followed by Rev. Messrs. Rugg, Thayer, H. C. Leonard, Deere, Spaulding, Bolles, and A. B. Fuller (Unitarian, whose life was afterwards given for his country in the war of the Rebellion). Mr. Whittemore writes of the meetings: "One thing which gave peculiar power to the public meetings of Anniversary Week, was the fact that the speakers were all taken from the young men. The Universalists never had a better series of speakers. And the best is yet to come. There is a batch of young orators at Tufts College who will confer great honor on their parents, friends, and the denomination, who will surpass altogether the young orators of the late Anniversary Week. The noble banner of our church will be borne up well by the young men."

His friend and brother, Rev. Dr. Sawyer, entreats him to remit his labors, and take life more easily. "Nurse yourself. Do not think it your duty to wear yourself out as soon as possible. I beg you do not be in such haste. We cannot spare you for years to come. You are not an old man yet, and with proper care are worth half a dozen boys for twenty years to come." Mr. Whittemore acknowledges the kind and heart-touching exhortation. "We have had such admonitory words from Mrs. Whittemore and our children, on this subject. Our family physician has threatened us with sundry penalties. Our coadjutors in the active business of life have admonished us. But the trees will throw off their foliage at the winter's blast; the flowers will fall; man goeth to his long home, and the mourners go about the streets. Then shall the dust return unto the earth as it was, and the spirit shall return unto God who gave it."

His testimony against the use of the "vile weed" is sensible and manly. "Some person writes us, 'Do you use tobacco? Do you chew, or smoke, or take snuff?' We answer very readily that we do not. There might have been a time years ago, when we did chew tobacco slightly and sometimes smoke cigars. We believed at last that the practice did us no good, and we abandoned it, wholly, totally, and shall never resume it. It was offensive to personal cleanliness; it clouded the brain in some degree. In our case it was evil, and only evil. We never loved it; but, if we had loved it as the toper loves brandy, we should have abandoned it. This is all we have to say."

He notes a fact in reference to the connection of Forefathers' Rock at Plymouth, Mass., and Universalism. " Universalism is established on Forefathers' Rock more directly than any other religion. All the churches in Plymouth except the Universalist, are located at some distance from the Rock. In fact, it is not certain that a part of the original Rock does not lie directly under the Universalist church. We are speaking of the veritable Rock in its original place, and not of that piece which was split off and carried up into the village, and deposited in front of Pilgrim Hall. The very spot where the feet of the forefathers first touched the shore was precisely where the Universalist church now stands. There is a narrow street between the outer face of the Rock and the Universalist church ; but it is probable that a part of the original Rock, in the place of its formation, lies under that church. The Universalist church in Plymouth, then, is the real Pilgrim church. Its preacher stands on Forefathers' Rock on every Sabbath day, to break to the people the bread of life."

In June, Mr. Whittemore visited Newport, N.H., to attend the New Hampshire Convention. " We went up," he says, " for the benefit of health, for the fresh air of the New Hampshire hills, for the society of friends, for the diversion of the mind to inspiring subjects. The Sunday-school meeting was full of interest. That excellent Superintendent, Brother Parker, of Nashua, presided. One after another, the Superintendents arose to make statements respecting the schools. The Methodist clergyman was present, and made an address in union with the spirit of the meeting. The writer tried to preach on the last afternoon of the session. He did not faint, but went through to the end. Perhaps this may be regarded as a violation of his promise. If so, he hopes it will be forgiven him. The journey did him good."

In August, he made his first visit to the Isles of Shoals, nine miles from Portsmouth, N.H. His wife accompanied him; and, aside from a short but severe sea-sickness on her part, the trip was a very enjoyable one.

At the last of the same month, he visited Vermont, and attended the State Convention at Cavendish. The visit was exceedingly enjoyable to him. The meetings were very large, and the services of deep interest. Mr. Whittemore made an address on the morning of the second day. He spoke for nearly an hour without fatiguing himself. In his account of his visit, he gives a glowing description of Vermont and its staid and thriving people. Of those with whom he mingled most, he writes: "There are no better people in the world than the Universalists of Vermont. We do not say they are perfect, but they come as near to it as any people we have ever seen. Perhaps our picture is too glowingly painted; but remember we go among Universalists; and, if our picture is too bright for people in general, attribute it to our keeping the very best of company."

He has some pertinent remarks elicited by King Agrippa's word, " Almost," in his saying to Paul. " *Almost* thou persuadest me to be a Christian : —

" Agrippa was nearly balanced on the pivot of conviction; but the beam did not gain an equilibrium. The kingdoms of this world outweighed the heavenly kingdom. Touching Paul, 'Almost' was a confession of his success: but touching Agrippa, it was a record of defectiveness, shortcoming, irresolution, a yielding to temptation, a controlling worldliness; in short, *failure*. To confess one's self *almost* persuaded is to confess one's self unpersuaded, — *almost* a Christian, *not* a Christian. The man who is only *almost* able to take up his note at the bank fails, and is reported as bankrupt. He who is almost persuaded to relieve the needy leaves them in want. The navigator that can almost keep his reckoning drives upon the rocks and is a castaway. ‘ Almost ’ has a certain warmth in it, a certain coloring, a certain temper quite its own. It is a prophecy of what might have been, a confession of what ought to be; but as a record of what is, it is a synonyme for failure.

“ But it is not simply failure. It is a precursor of failures to come. It tells of duty neglected, of moral commands disobeyed, of promptings of conscience disregarded. A neglect of duty is the deadening of the moral sense. He who hears often the plaint of the poor, and heeds it not, will cease at length even to hear it. The unemployed husband, or unfilial son or daughter, who sits by the fireside and lifts not a hand to ease the burdens of the wife and mother in her daily toil, comes at length to feel that she is by right the servant, while they are practically guests in the mansion. They fail to read as they ought, their own self-condemnation in the lines of care upon her toil-worn face. Duty neglected darkens the understanding, blunts the sensibilities, and chokes out the life. Duty performed clarifies the perceptions, quickens the conscience, and strengthens the whole man in good. Let us beware of joining the school of Agrippa; but rather yield to Paul’s persuasiveness, — ‘ I would to God that not only thou, but also all that hear me this day, were both almost and altogether such as I am, except these bonds.’ ”

The United States Convention held its annual session this year in Boston. Mr. Whittemore writes of it: “ The occasion has come and gone. Boston has been flooded with Universalists. Individually, we had as much as we could do in receiving the brethren and friends from the country at 37 Cornhill. Our own house at Cambridgeport was well filled with friends from a distance, and we took great pleasure in having them there. The happiest hour of the week was on Wednesday evening, after the lecture, when in our own parlor, with the accompaniment of the piano, we all joined in singing conference hymns. It seemed to us that we were *well*. We felt that we had health and strength to preach. We longed to be in the pulpit. [He was not strong at the time.] So much for the influence of our friends upon our heart. Their presence did us good. We have no doubt that, in all the Universalist families hereabouts, there was much joy."

In a brief article entitled "Three Ways to Live," he has some pleasant and profitable thoughts : —

"I have three ways to live : I live in the present ; I live in the past ; I live in the future. I live in my labor, in my enjoyments, at the head of my family, as editor of the *Trumpet*, as a preacher of the Gospel ; these are present things.

"I live in the past ; and how? I am continually living my life over again. I forget little that I have done. I remember the scenes I have witnessed ; the men and women I have known ; the aged fathers in our ministry ; the Conventions of olden time ; the controversies of those days ; men now in the middle of life I remember as very young men, and their children, now twenty-five and thirty, when they were babes in their mothers' arms. In this way I live in the past. Why should the past be forgotten? It is the only thing we have to remember. We cannot remember the future, neither can we remember the present until it has passed. Why did God give us our memories? It is that we might remember what has gone by us. How unwise are those who speak of past things as unworthy of our remembrance !

"But there is still another way to live ; I mean in the future. I live in faith and hope. I believe what the Word of God declares. I believe that if I die I shall live again. When I lie down at night, I believe I shall awake in the morning; and when I shall lie down upon my death-bed, I shall hope to awake in the resurrection. But the sceptic will say, You do not *know* these things. We did not say we did know them. We said they were matters of faith and hope. I know them better than I knew what I was to have in this life before I was born. I have never believed too much; I have always believed too little. God has surprised me with my present existence; he has brought me out of darkness into marvellous light. I thus live in the present, in the past, and in the future."

CHAPTER XVII.

1860–1861.

Aged 60–61.

Prostrate again — His Last Sermon, in Malden — Resolutions from Massachusetts Convention : Reply — Expressions of Sympathy — Sale of the *Trumpet* — Question, " What am I? " considered — Interviews with Friends — Revival of Strength — Decline — The Departure — Funeral Services — Discourse by Rev. C. A. Skinner — Other Tributes to him.

In the *Trumpet* of Oct. 13, there is an editorial notice headed " The Editor Prostrate Again." He was taken down soon after the Convention. On Sunday, Sept. 23, he rode with Mrs. Whittemore to Malden to spend the day with Rev. Mr. Greenwood, not to preach, but to see his old friends in that town. He heard Mr. Greenwood preach in the morning, and took part in the service. In the afternoon, with but little urging, he consented to preach : it was so hard to deny himself that enjoyment ! But it was too much for him. He was taken down on the following Wednesday. The family insisted that a consulting physician must be called, and his opposition yielded. Dr. Thompson of Charlestown, his long tried and excellent friend, was sent for, to meet Dr. Allen, his family physician. After a very careful examination, they decided that there was no enlargement of the liver, nothing of a scirrhous nature in the stomach, but possibly a slight irritation of the mucous membrane. They advised that there must be quiet, especially of the mind, which had been too much worked. He should lie by for a time, and good treatment might bring him up. If he fell any lower, they could not reach him. They thought him in that respect in a dangerous condition.

The Massachusetts Convention held its session this year at Springfield. Mr. Whittemore was missed there, and the fact of his severe illness caused much sadness on the part of his ministerial brethren and many friends. The following resolution, offered to the Convention by Rev. A. G. Laurie, was unanimously adopted : —

" *Resolved*, That this Convention hears of the serious illness of Rev. Thomas Whittemore with great sorrow, that they send to him on his sick-bed the sympathy of their brotherly love, and their earnest hope that the human skill and love which are now contending with disease for his health and life may be blessed by our Heavenly Father to his recovery, and his restoration to his former duties." Rev. N. M. Gaylord was appointed a Committee to convey the resolution to Mr. Whittemore.

It was gratefully received, and tenderly and affectionately answered. He writes in the *Trumpet* to his " Dear Brethren of the Massachusetts Convention :" " On Thursday, Oct. 18, as I lay upon my bed, Rev. N. M. Gaylord was announced as having a desire to see me. He was immediately invited to my chamber, when I expressed to him my astonishment that he had not been to Springfield in attendance on the Convention. 'But I have,' said he; 'I have just returned from there; and have come down to bring you a letter from the brethren assembled in council; a letter of sympathy and love, expressing a hope that you may be restored to health. It is one of the pleasantest duties I ever was charged with by any Convention, to bear this letter to you.' I thanked him out of my heart.

"It does me good to know that I am not forgotten by my ministering brethren in my season of weakness and weariness. All I can do is to lie still, looking upward to heaven. I have great time for reflection. I have tried my faith over and over again. I have tried it in every form. I can try it without actually passing through the veil. It sustains me; it gives me hope and strength and life. With an opposite faith, it seems to me that I should be the most miserable being in the world. The stronger my faith grows, the happier I am.

"I accept, dear brethren, your sympathy. I do not feel worthy of your remembrance. I am weak and feeble, and cannot make any suitable reply. Where could I find a band of brethren whom I could love as I have loved these Universalists? They have had my whole life. Very little of it is left to me now. You are my brethren, and I can never, never turn away from you. 'May the Lord bless you, and keep you; may he make his face to shine upon you, and be gracious unto you; may he lift up the light of his countenance upon you, and give you peace. Amen.' I subscribe myself, most affectionately, your brother in Christ.

"Thomas Whittemore."

Rev. A. G. Laurie, of Charlestown, wrote in reference to this action of the Convention: "When the resolution was proposed, it was supported by every member of the house rising to his feet. Many persons among them dissented from the published sentiments of the *Trumpet* in reference to the Constitution of the new Convention; and, indeed, the motion was made during a somewhat excited state of feeling on that very subject; but instantly the simultaneous expression of respect and affection from the whole body made by that action, declared how firm is the attachment of the Universal-

ist clergymen and laity to one who has been so long and usefully
a chief worker in the common cause ; and with what gratitude
for his past services, and with what an interest of love in his
present illness, the sympathies of the brethren gather round
a life whose preservation is of such great value to us all."

Letters of sympathy come in to him from various sources ;
from his ministering brethren especially. They are greatly comforting to him. His views of Christ are fervently expressed in
a reply to a letter from Rev. J. G. Forman, of Alton, Ill. :
" I thank you when you pray that the Restorer and Saviour
may stand at my side. I have long had some acquaintance
with this Saviour. I was taught to lisp his name in my
tender youth. He accompanied me through my boyhood,
like a bright angel at my side. In my twenty-first year, he
sealed me (although very unworthy) as a preacher of his
grace ; blessed be his name ! Praise him, all ye angels ! From
that time to the present, he has been near me. For the little
that I have done for the cause of his truth, I desire to be
very thankful."

When lying very weak and low, his son-in-law said to him,
" I am about to write to Dr. Chapin : what shall I say to him
for you?" "Oh!" said he, "I will try to write one more
epistle, and it shall be addressed to Brother Chapin." He
sat at his bedside, and with his own hand wrote the letter.
It was a farewell to his esteemed brother. Dr. Chapin's engagements brought him soon to Worcester, from which place
he wrote the following epistle : —

" Worcester, Nov. 15, 1860.

" My dear Brother Whittemore, — I write, not knowing
whether this will find you on the shores of time or not. Should
it do so, accept my heartfelt thanks for your letter. I assure
you that the love which you express in it for me is fully re-

ciprocated. My thoughts have been much upon you of late. I should like to have seen you, but am forbidden by engagements. But you need no consolation or encouragement from me. Your faith is sufficient for you, and I rejoice at it. Our intercourse has been very pleasant; not interrupted by a single harsh word or any unkind feeling. May it be renewed where —

> " ' Congregations ne'er break up,
> And Sabbaths never end.'

> " Affectionately yours,
>> " E. H. Chapin."

In the *Trumpet* of March 23, 1861, a notice appears stating that this paper has passed from his hands. He feels that the labor, care, and anxiety attending the publication of it is more than he is able to bear. His family, his friends, and his physician think he ought to be relieved of all labor and care not positively necessary. He feels anxious for the paper. " Acting in accordance with this conviction, he has sold the *Trumpet* establishment, with all its accounts for subscriptions and advertising, to Rev. James M. Usher, who has the best wishes of the retiring editor and publisher, that he may be successful in the new enterprise which he has already assumed. May the paper deserve and receive a more extensive patronage than it has ever enjoyed in the past." The paper was, in after years, united with the *Christian Freeman*, published by Rev. Sylvanus Cobb; and was subsequently purchased by the New England Universalist Publishing House, who continue to issue it from the same office, 37 Cornhill, under the name of the *Universalist*.

During the winter, he was confined most of the time to his bed. There he met his friends with cheerfulness, and gave them repeated evidences of his firm faith in the principles he had so long and so earnestly advocated. The faith which had sustained him in life now shed its radiance upon him as he neared the confines of "the morning land." His walk through the valley of the shadow of death he did not fear, for the rod and staff of the Lord gave him assurance and support.

"One day," writes his son-in-law, "my father called me to his bedside, and pointed out to me the following article, and said, 'I wrote that many years ago. It truly expresses my mind now.'"

"WHAT AM I?

"What am I if Atheism be true? A poor, blind creature of chance. My race came into existence I know not how; and, when I die, I am to perish for ever, like the beasts. The beasts have the advantage of me, for they have no desire for immortality; but I have a desire, which is to be mocked and tormented.

"What am I, if Calvinism be true? Perhaps one of the elect, perhaps not. I may be damned for ever; and if not, some of my dearest friends may, which is about the same thing. Miserable consolation!

"What am I if Arminianism be true? My eternal destiny in that case is committed to my own keeping, — to the care of a poor, blind, erring creature, who cannot tell what even a day will bring forth.

"What am I if Universalism be true? I am a child of God, a creature formed in his moral image, an heir of eternity, on whom God will bestow unfailing blessedness. I find myself in this world, but I know that this is not my home. It is only a temporary resting-place, the place of my journeying, the road on which I walk to the abode of the immortals. I find that I do not belong to earth. Death is 'the gate of endless joy.' I need not fear annihilation; I need not fear what is worse, — eternal woe; but I may believe without a doubt, and I may exult in this faith with a pure and holy joy, that I am a brother of angels and a child of God. This is what I am if the doctrine of Universalism be true; and I rejoice that all my fellow-creatures are the same. How should we live under the influence of this doctrine? What will be the natural effect of it in our hearts? Answer: It will promote love to God, love to men, even to enemies; it will enable us to raise our thoughts from the grovelling pursuits of life, and fix them upon heavenly things."

Many pleasant interviews with friends were held at his bedside. One was enjoyed by the writer of this memoir. He found the invalid in a happy frame of mind. He spoke of a rich season he had enjoyed with some of his ministering brethren and others, in the morning; as also of a call made upon him that day by his friend Mr. Green, Mayor of the city, who had once been a pastor in Cambridge. "You have fought a good fight, my dear sir," said Mr. Green. "Ah!" said the sick one, "let me say those other words in that passage of the apostle: '*I have kept the faith:*' that is my great blessing now." The whole interview with the callers at this time was deeply impressive, and gave to those present renewed assurance of the value of the faith and hope of the Gospel.

After this time, there came a brief revival of his powers. He was able to leave his house again, and even made a visit to the office in Cornhill. But after some weeks he began to fail, and the end evidently appeared near. Towards the last, he was calm and trustful. He said to a brother at his bedside, "My work is done; I leave my work behind me. What I have preached is the truth, nothing but the truth. I have nothing to take back — nothing — nothing. I am almost surprised at my frame of mind, that I view my approaching departure with so little dread; but my faith is as strong as it ever was. I have got so far on the way, that I do not know that I want to be called back again." And then he repeated the lines of the poet: —

"Vital spark of heavenly flame," &c.

His pastor, who preached his funeral sermon, truly said, "His victory did not come at his death-bed, it was wrought out before."[1] He breathed his last on Thursday night, March 21, 1861.

The funeral occasion was one of the deepest interest to the Universalist Churches in the neighborhood of his home, to the citizens of Cambridge, and to the community at large, by whom he was so well known and so highly respected. The service took place on the Tuesday (March 26) following his death. The relatives and intimate friends assembled at his residence at the corner of Washington and Cherry Streets, where private exercises were held, conducted by Rev. A. G. Laurie of Charlestown, who read appropriate passages of the Scriptures, and offered prayer. The funeral procession was then formed, and proceeded to the church, which was thronged. The exercises opened with a dirge from the organ, followed by a hymn from the "Gospel Harmonist," entitled "Anastasis," the music of which was composed by the deceased. Selections of Scripture were then read by Rev. C. R. Moor of Cambridge, another hymn was sung, following which a fervent prayer was offered by Rev. C. A. Skinner. The congregation was then addressed by Rev. Dr. A. A. Miner, of Boston, and Rev. T. J. Greenwood, of Malden. Of the man and minister Dr. Miner said: —

"He was not aged by the weight of years. But he was

---

[1] Rev. C. A. Skinner.

old by the weight of toil. He was old in the profession of his love. He was aged in those voluntary and unremitting labors, for the good of men and of the church, for the honor of God and the comfort of souls, to which he lived to devote himself. For full forty years has his name been, perhaps, quite as closely identified with those great principles of our holy religion that give joy to our hearts, as the name of any other; and I do not know that you, who are able in your own experience to call to mind the condition of this world as it was forty years ago, and contrast it with to-day, and who are able to observe the changes that have marked the intervening period, and recur to those by whose labor, and faith, and genius, and persevering devotion these changes have been wrought, — I do not know that in this survey you will be able to recur to any name that more readily presents itself than the name of the brother whose mortal remains lie now in our presence. Yet we cannot forget that during thirty years of this period he has not filled a pastorate. With many cares of the world upon him, with many labors and toils that would have absorbed the entire energies of most men, you have met with him in the chair editorial, and as an author, appealing to the religious mind, and as a preacher welcome everywhere, in all our churches.

.   .   .   .   .   .

"His life and his labors, varied and persistent as they have been, are left as a legacy to his family, to the Church, and to the world. His influence will remain with us. We shall not, indeed, meet him henceforth in the pathways of our toil; we shall not meet him when believers in our Zion are convened; we shall not meet him either in social conference, or at the Communion Table of our Lord. We shall not meet him personally, as in times gone by; but in what direction shall we look, which way shall we turn, where some memorial will not present itself to us, and bid us remember what he has done for us, and the joy that abides in our hearts? In the fruits of his labor, he shall long remain in our midst, to bless those who shall be led, through his instructions, unto the God of Hosts, unto the Father of the spirits of all flesh. His memory, embalmed in our affections, will be henceforth hallowed by the shadows of death.

.   .   .   .   .   .

" With little outward aid, with few favoring circumstances, with a persistence and vigor of purpose animated by a new discovery of divinest truth, he consecrated himself to his life-labor; his perseverance shining out steadily in the midst of all events, converting even obstacles into causes of success and triumph, because he took fast hold of God, and believed in the ordainments and the pleasure of heaven."

Rev. Mr. Greenwood said of him : —
" In the forty years that have marked his ministerial course, it has been my privilege, for more than thirty years, to be an humble toiler with him in the cause in which he labored; to be in his neighborhood nearly all the time, and thus to know something of the influences which moved his own spirit, and rendered him so faithful and so successful in the work which God gave him to do. And for years, in reference to him, as in reference to no other man that has ever lived upon the earth, there has been ringing in my ears a voice of instruction with regard to the power and influence of Christian faith as cherished by him, and as illustrated by his own life. I say that an influence has come to my soul from this consideration, as from no other man that has ever lived on earth; and I mean by this to say that he has put that faith to the test — to the severest test — as, within the range of my knowledge, no other human being has had the power or privilege to test it.

Notwithstanding the vigor of his frame, the indomitable energy of his being, the power which God gave him in the work allotted to him, they who knew him most intimately, know that, even for years past, he has been at least partially checked in his course, partially broken down, by the inroads of the disease — the mysterious disease — which has at length closed his life. Three times or more, under such circumstances, it has been given to him, with the faith he cherished, to walk down to the very borders of the grave, to take that look where, to the unchristianized mind, and to the soul of the faithless, nothing but darkness and desolation reign, and to catch glimpses there of the spirit-land : to hear the distant cadence of the songs which angels and enfranchised spirits sing, and go back to earth refreshed, invigorated, and encouraged for the labor which he was still to perform here upon the earth. And when our fears had well-nigh found their fulfilment, that the day of his departure was at hand, but a few months since ; when he himself had become aware of and prepared for the inevitable hour, and wife and children were at his bedside, and the pale messenger seemed ready to touch his lips with silence, — how expressive the power of the *faith* he cherished, as expressed in the language he uttered to a brother now in this presence : 'Gradually, calmly, sweetly sinking.' For him, death had no terrors ; the grave had no gloom. The victory had been pre-dated for him, and he met the hour, when it came, like one sustained by the truth he had borne to other minds."

At the conclusion of the addresses, prayer was offered by Rev. E. A. Eaton, of South Reading, and the benediction was pronounced by Dr. Miner. Some time was occupied in the solemn leave-taking, the congregation being so large that progress through the aisles could be made but slowly. As the audience dispersed, the funeral *cortége* formed. The pall-bearers were Hon. J. D. Green, Mayor of Cambridge ; Rev. J. M. Usher, of Medford ; Deacon Eben Francis ; Robert Douglass, Esq. ; Benjamin Tilton, Esq., of Cambridge ; and G. W. Bazin, Esq., of Boston. The remains were conveyed to Mount Auburn. As the procession passed the Episcopal Church, Old Cambridge, the chime in the tower played the tunes " Peace, Troubled Soul," " Pleyel's Hymn," " Tivoli," a Dirge by Pleyel, " Sicilian Hymn," " Dead March in Saul," and " Naomi." The family burial-lot is at Mount Auburn, No. 2007. It was a late hour before the mourners returned to their homes.

On the Sabbath following the burial, a Funeral Discourse was delivered in the church by Rev. C. A. Skinner, the pastor, entitled " The Christian Warrior," from the words of Paul to Timothy : " I have fought a good fight, I have finished my course, I have kept the faith : henceforth there is laid up for me a crown of righteousness, which the Lord, the righteous Judge, shall give me at that day ; and not to me only, but unto all them also that love his appearing " (2 Tim. iv: 7, 8). These words were chosen by Mr. Whittemore as a text of the last sermon he ever attempted to prepare. But little else beside the text had been written. The discourse by his pastor was a just and feeling tribute to the subject of it. The closing section is beautiful as it is appropriate : —

" It is Easter Sunday to-day. And as the sun rose bright and glorious this morning, rolling back the shadows of the night before its oncoming splendor, flooding, with its golden light, mountain and plain, and all the habitations of men, it was symbolical of the light that the rising of the ' Sun of Righteousness ' has shed upon the world, scattering even the shadows of the grave, and glorifying the humblest tombstone that lies to-day with the early grass and the first flowers of

spring.   Oh, what a grand fact is that bursting out from the
history of the ages!   What a great truth is that which breaks
in fresh significance upon us with the dawn of this Easter
morning!   What a fact for these friends to carry in their
sorrowing hearts, as they shall go to plant flowers upon the
grave of their dead.   Standing there by his sepulchre, the
voice that spoke to Mary in her grief shall be heard again,
borne through all the avenues and winding paths of Mount
Auburn, saying to them, ' He is not here, for he is risen.' "

Tributes to his character and memory came in on every
hand.   " For forty years," said the editor of the Maine *Gos-*
pel Banner, " he has been a prominent man, and, most of the
time, a leader in our communion ; and it will be a long time
ere we shall accustom ourselves to think of his absence without sorrow.   We shall miss his cordial greeting in Cornhill ;
his characteristic paragraphs in the *Trumpet ;* his genial wit
at our festivals ; his defence of our faith ; his advice in our
councils ; and his strong and earnest words in our religious
meetings."   " His business talents," writes the editor of the
New York *Christian Ambassador*, " were of an extraordinary
character.   As the fruit of his industry, he acquired a large
fortune in a manner the most honorable and commendable.
We ever found him a warm-hearted, loving, ministerial brother,
a true friend, and a zealous and sincere Christian."   The *Chris-*
tian Inquirer (Unitarian) bore this testimony : "As a self-made
man, as an author, as an editor for many years, as an earnest
preacher of his peculiar faith, the broad, honest, Luther-like, yet
tender and affectionate, presence of Thomas Whittemore will
long be remembered.   He did a great work in his day to prepare
the way for a more universal acceptance of the truth that God
is Love.   Peace to the memory of the brave old iconoclast !"
A Baptist clergyman of New Hampshire says of him : " Although I am a Baptist clergyman, and cannot believe that all

men will be saved, still I do cherish the memory of Mr. Whittemore, and esteem him highly for his work's sake. I cannot persuade myself that he was not a friend of God, as, unquestionably, he was a friend of men. How much he wrought in forty years!"

Discourses in reference to his departure were preached from Universalist pulpits, in Boston, Charlestown, Providence, R.I., and elsewhere. We note one passage of a discourse of Rev. T. B. Thayer, in the Warren Street Universalist church in Boston: —

"It may be justly said that it would be impossible to estimate the difference in our denominational position and strength, if Mr. Whittemore had not lived and preached and talked. Take out his activity, and zeal, and intelligence, and large information, from the last thirty years of our denominational life; take out the powerful influence of his sermons and conversation; take out the *Trumpet*, with its ringing notes of alarm and defiance against the hoary errors of the Church creeds; with its sharp, doctrinal discussions, and popular expositions of Biblical texts and phraseology; take out his books, several of which — as his ' Notes on the Parables,' the ' Commentary on the Apocalypse,' and the ' Modern History of Universalism ' — have been among our most valuable and useful publications; take out his missionary labors — so widely extended in his latter years — and his popular addresses on religious subjects; take out his varied experience, and counsels, and business talent, and executive ability in our conventions and public meetings; and the difference between what we are, and what we should be as a denomination, as a religious power in New England, in the entire land, would be immense."

CHAPTER XVIII.

His Person and Character.

In summing up our account of the departed in these pages, these questions are very naturally suggested: What were some of the leading traits in the character of Mr. Whittemore? What has he wrought? What instructions are given us in his words and deeds?

A thick-set, round-faced man, of ordinary height, was the preacher; with no outward grace of appearance, except that which savored of healthfulness and self-reliance. His large features indicated strength, if the beautiful was not prominent in them. There was genial humor and tenderness in his eye, and his strong smile lighted up his whole countenance, and gave it attractiveness. He was somewhat corpulent, and indulged quite freely when at the table, — for which in after years he had admonitions which led him to greater abstemiousness. He realized his need of bodily exercise, and for years was accustomed, as he has told us, when the weather was favorable, to walk every day from his home in Cambridgeport to his office in Boston, often returning the same way, — a distance of two miles. He had a clear, strong, ringing but not musical voice; sometimes accompanied with a slight huskiness when beginning to speak, but pouring itself out with great effectiveness as he became filled with his theme. In singing, especially when excited, his voice seemed almost like an accompaniment of reed music to the other voices. He could make himself at home wherever duty called him, and into whatever company : if with the polite and refined, none could be more watchful, reserved, or truer to "the proprieties" than he ; if with the less polished, an equal ; if with the jocose, as witty as the wittiest ; if with the sorrowing and suffering, none could be more tender. That he should have "troops of friends," and should leave the strong impression of himself upon them, is readily accounted for.

Upon whatever might have been deemed defects in his character, we can think and speak charitably. He was not faultless : that he knew, and was ever ready to acknowledge. He might have been and was wrongfully judged by those who could not realize what inward strife he had experienced in the formation of that character which, as a whole, made him stand so well with his friends. The wonder is, that with the waywardness which marked his early life, according to his own confessions, and the many adverse circumstances in the way of his spiritual culture, he became the man he was, — so true to principle, so firm in virtue. It is written that the author of the "Pilgrim's Progress" once said, on seeing a poor convict on his way to Tyburn to execution, "But for the grace of God, there goes John Bunyan!" Mr. Whittemore seemed fully aware of the influences that had kept him from the power of temptation, and from the destructive evils into which so many youth are drawn. It was once told him, while he was editor of the *Trumpet*, and had occasion to speak so often in exposition of the wrong-doings of the ministers of other sects, who were so ready to condemn Universalism for its lack of restraining power over those tempted to evil, that an over-zealous woman, quite aggravated at these exposures, said earnestly, "I wish that Mr. Whittemore might get into some such difficulty!" "Dear woman!" said he, when the account came to his ears, "by the grace of God she cannot be gratified." He attributed his success, in the formation of his character and in the walk of his life, to the renovating influence of that Gospel which it was his great purpose to promulgate. There were differences of opinion in regard to certain questions, theological and reformatory, which led to very plain words between him and not a few of his denominational brethren. But they were not alienated from each other on this account. They loved him for his work's sake, and he kept his course with them fraternally to the last.

The versatility of talent possessed by Mr. Whittemore was notable. He could do many things, and do them well. He was an apt and comprehensive business man; one of the ablest among the business men of his time. He was a careful financier. He looked well to his accounts, and knew how he stood in debt and credit with all men. Taking care of the littles made the great incomes more certain. This was his habit, such as men acquire who have had to begin life on smallest means, and struggle up into a competency. The business world seemed somehow of right to claim him. As a bank and railroad director, as a city officer or State legislator, he stood among the foremost. Wherever he undertook to act in good earnest, he seemed at home; and whether his appointments were according to bank hours or railroad or church-service time, he was in season at his post of duty. Some have thought that his secular cares at times might have trenched upon his ministerial work. Possibly it might have been so; but the ability and disposition to do these various works were in him, and could not easily have been suppressed. Few men would have served in all the capacities that he did with less complication of the different interests. He had time and place for each and all. He was a talented musician, a ready composer of instrumental accompaniments to be used by the members of his choir, and for years he was a member of the principal musical society in New England. Later in years he determined to become a musical author, and issued books of sacred music among the most popular and acceptable of the time.

The editor of the *Salem Observer* said of him: "His name adds one more to the line of famous shoemakers. He was, doubtless, a good cobbler in his youth, as he has been a good preacher since he dropped the waxed-end, and took up the thread of public discourse. To be at the same time a preacher, president of a bank, editor, and president of a railroad, and good at all, certainly gives evidence of great versatility of talent."

As a writer, he was plain, pointed, strong; sometimes quite attractive in his rhetorical and descriptive efforts. Although given to verse-writing in the beginning of his literary efforts, he never excelled as a poet, nor attempted to do so. And yet he has left us one of the most compact and literal versions of the Lord's Prayer in the language.[1] This versatility of talent helped him as a preacher. It gave freshness and variety to his public addresses, and especially served him in his editorial work. The *Trumpet*, whatever might be thought of its theology, was never a dull paper. It was usually alive with argument, fact, illustration; with that which could make a weekly journal a welcome visitor to its patrons. The eyes of its editor looked in all directions for what could give interest to it. Said an earnest solicitor of subscriptions for another paper once to an intelligent friend of ours, "There is no better weekly in the land than this except the *Boston Trumpet*, edited by Mr. Whittemore, and that cannot be excelled by any paper." Many thought thus when the chief attention of its editor was bestowed upon it in the vigor of his days.

[1] Adams and Chapin's Coll. Hymns, 438.

The industry of Mr. Whittemore is one of the most remarkable of his life lessons to us. This was untiring. His mind was seldom inactive. He undertook great tasks, and succeeded in accomplishing most of them. He did well to resign his pastorship when other duties as an author and editor claimed the chief share of his attention. His sermonizing then became comparatively a light labor. He preached much as an itinerant, and could use his powers for extemporizing with greater effect and less cost of effort to himself than though he had been called to bring from his mental storehouse new as well as old forms of appeal to his hearers, a work which the settled pastor finds himself so constantly impelled to do. Other ministers of less ability have made themselves highly effective in this itinerant course of ministerial effort, while others have rested too much on their past labors and have given but little attention to the renewal of their mental efforts by fresh supplies through study and meditation. But what work our preacher might have bestowed upon sermonizing was given to other pursuits, some of them of equal importance with his ministerial work. And, besides, his habits of inquiry and investigation kept him well stored with facts and illustrations with which to interest the many audiences to whom he ministered. In addition to his editorial labors, he had constantly before him some work of interest, as he deemed it, by which the cause of Christian truth might be aided. He entered upon the work of an historian. Mr. Ballou (afterwards President of Tufts College) had resolved to prepare the history of ancient, and Mr. Whittemore the history of modern, Universalism. Much of the ground to be surveyed in this work was new. It had not to this end been examined carefully and extensively by any other historians. The materials were in existence, and it needed only two such patient and untiring explorers and gatherers to collect and arrange them. The author of the Modern History did his part faithfully. His other works already mentioned were wrought with the same industry. What he lacked in his knowledge of certain languages to aid him in his researches, he attempted to gain by persistent effort, — to master at least the rudiments of them, that he might employ them as occasion should demand. Nothing of this kind of effort seemed to daunt him. Dr. T. J. Sawyer wrote of him years ago: " I have been expecting that, in the midst of all his other labors, he would study Greek and Hebrew for the purpose of writing a Commentary on the New Testament, or perhaps the whole Bible." When preparing to write the Modern History, he found it desirable to read French, and forthwith he put himself at work to acquire a knowledge of the language. His singing-books are resolved upon, and although a well-trained musician, he finds himself lacking a knowledge of thorough bass. He seeks instruction of one of the profoundest harmonists in New England, and is soon qualified for the work intended. His Commentary on the Apocalypse and on the Book of Daniel were written — large portions of them — amid seasons of bodily weakness and mental depression, when severe trials were upon him. But he seemed to seek refuge in these investigations of Divine Truth, and find the home-work and rest of his heart there.

His industry was inspired by his fondness for facts and his inclination to details. He was seldom wrong in reference to a date or an event which had once come to his knowledge. This made him an accurate historian. It was of especial advantage to him as a business man. He would have, as far as possible, personal knowledge of any important interest with which he was connected. While his physical powers were in full vigor, he wrought as little by proxy and as much himself as possible. His lone walk upon the railroad track

for personal examination of the road from Fitchburg to Brattleboro, when he had the supervision of its business, was an
evidence of this. The last of his years evinced this habit of
persevering industry in him. Partial paralysis does not find
him willing to yield. He clings to the pulpit, and attempts
to go on with his work there, when the benumbing power is
upon him. He pursues the task of revising his Modern History, to be enlarged into two volumes, one of which he succeeded in giving to the public; and persists in his ministerial
labors until physician, family, and friends prevail on him to
yield to the demands of nature and afford himself rest. A
sterling representative was he of that indomitable will and
endurance, undismayed by adverse influences of whatever
force or form, for which the New England character has been
so justly distinguished. In this he has been an example and
an inspiration to not a few in the past, as he will be to others
in the long time to come. His industry is for the encouragement of all toilers who would make good and effective their
influences in the world. "Seest thou a man diligent in his
business, he shall stand before kings: he shall not stand
before mean men." This virtue of which we have spoken
has, in the instance before us, nobly earned the tribute here
given to it in the Sacred Word.

His peculiarities as a preacher were mainly these; strength,
plainness, scripturalness, earnestness, vivacity. He was,
theologically speaking, a strong man. He grasped his subject as if by intuition, and could present its points with a
peculiar force, in the face of any number of objections. The
more the objections, the greater seemed his anxiousness to
meet them. He was not a metaphysician, nor did he assume to be. For the intricacies of logical study and exercise,
he had no great inclination. But he could reason with great
clearness, and usually with much effect on the subject which

he desired most of all to urge upon his hearers. Conscious too of the truth which he advocated, he had all confidence in the positions he assumed, and was ever inviting theological inquiry, and in readiness to answer its demands for himself and in behalf of the faith he cherished.

He was a plain preacher. His hearers could clearly see all the points he would urge upon their attention. He had learned this method in a good school; for, if he had any preacher as a model before him, it was Mr. Ballou. One difference in their methods was, that while Mr. Ballou seemed to think it well to leave something for the hearer to work out for himself, as if in deference to his logical perceptions, Mr. Whittemore would present it often by repeated illustration or enforcement, so that there seemed but little call for any extra mental action on the part of the listener. Said a shrewd and intelligent hearer once, after listening to both of them for the first time: "Mr. Ballou gives his hearers good food; Mr. Whittemore, after doing the same, seems determined to aid them in eating and digesting it." This was his habit, the endeavor to make all things plain to the humblest capacity. Said a friend who heard his last discourse in Malden, "I shall never forget how it interested the children. They talked of it after they came home more than of any one they had heard before." Although elegance of speech was seldom sought by him, he had that direct and common-sense utterance which made him understood wherever his discoursings were heard. He practised after the apostle's affirmation: "Seeing we have such hope, we use great plainness of speech." No attentive hearer went away from his preaching querying as to what the minister intended to present as his sentiments; so mystified with his indefiniteness, so dazzled with the imagery, or captivated with the manner of the speaker, as to be unable to identify the topics of the discourse. The points were made, and made to tell, too, upon the minds for whom they were intended.

He was a scriptural, a textual, preacher, whatever might be thought of his method of sermonizing in the face of modern changes. After the way of most of the old Protestant divines, he fortified his statements and illustrations of doctrines with a goodly array of testimony from the written Word itself. "To the law and to the testimony," was a favorite text with him in the earlier times of his ministry. It expressed his fondness for using a "thus saith the Lord" in defence of his faith. He had read his Bible diligently, and could make his quotations from it with the greatest readiness. Sermons having texts that were not used after being named in the beginning; sermons that were intentionally sparse as to Bible language, lest literary niceness should not be conspicuous enough, — he held in light esteem. He regarded the Script-ures as their own best interpreter, and was fond of showing to reader or hearer how one text could be made to shed light upon another. He believed that there was no greater need among men than an acquaintance with the real meaning of the Bible, — a need which, if rightfully met, would weaken scepticisms and partialisms, dispel the theological and spiritual hallucinations of many kinds, and bless man with "the light of the knowledge of the glory of God in the face of Jesus Christ." [1]

His earnestness was another peculiarity in his pulpit work.

---

[1] He writes of himself in a foot-note of Dr. Sawyer's Biographical Sketch of him, in the *Trumpet* of Dec. 25, 1852: "Almost all my discourses are founded on the Scriptures. I could not preach without the Bible. With me a 'thus saith the Lord' is not merely a *sine qua non*, but it is also a *ne plus ultra:* I cannot do without it; I ask nothing else. Although I do not write my sermons, yet I never preach without premeditation; and almost always have the frame of the discourse written out before me, and pinned to the leaf of the Bible."

His preaching had life in it. He never entered the pulpit as an essayist or reader of homilies, but as a preacher, a living man to living men, — or to those who ought to be alive in their inquiries after religious truth. His eloquence was in the truthfulness and earnestness of his preaching. When warmed with his subject, he had much power over an audience. If he had not scrupulously studied the graces of oratory, yet, filled with his theme, he was the orator who would hold the attention and usually the sympathies of his audience. His discourses, like the one on "Jesus and the Resurrection," or from the text, "They believed not for joy," were exceedingly effective.

His vivacity, combined with these other peculiarities, of course made his preaching attractive. His illustrations were often apt, if not always the most refined in conception and presentation ; and his wit would break out even in the midst of the most serious appeals and tenderest passages of his discourses. Hearers expected to smile at times when he preached ; and there were those, in heart-faith deeply sympathizing with the speaker, to whom this indulgence on his part was an offence. But it was never thus intended by him. He certainly did not design by any lightness to loosen the force of his appeals to the understandings and affections of his hearers ; and, if his wit and pleasantry were too exuberant at times for the more serious-minded of his audience, he never tried them with any forced exercises in the pathetic. Pathos with him was the utterance of the heart's sincerest emotion, and *his* bore that evidence so plainly with it that its genuineness could not be questioned. It may be truly said of him, as it was of one before him who spoke with more than human power, that "the common people heard him gladly." It was his aim to reach them, and he did.

Not only in the pulpit, but in the conference and prayer

meeting he was always at home. He took great interest usually, and more as his years increased, in the meetings of conference and prayer with his denominational brethren or with other Christian fraternities. He believed in the communion of Christians in the spirit of the apostolic benediction, " Grace be with all who love our Lord Jesus Christ in sincerity." He was in the truest sense a denominational man, a sectarian in the best definition of that word. He loved the name (next to that of Christian) by which we as a sect are called. To him it embodied a sublime idea, one in which the thought of the Christian world ought to be centred, — that of the Divine Paternity. His Universalism was based here, and he desired that all others might build their theology on this sure foundation. He was conscientiously and unceasingly opposed to any evasions, suppressions, compromises of sects or no sects, that would have the effect to keep this consideration out of sight. Living and dying, this was his conviction and this his testimony. He believed that as a church we should not go out of our way to seek the patronage of any other, but rather have dignity and consistency enough to do our own work under our own name, and to do it well, and thus gain the honor we deserved, and would sooner or later receive, from the wisest and sincerest of sister denominations. But he had great charity. His sectarianism was not soured nor frozen. It had good fellowship for all lovers of the great Christian Master.

Mr. Whittemore was not strongly inclined to put himself forward as an ecclesiastical organizer. That he had eminent ability for this work no one who knew him could doubt. Had he given that talent which made him so successful in the bank and railroad operations which he conducted, to the building up of a thoroughly planned and effectively working church organization, embracing the interests of our whole church fraternity, throughout the country, he might have proved himself a helper in our onward movement whose memory on this account would have been gratefully cherished. He seemed, however, to have not only little inclination to see his denomination assume an effective form and organized method of action, but was inclined to question such movements in this direction as were made by some of the wisest in our churches, and finally accepted and adopted by them. Carefully prepared reports on this subject made to the General and Massachusetts Conventions failed to receive his approval. That he was conscientious in this course it would be uncharitable to deny. But such action on his part seemed inexplicable when his usually clear perception and sound judgment in practical matters were taken into the account. His strong influence was greatly needed in preparing and rendering effective the present commendable organization of the American Universalist church.

None were readier than Mr. Whittemore to acknowledge the truth which other denominations held and proclaimed, and the good which they were accomplishing. He was a " liberal Christian." But this word " liberal " had definiteness with him. It did not signify any thing or every thing out of the line of the accepted orthodoxy of the past; but Christian truth, or what was believed to be this truth, held in Christian love for all. " In essentials unity, in non-essentials liberty, in all things charity," was an acceptable basis of Christian fellowship and action with him. A " Broad Church " that could take in all shades of belief from most rigid Calvinism to most latitudinarian pantheism, or transcendentalism, or spiritualism, he did not conceive to be exactly the church of the New Testament, " Jesus Christ himself being the chief corner-stone." This last-named church was the one which he loved most, and he believed that not a few of all the sects were worthy members of it.

As a theological controversialist, Mr. Whittemore must be fairly judged. He came into the field when the attention of the Christian community, in New England especially, had become seriously turned towards Universalism. The preaching and writings of Mr. Ballou and his contemporaries had set religious thought astir. It was beginning to be seen, and was in so many words acknowledged, that " Universalism was to become the prominent heresy of the times." Opposition to this rising heresy manifested itself in various forms, but chiefly in misrepresentation, ridicule, and satire. Papers especially anti-Universalistic were started, and lectures delivered and published, giving the advancing doctrine an ill name to the public. Mr. Whittemore was well prepared for this kind of warfare. If others could use wit and ridicule against Universalism, he could show how these very weapons might be employed against themselves. If they asked for arguments, none were readier than he to adduce them, and to give closest attention to any examination of them which a theological opponent might make. But when assertions as to the absurdity of the theological pretensions or immoral tendency of Universalism were put impudently forth, he had a way of " turning the tables " so as to make his opponents see themselves " as others saw them ; " which, doubtless, not a few of them remembered in after days.

The narrower theologies had so generally kept the ascendancy in New England, that the advocates of them, especially the ministry, were habituated to the feeling of contempt for Universalism, and were inclined to treat with something like arrogance those who were bold enough to avow and defend it. Against all such assumption, it was Mr. Whittemore's business to wage an uncompromising war. In his treatment of such opponents, he gave them to understand that their assumed airs of religious superiority had no acknowledgment on the part of the Christian fraternity which he represented; that he regarded them as equals, and deemed his own authority to judge them by their works as unquestionable as was theirs to denounce him and his brethren as heretics. One intention in his frequent exposures of the moral aberrations of ministers of other sects was that of humbling the pride of such as were ever in readiness to represent Universalism as tending to evil, and that continually. His hits in this direction told, and a better behavior on the part of the accusers was the result. He would not spare error. He indulged in no bitterness towards the errorist; but he would give his groundless accusations, his reckless assumptions, his shallow sophisms no chance of escape from exposure. He was as blunt as Luther, and equally fearless in defending what he believed to be the truth of God. But he outlived much ill-feeling on the part of religious opposers; and later in his ministerial course held pleasant Christian conference and communion with individuals and churches who once would have considered such fellowship of spirit impracticable.

We justly class Mr. Whittemore among the reformers of his time. It was to theological reform, however, that he gave closest and most habitual attention. In some of the philanthropic movements of the day he took deep interest. He spoke strong words for the abolition of the gallows, for the promotion of temperance, for the reformation of the offender, for the raising up of the fallen. He had a warm heart, and could from its depths say to the recording angel as in the vision of Abou Ben Adhem: " Write me as one who loves his fellow-men."

He believed in human progress. He was a friend to the cause of education. He advocated this cause in behalf of his denomination. He sought to aid it in good words and acts for institutions established under its fostering care, and especially in early and timely endeavors to place the new College at Somerville on a permanent foundation.[1]

If Mr. Whittemore was watchful of his financial affairs, he was disposed to be generous, also, in his bestowal of aid to the needy. If he would not be easily induced to give in answer to all the appeals that came to him, he had a heart open to the calls of those less blest with earthly goods than he. A ministering brother (Rev. A. G. Laurie) writes of him :

" 'Means he made and had, and he was a minister of Christ,' said the surface-seeing world. And 'means he had and gave, and he *was* a minister of Christ,' was the blessing of many ready to perish which came upon him. From no family source, but from one well knowing whereof she affirmed, I learned, years ago, how, from that house of which he was the head, flowed many secret streams of bounty into the dwellings of the neighboring poor. And I well remember how, when I came before him fifteen years since, asking only his influence, not his money, for help to our broken-down church in Canada, he equally surprised and gratified me — unknown, a feeble apostle from the wilderness — by putting into my hands the largest contribution I received from individual help, in the course of a weary mendicancy of three months through the chief cities of the North."

In his domestic relations, Mr. Whittemore found great enjoyment. Home to him was the dearest of all places ; and, however absorbed he was in business abroad, he gladly turned from its cares or perplexities to the delights of the family retreat. He was blest with a companion of rare worth, who was indeed a sympathizing and most efficient helper to him, and of whom he ever spoke in tenderest praise. Nine children were born to them, four of whom survive.

---

[1] Since his death, his large and valuable library has been presented by Mrs. Whittemore to Tufts College.

Such was the man, the minister, the toiler, who wrought diligently and did faithfully that for which he seemed so well qualified by nature, and by the improvement of the powers God had given him. He aided in a work in his day for which we have reason to " thank God and take courage." He lived to witness changes which his own persistent labors had helped to effect : lived to see religious sectarianism more tolerant than it had been ; his own church increasing in influence as in numbers ; opinions which he had discarded and denounced as error questioned, and in many instances repudiated by sects or parts of sects who had once held them ; and the very principles which are the basis of Christian Universalism boldly and eloquently advocated in many of the pulpits and in much of the popular literature of the day. He could afford to be thankful as he realized this change, and had a right to the conviction that his labor had not been in vain in the Lord.

Sturdy and indomitable Christian hero, — struggling up through early adversities with vigorous trust ; led by divine grace through doubt and darkness into the Gospel's marvellous light ; out of weakness made strong ; valiant in " the good fight," — how art thou speaking to us all as one of the world's heroic moral pioneers to whom we and our race are indebted : who lived for God's truth and the rights of a common humanity ; who died in the strength of the overcoming faith, and whose helpful works do follow him !

The Great Cause which as a Christian minister he advocated will triumph. All weapons formed against it shall fail to prosper ; and every tongue that rises in judgment against it shall be condemned. It is one of the grandest privileges we can have to contribute to its advancement. Discouragements there may be, — there are ; mountains of prejudices to be brought down, valleys of human ignorance and degradation to be levelled up, that the highway of the Lord may be laid for the redeemed to walk on. But humanity will not falsify itself nor the Almighty's purposes fail. What he has promised he will perform. There are hopeful indications and assurances. Helper after helper shall appear as the world is ready for them. All things shall aid us, the Divine and the human. Sects shall come to this light, and churches to the brightness of its rising; all truth-seeking minds, all hearts imploring for the Father, all souls crying out for rest and salvation. As we would honor our nature and bless our race, let us go on!

"For Right is Right, as God is God,
And Right the day shall win;
To doubt would be disloyalty,
To falter would be sin."

THE END.